I0819415

BURN DOWN MASTER'S HOUSE

BURN DOWN MASTER'S HOUSE

CLAY CANE

KENSINGTON PUBLISHING CORP.
kensingtonbooks.com

Content Warning: Child abuse, physical abuse, sexual abuse, parental death, murder, pedophilia, racial slurs, hate speech, rape, sexual assault, torture, and violence.

This book is a work of fiction. Names, characters, businesses, organizations, places, events, and incidents either are the product of the author's imagination or are used fictitiously. Any resemblance to actual persons, living or dead, events, or locales is entirely coincidental.

To the extent that the image or images on the cover of this book depict a person or persons, such person or persons are merely models, and are not intended to portray any character or characters featured in the book.

DAFINA BOOKS are published by

Kensington Publishing Corp.
900 Third Avenue
New York, NY 10022

All Kensington titles, imprints, and distributed lines are available at special quantity discounts for bulk purchases for sales promotion, premiums, fund-raising, educational, or institutional use. Special book excerpts or customized printings can also be created to fit specific needs. For details, write or phone the office of the Kensington Special Sales Manager: Attn. Special Sales Department, Kensington Publishing Corp., 900 Third Avenue, New York, NY 10022. Phone: 1-800-221-2647.

Library of Congress Control Number: 2025945757

The DAFINA logo is a trademark of Kensington Publishing Corp.

ISBN-13: 978-1-4967-5914-6
First Kensington Hardcover Edition: February 2026

ISBN-13: 978-1-4967-5916-0 (ebook)

10 9 8 7 6 5

Printed in the United States of America

The authorized representative in the EU for product safety and compliance
is eucomply OU, Parnu mnt 139b-14, Apt 123
Tallinn, Berlin 11317, hello@eucompliancepartner.com

To my ancestors of Goochland, Virginia—and to my love, my heart, Alexa Muñoz, rest well.

Introduction

Misinformation is an old, strong tool; it distorts history, manipulates narratives, and fuels power. Misinformation makes it possible to win elections, spark wars, and turn neighbors into enemies with the stroke of a pen or a simple click. The danger of being misled is more than ignorance; it's political and social vulnerability. A society untethered from truth can be easily controlled, its people divided by lies while the oligarchies consolidate their control. As Alexander Nix, former CEO of Cambridge Analytica, said in 2018, it doesn't "necessarily need to be true as long as they're believed."[1] Misinformation campaigns aren't just careful mistakes, they're surgical strikes against our ability to see how these systems' legacies infect our world.

Truth and facts are ultimately what make collective opposition possible. If people are swayed to believe resistance is hopeless, they'll surrender before the battle even begins. But once they learn of others who have resisted and won, the idea of rebellion transforms from a fantasy into a possibility. Just as contemporary purveyors of misinformation work tirelessly to keep others in ignorance, enslavers once strove to prevent

1. Carole Cadwalladr and Emma Graham-Harrison, "Revealed: 50 Million Facebook Profiles Harvested for Cambridge Analytica in Major Data Breach," *The Guardian*, March 21, 2018, https://www.theguardian.com/uk-news/2018/mar/21/cambridge-analytica-facebook-exploited-trust.

the enslaved from learning of successful revolts that might embolden them. There is a power in retelling stories of liberation. When a society reclaims its past, when it knows that rebellion has happened and can happen again, it steps closer to building a future in which oppressive systems can be undone. Remembering is an act of brilliant opposition.

America's new civil war is being fought on the battlefield of media, and more than 160 years after the abolition of slavery, the nation's greatest sin remains a central target.

The claims that U.S. chattel slavery based on race was a "necessary evil," or it somehow "benefited" the enslaved people, aren't just distortions of the past. They are tactics of erasure in the present. They shape how we see ourselves, see one another, and decide who is worthy of opportunity and dignity. These distortions don't just remain in rhetoric—they often result in policy. They appear in executive orders to rewrite the Fourteenth Amendment, eroding the foundation of citizenship and equality. They manifest in state laws designed to suppress voting rights, restrict the teaching of Black history, and roll back protections for marginalized communities.

Enter rapper Kanye West. In 2018, Kanye West proclaimed, "When you hear about slavery for 400 years . . . For 400 years? That sounds like a choice."[2] As if that weren't horrifying enough, in 2019, he said during a performance at Howard University—one of the most revered historically Black colleges in America, "If they throwing slave nets again, how about we all don't stand in the same place."[3] West, a fully

2. Adrian Horton, "Kanye West just said 400 years of slavery was a choice," *CNN*, Updated May 1, 2018, https://www.cnn.com/2018/05/01/entertainment/kanye-west-slavery-choice-trnd/index.html.

3. Dawn Onley, "Kanye West brings Sunday Service to Howard University, warns crowd to avoid 'slave nets,'" *TheGrio*, October 13, 2019, https://thegrio.com/2019/10/13/kanye-west-brings-sunday-service-to-howard-university-warns-crowd-to-avoid-slave-nets/.

grown, ignorant man-child, echoed the "Lost Cause" narrative that emerged immediately after the Civil War—a rewrite of history meant to glorify the Confederacy and romanticize the antebellum South. This narrative painted enslaved people as content and their enslavers as benevolent, conveniently downplaying the inhumanity of slavery. It's the same myth perpetuated by films like 1915's *The Birth of a Nation* and 1939's *Gone With the Wind*, movies that poisoned generations of Americans' understanding of slavery as something less evil than it was. Hearing such rhetoric from a Black man in the twenty-first century was nothing short of abominable. Scholars like W. E. B. Du Bois, Marion Thompson Wright, Lawrence Otis Graham, Julius E. Thompson, and Lerone Bennett Jr. were turning in their graves.

But it's not just Kanye. Another favorite tactic to downplay the horrors of American slavery is the tired refrain that "slavery existed everywhere." Parroted by everyone from Condoleezza Rice[4] to comedian Bill Maher,[5] this conveniently ignores the distinct brutality of race-based chattel slavery practiced in the Americas. Yes, slavery existed worldwide, even in ancient Africa, but *not* slavery based on race. While African kingdoms engaged in forms of servitude, those systems did not hinge on the permanent dehumanization of an entire race.

In African societies, enslaved individuals were often captured through warfare, but they were not enslaved for life or treated as property in the same way as chattel slavery dictated. Enslaved people in Africa were typically reintegrated into so-

4. CNN, "Rice rejects reparations for slavery," *CNN*, September 9, 2001, https://www.cnn.com/2001/ALLPOLITICS/09/09/rice.reparations/.

5. "New Rule: A Unified Theory of Wokeness," *Real Time with Bill Maher* (HBO), YouTube video, 2:26, posted September 16, 2022, https://www.youtube.com/watch?v=MgzW9T_G8N4.

ciety over time, and their children were not born into bondage. In contrast, European chattel slavery commodified human beings, binding them and their descendants into a legacy of slavery based on the color of their skin. Yes, Africans did sell other Africans into slavery, but let's not pretend they had any way of knowing what awaited those sold into the so-called New World. There were no social media alerts, no breaking news segments or trackers warning of "race-based slavery ahead!" A lifetime of bondage tied to skin color wasn't their idea—it was a uniquely European reinvention, a horrifying twist on human exploitation that forever altered the course of history. By the 1860s, the United States had perfected this cruel system, becoming the most profitable engine of slavery in the modern world, where generations of Black Americans were bred and traded like livestock. This context makes dismissive comparisons not only disingenuous but an attempt to absolve America of its singular, unique monstrosity. For over 160 years, there has been an unrelenting campaign to remix the history of slavery, finding its way into mainstream thought and education. Therefore, storytelling and truth-telling are never ending.

When I told a friend my next book would focus on slavery, he sighed and said, "*Another slavery story*?" I understood his reaction. For many Black Americans, the subject of slavery feels like a wound too infected to touch, especially when much of what exists in popular culture is created through the lens of White storytellers. These works often dive into "torture porn," masquerading as art, reducing Black suffering to little more than shock value. Yet, after finishing the book, he admitted, "This is not just another slavery story." His initial dismissal had almost stopped him from engaging with a profound human narrative.

On the other end of the spectrum, there are those—like certain lawmakers—who do not want "another slavery story," but for very different reasons. They argue that these stories make White children feel bad about the color of their skin. But let's be clear: In Germany, there is no glorification of the Nazis or the Holocaust. Schools aren't named after Nazi generals, and German children are taught this chapter of their history from a young age, so they understand the importance of never repeating it.

The problem isn't the stories of slavery—it's the discomfort they cause in those unwilling to confront the truth. The urgency of these stories has only grown. In July 2023, Florida's Black history curriculum included the audacious claim that "slaves developed skills" that could be used for "personal benefit."[6] Florida Governor Ron DeSantis proudly defended the curriculum, calling it "the most robust standards in African American history."[7] In December 2023, Republican presidential candidate Nimarata Nikki Haley refused to acknowledge that the Civil War was fought over slavery.[8] In April 2025, Mississippi Governor Tate Reeves once again declared April as Confederate Heritage Month. These are not isolated incidents. They are part of a campaign to erase Black history and sanitize the realities of America's past.

We've also seen efforts to suppress these stories in educa-

6. Kerry Breen, "Florida's new Black history curriculum says "slaves developed skills" that could be used for 'personal benefit,'" *CBS News*, July 21, 2023, https://www.cbsnews.com/news/floridas-new-education-standards-says-slavery-had-personal-benefits/.
7. Emily Anderson Stern, "DeSantis takes shot at Trump during Utah campaign event, says GOP wave can happen with 'no distractions,'" *The Salt Lake Tribune*, July 21, 2023, https://www.sltrib.com/news/politics/2023/07/21/desantis-takes-shot-trump-during/.
8. Meg Kinnard, "Presidential candidate Nikki Haley left out slavery when asked what caused the Civil War. Then she backtracked," *PBS NewsHour*, October 10, 2023, https://www.pbs.org/newshour/politics/presidential-candidate-nikki-haley-left-out-slavery-when-asked-what-caused-the-civil-war-then-she-backtracked.

tion, with lawmakers arguing that they create division or promote "wokeness." But these stories are not divisive—they are clarifying. They force us to reckon with who we are and where we come from. They threaten the comforting myths of equality and fairness many would prefer to believe. Perhaps, just perhaps, the real fear isn't Black and Brown people knowing their history—it's young White children being inspired. The possibility that they might see themselves not in the oppressors but in the rebels, the freedom fighters, the ones who dared to demand a better, more just world. That's why this novel is for everyone, a story not confined to race or ancestry but rooted in a universal struggle.

Slavery isn't just a story of brutality; it's a story of resistance and opposition. This discomfort isn't about the history itself, it's about what it forces us to acknowledge: that we are still grappling with a system built on the subjugation of Black and Brown bodies, not just admitting that slavery existed but refusing to see the humanity of those who survived it. Slavery didn't end because President Abraham Lincoln had a profound love for Black people; the sixteenth president cared only about preserving the Union. Slavery, as an institution, began to die on paper because the enslaved people said "no more" and the country had no choice. To quote Whitney Houston, "I love it when they have no choice."[9] That's why I wrote *Burn Down Master's House*.

Every main character was inspired by real people whose names history has forgotten, but whose spirits deserve to be remembered. There were two Josephines—one in Maryland and one in Mississippi—who poisoned their owners. I took their stories and reimagined them. Luke and Henri were en-

9. MTV News, "Whitney Houston reminisces about 80s music on MTV (2001). #TBMTV, YouTube (9:27), October 18, 2016, https://www.youtube.com/watch?v=IzZgor4981M&t=170s.

slaved men who endured horrific sexual violence. I give them love where history gave them pain. Charity Butler resisted slavery through the courts, only to have her life destroyed by Thaddeus Stevens—a man who would later become a leading abolitionist. Her story is a reminder of how allies can uphold systems of oppression. And then there is the deeply unsettling tale of a Black enslaver, a man whose actions ignited an uprising. These stories are interconnected, not just to recount history, but to explore the complexities of identity and power.

Yes, this book will make you uncomfortable, but discomfort is the extravagant price of truth. These are not sanitized tales. The characters teach us to remember, and to hope. There is no one way to resist, it's a spectrum. In these trying political and cultural times, *Burn Down Master's House* is my literary opposition against those who would erase the truth. And maybe, there's a house in your life you need to burn—chains holding you back, something keeping you from your own freedom. This book isn't just a reckoning with history, it's a call to action. To confront. To break free. To build something new from the ashes.

BURN DOWN MASTER'S HOUSE

CHAPTER 1

LUKE AND HENRI

"I have been dragged down to the lowest depths of human degradation and wretchedness by slaveholders . . . which I consider to be too vulgar to be written . . ."[10]

The cabin was beaten down by humiliation and despair, infesting every corner of the caged space. The filth was stitched into the walls, into the hay-strewn dirt floor, into the rusted hinges of the door that never closed all the way. The cramped room was a sweatbox and a stage all at once. "Please, Henri, just do it," Suzie begged. She sat hunched on the floor, clutching the remains of a blanket to her bare chest. Her eyes pleading with him more than her words ever could.

Henri's body betrayed him, as it always had in moments like this. He hated himself for the way he went limp, the way the thought of touching Suzie—of giving the master what he wanted—felt like a death he couldn't bear.

10. Henry Bibb (1849), "Narrative of the life and adventures of Henry Bibb, an American slave, written by himself." In: Gilbert Osofsky, editor. *Puttin' On Ole Massa* (New York: Harper & Row, 1969), 64.

Suzie sighed with unsympathetic frustration. "Why can't you just give me some babies, like Master said? You know what'll happen if you don't."

Henri stared at her. Suzie was the oldest girl on the plantation who hadn't birthed any property, and he was the lone man who hadn't fathered any field hands. They were nothing more: failed machines in an apparatus that demanded they work, produce, and abide. Suzie blamed the "African" in his blood for what she saw as stubbornness. Henri sat back, his hands resting on his knees, his broad shoulders slumping. "Think I don't know?" he said. "Think I don't know what happens when they don't get what they want? But it ain't just about babies, Suzie. We not making no children here. We making slaves."

Suzie whipped her head around. "And what you think happens to me if we don't? He gonna sell me, Henri! Sell me someplace worse. You think it's bad here? We don't go hungry. Whippings ain't every day. You don't know bad."

Suzie was right. He'd heard the horror stories: masters who tormented with glee, plantations where survival wasn't just painful, but near impossible. Henri, still a young man, had been on several plantations over his years, yet this one stretched the longest. In all his time in this strange land, five years or so, there were no degrees of benevolence among any owner. Some used the lash more, some used the lash less, but all were orchestrators of terror. Soulless hacks who patted their own backs for handing out an extra biscuit, as if that made them one of the "good ones." There were no good ones. No redemptive qualities. They were all sick as the first white hand that touched the shores of the Gold Coast—rot fermented in human skin. And now, every part of Henri shrunk from what was being demanded of him. It wasn't Suzie—he thought she was beautiful, even more so than she believed herself to be.

He pushed to try again. He could feel Suzie watching him.

He touched her where life begins. His blood pulsed through him in starts and stops, refusing to flow as it should. His body was caught in trickery, stuck between instinct and rejection. Henri willed himself to feel something, anything. The act itself, the thought of pretending to be a man who could breed, was a lie his body couldn't perform.

"I can't, Suzie," he said with defeat.

"You can't or you won't?" she spat. "I ain't good enough for you? Too black, too ugly? You can't even look at me." She turned her face away, biting her lip to stop it from quivering.

"You think this is you," Henri replied quickly. "But, no . . . I . . . can't explain it."

She stared at him as a thought crossed her mind. "Parts don't even work, do they?" she hissed. "You ain't a man at all."

The door kicked open before Henri could say another word. Master's pink, portly face was warped with anger. Suzie screamed, yanking the blanket up to cover herself. "Fifteen minutes I been outside," he barked. "You ain't done a damn thing! You gonna get in that girl or I'm selling you tomorrow, you hear me?" Master ripped away Suzie's blanket. "And I'm watching. Now do it!"

"Please, Henri," Suzie whispered, her voice shaking. "Please . . . just do it."

Henri couldn't move. His body locked, every muscle tensed to prevent him from lunging at Master and sealing his own doom. He sat motionless, even as Master struck him across the face, making him taste blood.

"Worthless," he snarled. "You going to Magnolia Row tomorrow—meanest damn plantation in Goochland—they'll beat the devil outta you. Had Mr. Ragland come 'round looking at you, and you too dim-witted to even notice. You a leak in my pocket. More trouble'n you worth." He turned to Suzie. "You staying, but you better find someone who gonna do what he couldn't, or you next." As Master stormed out, Suzie burst into sobs, curling into a fetal position on the floor. Henri didn't move, he was deadpan, edged with shame, anger, and helplessness, all of it torpedoed inside him.

The sun blazed as Henri sat in the back of the buck wagon, hands bound by tattered ropes. He didn't understand why they tied him up. He had left without struggle. Suzie watched the wagon pull away. Slight relief crossed her face; her burden was finally gone. But she also felt a sadness. Henri was kind. He was a shield in his own way, a reminder that pushback, no matter how small, still had a place here. His tales of his homeland. His obsession with stories of a place called Haiti. She couldn't decide if she was mourning his absence or dreading what it meant for her future. She wiped a tear away angrily. There was no time for emotion. Not here. Not now.

Master was determined to make a lesson out of Henri, a warning to the others who didn't produce. Yet, Henri paid no mind to the winks and waves from the souls he seemed to befriend. There were no friends or loves. He showed no sign of hurt as he sat upright in the back of the wagon, eyes glinting like a panther in repose. His thoughts were already far beyond the fields; his vengeance would one day shake Virginia. The old Master sold off his trouble, thinking distance would cool the flames. Henri let himself slump against the wagon bed as it rolled forward. His face turned toward the sun; he glared with unblinking eyes as the heat seared his dark skin. *Let it burn*, Henri thought.

Henri was mourning. The land he once knew was a dissolving flash. Although he could still chant prayers, Henri could no longer remember his true name, forgotten somewhere in the murky waters of time and grief. His age was somewhere in his late teens, though he couldn't be sure. Memories felt distant, but one imprint stained him. The pale men came with fire, their hands eager to snatch up all that breathed. His village burned, the air permeated with the stink of conquest. His father fought like a king, roaring against guns and steel, but his mother's voice rang in his ears, her screams piercing the chaos, shouting for her children to run. His sisters and brothers fled, their feet pounding the dirt, but Henri—Henri could not move, he was moored to his mother.

Peering from behind a tree, he saw them grab her, throw her down with a force that shifted the ground. His mother's cries turned raw as she struggled. Henri wanted to fight, but there were too many, too strong. They grabbed her by the skull and slammed her head against a rock. The crack of bone reverberated in his ears as her once-beautiful face shattered against the stone. Each blow splintered the image of her in his mind, her features crumbling.

Henri could've fled, but he couldn't leave her at his own peril. He walked to her body. Her blood seeped into the earth. The rock was jagged and indifferent. It had taken her last breath, just as the pale men had taken everything else. Yet, he stayed. His little boy hands trembled, reaching for her as though he could pull her back, as though his touch might bring life into her broken body. His heart burst open, not the slow, steady crack of erosion, but the violent shatter of something sacred. Then they came for him, wrenched him away; he didn't scream. He had no sound left, no voice to give—a kaleidoscope of loss.

Vast waters, the kind that swallowed villages and spit out spirits, churned in his mind. The floating tomb where his body survived but his soul imploded. The countless masters who wore their savagery like armor, each one carving new scars. And the rebellions—his rebellions—fierce, unapologetic, but always costly. He remembered the small, everyday uprisings, stealing an hour of extra sleep, letting a tool fall too hard, or staring at an overseer a moment too long. There was also folklore. The stories danced through the hull of the slave ship on that terrible passage from Africa to Virginia, captives who rose up mid-voyage and pitched the crew overboard and Haitians who burned their masters' fields. Those stories insisted fighting back was always an option, even when it meant risking everything. Still, all of it blurred now, like images through smoke. Only two things burned sharp and clear. His mother's eyes wide with pain and love as her body broke. And the flames, always the flames. They licked in the corners of his vision. Fire had taken his village and left him with the unsatisfying taste of survival. Flames consumed everything and became the only thing he could trust.

The wagon meandered down a serpentine road, and then, like a revelation, Magnolia Row appeared, an endless ocean of cotton fields and bondage. Henri had never seen a plantation so immense. The plantations he endured before had been small, scarcely housing no more than a handful of souls. As they drew closer, he saw solemn faces and felt their quiet energy. They moved like phantoms, shells of memory. The ride to the big house was distant, many steps from the fields. On larger plantations, the shacks were far from the big house. *This devil doesn't want to see his work up close*, Henri mused.

The big house loomed like a monument to permanence. Its stark white exterior gleamed unnaturally, a menacing perfection. Two imposing levels rose with supremacy, crowned by a roof that jutted sharply against the sky. Massive pillars lined the front, their smooth surfaces lending the house an almost temple-like quality. Expansive, unblinking windows punctuated the façade, their dark panes like watchful eyes surveying the fields and forests beyond. The symmetry of the house was perfect, each line too exact and each corner too sharp. The wagon stumbled along, and the closer they drew, the more Henri could feel authority pressing down on him, as if worship were required. The porch stretched the entire width of the house, its wooden boards painted in the same glaring white. Rocking chairs sat perfectly still, though they were less for comfort and more like spies keeping watch.

In the distance, Henri noticed a tall figure standing at the center of it all. He exuded a presence that matched the house itself, judgment and sadism. He wore high boots and overalls that hung loose on his bony frame. His thinning dark hair clung stubbornly to the sides of his head, leaving a bald, shiny crown. A long, pointed nose poured from his face, matched by unnaturally angular ears. His skin was ruddy and blotchy, the angry redness crawling across his face and neck. His eyes were pale and cold. He didn't just look at Henri; he dissected him. Henri was ordered to sit up taller by the driver. This was not a place where mercy lived, he realized. This was a place that devoured you whole.

"Here he is, Mr. Ragland! Henri!" the driver called, halting the horses. Henri was pulled out of the wagon while Mr. Ragland stood on the top step of the porch.

"I see," Mr. Ragland said in a raspy growl. He eyed Henri from his head down to his bare feet. "Listen, boy," Mr. Ragland began, "heard plenty 'bout you. Only bought you because you was cheap to be so young. We run a tight ship 'round here. No one asks questions, and the work gets done. I done broke in the toughest of y'all, but if you reckon you can try something different, just know I ain't got no qualms 'bout cutting my losses. You only cost me $300, and I done paid more for wenches. There's a river beyond them woods"—Mr. Ragland pointed to a wooded area—"that's been the grave for many fools. Got it?" Henri nodded.

"Ruby!" Mr. Ragland yelled. She appeared almost instantly through the door to the big house.

"Yes, sir?" She was a medium-sized woman, wrapped in a long cloth dress with a bandana tightened around her head. But there was something distinctive about Ruby's red skin and the kinky burgundy hair that peeked through her bandana. Henri knew she was Black, but she was a shade of black he had never seen. Clinging to Ruby's side, half-hidden by the folds of her dress, was a little girl no older than fourteen. Her curious eyes darted between Mr. Ragland and Henri. Her dark brown skin was smooth, unblemished, and radiant against the backdrop of Ruby's fiery complexion. She stayed pressed against Ruby as her eyes stared at Henri.

"Take this boy Henri to the fields," Mr. Ragland ordered.

"Yes, sir." Ruby walked off the porch and grabbed Henri by his arm as his hands were tied behind his back. They slowly walked away with the little girl following them.

"Goddamn it, Ruby! Untie him! Be sundown by the time you make it to the fields. Don't you ever get any smarts?" He gestured impatiently toward the girl. "And why Josephine always following you? You teaching her how to cook yet?"

Without looking up, Ruby called over her shoulder, "She learn to cook when she ready. Can't rush good help, Mr. Ragland. You know that better than anyone."

Mr. Ragland squinted at her but couldn't grasp the subtle edge in her words. "Well, make sure she not just lollygagging!"

Ruby turned Henri around, untying his hands, then mumbled under her breath, "Well, I was 'bout to untie him, you beet-faced rascal, but I just knew you go yelling, 'Don't you dare untie that boy while I'm standing right here!' One day, Jesus gonna do away with that man. Cut his throat while he's snoring louder than a hog at a trough!"

Henri's mouth dropped as Ruby spun him to face her. He had never heard an enslaved woman talk so ferociously about their master. Henri harbored those thoughts only in his mind, never daring to say them out loud.

"Why you looking at me like that?" Ruby didn't give him time to respond. "I say what I want. Ain't holding back just 'cause you new. Now get to walking 'fore that devil starts yelling that we ain't moving fast enough."

Henri nodded as Ruby and little Josephine set off on the long trek to the fields. They passed the ginhouse first, its presence casting a shadow over the land. Beyond the ginhouse lay the rows of cotton, the white tufts bobbing gently in the wind. Souls moved silently, their bodies weary, their faces downward, hands working methodically, plucking the cotton and stuffing it into the baskets strapped to their hips. Some led mules that pulled carts laden with the day's harvest. The white overseer, a hulking figure with a face as red as the setting sun, stalked the rows, his eyes on the workers. A rifle slung too comfortably at his side with a whip in one hand.

The walk was punishing, the suffocating heat pressing down. Ruby could feel the eyes of the souls on them, a few nods in her direction and eyes on Henri, fleeting glances that quickly turned away. The grip of Magnolia Row was inescapable.

"This is it," Ruby said, with Josephine still clutching her as they entered a doorless log hut. The floor was damp earth, with several blankets scattered around the single, large room. The smell was jarring, reeking of urine, feces, and other aggressive odors. "You got about ten folks in here, but they all busy working right now. You meet 'em later on. Work starts at sunup, small break at high noon, and don't stop till sundown. We going right back to the fields now, so be sure to remember how to get back. Mr. Ragland don't like anybody wandering."

Henri took in his new home. He already missed his cabin with Suzie. *Least Suzie and I had a wood floor and only two others breathing up the air*, Henri thought. Ruby's eyes narrowed slightly, curious why he hadn't said a word. "Ain't much, but it's all you got now." Her tone softened just slightly. "You learn to keep your head down, Henri. That's how folks survive here."

"Where you stay?" Henri asked.

Relief hit Ruby's face. "Sweet Jesus, you talk!" Henri felt a pinch of anxiety. He never knew how the remains of his accent would land and if it would give away pieces of his past he'd tried to hide. Direct connections to Africa were not celebrated in places like Goochland. Ruby caught the worry in his eyes, instantly regretting her quick mouth. "Well, best you stay quiet. Keep you out of trouble." She gave a soft smile. "I gotta shack out back of the big house. Josephine stay in there with me. Always work to do."

Curiosity tugged at him. "You work in the house?"

Ruby nodded slowly, stepping into the sun with Josephine hanging on to her dress and motioning for him to follow. She nodded. "Only reason is 'cause my mama used to work in that house. Before she got sold off back when I was so little I can't even remember her face." Ruby let out a dry, humorless laugh. "But don't think it's all pretty, ain't no kindness in it. Ain't no safety." She turned to face him, hard and direct. "Working in that house means you pay your dues in different ways. But you learn how to move so they don't see you too much, and you make it through another day. That's what I do. That's what my baby girl Josephine do." Ruby looked down at Josephine and smiled.

Henri glanced at Josephine, who was still at Ruby's side. "She your child?"

Ruby shook her head, her smile fading. "I ain't her mama, but I might as well be. Her mama died giving birth to her. I been taking care of her ever since she drew her first breath. Nobody else gonna look out for her like I do." Josephine peeked out at Henri for the briefest moment before looking away.

Henri watched her. "She talk?"

Ruby chuckled softly. "Not right now," she said. "But she will. When she ready. My Josephine's got a lot to say, just need the right time for it to come out." Henri's eyes remained on Josephine, noting the intensity in her dark eyes and the way she clung to Ruby as if she were her entire world. She wasn't just shy, she was waiting, Henri thought. Waiting and watching, taking it all in, as if she were storing it away for a moment only she could see coming.

"Come on," Ruby said to Henri. "Time to work. Sun ain't waiting for nobody, and neither is Mr. Ragland."

Henri was put to work immediately. The souls were draped in tow cloth, shirts hanging like sacks down to their ankles, while a few men stood bare-chested, their tattered trousers stuck to them like a second skin. The sight of their backs, necks, and chests, crisscrossed with the scars of whippings and brandings. Those etchings were a mirror of his own.

He was ordered to break up and turn the soil. The plow tools were rusted and dull. What would have taken Henri a single sweep at the previous plantation now demanded three times the effort, each motion a struggle against the dirt. Then there was the oppressive silence of the fields. No voices rose, no songs drifted in the air, only the occasional crack of the overseer's whip.

By the time the sun sank, Henri was delirious with exhaustion. His limbs trembled, and his hands were raw from the day's labor. Yet, he felt a small spark of relief at the thought of food, however meager. He followed the others, their silent procession leading to the center of the quarters, where the evening's sparse meal was handed out. An old woman stood at the makeshift table, her hands unsteady as she doled out the portions. When she dropped a small lump of cornmeal into Henri's outstretched hand, he stared with disappointment. The grainy mound mocked his hunger, his stomach growling loudly in protest. Henri needed meat, anything substantial. He was starving.

"What you want?" Her voice was sharp but tired. "A feast? Eat or don't but move on. Ain't no more for you."

Henri pushed down his frustration, stepping aside to let the others behind him take their portions. As he turned, two men approached. They were near enough in age, their faces were marked by overtiredness and frames stocked with abnormal muscle from work. One of them, the taller of the two, spoke first, his tone laced with sarcasm. "You the new one Ruby brought in, huh? Thought you be bigger, the way she was talking."

"Bigger?" Henri questioned.

The other man snorted. "Don't mind Solomon," he said, jerking his head toward the taller man. "He like to size folks up. Thinks he can tell what a man's about just by looking." His eyes lingered on the rawness of Henri's hands. "Guess we gonna see soon enough."

Solomon smirked, and for a moment, Henri was struck by his gray eyes, stormy like the sky before rainfall. "Where you come from?" he asked, his tone casual but probing. "You don't look like you from 'round here."

Henri hesitated, the pitiful lump of cornmeal in his hand. "Don't matter much where I'm from now."

Solomon turned to his friend. "Got a sharp tongue, don't he, David?"

David shook his head. "Let the man eat, Solomon. He's just trying to figure things out, same as anyone else." He turned to Henri. "Name's David. That one's Solomon. Don't take nothing personal."

"Henri," he said simply.

Solomon gave a slow nod. "Well, Henri, guess we gonna see if you can keep up. We don't take too kindly to slackers."

David shot Solomon a warning look but said nothing more. The two men moved on. Their sarcasm felt less like hostility and more of a test, as if they were trying to figure out where he fit in the structure of this place. Henri looked down at the cornmeal in the palm of his hand, his stomach growling again. With a sigh, he shoved the grainy lump into his mouth and chewed slowly, forcing himself to swallow.

Still hungry, Henri returned to the sweltering shack, overcrowded with men and women packed together on the dirt floor, sharing old blankets. Most were already asleep, their exhaustion heavier than their hunger. A few coughed and wheezed in the darkness. As Henri tiptoed to an empty space, he caught snippets of conversation. Someone murmured that the next day was the Sabbath, which thankfully meant no work. Church service would be held in the barn. Henri didn't care much for preacher men, but the thought of escaping the suffocating cabin, even for a few hours, was enough to convince him. He would be at the service, if only to see what kind of salvation they could offer.

Squeezed into a corner on the dirt floor, Henri's throat bit against the cabin's stench. He adjusted his position, his eyes slowly acclimating to the glow of moonlight that seeped through the cracks in the wooden walls. Above him, the ceiling was filled with spiders, mosquitoes, and other unfriendly critters. Nearby, he briefly locked eyes with David and Solomon sprawled shirtless on the dirt floor. In the moonlight, their frames looked both imposing and vulnerable. David was deadpan, but Solomon's gray eyes held curiosity. Solomon nodded. The moment passed as quickly as it had come.

As Henri lay back, staring at the ceiling, a pink-colored snake slithered by his face on the dirt floor. He didn't flinch. Moving swiftly, he grabbed the snake. Solomon's eyes followed the scene as he saw Henri squeeze the reptile with his black hand. The pink serpent fought for its life until it finally went limp in his grip. Solomon watched as Henri released it, tossing the lifeless body aside. *He's not like the others*, Solomon thought.

Henri tried to rest but his mind raced, regretting his constant disobedience at the last plantation. In that act of stubborn courage, he hadn't fathomed the cost. Suzie's face was in his mind. He wished he could have performed, ached that he was not what she needed. He wondered how she was now. Did Master take out his anger on her the moment Henri was gone? Did she sit curled in that shack, weeping for herself or for him? Or had she steeled herself as she always did, cloaking her pain behind a wall of anger? The thought of her suffering hurt him, suffering that he might have spared her if only he had been different. Tears streamed down his face as he began to sob, his voice breaking into a prayer of his mother's name in his native tongue. Around him, the shack echoed with the sound of other tears. A dreadful lullaby.

The next day, Henri trailed behind a small group toward the barn, where the rafters were half buckled and cracked lanterns lay in corners. The preacher, another field hand draped in the guise of holiness, launched into his dramatic, atypical sermon. His palms cupped a tattered Bible as he stood atop a crate and ranted about salvation. "Brothers and sisters," he cried, "ain't no man or woman so broken the Lord's Word can't fix 'em!" Heads bobbed in agreement with "Amens" and "Yes, Lords." The souls were seeking comfort from anyone or anything.

"We must keep our eyes on His promise," the preacher insisted, "for He will deliver us in His own time."

Henri stood in the back, hands in his pockets. He heard the preacher's voice and knew each line by heart. He'd listened to this sermon, or one just like it, more times than he could count. All that holy talk about waiting on heaven's reward never reached him, not in the way it inspired others. Their swaying bodies and lifted hands only reminded him how easily folks could be lulled into hope. Henri wanted purification by fire in the here and now, not a faraway promise from a book. He flexed his shoulders and exhaled as the preacher got more animated, jumping and shouting with tears. Henri couldn't take it any longer. He had his fill of Jesus and the Sabbath, enough of waiting for a sign that never came.

As Henri emerged from the barn, he saw Ruby perched on a stool, her lively conversation with a tall, young man catching his eye. He was a stark contrast to most others, still rough around the edges, but wore knee-high boots, a shirt that wasn't torn, and his face, though not immaculate, was relatively clean. Henri hoped Ruby would introduce him.

"Hey now! Where you headed? Don't you like Jesus? You might end up in hell if you don't listen to preacher man!" Ruby's hearty voice rang out, mingling with the young man's laughter. Henri continued walking, hoping Ruby might call out to him again.

"Don't you hear me talking?"

Henri turned around. "I hear you," he said.

"What'd you say your name was again?"

"Henri."

"Well, if you forgot and I don't know how you would, I'm Ruby and this here is Luke." Luke laughed at Ruby and extended his hand. Henri was taken aback. He couldn't remember someone shaking his hand.

"Nice to meet you," Luke said with a nod as Henri felt his palm and fingers.

"Why your hands soft like that?" Henri asked, the question escaping before he could catch it, even his accent slipped out. Ruby erupted into a cackle, nearly toppling from her stool.

"They should call you Soft Luke! Hands soft as cotton!"

Luke ignored Henri's question and asked, "Why do you talk like that?"

Henri cramped up, always uncomfortable when his accent showed up uninvited.

"Yeah, you talk a little different," Ruby added.

"I'm from Africa."

"Africa!" Ruby exclaimed.

"We are all from Africa," Luke added. Henri stared back at Luke, appreciating his acknowledgment of their roots.

"I ain't from Africa," Ruby said.

"Yes, you are, Ruby," Luke insisted. "Unless you're telling me God built you separate from Eve." Ruby laughed as Luke looked down at Josephine, who pulled at his hand. She was crouched in the dirt, her little fingers holding a stick as she drew lines and shapes. He pointed at the ground. "Now, make three more, just like that one." Josephine obeyed, her tongue peeking out slightly as she concentrated, carefully scratching out another set of matching lines. Henri tilted his head, puzzled. Luke wasn't just talking to her, he was teaching her.

"What's she doing?" Henri asked.

"I'm showing her how to do her numbers," he said, turning back to Josephine. "Good. Now add two more. How many does that make?" Josephine looked up at him for reassurance before scratching out two more lines. She paused, then wrote out a seven.

Luke nodded approvingly. "That's right. Seven." Josephine beamed. "See, nobody can take that from you. Don't let them take what they can't touch."

Henri's brow furrowed. "You teaching her? Numbers?"

Luke shot a look at Ruby before answering, questioning if he could trust Henri. "It's no harm in knowing how to count. It'll be something she'll need one day."

Ruby chimed in, "He's good with that kinda thing. Been

showing her little by little when there's time. My Josephine's sharp. Pick up things faster than most." Henri stared at Josephine, who had gone back to her drawing, adding more lines and shapes. He couldn't hide his surprise.

"Didn't think . . . we could learn that kinda thing."

Luke straightened slightly. "We can learn plenty," he said. "We just need to make sure the right people don't see."

Ruby gave a small smile, her eyes on Josephine. "She's gonna learn more than just numbers if I got anything to do with it. This girl ain't just gonna survive, she gonna know how to think."

"How did you learn?" Henri asked Luke.

"Well!" Ruby interjected. "Luke don't work in the fields, he works in the house. That's why he don't talk like one of *us*."

"Ruby," Luke snapped. "Why are you always speaking for somebody? I can speak for myself."

"I know how you get when Junior come up, just wanted you to get to the point," Ruby said with a wink and turned back to Henri. "But don't you think he's got an easy life."

"Who's Junior?" Henri quizzed.

"The 'princess of Magnolia Row'!" Ruby guffawed.

"Junior is Mr. Ragland's son," Luke said with a sigh. "Ruby, you always have to mock something."

Ruby turned to Henri as if Luke had vanished. "See, Luke's been Junior's slave since he was a child. Luke knows how to read, write, and ain't never been hungry."

"Ruby, I wish you'd stop running your mouth about all my business. There are plenty of folks who already hate me on Magnolia Row."

"Don't nobody hate you, Luke. They just wanna be you."

"I have to get back to the house. Junior's waiting on me. Nice meeting you, Henri. Don't pay too much mind to Ruby; she'll have you in a heap of trouble in no time." Luke offered a nod and gave Josephine a kiss goodbye on the forehead. Henri watched him walk away. There was something in the way he moved. A dignity that was impervious to the fragility of their lives. He reminded him of the certainty of the boys from his village, the way they stepped on slippery rocks with assuredness. That same aura surrounded Luke.

"That boy's as touchy as a hive of bees!" Ruby said, shaking her head. "You doing alright?"

"Never alright," Henri replied.

"Lord, you gonna be one of them?"

"Not too excited about being in a new place."

Ruby stood from her stool and fixed him with a stare. Although they were around the same age, her wisdom bore down on him. "You listen up," she said. "This here's all you got. Don't matter what you had before or what you thought you deserved. This"—she gestured to the dusty fields and sagging cabins of Magnolia Row—"this is it. So, you best make something of it. Ain't no point in dreaming about what ain't gonna be." Henri looked about frowning. "Don't you go making Magnolia Row a hotter hell than it already is. That fire burns up everything around you." Ruby turned to Josephine. "Come on, Josephine," she said, her tone softer. "Time to get back to the house and get supper ready. No meal gonna make itself."

Henri stood in place. Ruby's words stuck with him. *That fire burns up everything around you.* Ruby's words weren't a warning, they were a prophecy.

Time was an abstraction to Henri. The fields gobbled his days, and while others were often chastised with a quick lashing for fainting from an empty stomach or heat, Henri managed to go unnoticed. The other souls in his shack insisted that if the White overseer, who did not live on the plantation, didn't know your name, you were doing well. Henri aimed to keep it that way. On another muggy day, as the humidity threatened to overwhelm him, Henri barely dodged the crack of a whip. He cried out, falling onto the dirt as the overseer's horse stood over him. "Don't you hear me calling you?" Henri shook his head no. "Mr. Ragland wants to see you—now!"

"For what?" Henri wondered aloud.

"Don't you ask me no questions!" the overseer snapped, his whip cracking. Henri avoided the lash again, causing a collective gasp from the other souls, including the overseer. The man's nostrils flared. "Go see Mr. Ragland!"

Henri made the long walk to the big house, his heart racing with anxiety. What could he have done wrong? Perhaps Mr. Ragland wanted him to breed. The thought of it made him nauseous. Ruby met him on the front steps of the house as Josephine was sweeping. It was his first time at the big house since arriving; he stared at the structure, resplendent and statuesque, its grandeur a gilded scar of the Antebellum South's unbroken hegemony.

"Mr. Ragland wants me?"

"Sure does," Ruby said, swinging open the door.

"Why?" Henri asked.

"If you don't know, then you don't have nothing to worry about." She guided him into the majestic interior. High ceilings arched above them, hardwood floors stretched beneath their feet, and a grand staircase featured a mahogany banister. Walls adorned with portraits of pale faces from every corner. The air was clean, free from the dirt and critters of the fields. Henri had never seen a house so grand. "Gonna let Mr. Ragland know you here." Ruby disappeared through a set of double doors, leaving Henri to stand alone.

"Come on now!" A high-pitched voice called from the top of the stairs. A tall, chubby, young White man, his attire snug and his black hair slicked back, pranced down the stairs. His tight pants and buttoned-up shirt struggled against his girth. "Did you have them get the carriage ready? I can't miss my train—God, I'd just die of shame!"

Luke appeared at the top of the stairs, juggling four trunks. "Yes, Junior, everything ready for you."

" 'Everything *is* ready for you,' " Junior corrected, sashaying down the steps. "I know your mammy didn't teach you how to speak, but Christ—listen to you, you sound like somebody raised you in a tobacco row." Junior turned and saw Luke struggling with the trunks. "Oh, Lord! You're going to tip over trying to handle that yourself. Sometimes I think you're as delicate as me!" Junior's squeaky laugh echoed as his head threw back. "You"—he pointed at Henri—"help Luke. I really can't be late for the train," he said, adjusting his white gloves.

Henri darted up the staircase and grabbed two of the heavy trunks. Luke offered a reassuring smile and wink as they descended the stairs.

Ruby returned for Henri with Josephine right behind her. "Oh! Ruby!" exclaimed Junior, his Southern dialect dropping as he examined himself in a mirror. "Fetch Daddy and tell him I'm leaving. I've already said my goodbyes to Mother and must bid farewell to Daddy."

"But . . . Mr. Ragland is busy."

"I don't care if he's with the latest whore on the plantation! I'm leaving for weeks, and he needs to say goodbye to his only White child!" Henri looked to Ruby and Luke for their reactions. They were stone-faced. "Boy, be careful with that trunk!" Junior screamed at Henri, his Southern drawl thickening with his anger.

"Gonna get Mr. Ragland," Ruby said, her composure unshaken as Josephine followed.

"I swear, Luke, I don't know what you see in Ruby. She's dumb as a tick, and she got the gal following her like a damn dying puppy!" Junior lusted at himself in the mirror again, admiring his appearance. Henri controlled a laugh as Luke shot him a quick look.

Mr. Ragland appeared from another room. A look of repulsion crossed his face at the sight of Junior. "Daddy! You weren't even going to say goodbye!" Junior whined, slipping back into his affected speech.

"I'm running a business!" Mr. Ragland's voice echoed. "A business that's letting you go to New York City to do God knows what!"

Junior sighed.

"Junior!" Another high-pitched voice called. A stout woman in a revealing dress came down the stairs. "Don't make your departure a big scene!"

"But, Mother—"

"Shut up!" she snapped. "It's hot, and I need a drink. Ruby, get me some brandy!"

"Yes, ma'am," Ruby replied, hurrying off with Josephine.

"Goddamn it! Don't call me 'ma'am' anything. Just call me Mistress Kitty!"

"You don't need to be drinking right now, Kitty," Mr. Ragland said, his frustration evident.

"Quiet, Montgomery. I am the one who should be in New York City, visiting my old friends. I was quite the dish in my time," Kitty said, patting her moist chest.

Kitty's vacuous chatter bored Mr. Ragland. He turned to Junior. "I don't approve of this trip, Junior."

"You don't approve of anything unless it's about this dirty plantation."

"You need to learn about the working of this plantation instead of prancing in New York City," Mr. Ragland snapped. "And why you wearing those white gloves?"

"I'm looking into a suitable college!" Junior spat, dismissing the question. "I'm eighteen and don't want to be tied to the fields. I have no interest in managing begrimed slaves." Junior embraced his father to say goodbye.

"You smell like a French whore!" Mr. Ragland snapped.

"It's jasmine!" Junior retorted.

"Leave Junior alone!" Kitty demanded. "He's a creative child. Stop trying to turn everyone into a servant."

"Ma'am—I mean, Mistress Kitty," Ruby said, appearing quietly. "No more brandy."

"What! Now what am I supposed to do?" Kitty whined, giving Junior a brief hug before retreating up the stairs.

"I'll see you in a few weeks, Daddy. I left a long list for the servants. I want *everything* done when I arrive from cleaning my room to building me a vanity. Come on, Luke; get my bags in the carriage." Junior's hips swayed as he strutted out of the big house.

Mr. Ragland fumed. "Don't know why his mother allows him to act like this!" He pointed at Henri. "Follow me." Henri cast a fearful look to Ruby.

Henri stepped into a den that stunk of cigars. Mr. Ragland slumped into a horsehair chair, fanning himself with his hat. Between his thick fingers, a drawing pin glinted as he rolled it over a folded deed—pressing, lifting, pressing again—as if testing its point. Henri stood in the center of the room, head bowed and hands at his sides. Mr. Ragland threw his hat onto a nearby chair, then flicked the drawing pin onto the desk before pulling out a cigar and matches from his baggy overalls. He lit the cigar, took a deep puff and glared at Henri, smoke curling around his eyes. "David and Solomon ran away."

Henri racked his brain, trying to remember who David and Solomon were. "Don't know David and Solomon," he said, masking his accent.

"What you mean you don't know David and Solomon? You boys sleep in the same shack!" Henri moved uncomfortably. Then it came to him, the two men sprawled shirtless on the dirt floor. David, the one who seemed quieter, more observant. Solomon with the gray eyes, sharp-tongued and testing. He remembered the brief moment on his first night when they had locked eyes, and how intently they were sizing him up. They hadn't spoken since.

"Sorry, sir. Forgot their names."

"You see anything, hear anything?"

"No, sir."

"You see them when you got up?"

"No, sir."

"You lying to me?"

"No, sir. Don't know nothing. Just do my work." Mr. Ragland scrutinized Henri's face, seeking any sign of deceit. He had been warned of Henri's reputation, but with no previous encounters to judge, he didn't know what to think. Henri's silence left him puzzled. "Go back to Ruby. She got a job for you."

Henri left the smoky den, calm washing over him. Despite his fear, he admired David and Solomon for their escape. "Everything okay?" Ruby asked.

"Don't know nothing, honestly," Henri said.

"I believe you. Nobody likes you enough to tell you they running away!" Ruby's laughter rang out, making Josephine softly giggle.

"Don't care if nobody likes me."

"Boy, I'm just messing with you. Mr. Ragland wants you to help Luke clean Junior's room."

"Clean his room?" Henri was confused.

"Might be wondering why you gotta clean somebody's room, but lemme tell you—it's a pigpen. It's 'bout the nastiest sight you ever gonna lay eyes on." Henri followed Ruby and Josephine up the staircase. He marveled at the kerosene lamps built into the walls. The hallway was lined with more portraits of the most colorless, grayest people he'd ever seen.

Ruby opened the door to Junior's room. Clothes were thrown across the floor, spoiled food in every corner, slop jars, some overturned, where flies danced. A sheetless bed on a wooden frame stood in the middle of the room. A single small window struggled to shed light on the disarray, while kerosene lamps stood atop the dresser. Henri stood, stunned and overwhelmed, unsure where to start. Just then, Luke entered, panting and burdened with cleaning supplies.

"I sure am glad Junior's gone," Luke said with relief.

"Surprised he didn't take you with him," Ruby remarked.

"In New York City, slavery isn't classy. That would make him look like Southern trash, if he brought his slave boy," Luke replied.

"You remember Henri?" Ruby asked.

"I do." Luke nodded. "How come you aren't helping me clean, Ruby?"

"'Cause I'm going dancing in the river! What do you reckon? Me and Josephine gotta cook and clean." Josephine nodded. "With David and Solomon gone, I got even more work to do. They did so much in the house." Ruby turned on her heel with Josephine mimicking her and closing the door, leaving Luke and Henri to tackle the mess.

As they locked eyes, the world around them paused. They stood in silence. They were of similar height, their builds nearly identical. Henri stared into Luke's pupils. They had met only once before, yet the familiarity was palpable.

"Did Mr. Ragland ask you about David and Solomon running away?" Luke asked, breaking the silence.

"Don't know nothing."

"I knew they were up to something. They were whispering in corners and food was missing. They worked in the fields but also in the house. They did some good work, but they had enough of Magnolia Row. God be with them." Henri shrugged, ready for his orders to work. "You're from Africa, right?"

Luke asked as he approached the soiled bed with a bucket of water.

"Yeah. You know where Africa is?" Henri responded, trying to erase his accent while following Luke to the bed.

"Of course, I know where Africa is," Luke answered.

"I wasn't born a slave. Born in Africa. Wasn't meant to be here."

"None of us meant to be here," Luke said, his hands working as he poured powdered soap over the stains. "None of us are meant to be slaves."

"Well, you ain't really a slave," Henri said.

"You think I'm free?"

"You ain't on the fields."

"I do work, though, and I always have Junior on my back."

"I rather be working in the house."

"I reckon we all want to be somewhere else. I know Ruby does. They got her in a small cabin in the back of the house so Mr. Ragland can do . . . what he wants with her."

"Do what he wants?"

"You know what that means, Henri," Luke said with a dead stare.

Henri paused. He knew. He saw the vile acts at every plantation he suffered through. He could smell the scum in Mr. Ragland's grin before the man spoke. "You sleep in Ruby's shack?" Henri asked.

Luke paused from scrubbing. "When Junior's here, I sleep in this room on the floor." His hand motioned to the grimy shackles near the end of the bed. "Sometimes I'm chained to his bedside. Not allowed to wear nothing but a shirt . . . When Junior is gone, I sleep in Ruby's cabin."

Henri could see the scars on Luke's wrists and neck. The cruelty was clear. Captivity was more than metal. They were tools of degradation. Luke felt Henri's pity and grew uncomfortable.

"Tell me about Africa," Luke said, shifting the conversation. "I don't know anyone who remembers Africa."

No one had ever asked Henri about Africa. On the other plantations, he was cast aside as an enigma wrapped in the dark skin of a troublemaker. They said he had too much African in him, as if it were a curse, but Luke was different.

As they scrubbed and cleaned Junior's foul room, Henri spoke of the smell of his village. Something you'd never find on Magnolia Row. Sweet and intoxicating, a rich aroma easing the storms inside you even on your harshest of days. It was the smell of life, earth and sun. Henri described the colors of his homeland. Vibrant yellows, forest greens and browns that spoke of the earth itself. Everything was a part of the land, a living, breathing canvas of life. Every hue had a voice.

The food. Even when it was days old, it always looked and smelled fresh. The flavors were rich, like tasting the very spirit of the land. His thoughts drifted to his family. Henri was the youngest out of his brothers and sisters. Their smiles were sunbursts, laughter filled the air like drums. They were his world, each of them with their own way of making him feel loved and protected. They always said one day he'd earn a village of his own, perhaps become a king. They knew he was stubborn. He'd never be content as a mere follower.

The ache in his voice grew as he spoke of his father, whose presence had been as commanding as a god. A loud man, his voice booming across miles, a force of nature. He loved to sing and dance, leading ceremonies with a spirit that could make the ground shake. And his mother, she ruled with a quick tongue and a heart full of grace. Lost in the sorrow, he wondered out loud where they were today. How they managed after his mother's death and how they handled their grief after he vanished.

A thread of vulnerability connected Henri to Luke, the pain of it all was a lump in his throat. "I want to go home."

Henri and Luke found themselves sitting on the floor of Junior's room, now half-clean. Luke placed his hand gently upon Henri's. A spark shot through Henri; he could not remember the last time he felt someone's touch. He took in Luke, studied the movements on his face. He looked perfectly drawn, no lines, like a painting. *He could be a friend in my village*, Henri thought.

"It's alright." Luke's voice had a soothing cadence. "I know how it feels. I may not come from Africa, but I understand."

Henri's response was a nod. "You know how many years you got on you?" he asked.

"Mr. Ragland's records says I'll be nineteen on August twenty-first. Just a couple months away."

"Don't know mine."

"Well then," Luke declared with a squeeze of Henri's hand, "we'll be the same age from now on."

"And when is my nineteen?"

"Same day as me, August twenty-first. So now we got the same birthday and age."

"Fine by me, Luke," Henri said, a smile breaking through his face. As Luke withdrew his hand, they both stood, matching each other's height.

"We better get back to work before Mr. Ragland starts asking questions," Luke said. "I'll be walking back with you to the fields tonight."

Henri stayed quiet as they turned back to their work.

With the sun setting, Luke and Henri slowly walked back to the fields. Luke carried a bucket of water, a kerosene lamp, and a full knapsack.

"Why you got all that with you?" Henri asked.

"For my momma. She's dying," Luke said with a sigh. "Mr.

Ragland doesn't want her around anybody. Not sure what ails her. She's in a shack by herself, all the way down at the end of Magnolia Row. I check on her once a day, but when Junior's gone, I get to stay the night with her sometimes."

Henri nodded, wishing he had one more night with his mother. He wanted to ask more, but they were both in their heads, broken only by the sound of their steps, the water sloshing in the bucket, and the jumbling of items in Luke's knapsack. That familiar feeling returned. Henri wasn't used to listening or being heard; his emotions were tightly bound. Talking with Luke felt both natural and uncomfortable, a strange mix of ease and vulnerability. He had learned to survive by keeping his feelings locked away, but in this moment, the struggle for emotional intimacy was real.

As the sun dipped lower, they reached Henri's shack, which he dreaded entering. He could hear the rumbling inside and knew the stench was waiting for him.

"How far is your momma's shack?" Henri asked.

"Way down." Henri stopped in front of his shack as Luke kept walking. "Mighty good working with you today, Henri," Luke said. "I'll see if you can do more work in the house. There's always something to do."

Henri gave a slow nod, watching as Luke disappeared into the night.

In one of the last shacks, the reaper's cabins, Luke's sickly mother waited, far from everyone, near the ghostly woods where souls were sent when they were expected to die. The woods represented both death and freedom. Death—because that was where Mr. Ragland disposed of the bodies—and freedom—because it was the portal souls had to cross to escape their physical bonds.

Opening the flimsy shack door, Luke's heart pounded with excitement and fear. He was eager to see his mother, but each time, she was much worse. Lighting the tiny room with a kerosene lamp, he said, "Mama?"

Miss Emily opened her eyes, finally finding sleep through all of her pain. She knew it was her child's voice. "Luke?" she asked, trying to sit up on her elbows.

"Mama, no. Don't push yourself." Luke sat on the floor. His sickly mother rested on a humble bed, handmade from scrap wood and straw, with a quilt carefully spread on top and a thin sheet drawn over her as she breathed slowly in and out. One of the souls had helped him build it, so she wouldn't have to lie on the dirt. Her illness and the engulfing summer heat kept her drenched in sweat. While she appeared more lucid, the bones in her face pierced through her skin. Her once-beautiful, jet-black eyes were sunken. She was more bones than woman. The tumors had grown, especially the angry swell beneath her ribs. Luke choked on his tears as he knelt beside her, wiping the sickness from her paper-thin skin.

"Luke," she whispered, her voice frail, as she gripped his hand with what little strength she had left. "Your mama is in so much pain. Can't move. Can't breathe. In so much pain, even hurts to pray."

Luke sucked up his cries, his heart in a state of helplessness. "Mr. Ragland didn't send the doctor, Mama?"

"He did," she replied, her voice bitter. "Doctor said he might as well shoot me because I'm no good. Put me out of my misery. Mr. Ragland put a gun to my head, but I told him no. That man stole everything from me. Wasn't gonna let him take my own life. Only reason he got that doctor is 'cause Ruby begged."

Luke laid down beside his mother. He wanted her to feel human, to feel loved. Miss Emily took a labored breath. "How little Josephine? You still teaching her numbers?"

"Yes, Mama."

"So sad any child gotta live like this." Miss Emily began to sob.

"Mama, you need to be calm." Miss Emily tried to breathe. "I'm going to clean you up some. I got this bucket of water, clothes, and Ruby wanted me to give you a new quilt. I got some good food, too." Luke undressed his mother and gently washed her with warm water. Her body told a story, lash marks of decades past and the ravages of her disease. Though not even forty, Miss Emily looked ancient, her body emaciated.

After changing her into clean clothes, plaiting her hair, and feeding her, Luke carried his mother outside for fresh air. A drowsy breeze washed over her, momentarily easing her fever and pain. She studied the darkening sky. "If there's a God, I'd die right now . . . But there ain't no God . . . ain't ever seen no God . . . Ain't seen nothing that even looks like God."

Luke's heart broke. "Mama, I'm so sorry I can't be here more."

"What you sorry for? Sorry for being on Magnolia Row? This ain't your fault. Others come by and check on me, always passing me something." Miss Emily still conveyed the maternal comfort she had rarely been able to provide. "We in this life. A life that ain't no life . . ."

Miss Emily took in her son, his eyes catching the lamp's light in that familiar way, just like his father's. It was uncanny, the way Luke could carry his father in his eyes. Luke's father had been a man who was never meant to be enslaved, a man who stood tall even when the lash cut him down. He was the sort of man who made White folks uneasy, the kind who refused to let Magnolia Row break him. His back was a roadmap of scars that Miss Emily had memorized in the dark, tracing each line with her fingers as though trying to ease the pain that lived there. When Luke was born, with those same fierce eyes, his father would carry him for hours, sometimes humming melodies from a land long ago. Miss Emily would watch, her heart full and breaking all at once. He'd stare at his son like he knew he wouldn't have much time and say, "Don't let them take what they can't touch." He held his baby boy close, as if trying to pass his strength into the child, to make him remember something he was too young to know. Mr. Ragland had seen it too, the father's stare—and it unnerved him. Mr. Ragland had made his decision within a few months of Luke's birth. "Don't need no more trouble from that one," he'd said coldly. Other souls warned Luke's father so he could say his goodbyes.

He came to Miss Emily's shack—the one Mr. Ragland had let her keep, so she could tend to baby Luke. His voice was calm in a way she'd never heard before. After a thousand kisses, he held a shotgun loosely, like it was an extension of himself. "Ain't being sold again, Emily," he told her. "Leaving this plantation a dead man."

She begged him not to do it. Pleaded with him to wait, to think. But he only smiled, a bitter curve of his lips. "Nothing to think about," he said. "A man's got a choice, live on his knees or die on his feet. Done kneeling."

The bullet tore through his chest, but Miss Emily didn't cry. Across the cabin, baby Luke slept on, his breath steady as river water. Miss Emily sat with him, her hands pressed against the wound, feeling his blood, warm and thick between her fingers. For the first time, his face was peaceful. She stayed with him through the night, watching his body grow cold, knowing Mr. Ragland would have dragged her love off and dumped him in the woods like trash. She couldn't stop his death, but she kept him with her as long as she could.

When Mr. Ragland came the following day, he found her sitting by the body. "You one nasty animal," he spat. "Knowing he dead and not saying nothing." She didn't respond. What was there to say? No words could resurrect him or stop Mr. Ragland from throwing him in the forest.

Mr. Ragland didn't believe in families. Mothers or children were sold off as soon as the babies were weaned. Miss Emily had seen it happen time and time again, but Mr. Ragland kept her close. She learned early that fighting only made it worse. She shouldered all the violence, the humiliation, and gave birth to eight children, each ripped from her arms before she could see them crawl.

Luke was the only one she was allowed to keep, the only one not born of rape. He was her son, hers and his father's. And because of that, she cherished him fiercely, even as Magnolia Row claimed him piece by piece. In some ways, Luke was nothing like his father. Magnolia Row had molded him. He didn't carry the same restlessness. He was a child of this place and bound by its rules. When Junior decided he wanted Luke as his servant, Miss Emily lost her son in a way that felt like a death of its own. But at least he wasn't sold. That was the only solace she could cling to, thin as it was. Luke was born alongside Junior, raised as his playmate. But as they grew, Junior's boyish games turned possessive, his cruelty sharpened by privilege. He didn't want Luke to exist outside of him, didn't want him to see his mother unless sickness forced him back into her arms. Miss Emily could only watch. Yes, Luke carried his father's eyes, but the fire behind them was dim, smothered by the pressure of Goochland's Magnolia Row. Yet, she held on to the memory of his father, hoping that somewhere, deep inside, that same spirit lived on in her son.

Miss Emily shook with pain from the memories. "Mama?" Luke kissed her forehead, overflowing with sweat beads.

"Take this pain away, Luke . . ."

"What do you mean, Mama?"

"Free my soul."

"Mama, I can't . . . Time to set you back down." He walked back into the shack and laid her gently on the fresh quilt. Luke's eyes filled with tears as he stared, the lump in her chest pulsating with every breath.

"Don't leave me tonight on Magnolia Row. . . ." Her eyes, though clouded with pain, were resolute.

"Mama, please . . ." Luke pleaded, his tears flowing. He remembered running into her arms as a child. The early whippings haunted him. Those first lashes, which came when they tore him away from her, were seared into his memory. He recalled the confusion as she explained why they had to obey, why they were not free people. The stories she told him of his father painted him as a warrior, a soldier, a hero. In his childlike mind, he believed his father would one day rise up and rescue them. As he grew, the realization sank in that they were property, and there would never be an escape. Wherever he looked, there were only fields and trees, no glimpse of what freedom could be. He never once set foot off Magnolia Row. His mother was the only love he had known.

His tears mixed with hers. "Love you, Mama." He lay beside her, praying for sleep, grateful he wasn't chained to Junior's bedside. He hoped his presence would comfort her enough to rest, but she couldn't endure much longer. The end was coming.

Luke woke up early the next morning, his mother still asleep, her face softened. He kissed her on the forehead and made his way to the big house. The air was filled with the smell of cooking as Ruby worked in the kitchen, damp curls from sweat sticking to her neck. Keeping his promise, he approached her about Henri working in the house. There was so much work to be done—from gardening to serving meals, to Junior's endless list of demands to be completed upon his return. Moreover, Luke was now Henri's friend. He wanted him closer. Ruby agreed to ask Mr. Ragland.

"That boy's only been here a few weeks and you want him in the house?" Mr. Ragland said to Ruby in his den. Josephine was behind Ruby, always avoiding being directly in front of Mr. Ragland.

"He quite the worker, sir. Did you see how clean he got Junior's room?"

Mr. Ragland snorted. "Yeah, not even Jesus Christ himself could get that room clean."

Ruby persisted. "There's a mighty lot to be done. Junior left a long list, and without David and Solomon here, it's just me and Luke trying to manage. It's more than we can handle right now, sir. Junior's asking for a vanity. Reckon Henri could see to that," although she was unsure if Henri knew a thing about building.

"A vanity!" Mr. Ragland fumed. "That boy don't need nothing fancy to be fussing over!"

"We still need the help, sir," Ruby insisted.

Mr. Ragland hesitated, then his attention settled on Ruby. She was young. Mistress Kitty was old and spoiled, just like his first wife. Mr. Ragland, an old man himself, didn't like old women. *Young keep you young*, he thought. Ruby's eyes shot to the floor. Her womb ached with the memory of the last time, a pain that never leaves, and now it flared up again. Mr. Ragland's eyes salivated for her shape. Ruby fought the urge to run. It was a violation she knew too well. "Josephine, go clean up that front porch," Mr. Ragland ordered.

Mr. Ragland agreed to let Henri work in the house. The new role settled over him like a mantle of both burden and privilege, the walls of the big house closing in around him, offering a strange, confining freedom. There was an unease in his chest whenever he passed by the chains at the foot of Junior's bed, a ghostly reminder that even the comforts of the house were fitted with shackles. But day after day, Henri worked, his hands becoming tools of their own. Despite Mr. Ragland's saying no, Mistress Kitty insisted on the vanity. Henri built Junior's vanity, each piece of wood perfectly carved, knowing that even the smallest error could spark a full-blown brouhaha when Junior returned home. He fixed everything that needed mending, repaired broken furniture, and scrubbed the floors until they gleamed. The tasks were unceasing, a cycle of labor that left little time for rest. But amidst the work, there were moments that made it bearable, the rare minutes he could steal away with Luke. When they were together, Henri felt a spark of life that the big house could never take away. Sometimes, after the hardest days, they would slip away to tend to Luke's mother. Although she was a frail woman, there was a loud strength in her eyes that Henri admired. Each time he saw her, Luke would bring whatever food he could gather from the kitchen, slipping her a warm biscuit or a small piece of ham. He'd help her with what little clothing she had, making sure she was dressed for the heat, his hands gentle as he massaged her body to relieve pain. The sight of Luke caring for his mother moved Henri in ways he couldn't put into words. Miss Emily loved seeing her son have a friend.

"Henri," Miss Emily would say, "tell me 'bout Africa again. Tell me what it was like."

Henri would sit by her side. "It was . . . different," he said, his accent thickening. "The air, eh, it warm like the cloth we wrap ourselves with at night, soft and close. The earth smells full of life, like it been feeding us forever. The trees, ah, so tall, you look up and your neck go tire' before you see their top. And the rivers? Hmm, they no just flow, oh—dey sing, like dem get plenty stories to tell, stories that go make your heart dance and your mind wonder."

Miss Emily would close her eyes as she listened, her mind

painting pictures of a world far removed from the one she knew. "A place full of life," she whispered.

"It was." Henri's chest tightened.

"You a good boy, Henri. Y'all gotta take care of each other," Miss Emily said, nodding to them both.

After making sure Miss Emily was comfortable, they would run, their feet moving through the fields, the plantation falling behind them. Luke knew every twist and turn of Magnolia Row to escape the eyes of the souls. Henri hesitated at first, glancing back, but Luke pressed a hand to his shoulder. *"Nobody's watching. Just follow me, Henri."*

And Henri did.

They ran with the kind of freedom that existed only between them, the air vibrant against their skin as they raced toward the river. Once they reached the bank, they collapsed onto the grass, breathless and spent, their voices harmonizing with the rushing water. The river danced, intoxicating them with the smell of fresh currents. Luke drank in Henri, his chest softly moving up and down through his cotton shirt. He could see his bare black skin etching out his sharp collarbone. A fever rose in Luke, going from a simmer to a boil. Feelings stirred. He wanted to touch him.

Henri turned to Luke, seeing him stare at his chest. He moved his leg and bumped Luke's. They locked eyes. Luke could hear his heart beating. Henri stretched out his fingers, slightly touching the tips of Luke's fingers. "What you thinking?" Henri asked.

Luke turned fully toward him. His cool breath danced across Henri's lips, causing a shiver of anticipation. Henri's eyes gleamed like jewels, his stare intense and familiar. Luke couldn't speak. His fingers found their way to Henri's hand, his hot skin was a contrast to the coolness of the river's edge. Henri moved in closer, their lips brushing together. Henri's heart raced. The only other person he had kissed was Suzie, and that had felt like duty, an act he was supposed to perform. It didn't feel natural. Didn't feel like this at all. This felt real, like it belonged to him, like it was meant to be. Luke crawled on top of Henri, running over him like the river. For Luke, this wasn't like before, not the assault of Junior, not the violence that left scars. This was different. It wasn't taking; it was giving. It wasn't pain; it was comfort. For the first time, for the both of them, there was no shame, no expectation. This moment wasn't stolen or forced, it was freely given, an act of God.

They kissed again. Henri wrapped his arms around Luke and thought he would cry. He was never able to show affection. He was never able to feel intimacy or the purity of attraction. For once, he didn't feel like an animal. Their clothes peeled off. They were alive as their bodies intertwined; long black legs wrapped around each other. They were like the river, going where they pleased with no inhibitions, as natural as the sun rising and setting.

Henri and Luke bobbed in the deepest part of the river, forcing them to tiptoe to stay afloat. They were inches away from each other's face with the water up to their chins. There was a smile in their eyes as Henri's hands made waves against the current. The heat felt alive with a warm air over their faces, drying their brows. The door of their hearts cracked open, wide enough for the river to flow in and climb to the crown of their heads. "We been gone for a long time now," Henri said, his lips wet with the river.

"We should get back," Luke said.

"Can't be free too long."

"This is free, ain't it?"

"Can't think of nothing more free than this," Henri said, his eyes welling up. He never cried at a whipping, but he cried here.

"Things are going to change when Junior comes back," Luke said with a sadness in his tone.

Under the water, Henri slid both of his hands into Luke's. "Maybe . . . but I ain't ever really gone," Henri affirmed. Henri and Luke returned to the riverbank for the next several days, always after visiting Miss Emily. Beneath the open sky, they splashed in the water, kissed, and caressed like old lovers.

Luke and Henri were tending to the front of the big house. Ruby was sweeping the porch, with Josephine counting each sweep, making all three of them smile. The sound reached them first. Dragging, boots against dust, something was broken but still alive as Mr. Ragland stomped ahead. Behind him, barely upright, was another man, tripping over his steps. Luke and Henri couldn't place him. The man's skin stretched tight over sharp cheekbones, his face covered in grime and flecked with dried blood. His clothes, torn to rags, hung in strips from his shoulders. The iron collar around his neck was a monstrous thing, spiked edges sprouting outward, each movement threatening to stab the man's face. A thick, rusted chain extended from the collar.

It was Ruby's gasp that made the truth settle in their bones. "Solomon," she whispered, grabbing Josephine's hand as though to shield her from the sight. Yes, it was Solomon—the man with gray eyes who, alongside David, had sized Henri up his first night on Magnolia Row. Solomon and David had slipped away into the night not long after. But now, here was Solomon. His eyes were swollen, only a sliver of his stormy gray irises visible. And David? Nowhere to be seen. Henri wanted to look away, to pretend this wasn't Solomon. He felt the heat of failure, even though he had no part in Solomon's escape or capture. Henri's eyes locked with Luke's. Henri knew they were both thinking the same thing: *Solomon was supposed to be free. Not this. Not back here.*

Mr. Ragland's voice erupted, "Gather 'round! Y'all come on now, quick-like! Your dear friend Solomon is back. Took some time, but he's back and he's got a debt to be paid, oh yes, he does!"

The souls within earshot moved reluctantly toward the front of the big house. Luke had seen this before, but Henri had not. Mistress Kitty stumbled out of the front door. "What's all this fuss about, Montgomery? You catch yourself another runaway?"

Mr. Ragland ignored her. "No runaway now! He's back! Thought he could run from me, but ain't nobody run from Montgomery Ragland for long!" He turned to the gathered souls. "Now, y'all gon' see what happens when one of you gets ideas. This here's a lesson for every last one of you!"

Ruby covered Josephine's eyes, which Mr. Ragland saw. "Don't you shield her eyes, Ruby! She gon' look. She gon' *see* what happens to fools who think they smarter than me."

Ruby put her hands down. Josephine whimpered softly.

Solomon stood as Mr. Ragland circled him. "You thought you could run from me? Thought you could take *my* money and just vanish? Where's David?"

"Don't know," Solomon said, struggling to keep his balance, his bare feet in the dirt.

"You don't know?" Mr. Ragland howled, spit flying from his mouth. Solomon lengthened his neck despite the iron collar.

Mr. Ragland paced, spitting out curses about money lost, paying bounty hunters, and "uppity boys" who needed breaking. He ordered the collar to be removed, which the White overseer did quickly. And then, without warning, he crouched low and pulled a shiny blade from his pocket. "Hold him," he ordered the two souls closest to Solomon. They grabbed Solomon by the arms. At first, he didn't struggle. Not until Mr. Ragland dropped to his knees and pinned his left foot against the dirt. "Keep him still!" The blade flashed once as it came down with precision, bit through flesh and bone with a grinding as his big toe was severed. Solomon's scream split the air as blood gushed. Mr. Ragland tossed the toe in the dirt. Solomon's arms jerked against the souls holding him as he fell to the ground.

His cries turned to shuddering gasps, sweat pouring down his face as Mr. Ragland stood. "*Now*," he seethed, "where's David?"

Solomon's chest rose and fell. "Don't know, he got away. Went different ways. Ain't seen him," he whispered.

"You ain't *seen* him? Well, I'm gonna make sure them gray eyes don't see right again." Mr. Ragland pulled a small drawing pin from his baggy overalls, the same drawing pin Henri had seen in his den when he was questioned about David and Solomon. He leaned in close to him on the ground. "One of you, hold his head!"

Solomon's head was trapped between two arms. Mr. Ragland held the tip of the drawing pin. Ruby turned, but she couldn't stop hearing it—the squelch of a pin touching down at the corner of Solomon's left eye. Mr. Ragland worked slowly, his tongue hanging out of his mouth as the pin sank deeper. Mr. Ragland paused, adjusted his grip, pushed farther and turned the pin, but not enough to kill. Solomon thrashed against the hands that held him. The screams were no longer words. Just sound. Just pain made real. A clear liquid pool leaked from Solomon's eye as he blinked a thousand drops of blood.

Tears streamed from the souls. Luke squeezed his eyes shut. Josephine covered her face with the hem of Ruby's dress. Henri imagined he was living under another sky. Ruby fell into a cry. But from the porch, Mistress Kitty watched, googly-eyed with the corners of her mouth lifted, like she was soaking in a theater production.

Solomon lay defeated in the dirt. Blood seeped from the gaping wound where his big toe once was. With his hand, he covered his swollen and mutilated left eye. His chest heaved, each breath rasping like sandpaper against his throat. The once-proud man was now barely human, ruined in ways that went beyond his flesh.

Mr. Ragland stood over him, wiping the blade clean on his overalls. He looked around at the gathered souls. "That'll learn you," he sneered. "That'll learn all of you. Don't cross me. Not ever." Mistress Kitty smirked as though pleased with a fine performance. She returned to the big house.

Solomon was still alive, but his body was limp. "Clean him up," Mr. Ragland said as he wiped his hands on a soiled rag. "Y'all best make certain that boy's back in them fields by week's end. He ain't never working in the big house again, that's goddamn sure. Luke, Henri, drag him to one them back cabins. Ruby, you tend them cuts good enough so he can work, but don't waste no liniment on him. Rest of you get back to work."

Luke and Henri carefully walked Solomon to an abandoned shack near the reaper's cabins, his body swaying as he leaned heavily on them, barely able to keep his feet beneath him. Blood trailed behind him as Ruby and Josephine followed, their arms cradling baskets filled with rags, twine, honey, salt, and a basin of well water. The other souls watched in heartbroken silence, their eyes heavy with pity. They arrived to a barely standing shack. The floor was uneven with debris, dead leaves, and the skittering movement of unseen creatures that had long made a home there. Little Josephine wasted no time, immediately grabbing the nearest makeshift broom, perhaps an old branch, to sweep away the layers of filth, dust, and crawling things that had claimed the floor. Spiders retreated into the corners, beetles scurried beneath the rotted floorboards, but Josephine pressed on.

Luke and Henri laid Solomon carefully onto a rough pallet that served as a bed, its surface barely softer than the floor itself. The fabric was coarse, reeking of age and mildew, but it would have to do. Ruby knelt beside him as she worked. Her hands moved quickly but gently, first cleaning the stump of his big toe with salt water and honey. Then wrapping the wound with a clean cloth. Blood seeped through, but she pressed hard. Josephine knelt by Ruby's side, holding the basin of water and passing cloths as Ruby cleaned the wound. "Keep this cloth wet," Ruby said. "We gotta stop the bleeding best we can."

When the toe was bound, Ruby turned to Solomon's damaged eye. She tilted his face toward the sunlight creeping through the wooden roof, her fingers trembling as she inspected the wound. The skin around the eye was already swollen, streaked with blood and fluid that didn't stop leaking. With a soft sigh, she began to clean, dipping a rag in the water and dabbing it carefully. Solomon winced but didn't cry out. He just stared at the wooden ceiling with his good eye.

Henri and Luke hovered nearby, their faces sagging with worry. Luke held Solomon's shoulders steady as Ruby worked. Henri stood at the edge of the pallet. "What happened, Solomon?" he asked quietly. "How did David get away?"

Ruby shook her head no at Henri as she tied the strips of cloth into place. She reached into a small box and pulled out a piece of fabric and some twine, crafting a makeshift eye patch. With Josephine's help, she tied it around Solomon's head, covering the damaged eye. The patch hung slightly loose, but it worked.

Henri leaned closer. "Solomon," he said again. "What happened?" Solomon didn't answer. He was far away, lost somewhere beyond the affliction and the grief.

Ruby exhaled deeply. "Leave him be, Henri. Not ready to talk." Josephine pressed a damp cloth to Solomon's forehead. "He'll live," she said. "But he ain't ever gonna be the same."

Days passed, and Solomon began to heal, but he was no longer the man he had once been. He walked with a limp now, each step uneven, the scarred stump of his toe forcing him to stumble. His eye was swollen and ruined. His good eye stared blankly at the ground. Henri and Luke watched from a distance. The other souls would pause their work to help when he tripped, catching a handful of the cotton that slipped from his grasp. He would whisper a hoarse "thank you," his voice barely audible, accompanied by a nod. Solomon shuffled between the aisles of cotton, the fields always waiting like an open mouth ready to chew him up.

Magnolia Row was solemn, even more than usual. The souls who hadn't witnessed Solomon's torture felt the change. He limped through the rows of cotton like a ghost, a reminder and an example of the Raglands. Then there was the return of Junior. In the early evening on the first Friday in July, the princess of Magnolia Row, as Ruby would say, made his grand return. The minute he stepped out of the wagon there was a flurry of souls surrounding him to take his trunks. Mistress Kitty and Mr. Ragland met him on the porch. "Momma!" Junior said, embracing her. "Daddy!"

"Hope you got all that traveling outta your system now," Mr. Ragland said. "Got lots of work to do."

"Good heavens!" Junior exclaimed. "Why, I haven't even stepped off the carriage for thirty seconds, and already you're prattling on about work! Work! Work! I'm not White trash nor am I one of these . . . slaves. You don't own me!" he cried as he paraded in the house and slammed the door shut. "Luke!" he screamed. Luke appeared at the top of the stairs with Henri next to him. "Praise the Lord you're here! Daddy is already yammering about work. I haven't even had a chance to relieve myself! What is *that* standing next to you?"

"This is Henri. He's the newest house boy."

"Another one?" Junior questioned, pulling off long white gloves. "I guess Mother needs some new meat." Henri's eyes bulged. He met Junior one time before and that was right before he left for New York City. However, he was now even more flamboyant. His cheeks appeared to have been patted with a touch of blush, giving him an almost cherubic glow, though the smirk on his lips was anything but angelic. The lavender slacks he donned were skintight, hugging every lumpy curve and tapering into what appeared to be pumps with flat heels. A silk violet scarf loosely tied at his throat added a final splash of drama. A sassy peacock daring anyone to look too long or say too much.

"Well, don't stand there!" Junior blurted out as he stomped up the stairs. "Take my things this instant, and heat some water for my bath! This Goochland heat has me reeking like one of you. And my vanity better be good and ready, or there'll be the devil to pay!"

Henri watched Luke walk away with Junior's trunks. Luke missed him already and was terrified at how things would change.

Luke sat on a stool near the metal tub, his stomach burning as he tried to keep his eyes anywhere but on Junior's bloated, naked body. Since he was a child, Luke was with Junior as he washed. He despised Junior's blotchy skin and loose fat as he sat in the tub like a skinless chicken. The tub protested under Junior's weight, the water sloshing over the edges as his flabby flesh oozed against the sides. The rolls of his body wet with the murky bathwater were a mixture of soap scum and sweat pooling in the creases of his skin. Junior leaned back as though he were an empress instead of a man crammed into a tub too small for his indulgence. His flesh rippled as he moved, making Luke recoil inwardly, his hands in fists on his lap.

Luke hated the way Junior's colorless, greasy skin caught the light, hated the sound of his breathing, like a hog wallowing in the mud. But most of all, he hated the feeling of being trapped. Junior rambled away, "New York City was just divine! So many sophisticated, educated people, and I just fit right in! I don't know why I was born in the South! I should've been born in Connecticut or Vermont! Not Virginia!" Junior grabbed Luke's hand and placed it on his chest. "That feels lovely, Luke . . . I've missed your company."

Luke held his breath and closed his eyes. He hoped Junior had satisfied his urges in New York City, but he suspected otherwise. These were the dues he repeatedly paid that the souls in the fields never saw. He would've rather slaved among rows of cotton than suffer with Junior as he lay back in the tub, opened his legs, and gently stroked himself. "You know what Junior likes." He moaned and played with his fat nipples.

Junior wrapped his wet hand around Luke's neck and demanded, "Come on. If you scrape me, I'm beating you."

Luke went down in his soul. He placed his mouth on the flesh that felt like a half-grown, skinless snake. Tears dropped into the dirty bathwater. He wanted to pretend that he wasn't there, somewhere else, but the shame was inescapable. Junior grunted, shaking his vile body, causing water to splash over Luke's clothes. He thought he would vomit. He was about to purge all over Junior and knew what the punishment would be. Suddenly, Junior pushed him off, as he fell deeper into the tub. "Leave me be, Luke."

Wet and debased, Luke turned and saw Ruby and little Josephine in the doorway of the washroom, which was beside the kitchen. She stood with a towel gripped in her hand, her eyes reflecting an unspoken understanding. Luke didn't know how much they saw as he walked past them.

For Henri, Luke was a universe away. Though they shared the same oppressive space of the big house, the distance between them felt infinite. Luke was attached to Junior by more than chains, it was a demonic force that drained his spirit. Whenever Junior was near, Luke avoided Henri's gaze, his subjugation too much for him to bear openly. Junior's eyes would fixate on Henri with an envious intensity. He could sense the connection between Luke and Henri, stirring within him jealousy and hatred. The very presence of this bond seethed through Junior's veins. The more he watched, the more his blood boiled. Henri could feel Junior's fury and feared his time in the house would soon end.

"Don't think Junior likes me," Henri said to Ruby as he was helping her prepare dinner.

"He don't like nobody," Ruby said in a rare monotone voice as Josephine sat at the table, cutting greens into a bowl. Ruby watched her for a moment, then pointed to the pile of greens still waiting to be trimmed. "Now, when you cut them, make sure you get all the tough stems out. Nobody wanna bite into something bitter," Ruby instructed as she leaned over to demonstrate. "See? Just like that. Clean and quick."

Josephine nodded, mimicking Ruby's movements. Ruby gave an approving hum, stepping back. "Good. After you finish that, you gonna watch me again with the cornbread and chicken. Gotta get that right, too. Can't have no dry bread or meat."

She turned toward the hearth, but as she reached for a heavy cast-iron skillet, her hand froze midair. A wince crossed her face. She clutched her belly, her fingers pressing against her side.

"You okay?" Henri asked.

"Nothing, just a little stitch, that's all," she said, brushing it away like a fly. But the pain in her voice betrayed her. She leaned against a table, gripping its edge for support. Ruby grabbed her stomach and squealed. "Get Luke," Ruby cried, and doubled over. Henri dashed upstairs and screamed for Luke. Luke jumped out of Junior's room, shirtless, which confused Henri.

"What's wrong?" Luke nearly yelled.

"Ruby needs help."

They heard Ruby scream.

"Slaves usually better built than this," said a doctor standing above Ruby lying in her wooden bed with feathers. Mistress Kitty stood in the cabin with Henri and Luke by the door. Josephine sat in the corner, her knees drawn up to her chest, staring at Ruby. "A miscarriage," the doctor said. "She looked pretty messed up inside. Probably barren now. What a waste."

"I see," Mistress Kitty said, her voice deadpan. Mistress Kitty stood at the edge of the bed, looking down at Ruby. She didn't want to be there, but her husband had made it clear this was "women's business," and she was to tend to it. Mistress Kitty knew the truth. She knew whose child grew in Ruby's belly, whose seed had taken root. The truth was a stone in her gut. Her lips pressed into a thin line as she glared at Ruby, the woman who was both her husband's property and his mistress. She crossed her arms tightly, feeling the heat of her own skin, the blotches spreading across her chest, as if her body was rebelling against the sight of Ruby.

Mistress Kitty had convinced herself Ruby held a power over her. She was blind to her complicity. Her unearned place in a world that valued skin over character was her cover, her shield. But she was also a woman, and that meant she was not a full citizen. She was owned by a man who saw her as a keeper of his house and nothing more. Her womanhood was a brand, marking her as property, but she saw no solidarity with Ruby. Mistress Kitty was both the oppressor and the oppressed.

"She'll be okay, though, Mistress Kitty. I gave her some medicine and she'll be right back to work." The doctor left with Kitty still fixed on Ruby with her eyes shut, her breath labored.

"Look at me," Mistress Kitty ordered, her voice tight. Ruby opened her eyes, meeting Mistress Kitty's green pupils with a hard stare. Mistress Kitty didn't want to feel pity, didn't want to feel anything at all. She only blamed Ruby and could not accept the part she played. "Need you back up. Work needs to be done." Kitty turned to Henri and Luke. "Y'all clean her up, then get back to the kitchen and work. Josephine gonna have to cook in the meantime. She been watching long enough. Wood needs to be chopped, animals got to be fed before nightfall."

"Yes, ma'am," they both responded as Mistress Kitty walked out.

Henri and Luke stared at Ruby. Her eyes were bloodshot as tears streamed down her face.

"Why didn't you tell me?" Luke softly asked. "I could've helped you work. Henri would've helped."

"Didn't need help," she answered, looking at no one. "Knew what was gonna happen." Ruby paused. "You two lucky to be boys. Being a woman ain't nothing but hell." She turned to Josephine, terrified at what lay ahead for her. "Rather be dead. Dead with the rest of my family." Ruby took a deep inhale. "But this time I made sure I wasn't gonna have no more babies. I drank some castor oil, tons of it, and took care of that. Hope my insides all messed up forever. I die before I have another child from Mr. Ragland."

"That White man gonna rot in hell. All these White folks gonna rot in hell," Henri said, feeling so angry that tears welled up in his eyes.

"How will they rot in hell if we're already in it?" Luke said, more to himself than anyone else.

Henri thought of the women in his life—a reminder of all he couldn't change, of the ways he had been powerless to protect them. His mother came first. The fear in her eyes was an image he couldn't shake. Then Suzie, he remembered her begging him to perform, to save her from a fate neither of them could control. Miss Emily, Luke's mother, her spirit locked with sickness. Then Ruby, freeing her unborn child. He turned to Josephine, who sat in the corner, unable to utter a single word. They all deserved peace. A soft life. He wanted to be the shield they needed, the weapon they didn't have. But each memory reminded him of his helplessness, of the way others had taken and taken and taken. They had stolen dignity, lives, and love. They had stripped away everything these women deserved. "One of 'em's gonna bleed. They gonna feel it. Feel what they done." Henri's rage wasn't aimless. It had a purpose, a direction. For himself, Solomon, and Luke.

Ruby stared at her two boys. She took in Henri, biceps flexed and brow sweaty. Henri was a man with a spirit too wild to be caged; no amount of punishment, no beating, no harsh words could bend him into the shape of a proper field hand. His rage was a monsoon, a rage he could not cast aside like she or Luke could.

Luke's hand rested gently on Henri's tight shoulder, a touch that drew the heat from Henri's anger, like a flame blowing out beneath a pot of boiling water. Henri's breath steadied as he turned toward Luke, his rigid features relaxing. Luke's mouth curved into a tender smile, his face—already kind—easing into a warmth Ruby had never seen. At that moment, Henri and Luke were oblivious to Ruby's presence, as if the world had narrowed to just the two of them. Ruby watched. She didn't move, didn't speak. Any sound might shatter what she was seeing. Ruby felt an unfamiliar sensation. She had never known a touch that didn't bruise, never felt a presence that didn't demand something from her. But now, as she lay there, she saw something pure. It was love, as natural and vibrant as the green sheen of the forest or the soft yellow glow of the moon. She saw it, felt its presence, and it danced within her. In that fleeting moment, she was witnessing love. In this quiet, she absorbed something that healed and hurt all at once. This wasn't just something to see; it was something to feel.

Henri stared at Luke as he chopped wood. It was their first time alone in weeks. He thought of Solomon, Ruby, and Luke, the horrors they endured. There was no freedom, not even of your own body.

"Junior touches you?" Henri asked as he chopped. The question brought on a mess of memories. Junior's fleshy stub, making his insides burn. Junior forcing himself on him for years, even when he was a child. The years of violation and nightmares were demons in Luke's life.

Luke nodded, struggling with the shame as he looked to Henri. "But being with you, Henri . . . it's the first time I ever felt good with somebody. You make me feel like there's something more out here. I was born and raised on this plantation, never left. But you, you're from Africa; you remember home. You remember a family, a life before all this. If I knew how to love, I'd tell you I love you. But I don't reckon I know how, Henri. I'm not even sure we're supposed to love."

"Everybody's s'posed to love. All we had was love back home."

"That home is many miles away."

"Maybe that's a sign we oughta leave Magnolia Row." Henri

tossed down his ax. "Right now, all we need is something different. You wanna be stuck for the rest of your days?"

"Look what happened to Solomon." Luke shook his head. "I don't know how to travel through woods and rivers. And I know Junior would do everything to hunt me down. I'd be a dead man. And you would, too."

Henri put his hand on Luke's neck. "David did it. And you know how to read, you can write us a pass. *We* can do it."

Escape was something imagined rather than lived. Luke had never left Magnolia Row, not once in his entire life. The world beyond the plantation was no more real to him than the stars, beautiful but unreachable. The closest he'd ever come were Junior's stories. He knew of others who'd run wild like cornered animals. Some returned, broken in ways that didn't heal, their scars a warning to everyone who dared think of fleeing, like Solomon. Most, though, were simply never heard from again. And in Luke's mind, silence meant death. What other fate awaited someone who stepped into the unknown with nothing but hope to guide them?

The other souls spoke of freedom like it was a shaky promise. Up North, they said, freedom came with chains of its own. It wasn't as sweet as folks imagined, maybe no sweeter than the bitter air of Magnolia Row in Goochland. Luke didn't know what to believe. Maybe it was a lie whispered by men like Junior to keep him bound here. Maybe not. But how could anything be worse than this? Was the risk worth it? Would the reward—freedom, or whatever it really was—be sweeter than the horrors of being caught? The stories of those who'd made it haunted him almost as much as those who hadn't. They sounded so brave, so certain. Luke didn't feel brave. All he felt was a clawing fear.

Luke traced Henri's face with his eyes, and for a second, he saw it. Luke saw himself on the other side of something else with Henri. He was unsure what the "else" would be. But

Henri's eyes were full of distant hope. Luke wanted to believe, to feel that same spark of possibility. He also trusted Henri. He knew the world; if he were ever to escape, it would be with him and him only. He also knew that he would never let Henri leave alone.

Night had come down and Luke persuaded Junior to allow him to stay the night with his mother, who everyone knew was in her final days. He had told Henri to wait for him by his mother's shack, instructing him to remain hidden until he arrived. Before leaving the big house, Luke had hurriedly gathered what he could—clothes, food, water, and a kerosene lamp. He told Ruby the supplies were for himself and his ailing mother for the night. Ruby's brow furrowed with confusion, but she said nothing. Luke wanted to bid Ruby a final farewell but was determined to keep their plans concealed. He feared that Mr. Ragland would pressure her into betraying their escape. It was safer if she remained in the dark.

Outside of the shack, Henri breathed when he saw Luke. Henri prayed tonight would bring their escape but Luke's nerve wavered. Luke had his doubts, but he needed the wisdom of his mother. Luke pushed open the creaky door to the shack. He moved toward his mother. She lay in bed—the sickest he had ever seen. Her mouth hung open, thin fingers curled as if clutching something invisible, eyes half-lidded, and each breath a sustained drag. Henri, right behind him, nodded solemnly as he approached Miss Emily, offering her a respectful greeting. Luke dropped to his knees beside his mother, his hands gently brushing her bony forehead. Miss Emily, her eyes clouded with both the haze of illness and the clarity of knowing, listened as her son explained he was considering running tonight with Henri. He laid out their bid for freedom. The night was their god, the darkness their ally, but only if she agreed. Only with her blessing.

"Go," Miss Emily said weakly. "Just like your pa," her words barely more than a breath. Her eyes met his with a look of resignation and unbearable pain. "Leave . . . but don't . . . leave me here."

Luke knew what his mother meant. Her plea was not just for him to escape but for him to end her suffering. Miss Emily was ready to die, the years of hell too much for her any longer. Her life had been a torment, and now, she saw no way out but through death. Luke felt a wrenching conflict within him. The thought of granting her release from agony nearly crushed him. He understood what she meant by "don't leave me here"—it was a request for mercy, an end to the suffering. Luke, caught in a maelstrom of love and sorrow, guilt and dejection, felt himself drowning.

Miss Emily sobbed. The lump in her chest looked as if it might burst. Not even dying animals were in this much pain, he thought. Miss Emily grabbed on to the back of her son's neck and said, "The blade." A shaking finger pointed to the corner of the tiny shack. A long blade that was used for skinning animals leaned up against a flimsy wall. Miss Emily wasn't afraid. She wanted the peace she saw in his daddy's face when he shot himself. There was no heaven, no purgatory, no hell. She wanted only to be nothing—empty—and let her traitorous body sink with the damned earth.

Henri's voice deepened as the words rolled from his tongue, "Don't let that devil Ragland steal her last steps. You give her proper passage."

A terrible truth in Henri's words. The thought of his mother dying alone by sickness or a bullet from Mr. Ragland shook him. Her last moments should be with her son, not that wicked man's cruelty. Luke looked at the blade and back to his mother. "You won't hurt me, Luke . . . already in too much pain."

Luke cried, his voice cracking with tears. "I know you're hurting so bad. I just don't want you to go . . . I can't stand Mr. Ragland. I hate all of them. No God in them. No God at all. When I look in their eyes, all I see is pure evil."

Miss Emily whispered, "All the devil's power came from God himself." Luke kissed his mother's forehead.

"Love you, Mama."

"Love you the whole wide world," she murmured, as she motioned to the blade.

Luke's tears flowed freely as he looked to Henri, who grabbed the blade. Grief bore down as Henri softly placed the handle in Luke's hand. Henri began to chant a prayer to guide the crossover. Luke locked eyes with Henri through tears. "I chant so Miss Emily is not stuck in the in-between."

Luke gripped the blade as he took in his mother. Miss Emily's eyes met his with a serene acceptance. Her face was bathed in calm. Henri chanted louder as Luke's heart thundered. He drew in a breath, the blade tight in his hand, and with a clean motion, sliced across Miss Emily's throat. The skin parted to reveal a flood of maroon, pouring forth as if a dam had given way. The flow was as inevitable as freedom itself, a visceral release. There was a slight flinch, but no discomfort—only a mystical relaxation: her jaw went loose, cheeks softened like wax, brow smoothed of its storms. And her eyes . . . they didn't close so much as still, the pupils widening into pools. In seconds, she looked younger, as if she were aging backward. Luke could feel his mother's soul slip away, unraveling like a finished spell.

Shaking uncontrollably, Luke let the blade fall from his hand, its edge now slippery with his mother's final moments. He sank down beside her, fixed on her form. With a kiss to her limp hand, Luke covered her body with a crisp sheet he took from the big house. As he sat there, he could still feel her, guiding him, urging him. Pushing them both. Luke imagined the freedom that now awaited her, a freedom that eluded them all in life. He had set his mother free out of love. It was a love that only souls who experienced love could understand.

"Free. No more pain."

Luke and Henri stood in the shadows outside of Miss Emily's shack. Luke wiped at his tears with the back of his hand, trying to control his breath. It was time to move, time to try. With Henri by his side, he believed it could be done. Still, his thoughts strayed to Ruby and Josephine. In another world, maybe he could come back for them, find a way to carry them to freedom too. But tonight, it was just the two of them. Henri pulled Luke into a tight embrace, their hearts beating against each other. For a moment, they stood, letting the connection ground them. But the shuffle of footsteps broke the quiet, pulling them back to the present.

Henri stiffened first, his head snapping toward the sound. Luke turned slower, his hand instinctively hovering near the small knife tucked into his waistband.

"Relax," came a familiar voice. "No danger here."

From the darkness emerged Solomon. His limp more pronounced in the night, his eye patch darker against his skin, and the moonlight catching his one gray eye.

"Solomon," Henri whispered. "You scared the hell outta us."

"What are you doing out here this late?" Luke said in a low voice.

Solomon took a few steps closer. He eyed their uneasy stances. "What y'all doing out here is the real question?"

Luke held Solomon's stare. "Just walking," he said. "Clearing our heads."

Solomon huffed a quiet laugh. "Y'all can try lying, but it ain't gonna work on me." He tapped his temple lightly. "I know it. You running."

Henri's mouth opened to protest, but Solomon raised a hand. "Don't bother. I know the look. I had it, too."

Henri stepped forward. "What about you? Why you roaming 'round Magnolia Row at night?"

Solomon glanced toward the fields. "I walk when nobody looking at me. Just wander in the night," he said. "When the stares ain't digging into my back. Makes me feel . . . normal, I guess." He turned back to them. "This time of night, I ain't Solomon, the one who ran and got caught. I'm just a man with two feet on the ground." Solomon stepped closer. "Y'all can do it," he said. "You can get outta here."

"How'd it go wrong for you, Solomon?" Henri asked.

"Ain't listen to what the land was telling me," he said, mulling all that led to his capture. "Thought I was smarter than it. Stuck to the rivers, thought they'd keep me hid. But the patrols know them waters better than anyone. They was waiting there. Got into a spat with David and said the rivers was the shortest way to go. I went into the waters, he didn't. I got caught." He paused. "Don't go near the rivers. Take the high ground, even if it takes longer. You see a tree with broken branches leaning west? Follow it. The land is gonna be rough, though, real rough. You gotta push through. The rougher the land get, the harder it is, the closer you get. Don't stop . . . and keep the wind at your back. You can smell trouble that way." Solomon looked at them both. "If I can't be free, somebody else oughta be. Maybe you come back for me, one day."

"Thank you, Solomon," Luke said.

Solomon smiled faintly, then lifted his hand as he placed it on Luke's shoulder. "Be anxious for nothing, but in everything by prayer and supplication, let your requests be made known to God."[11]

[11]. *Philippians* 4:6, New King James Version.

They nodded firmly.

Solomon stepped back. "Y'all take care. Hope to never see you again." His limp carried him into the darkness, his figure vanishing into Magnolia Row.

They slipped into the night, the heat of the day still clinging to their skin like a second layer. Their spirits were high. Solomon's advice had proved wise. Avoiding the rivers helped them dodge patrols, and by the time they reached higher ground, they felt nothing but hope. Even in the darkness, the stars spread overhead like a map promising deliverance. Every now and then, Luke would glance skyward, analyzing the stars.

"What are we gonna do once we get free?" Luke asked, carefully placing one foot in front of the other on the rocky path.

Henri took a moment before answering. "Don't know," he admitted. "Long as we ain't chained to nobody, that's all I can figure for now."

Luke nodded, a small smile pulled at him. "Me? I've been thinking about maybe acting in plays." He paused with a hint of embarrassment. "Junior used to make me read those old books of plays with him. That's how I first learned how to read."

"Plays?" Henri echoed.

Luke chuckled self-consciously. "Yes, sir. Shakespeare. I didn't always know what the words meant, but I'd do my best." He lifted his chin, trying for a regal tone. "'We are such stuff as dreams are made on . . . and our little life is rounded with a sleep.'"[12]

Henri blinked, then let out a sudden laughter. Luke grinned

12. William Shakespeare, *The Tempest*, Stephen Orgel, editor (Oxford: Oxford University Press, 2008), act 4, scene 1.

wide and nudged Henri's shoulder. "That's the first time I heard you laugh."

Henri shook his head. "Don't go worrying, I might do it too often," he teased, then exhaled. "Thank you, Luke."

They walked on in companionable silence for a few minutes, picking their way through brambles and sharp rocks. Luke spoke up again. "What do you wanna be, Henri, when we break free?"

Henri didn't take his eyes off the star-streaked sky. "Never really thought on it. Don't even know what I like or what I'm good at, beyond surviving." He paused. "All I do know . . . being around you, Luke, that makes me feel like maybe I can figure it out. Makes me the happiest I ever been."

Luke reached out and briefly gripped Henri's arm. For a fleeting moment, the punishing ground underfoot and the darkness pressing in all around them seemed conquerable. The risk was worth it, and they were going to make it. The words felt prophetic now, heavy with meaning: "*We are such stuff as dreams are made on.*" He almost wanted to laugh at the bitter irony of it all. So many dreams had never been dreamt, a billion reveries of hope, lost before they began. They were traveling in search of the dream, yet living in the nightmare. Freedom had to be close, it felt like they traveled so far.

But the climb became more grueling, each incline stealing their breath and sapping their strength. Rocks poked out in hidden places, slicing open their palms and soles, slowing them down. Tangles of thorns snatched at their clothes. Still, they pressed on, buoyed by small victories. There were no howling dogs at their backs, no torchlight cutting through the trees. They paused in a dark hollow to catch their breath. Luke managed a shaky grin. "We put some good distance behind us." For just a few heartbeats, it felt like they might truly get away.

By the time dusk turned to dawn, the paths and looming ridges began to look the same. Delirium set in, making every turn feel like a step backward. Landmarks they could've sworn they passed hours ago reemerged. "Don't make no sense," Henri said, pausing to lean against a crooked pine. "This ain't right."

"We just keep going," Luke insisted, though, for the first time, uncertainty was in his eyes. "We got to."

Weariness was in their bones. Their knapsacks were heavy. The farther they trudged, the more each step felt like a strike against their bodies. They pictured the bright fields beyond the enemy lines, but as the sun's rays peeled back the edges of night, the hope that had sustained them began to close.

It started low, almost indistinguishable from the wail of wind through the trees. They prayed it was a hallucination, but it was the baying of hounds, so sudden that Luke froze in midstep, his heart hammering against his ribs. Desperation shot in Henri's chest. They'd avoided the rivers, they'd taken the hard path through the hills—surely they'd gained ground. The frantic barks and snarls drew closer. In what felt like an instant, the bloodhounds were upon them, fangs bared and snapping. Henchmen followed with shackles in hand, their voices gruff commands. Luke and Henri fought with every ounce of strength, but the overwhelming numbers of their captors could not be bested. Blows rained down: lashes, fists and boots thudding into their bodies. Rusted iron tore into their wrists and ankles. Luke was thrown back to the nights he was chained to Junior's bed.

Luke had seen the scene many times: a runaway, bound to the back of a wagon, a collar biting into his neck, his hands tied so tightly that his wrists were raw. What he never imagined was that it would be him. A rope was fastened around his waist, tethered to the wagon, forcing him to stumble and drag his feet in a bid to keep pace. Each step was a battle; he collapsed repeatedly, but the wagon never slowed. Whether he was being dragged or struggling to walk, the movement was unceasing. Henri, by his side, was a picture of battered insurgence. Blood stained his chest where he had fought back fiercely, his face a mask of swelling and bruises.

The walk behind the wagon felt like hours, but soon everything began to look familiar. The ocean of cotton fields appeared before them, making Henri remember his first time on Magnolia Row not too long ago. His head was pounding. His heart shook. Henri could take a whipping, but he knew this time would be much worse. He looked to Luke, stumbling every few seconds and a torn shirt exposing his lashes. The wounds gorged with blood.

They could see the big house. There was a crowd surrounding the front. He had never seen so many souls this close to the house, even more than when Solomon was captured. Ruby stood at the edge of the crowd. Lips moved silently as her prayers fell into the air, begging any God who might be listening to spare her beautiful boys. Josephine wrapped herself around Ruby's leg. Her small face peeked out. Solomon stood nearby. Hands shoved into his pockets to keep them from shaking. His one good eye twitched. Solomon didn't need to see this to know what was coming—he had lived it just weeks ago.

Mr. Ragland, Mistress Kitty, and Junior stood on the front steps. The closer they got, Luke glared in Junior's face. He saw the rawest of evil, even worse than Mr. Ragland. His cheeks were flushed, his small, piggish eyes glinting with a cruelty that oozed from his pores. There was a long blade in Junior's hand. Luke knew the blade. It was the blade that freed his mother. "Luke . . ." Henri mumbled. "I'm sorry. So sorry." Mr. Ragland, Mistress Kitty, and Junior were on the top step of the wide porch, standing motionless, eyeballing them both. Luke uncontrollably screamed. Henri began to sob. "Luke, please. Please, Luke . . ."

Luke tried to breathe. "Henri, they are gonna cut us open . . ."

Henri and Luke kneeled in the dirt before Mr. Ragland, Mistress Kitty, and Junior. The souls surrounded them. Luke was unrecognizable with his bruised face and chest bitten by dogs. There was more blood than exposed skin on Henri as he breathed in and out, fearlessly staring directly at Mr. Ragland. If he wasn't chained and tied, Mr. Ragland would be a dead man.

"Saddest thing I ever seen," Mr. Ragland said.

Mistress Kitty nodded in agreement. "You ain't ever treated two slaves better and they ran away on you."

"You don't know the money you cost," Mr. Ragland continued. "The folks I had to pay to get you back. Known you since you was a baby, Luke. Took care of your mama. And you do this? To Junior? Ain't ever been more disappointed in any slave than you." He paused. "Your mama. Emily. Throat was wide open . . . Either you or that African did that to your mama."

Luke's insides steamed.

"I threw Emily in the thorn bushes," Mr. Ragland said. "Sho' did. She still out there, not too far away. Got the animals gnawing on her black body. You think on that, boy. You think real hard on it."

"Here, Daddy," Junior said in the deepest voice anyone heard him speak, passing him the blade. "You take this, I don't want to get my hands dirty."

Mr. Ragland grabbed the blade from Junior and walked down the steps. Luke lowered his head, bracing himself for Mr. Ragland's next move. "Whippings too good for you. Need stronger if you gonna learn. And everybody," he let out, his voice turning into the familiar roar, "need to be reminded that you need to know your place."

Mr. Ragland seized Luke by the head, forcing him down into the dirt. He smashed Luke's face into the ground with one hand, while the other gripped the blade. He pulled his ear and began sawing mercilessly. Mr. Ragland's violence would not be rushed. Henri broke, tears streaking through the grime on his face. Little Josephine turned into Ruby's dress, her tiny fists clutching the fabric. Solomon stood with his head low, his eye twitching, his left foot squirming. Ruby stared with prayer—not the meek kind, her prayer wasn't a surrender, but a simmering rage. Luke could feel the flesh being torn from his head, his screams piercing as Mr. Ragland worked. Each grind was an assault on his senses, the sound of tearing bone and skin reverberating in his skull. Blood erupted from the wound, pouring into his ear canal.

Mr. Ragland held half of Luke's ear in his hand, shaking it to the sky, showing it to the horrified souls. "This is what you get when you run away! And this is easy!" Luke rolled on the ground, screaming from pain. "Ruby! Get that boy up before I have a dead field hand." Ruby was ready with her cloth, water, honey, and salt. She only hoped her boys would survive as she tried to patch up a delirious Luke, who lay with his face in the dirt, shaking and sobbing.

"You four—hold that boy down!" Mr. Ragland shouted, pointing at Henri. "Spread open his arms and legs!" The four souls obeyed as they forced Henri to the dirt, his limbs spread wide and vulnerable. Henri didn't resist; he lay still, his once-tattered pants now torn away, leaving him exposed.

Henri's legs were spread so wide it seemed they might snap from the strain. Mr. Ragland stood over him as he brandished the long, sharp blade. "You know what it means to be whipped. Ain't nothing gonna scare you?" His voice dripped with satisfaction. From the dirt, Luke turned his face toward Henri, his eyes filled with anguish.

"Cut 'em off!" Junior's voice demanded from the porch. "Daddy, cut 'em off!"

Mistress Kitty giggled, "Do it like the hogs, Montgomery!"

Mr. Ragland's hands gripped and tugged at Henri's testicles. In a savage, immediate motion, the blade descended. Henri's most primal scream cracked from the back of his throat as the violence sliced through him. The world spiraled into a dizzying blur; his mind overwhelmed. He stared at the bluest sky, which vanished into an oppressive white.

Luke and Henri were barely clinging to life. The souls who witnessed their suffering heard the shocking words from Mr. Ragland: that Luke or Henri had killed Miss Emily. This malicious gossip spread, further tormenting them as they lay in the very shack where Miss Emily was set free, another form of punishment from Mr. Ragland—or so he thought. Somehow, in that cursed place, they felt shielded. Miss Emily was free, but she was not gone. She lived in between their short breaths, in the way the walls hummed when their strength waned. They prayed to her. Called her name like a hymn, summoned her warrior spirit to flood their bodies. Miss Emily, who had damned the shell that failed her, now became the vessel for their survival. With the scent of old blood in their noses, they swore they heard her whisper: *Live*.

The process of healing was a torment. Solomon, his own wounds still raw, checked on Luke and Henri daily. He would slip into the shack during the quietest hours and bring small scraps of food he'd hidden from his own meager rations. Other times, his presence was enough to remind them they weren't entirely abandoned. His hand would tarry briefly on their shoulders before he left, a gesture of solidarity. He held no judgment against them for Miss Emily. He understood the freeing; often, he dreamed of freeing himself in the same way.

Ruby came every morning without fail, bringing fresh

clothes, clean sheets, water and food. With Josephine at her side, she cleaned their wounds with salt water and honey, all supplies stolen from the Raglands' pantry. "Hold still," she said, as she dabbed. "This'll burn, but it's all we got." The salt water bit into their flesh and the honey stung as it sealed the wounds, but neither Luke nor Henri complained. They couldn't afford to.

Solomon stood at the doorway, his face grave as he whispered to Ruby. "Don't know if Henri gonna make it," he said one evening. Henri's wounds were severe, his body fevered and raw. But when Ruby looked into Henri's eyes, she saw no trace of doubt. Henri could feel their worry, but there was resolution in his expression. "Don't waste your tears for me," he said to them both.

Henri fought. Believing in Miss Emily's spirit. Believing in where he came from. At night, when the fields were silent, he forced himself to stand, his body trembling as he leaned against Luke. "We gotta move," he told Luke. "Wounds heal better with blood flow." Luke, with a patch covering his ear and a stiffness in his step, didn't question him. They shuffled through the darkened fields, the moonlight tracing their battered silhouettes.

"Ain't our birthdays coming 'round in a few weeks?" Henri said as they leaned on each other in the night.

Luke scoffed softly, turning toward him. "We got the same birthday, August twenty-first."

Henri kept his eyes on the ground. Not too long ago, Luke had given him a birthday, handed him something he'd never thought to claim for himself. *August twenty-first*, he repeated in his head, letting it settle.

"Nineteen," Luke said as Henri pushed to make wider strides.

Henri didn't know if nineteen felt right, but it didn't matter. What did was the way Luke had said it, so sure, like it was his to give, as if he could share something as simple and precious as a date with no strings attached. It was a strange thing, Henri thought, to feel ownership over time, over a day.

"We oughta celebrate," Henri said.

Luke gave a dry chuckle that turned into a wince. "Celebrate what? We barely living."

"Celebrate what's coming. We gonna make it. And when we do—" He paused, facing Luke and wrapping his arms around him, resting his head on his shoulder. "We celebrate with fire," Henri said in his ear.

Luke cupped the back of Henri's neck. "Fire it is."

Beneath their exteriors, a ferocity smoldered. Rebellion was in their blood. Luke carried it in his veins, the fire of his father. Henri had been ripped from his homeland that had nurtured him free, only to find himself in a nation that caged his body. For the weeks they were healing in the shack, they made their plans, biding their time. They knew the risks, but ironically, isolation became their ally, granting them the time and secrecy to strategize when no one was listening. When Luke and Henri were forced back into the fields, their bodies still aching, they worked through the pain, their movements robotic but their minds sharp with purpose. The stories of others who fought back never stopped circling their plans. Retribution was inevitable. Justice was fated. Capitulation was unthinkable. Through their healing, Luke and Henri plotted, they would strike again despite a failed first attempt. They refused to let defeat turn into despair. The curtain call was to coincide with the day of Luke's birth and the day he had given to Henri. The Raglands were determined to break them physically and mentally, to keep them subdued for their labor, but healing was more than a mere physical recovery.

Shortly after midnight, on August 21, Luke and Henri moved across the land toward the Raglands' great house. Luke knew every plank, every loose latch—knew the house's weaknesses better than the Raglands themselves. There were always ways in: a warped window, a door left unbarred, small oversights from the privileged who never thought to fear what crept in the dark. Ruby's cabin sat close to the back door. They couldn't risk waking her. Instead, they slipped toward the kitchen entrance. A gentle push was all it took. The door swung open without a sound, as if the house itself were inviting them in.

The grand, cold walls of the big house were eerily quiet, except for the sporadic creak of the old timbers. The smell of kerosene and old grease clung to the walls, a burnt odor. They moved through the halls, the walls aglow with the shifting light of oil lamps. The flames cast prancing shadows, making the portraits hanging on the walls come alive in a nightmarish ballet. The paintings were unsettling, each face rendered in ghoulish grays and pale blues.

Their movements were inconspicuous with Luke carrying a broadax. The walls tightened around them as they tiptoed up the stairs to Junior's room, the epicenter of the first comeuppance. The door, half-open, creaked with a haunting groan as they nudged it aside. Inside, the room was bathed in the unnatural light of a kerosene lamp on a bedside table, shining over Junior's mess, clothes across the floor, an unemptied chamber pot reeking in the corner, and at the foot of the bed, iron chains lying in a heap. Amid the chaos stood the vanity Henri had built. On its surface rested a single, unmoving thing: a Bible, its leather cover obviously untouched. *There is no peace, saith my God, to the wicked.*[13] A sleeping Junior, deep in his dreams, was unaware that judgment was ready to strike.

Luke and Henri stood over Junior in the bed, his naked body sprawled out. His fat belly spilled out like a bloated udder. Junior's pink fleshy nipples jutted out. Henri's groin

13. *Isaiah* 57:21, New King James Version.

ached with a phantom pain. He recalled how Junior demanded that he be mutilated. He glanced at Luke, barely recognizable, his face a patchwork of healing scars, a permanent reminder of the torment. His missing ear would never grow back. "Kill him," Henri said in a venomous whisper.

Luke raised the broadax as high as he could, his mind a cacophony of images. The kerosene lamp allowed him to see his target. He could still hear Junior's voice as he was inside of him. The memories of being choked, penetrated, and defiled were his recurring nightmares. The chains at the end of the bed. All of it shot into his muscles, spread in his veins, and settled right in his soul. With all the strength he could muster, Luke brought the broadax down. The blade cleaved into Junior's abdomen, flesh tearing in a grotesque symphony. Henri watched with glee while Junior's eyes broke open. They relished in his terror and let him yelp for a few seconds. They wanted to hear his pain. Henri smashed a pillow in his face. Junior tried to fight, his chubby arms swinging like a pig being slaughtered. Luke hacked again, blood splattering on their bodies and decorating the walls. Henri laughed as Luke shredded Junior's legs, each primal scream vibrating through the pillow. Junior's manliness was exposed. Covering Junior's face with the pillow, Henri grabbed his penis, squeezing and twisting, reminding him of the pink snake in his foul shack from that first night on Magnolia Row.

"Move that pillow," Luke demanded as Henri yanked it away. Junior's shrill, inhuman wail filled the room. Swiftly, Luke swung the broadax into his mouth. Junior's face shattered like a porcelain doll; eyes impossibly wide, a waterfall of blood and tissue ruined his cheeks. They stepped away, admiring their work, soaked in blood. Junior lay in disemboweled pieces, a rightful mess. Luke felt a rush of liberation, the scent of his oppressor's blood filling him up. He met Henri's gaze, both of them grinning. They had killed the devil's spawn.

A high-pitched scream pierced their birthday night. Mistress Kitty stood in the doorway, her white skin shining in the dim light. Henri grabbed the ax from Luke. She tried to flee, but fear rooted her where she stood. Kitty's knees knocked together, nails scratching the doorframe. She whimpered as Henri's ax buried itself in her shoulder. Bones snapped like dry twigs. The next blow struck her neck, blood spraying in a scarlet crescent. Kitty collapsed in the hallway, clutching her throat. The roles had reversed; now she was defenseless.

Henri followed her, chopping away at Kitty like she was firewood. Luke watched, seeing Kitty's beastly soul driven out of her body. She deserved to die. His only regret was not killing her sooner. He walked to Luke, smiling, proud and strong. Biceps bulging, chest heaving, half his face splattered with blood. He reached for Luke, but a gunshot rang out. Henri's body jerked, smoke curling from his shoulder. The ax clattered to the floor. Another shot, and Henri's hands uncontrollably flew up, blood shooting as he fell to his knees, collapsing atop Kitty's mutilated body. Standing a few feet away was Mr. Ragland with a smoking shotgun in his hand.

Luke thought it was unreal. The scene before him, a premonition of blood and violence rather than reality unfolding. The metallic click of Mr. Ragland's rifle being reloaded echoed like a death knell. As if jolted from a trance, Luke seized the broadax and charged forward. Mr. Ragland's attempts to ready his shotgun were clumsy, frantic. "Stay back, boy!" he shouted, but fear robbed his voice of authority. Luke swung the ax with a wild fury, slicing into Mr. Ragland's left shin. The impact sent Mr. Ragland sprawling to the floor as he fell onto his back.

Luke was upon him in an instant, driven by a fire that transcended his own strength. He raised the ax high and brought it down, severing Mr. Ragland's arm with a crunch. The hate that had been bottled up for so long poured out of him in a torrent. He had dreamed of this moment, imagined it in countless ways, and now he was striking not just flesh and bone, but the very embodiment of his torment.

Luke's hands were dripping with blood, determined to obliterate the face that had haunted his nightmares. That face—once a symbol of his suffering, the man who had stolen his mother and his dignity—was now his vengeance. But the eyes. Luke could still see those wicked orbs as they bulged freakishly wide from the pain. Under the light of the kerosene lamp, Montgomery Ragland's eyes glistened like wet marbles, the veins within them a map of all the souls he had killed, raped and tortured. The eyes pleaded—yet still carried a touch of arrogance, as if even now he believed he was omnipotent. He thought of Solomon. Thought of the pain in that lone eye hidden behind the crude patch. Solomon wasn't here to see this, to feel the reckoning he deserved, but Luke would deliver it for him. For Solomon, for his mother, for his father, for every soul who had been broken under the Raglands on Goochland's Magnolia Row.

Luke dropped the ax and fell to his knees, straddling Mr. Ragland. Luke's thumbs hovered over his master's goggle eyes for just a moment. Then he pressed. The taut membrane of the eye pushed back against his thumbs. He pressed harder, his thumbs sinking deeper. The wet squelch of the eyeball ruptured and squirted. A spray of clear fluid mixed with blood burst, splattering Luke's hands and Montgomery Ragland's cheeks. He let out a cry, bleating like a frightened sheep. Luke didn't stop. Farther as the tissue gave way, his thumbs sank in. Another sickening pop, followed by a gush of fluid that trickled down Mr. Ragland's temples like tears. He twisted inside the sockets, ensuring that nothing remained intact, nothing recognizable. Even if he survived by the grace of Satan, he would never see a soul again. Luke pulled his hands back. They were caked with blood and viscera. The devil he had longed to overthrow was at his mercy, and tonight, the master would be vanquished. Mr. Ragland's body convulsed in a final desperate, spasmodic dance of death.

Luke's senses were skewed. A sound cut through and he shot up. He turned, and there on the unforgiving floor of the hallway lay Henri, sprawled over the cracked remains of Kitty. Luke staggered forward. He pried Henri away from Kitty, laying him easily onto the floor, and knelt beside his friend. The light of the oil lamps showed a hole in his chest.

"Luke." Henri's voice was still strong. Luke's hands were tremulous as he reached out, gripping Henri's wounded body, the heat of his blood melting into Luke's skin.

"Hold on, Henri. Please, hold on. Let me get you outside." He scooped Henri in his arms, blood gushing out of the hole as he rushed down the stairs, kicking open the door to the front porch.

"Put me down," Henri croaked, coughing up blood.

"We can make it. Ruby can patch you up," Luke said through tears.

"Down, Luke. Gotta talk." Luke reluctantly laid him on the front porch.

"Henri, please." Luke clutched him. "You can fight. You got it in you."

"Ah love you, Luke. You be a king." Henri's eyes softened, his tone almost carrying back to his native tongue. His grip on the back of Luke's neck was strong. "Set Magnolia Row on fire. Leave not'ing. Burn it down like how my village burn. Burn it down like Haiti. Don't let nobody stop you. Burn down master's house. Burn it down, Luke."

"Henri!" Luke screamed. "Don't you leave me now, I'm begging you!" Henri's final breath broke free as Luke felt his soul drift away. Henri's body went limp, his hand slipping from Luke's neck as his final words hung in the air like smoke. His command settled on Luke's shoulders. Henri's eyes, once fierce and burning with the fire of rebellion, now rested, wide and peaceful. A cry tore from Luke's depths, a cry so extreme that it ripped his voice. He held Henri close, feeling the heaviness of his body press against his own. Luke's mind raced, torn by the urgency of Henri's call for fire. Their memories charged through his mind. First, meeting Henri outside of the barn, the kindness he showed his mother, their time at the riverbank, long talks about his homeland, and their moments of freedom in the mountains.

"Gonna burn it all," Luke vowed.

Carefully, he let go of Henri and kissed him on his bloody lips. A scream made Luke jolt up to see Josephine, the first sound that came from her mouth. She stood near Ruby, just as stunned. She pulled Josephine close to her side, trying to quiet the girl's cries.

Luke stood. "Henri's gone," he rasped. "And this place—this place is going with him. I'm gonna burn Magnolia Row down, Ruby."

Ruby took in Henri. Her knees weakened, and for a moment, she teetered but no tears. No more tears. Instead, an inflamed anger. She untied the tattered bandana from her head, staring at it for a moment before tossing it to the ground.

"Then we burn it down together," she said, smoothing down her hair. "Ain't letting you do this alone."

Luke hesitated. "Ruby— "

"I said *together.*" She cut him off, stepping closer to him. "We both been in this hell. We both gotta end it."

Luke locked into Ruby. They weren't bound by blood. Blood meant nothing here. They were bound by the same mortal coil, the same rotted-ripe hope that kept them alive. Luke turned toward the front door, the two of them stepping into the master's house side by side. From behind them came the sound of footsteps. Luke turned to see Josephine in the doorway, her unblinking eyes fixed on them. "Josephine, no," Luke said. "You don't need to see this."

"No, she do, Luke," Ruby said firmly. "Needs to see what

it means to take something back. What it means to end something that should've never been." Ruby walked over to Josephine and crouched down. "You stay close to me, you hear? You need to see this, so you know what we fought for. What *you'll* fight for someday."

Josephine nodded. Ruby took her hand and led her back to Luke, who let out a breath. "We start upstairs," Luke said.

Luke ran for a matchbox and two kerosene lamps from the kitchen. They bolted up the same steps they'd climbed a thousand times before—weary, sick, or with stabs of hunger, always at the Raglands' command. This time, their feet carried no obedience. In the hallway, the sight of the mutilated bodies of Montgomery Ragland and Kitty Ragland lying just feet apart gave Ruby pause, but she pressed on. Luke stood beside Mr. Ragland's corpse and emptied one of the kerosene lamps across the floor. He struck a match and dropped it. A small flame danced, making its way to Junior's room. Ruby stepped forward as she grabbed the other kerosene lamp from Luke's hand. "This one's mine," she said, Ruby hurled the lamp against the far wall, the glass shattering and igniting instantly. Josephine flinched at the explosion of fire, her tiny hands flying up to cover her ears.

Luke stepped back, his eyes on the growing fire. Ruby watched the fire climb, its light on Mr. Ragland, his face contorting as the heat reached his skin. Kitty's body began to sizzle. Ruby looked to Josephine and nodded, "Watch, baby," her voice above the crackling flames. "Burn," Ruby spat. "Burn for every scar, every scream, every soul you stole."

Blue flames crackled into the portraits of the pale, gray people who were always watching. Their senile smiles and stares melted from the walls. Luke wondered who they tortured and how they passed on their depravity to their kin. Bright colors licked, crept into corners, and soon engulfed Junior's room. This house, Junior's room, was his deepest hell since he was a child. The years of torment began to disintegrate. Ruby took a deep breath, cherishing the acrid smell of burning wood and flesh filling her lungs. Josephine let go of Ruby's dress, stepping closer to the fire. Her small hands hung at her sides. Her lips parted. "They gonna remember us."

Ruby nodded slowly. "That's right, Josephine," Luke added.

Luke, Ruby, and Josephine descended the stairs, coolly walking out of the big house, their final exit. They returned to Henri's shell on the front porch. Luke knelt beside his love. Henri was home. Freed, unencumbered by his Judas of a life.

As the heat of the master's house began to rise, souls gathered at the front. Luke lifted Henri's body, cradling it in his arms. Flames of every color lit up within the big house, breaking through the windows, writhing like tormented souls finally released. Luke's mind spun, the whippings, the stolen children, and the faces of the lost. He thought of his mother, her worn hands and tired eyes. He reflected on his father, a warrior he couldn't remember, but knew he would be proud. Magnolia Row would end here, consumed and cleansed. He walked down the porch steps, Ruby and Josephine by his side. With Henri in his arms, both drenched in blood, he pressed his lips to Henri's cheek. The souls watched Luke in silence, watched him mourn, thinking of the loves they had missed, lovers lost in real time, lovers snatched from them quietly in the night. They could feel his loss. They were with him. Their quiet was a surrender to his pain. Luke stared at his brothers and sisters with Solomon at the center.

"The Raglands have gone to hell, and the devil's finally got his due," Luke said. "They killed Henri . . . just like they killed my mama." He paused. "I know what y'all might think of me, but my mama wanted her soul free. I freed her." He drew in the scent of the flames and let the fire's rhythm play in his ears. "And I'm setting more souls free tonight. Magnolia Row's going to hell. Burning every inch of it to the ground. Stand with me or get gone while you can."

The faces of the souls reflected the inferno consuming the

master's house. Some stared, unblinking, their expressions compounded with awe and shock. Mouths hung open, not in fear, but in wonderment, as the flames climbed higher, devouring the pillars, the roof, the very walls that had held their suffering. The house, once a monument to supremacy, stood ablaze like a colossal effigy. Its proud symmetry warped in the heat, windows bursting outward with a crack. The fire was a soul coming alive, roaring and snarling as it tore through the boards and shattered the glass panes that once surveyed the fields with unyielding authority. The white exterior darkened and crumbled, the flames stripping away its façade of permanence. For years, this house had beat against their backs, its towering columns like demons watching over their pain. The souls watched as the master's house collapsed inward, its perfect corners and smooth surfaces giving way. They could feel it, the unraveling. The house was no longer a temple but a scorched tomb.

On that August 21, a wall of wildfire enveloped Magnolia Row whole. Every row of cotton, the ginhouse, every shack, the barn, everything the souls didn't take was engulfed by fire. There was a jubilee in destroying this place of terror. Children laughed; men and women danced and sang. The fire cleansed their spirits. And before sunrise, every soul was on their way to somewhere else. Many were captured, many escaped. But as the sun rose over the smoldering ruins, the ashes marked rebirth.

Word of Magnolia Row spread like the fire that captivated it. The news arrived on horseback, in ink-stained papers trembling in the hands of those who read them. White women clutched their pearls and pulled their children closer, their eyes jumping toward the souls. Ministers fell to their knees in churches, praying to their version of Christ. Men who once spoke with the arrogance of kings now stood in doorways, rifles shaking in their grip. Planters locked their doors in broad daylight. One newspaper headline screamed: THE FIRE OF REBELLION: NO MASTER SHALL SLEEP SOUNDLY AGAIN.

It wasn't justice on paper that haunted them. It was justice in flesh. The enslavers from Goochland, Virginia, to the deepest part of the South shuddered. The reckoning had begun, and for the first time in their lives, they considered: Vengeance was not theirs. They were sleeping with the enemy. The once-unshakable foundation of their power now felt fragile. Souls were activated. Not just on paper, but in flesh. How long could this institution survive? Its days were numbered. The Lord's judgment hovered over them, as if it were biding its time to deliver its reparation. America would be dragged, bloodied and gasping, into a hard-won glory.

CHAPTER 2

JOSEPHINE

"Make a change there before long."[14]

The clock ticked softly on the kitchen wall, its face worn and stained with time. Each measured beat filled the space, a rhythm that taunted her. The time didn't matter. It was another day, she told herself. Another endless, merging day in Goochland. Magnolia Row, the plantation where she had spent her childhood, was long gone. No matter how many seasons blurred together, she could still see the flames. The heat of that night stayed in her bones. Ruby had taught her so much: how to notice everything without being noticed, how to protect herself even when she was powerless. Luke and Henri had shown her what it meant to fight, even when the odds were built against your very right to exist. *Don't let them take what they can't touch*, Luke would say. And the

14. "Distressing Homicide," *Baltimore Sun*, July 18, 1855.

fire—beautifully teaching her that even the worst hell can burn.

She was no longer a child, but she couldn't say how long it had been since that night. She was told she was eighteen, but time had no meaning here. Not with the Baynard family. What mattered was survival. The days, weeks, months, years after Magnolia Row were a fog, a series of disconnected moments she couldn't—or wouldn't—piece together. She remembered the shouting and the running. Ruby's face, Luke's voice—they were still with her in flashes, but they felt as unreachable as the moon. She couldn't keep up. She remembered the commotion of being seized and how the chaos carried her to this place. Waking up somewhere new and alone was the only ending she could recall. She didn't ask where Ruby and Luke were now, not even in her own mind. Some questions were too dangerous to answer. As the clock ticked on, its sound pulled her back into the present.

Josephine. What did a name matter? She hadn't been called Josephine in years. Here, she was "girl," "gal," or "you." Sometimes, "lazy" or "stupid." A name was a thing of freedom, and freedom was far beyond her reach. She shifted her focus from the clock and looked out of the window, her eyes on the fields where the souls moved, preparing for a vicious day under the July sun. They bent low over the Goochland soil, their bodies already sheened with sweat.

It was going to be a hot Saturday, she could feel it in the air, even at this early hour. The Fourth of July had come and gone three days ago, the so-called Independence Day. Josephine had watched the Baynards celebrate, their laughter and fireworks lighting up the night. She could still hear their voices if she let herself think too hard, the drunken shouts of "liberty" and "justice." The irony of it had burned hotter than the sparklers the Baynard children waved in their small, careless hands. Freedom for some, bondage for others.

Josephine tried to focus on breakfast. Her mind tended to wander early in the morning. The bacon cooking in a cast-iron pan, its smoky scent filling the brick kitchen. Lady Baynard wanted her breakfast at the same time every morning. She glanced at the clock on the kitchen wall. It was nearly half-past six, the time Lady Baynard always expected her breakfast to be served. Not a moment sooner, not a moment later. The routine was as precise as the ticking clock. Josephine had come to mark time by it, her days carved into pieces dictated by someone else's hunger. By now, she knew without thinking how long it took for the bacon to crisp just right, how to fold the eggs into neat curds that would sit perfectly on Lady Baynard's fine porcelain plate. Yet this morning, her hands moved a little slower. Her mind drifted back to the fireworks just days ago, the way they lit up the night sky, a lie she couldn't unsee. *Independence.* Josephine wiped her hands on her apron. There was no time for wandering thoughts. Lady Baynard would be waiting, her appetite as sharp as her expectations. Anything less would earn her a slap or worse.

As she turned to set the eggs on the table and go for Lady Baynard, Josephine felt a familiar chill crawling up her spine. Mr. Lafayette Baynard in the doorway of the kitchen. His eyes held a darkness that the brightness of morning could not erase.

"You up early," he slurred, his voice slick like oil on water.

Josephine nodded, "Always up early." She kept her gaze fixed on the plate in her hands. "Lady Baynard likes her breakfast promptly."

He stepped closer, the space between them shrinking. The scent of whiskey stank on him, even at this early hour, and something else—something that made Josephine's tummy ache.

"Seems she ain't the only one who could use some tending

to—promptly," he said, his fingers brushing against her arm. The touch burned like a brand.

She pulled back. "Best not keep her waiting," she said, trying to move past him. He blocked her path.

"Now, now, no need to rush." His drunk breath stung her skin. "Plenty of time before she stirs."

Josephine's heart hammered. At only eighteen, she knew the dance all too well. "Please," she said, her voice steady despite the fear. "Eggs gonna get cold."

"Let them," he said, reaching out to tuck a loose strand of her hair behind her ear. "I gotta taste for something else this morning."

"Mr. Lafayette," she began, choosing her words carefully, "Lady Baynard will be waiting for me."

"The lady of the house will do what I say." He grabbed the back of her neck.

Time fractured, each second a lifetime as Josephine's mind began to slip. She thought of Ruby, how she would cling to her dress for safety, but that brought her sadness. She reached for something else, anything else. The garden outside unfolded in her mind, a sanctuary she willed into existence. She could see it now—the way the sunlight broke through the trees, dappling the earth in golden patches. She imagined the scent fresh blossoms carried, cool and cleansing as it kissed her skin. She was no longer in the room. She was outside, barefoot, the grass soft and damp beneath her toes, grounding her in a place where nothing could harm her. She focused on the sound of life there: the bees drifting lazily from flower to flower. She reached out to brush a bee away but paused. She stared, small and harmless, yet carrying something invisible, something hidden—*venom*, she thought. She didn't know why the word struck her so sharply, but the world she created felt so real, more real than the suffocating air around her now. She knelt by the garden bed, her fingers digging into the soil. A bird trilled above her, a melody so pure it lifted her spirit, carrying her higher.

The pressure and noise around her dulled, fading to a murmur, like something happening to someone else far away. Here in her garden, she was featherlike, untouchable. She looked up at the open sky, endless and blue. She was safe. She was whole. She was free. And when Josephine opened her eyes, the vision didn't fade. She refused to let it. Every detail ingrained into her mind, her body, in the soil of her imagination, even as the world outside her pressed on. She was no longer there.

Her mind went black, black as a forgotten dream. As Mr. Lafayette walked away, the sound of his belt jangled. Josephine shrunk into the rough wood of the kitchen floor beneath her. She sat there, knees drawn up, as if the wood itself could lock her to something solid. She remembered this position when she saw Mistress Kitty look down on Ruby after she miscarried. Josephine hadn't understood it then. She did now.

The room was still except for the ticking of the clock on the wall, its rhythm marking the seconds she couldn't feel. Time was slippery in moments like these. The smell of the kitchen was all wrong now. The sharp tang of eggs, once comforting, now sickened her. The charred bacon made her insides fight. She thought she should rise, but her body refused to obey. Her arms hung limp at her sides, her fingers twitching slightly, as though the only thing they could still feel was Lafayette's grip.

The sharp clatter of a plate striking the table jolted Josephine from her thoughts. Lady Baynard towered above her, shifting the plate.

"You're late," she snapped.

"Apologies, ma'am," Josephine replied, bowing her head.

Lady Baynard eyed her breakfast with disdain. "The eggs and bacon are cold," she hissed.

Josephine opened her mouth to respond, but no words came out. What could she say that would not invite further ire? That the delays were not of her making?

"Useless girl," Lady Baynard muttered. "Stand up!"

As Josephine slowly stood, Lady Baynard slapped her with an open hand. Josephine felt her skin tear, the metallic taste of her blood touched her tongue. Lady Baynard's diaphanous fingers, streaked now with Josephine's blood, quivered as she flung the plate to the ground, causing it to shatter.

Lady Baynard growled, more feral than woman. "That food was cold!"

The slap and taste of blood switched on a rebelliousness in Josephine. Her lips curled into a smile. "Cold as you," she spat, each syllable slicing the air.

Lady Baynard's thin nostrils flared. Her skin flushed like a bag of blood. She raised her hand again, nails long, and scratched on Josephine's neck. Josephine staggered but stood her ground, her hand instinctively reaching for her throat. She felt the warm, sticky blood trickle over her fingers and brought her palm up to Lady Baynard's face. "And you call me the animal?"

Lady Baynard recoiled, her mouth opening and closing like a fish gasping for air. "Lafayette!" Her voice struck the air like lightning.

The hesitant steps of Lafayette Baynard sounded from down the hall. His disheveled form appeared in the doorway, shirt half-buttoned, eyes rimmed with exhaustion. Josephine's body stiffened at the sight of him. Lafayette met her gaze. He saw the blood on Josephine's neck and the mark on her cheek. He glanced at his wife.

Lady Baynard pointed a finger at Josephine. "She lets the eggs grow cold because she's lazy, because—" Her voice cracked, and her fury turned on Lafayette. "And you, Lafayette! Lying down with that wench!"

Lying down. That's what Lady Baynard called it? As if it were anything so gentle. As if Lafayette didn't crawl under her skin. The cold bacon and eggs weren't a choice. They were the consequence of a man's insatiable appetite and of a mistress's simmering cruelty.

Josephine's hand fell to her side, the blood now drying, sticky against her palm. Lafayette slumped against the kitchen table, reeking of whiskey and sweat.

"Lafayette!" Lady Baynard snapped. "You're too drunk to be of any use. Get up and whip this girl right!"

Lafayette groaned, his bloodshot eyes barely lifting to meet hers. "Leave me alone, woman." He waved her off with a clumsy hand. He tried to stand, but his knees buckled. He stumbled toward the back door, bumping into the frame before sliding down the steps in a drunken heap.

Lady Baynard stormed to the wall, grabbed the cowhide whip, and turned back toward Josephine. "I'll do it myself," she hissed.

Josephine stood silent as Lady Baynard shoved open the back door. "To the post," she ordered. "Now!"

Josephine didn't hesitate. She held her head high as she walked across the kitchen and out into the yard. The heat of the morning hit her skin. The warmth was a reminder that she was still alive. Her bare feet pressed against the dry dirt as she approached the whipping post, its weathered wood a hated sight.

Lady Baynard followed, the whip coiled in her hand like a predator waiting to strike. She marched across the porch, sparing a glance at Lafayette, who had slumped against the steps, muttering incoherently in his drunken stupor. "Useless," she spat under her breath.

Josephine reached the post and lowered her dress without

hesitation. The rough wood pressed against her chest as she wrapped her arms around it, her fingers gripping tightly. The scars on the post, the dark stains, all told the story of what was to come—but Josephine refused to let that story break her.

Lady Baynard's mouth curled into a cruel smile, a glint of something unholy in her eyes as she released the whip. The leather slid through her fingers, serious and sensuous. Her washed-out dress billowed slightly in the breeze, the fabric catching and snapping with each movement. The hem swirled around her ankles like a living thing, matching the rhythm of the weapon in her hands. Her face, once powdered and pristine, was contorted with a manic glee that bordered on madness. The harsh, cracking lines of her face became more pronounced. The carefully crafted mask of refinement she had worked so hard to maintain disappeared.

With a sharp snap of her wrist, she raised the whip. The leather cracked through the air before striking Josephine's back with a resounding smack. Lady Baynard took in a breath as the whip bit into flesh, leaving a bright, angry welt that oozed blood. Again, she struck harder. The whip coiled around Josephine's shoulder before snapping back, its tip leaving a mark. The force of it reverberated through Lady Baynard's body. She tilted her head slightly, her hair catching the sunlight, but the shadow across her face made her look demonic. Lady Baynard found a sick rhythm in the act.

Her dress whipped in time with her strikes, as though it, too, had come alive to join in her frenzy. There was nothing human in her expression, just unbridled malice. Each lash was more than violence—it was her revenge against everything she couldn't control: Lafayette's drunken ineptitude, her lack of true status, the grasping at power that was just out of reach. Here, in this moment, she wasn't a woman desperate to hold on to what little control she had. She was power incarnate, reveling in her ability to command pain, dominate and destroy.

Josephine's breath remained steady. Her nails dug into the post, but she didn't cry out. She didn't beg. In her mind, she could see Luke and Ruby, she could feel Henri. They were there, standing beside her, blocking her soul from the pain. They wrapped her in their presence, their courage fusing with her own, keeping her upright. She could feel Luke's hand on her shoulder: *Don't let them take what they can't touch.* Ruby's big laugh rang, a reminder of her spirit. They were gone, but not lost. They lived within her, their fire refusing to die.

"You're nothing. Just like the rest of them," Lady Baynard sneered.

You're nothing. Josephine almost laughed at the absurdity of it. *I am everything you fear*, she thought. But she didn't speak. She held tightly to memories. Then she saw it—a bee. It hovered just above the splintered wood of the whipping post. Josephine's focus locked onto it, a small, trembling thing with the power to wound. Josephine thought of the venom it carried, invisible until it struck. The pain of its sting wouldn't come with fanfare, it would creep in and its harm revealed only too late. Another strike landed, but the bee didn't fly away. It remained with a determination that mirrored her own. The venom in her own heart stirred—a stealth weapon. Luke and Henri burned brighter. Lady Baynard could strike her body, but she couldn't touch the steel in Josephine's spine. The pain? It would not break her. It would be her fuel. The bee lifted off the post and disappeared.

From the edge of the yard, Old Mama Bess watched the scene unfold. Her back was bent with age, but her eyes missed nothing. She saw Lady Baynard's strikes, a whiskey-blind Lafayette still sprawled on the steps, and the strength in Josephine. Bess gripped her shawl tightly, her mind wandering back through decades. She thought of her own scars, the lashes she had worn when she was Josephine's age.

Mama Bess's mind traveled, as it often did when she stood in the shadows of this place. She'd been here longer than anyone, long enough to remember Lafayette Baynard as a boy. Even then, he had a meanness in him. She remembered him chasing the kittens around the yard with sticks, laughing when he made them yelp. He'd grown up evil, spoiled by a mother who loved him too much and a father who saw him as nothing more than an heir.

And Lady Baynard—Bess giggled to herself at the thought. She hadn't always been "Lady." No, she'd been just plain Lila Anne before she caught Mr. Baynard's eye. Hillbilly trash, that's what folks called her, from up in the hills where people lived off wild hogs and moonshine. She'd married up and now flounced around like she'd been born into all this, insisting that she be called *Lady* Baynard. This was no extravagant farm, but to Lila Anne, she was an empress. Bess saw through her. She was just as barbaric as Lafayette, maybe more, because she'd had to scrap her way into this life and was terrified of losing it. Lila Anne might dress the part, but she wasn't born into nobility. No matter how fine her clothes or polished her manners were, she'd always be garbage at her core.

Bess's memories darkened as her sight settled on Josephine. She saw herself in that girl, witnessed the fire that had once burned in her own eyes before years of grief had tempered it. Bess had been young once, too—strong, sharp-tongued. She'd been taken from her family and sold so many times. And she'd fought, oh, how she'd fought, until the fight was beaten out of her one lash at a time. Nonetheless, she had some wins. But Josephine? She had something Bess never did, an unshakable belief that she could survive this, and maybe more.

Bess had learned to endure. She'd learned to bend under the

pressure, to hide her rage. But she'd never stopped watching, never stopped planning. She knew the weakness in the Baynards' armor. "She the one," Bess muttered under her breath. "She can do it." The arsenic was tucked away in the clock on the kitchen wall, its unassuming presence hiding a deadly secret. She'd been saving it, waiting for the right moment, the right hands to pass it to. And now, watching Josephine, she knew. That fire in her wasn't just flames, it was destiny.

Bess's eyes hardened. "Lila Anne," she said to herself, using Lady Baynard's old name like a curse, "you ain't nothing but the dirt under God's feet. And Lafayette—" She stopped herself. No point wasting words on him. His time was coming. The Baynards thought they were invincible, but arrogance would be their downfall. Bess turned away, heading to the edge of the fields, where the souls would gather after a whipping.

Lady Baynard delivered one final strike as the whip fell to her side. She was panting now, hair sticking to her brow. Josephine sagged slightly against the post. She peeled herself off the wood as she straightened her posture. She pulled up her dress to cover herself. Her back burned, every nerve alive with pain, but her face remained stoic. She stumbled from the post without a word.

Lady Baynard sneered. "Get Bess to clean you up. You got work to do." Josephine didn't respond. She didn't need to. The fire in her chest was stronger than the pain in her back.

Josephine returned to the fields, the whipping against her back like a hot brand. The other souls worked in silence, but watchful as she approached. There were only a handful of them on the Baynard plantation—no more than ten in total. The farm was modest, not even an overseer, a far cry from what Lady Baynard liked to imagine it to be. But the smallness didn't make it any less cruel. If anything, it sharpened the pain, made it personal. Here, there was no hiding, no blending into a sea of faces. Every wound, punishment, and humiliation was felt by all.

When Josephine reached the edge of the field, Old Mama Bess was the first to come to her side. She was the anchor of their small, heartsick world. She was the oldest among them, her back curved and her hair a cloud of white. They turned to her for comfort, wisdom, and the stories that reminded them they were human, whole in ways the Baynards could never understand.

Her gnarled hands, rough from labor, were gentle as she removed part of the dress and saw the blood on Josephine's back had begun to crust. The welts were raised and aggressive.

"You don't never cry, gal," Mama Bess said. "You made of iron."

Josephine didn't answer. A few others gathered close. Among them was Larkin, the youngest boy on the Baynard plantation. "Nobody hold their head like you," Larkin said, with the composure of a much older boy. Josephine was five years older, yet she was almost like a mother to him. "If they can't break you, they ain't got nothing, Miss Josephine," he said as he shuffled away.

Mama Bess gave her a long look, her eyes filled with something between pride and worry. "Come on now," she said. "Let's get you cleaned up."

She led Josephine to one of the three small shacks where the souls slept, its roof drooping and walls patched with scraps of tin and burlap. Mama Bess guided Josephine to a corner where a bucket of water sat on a rickety table. She dipped a rag into the cool water and began to clean the wounds. "Wanna hear it again, don't you?" Mama Bess asked, a smile tugging at the corners of her mouth. "The story of when you first come here." Josephine nodded. Mama Bess chuckled. "Remember it like it was yesterday. It was August. A cool day for August. They brought you in the back of that wagon, skinny as a rail, but them eyes—Lord, them eyes was full of fire. Just sat there staring at us, like you was trying to figure us all out."

Josephine closed her eyes, the memory just barely in her mind.

"You didn't take to none of it," Mama Bess continued. "Not the work, not the rules. When Lady Baynard said you was to serve her eldest boy, you stood there and said, 'I ain't nobody's servant.' Lord, I thought she was gonna faint right there."

Josephine's lips twitched into a smirk. "And then she called Lafayette."

Mama Bess nodded. "That's when I knew you was different. Most woulda broke by then, but not you. You took what they gave and walked outta there with your head high."

Josephine opened her eyes. "Wasn't no choice, Mama. Just what I had to do."

Mama Bess finished cleaning the last of the wounds. She took a step away, faced Josephine, and placed a hand on her shoulder.

Mama Bess's eyes clouded with an intensity that made Josephine pause. There was something stirring in her expression, as if Mama Bess were deciding how much to say of what lurked in her heart. She spoke, her voice gravelly. "You strong. Stronger than any of them know. But strength ain't just about standing there taking it. Sometimes, strength is knowing when to strike back." Josephine nodded. She knew what it looked like to fight back. Mama Bess let out a sigh. "I been here too long. Too many years watching, too many years holding on. I see things. Things that tell me my time ain't long now." She wrapped her fingers in Josephine's. "You think I don't know what you carry? Seen it. Feel it in my bones every time that devil Lafayette looks your way, every time that witch of a mistress raises her hand. They take, till there ain't nothing left. But you? It's something they can't take—something the good Lord gave you. And I aim to see you keep it."

Josephine squeezed her hands back. Mama Bess drew in closer. "You know what the Good Book says—'No one can serve two masters.'[15] But here, every day, we doing just that. Pretending we can serve the Lord above while bowing to the Baynards. They ain't no God." She shook her head, tears filling up. "We feed their sin. How can we serve the Lord Almighty and serve evil all the same? Don't sound right to me. Don't feel right neither." Josephine recognized this tone. She heard it in Henri, different but the feeling was familiar. Mama Bess wiped away the tears forming. "I want you to end it. *End them.*"

Josephine's breath caught in her chest. "I got some brew," Mama Bess continued, her tone calm, as if she were talking about bread or tea. "Some bad medicine. Plenty of it. Been waiting for the right time, the right person. You just put it in their food, in they tea . . . couple hours or so, the Lord gonna call 'em home."

Josephine's eyes widened, a cold sweat breaking out along her neck. "Poison?"

Mama Bess smiled. "Child, you think I ain't done it before? My hands been washing white folks clean since I was a slip of a girl. Kill just one at a time—sometimes the baby, watch them white faces go blue . . . Next place, I give the daddy too much of my 'medicine' in his whiskey. Folks never did put it all together. Long as I played the quiet little girl. But once I got grown, I had to stop. A grown woman draws suspicion when folks keep dropping dead. I ended up at the Baynards, keeping my secrets close, waiting on the

15. *Matthew* 6:24, New International Version.

right day to use 'em again." She closed her eyes and nodded. "I call it an act of God."

Josephine couldn't look away. "Act of God?"

Mama Bess cracked her eyes open. "*Let your requests be made known unto God.*"[16]

Josephine searched Mama Bess's face. Could God strike a person down in the name of freedom or justice? She wasn't sure—but if He did, where did that leave Luke, Henri, or Ruby? She never told Mama Bess or anyone about the flames of Magnolia Row. Those memories were too precious. She had learned early on that survival demanded silence—words could bring questions, and questions could lead to cracks. But for Josephine, it was more than that. Magnolia Row was hers. To speak of it was risking its sanctity, letting it become something others could prod, even Mama Bess. Josephine knew the fire of Magnolia Row hadn't just burned away the old, it had shown her a truth. "How you know it's His will? Ain't the Lord supposed to forgive, not punish?"

Old Mama Bess grinned, her crow's feet becoming more detailed. "I believe the Lord put it in my hands to do His work. No sin in fighting for your freedom. No sin in taking back what they stole. You think they care about your soul? They don't. But I do. And I'll be damned if I leave this world without seeing you free."

Josephine sat, mulling over Mama Bess's words. There was something about the way she spoke, certain and holy. *Ruby would like her.*

"Why me? Why not you?"

"I'm a old woman. I know you got it in you. I know where you from . . . Magnolia Row."

Josephine's eyes lit up. "All of Virginia heard about it. Y'all

[16]. *Philippians* 4:6, King James Version.

scared the hell out of these White folks. You was spared 'cause you was young. The Baynards bought you 'cause you was cheap. They thought you was just a child, too young to understand what happened," Mama Bess paused, "but White folks don't know us like that . . . When I saw you on this land, I saw flames in your eyes—yes, I did. I still see it." Bess put her hand under Josephine's chin. "You got fire in you, fire that could burn this place to the ground, if you let it."

"I watched 'em burn," Josephine said proudly.

"That's a blessing," Bess said with a smile.

Josephine's head dipped. "Luke, Henri, and . . . Ruby, took care of me," she reflected. "Henri died . . . don't know what happened to Luke. And Ruby . . . she was something special."

"It's alright," Bess soothed. "That happens in this way of life. You lose people quickly."

"Don't let them take what they can't touch," Josephine said.

"That's right. You be sure to tell Larkin and everyone here that. And as for the Baynards, you deserve the glory to send them to hell."

The Raglands have gone to hell, and the devil's finally got his due, she remembered from Luke. "Why now?"

"I been watching you for years. You ain't a child no more, Josephine. You got the strength to do what needs doing." Josephine knew the strength was hers, but the right moment eluded her. "I feel it in my soul," Bess said. "Like the air 'fore a lightning strike. It's time. And wouldn't it just be the Lord's own justice to do it days after *they* Independence Day? Them Baynards, they been living high too long."

Josephine swallowed, her throat tight as a drumskin. "But how we know for sure? What tells us today's the day?" Josephine's voice wavered with doubt.

Old Mama Bess shifted. "We ask," she said simply. Reaching into the pocket of her faded dress, Bess pulled out four cowrie shells with smooth, cream-colored surfaces. They sat in her palm like tiny, split moons. Josephine had seen Bess carry the shells for years but never saw her use them. Bess cupped the shells in her hand, squeezing them tight. Eyes closed, she pressed her closed fist to her heart, then to her forehead. With a flick of her wrist, she tossed the shells onto the floor. They rolled, coming to rest in a scattered pattern. Two shells lay faceup; two lay facedown. Old Mama Bess studied the shells. Her eyes sparkled as she looked up at Josephine. "Ain't no cheating this, Josephine. The shells don't lie. The ancestors say yes, they say it's time. You feel it too, don't you?"

Josephine nodded slowly and felt relief. She did feel it. Not just in the shells or in Bess's words, but in the sting of her back, the ache of her cheek, the fire that had been burning in her chest for too long. How many more mornings must pass? How many more afternoons? How many more nights? Old Mama Bess never steered a soul wrong. Her wisdom was unfaltering. Yes, the ancestors had spoken. And now, so would she.

Josephine looked into Mama Bess's eyes. "Where is it? The bad medicine. Where you keep it?"

"Behind the face of that old clock in the kitchen. All you gotta do is open it up. There's a little tin can tucked inside, enough arsenic in there to kill a thousand horses."

"The clock," Josephine murmured, her voice tinged with awe. She had always been drawn to that clock, its ticking. It had felt like a jailer, each tick a sentence, each chime a taunt. She had hated the clock for years. And yet, all this time, it had held the key to something far greater.

Mama Bess gave a small nod, her expression knowing. "Funny how things work. That clock been marking every second of our misery, but now it's gonna set us free, if you got the courage to use it."

Josephine didn't need more convincing. She finally felt the stirrings of something she hadn't allowed herself to feel in years: hope. A hope that maybe, just maybe, she could make a change. Hope wasn't enough on its own, it demanded destruction. That's what she learned from Magnolia Row. And to know that all of Virginia, beyond Goochland, heard about those flames made her feel proud and more powerful. As Josephine said when she watched Mistress Kitty and Mr. Ragland's skin melt, *They gonna remember us.* Josephine felt the elders in her spirit, and fueled by vindictiveness against the Baynards for the abuse she had suffered, she set her plan for revenge into motion. She declared, "I'm gonna make a change there before long."

That afternoon, Josephine stood at the threshold of Lady Baynard's parlor, her head bowed. "Mistress," she said softly, her voice performing the humility that she knew would please her. "Sorry for this morning."

Lady Baynard turned toward her. *This wench has never apologized. Took a whipping to give her some sense*, she thought. "You finally learning your place."

Josephine nodded. "Yes, ma'am. Mama Bess ain't feeling well. Can I cook supper tonight?" Steeped in her privilege, Lady Baynard never saw the spark in Josephine's eyes, never guessed that the obedient servant was plotting her downfall.

"Yes, you may. Now go clean that kitchen. The whole family will sit at the dining room table. We will make it a beautiful evening and continue to celebrate our country's independence."

Josephine curtsied and walked away, heading to the kitchen. Her head was down but as soon as she was out of sight, her body lifted. Each step felt lighter. She felt not just alive, but *awake*. Her mind buzzed with promise; the plan in her thoughts was a seed bursting through soil. The satisfaction charging through her veins was electric, warming her even as the sting of her wounds still stung with each movement. She didn't care. She was no longer just surviving; she was *acting*. Every chore, every step had a new purpose, part of a rebellion that the Baynards would never see coming.

Josephine began to manically clean. The broken dish was still on the floor with the eggs and bacon splattered. Her hands moved; she let the pulse of the labor guide her thoughts. Josephine's mind replayed Old Mama Bess's words: "*You just put it in their food, in they tea . . . couple hours or so, the Lord gonna call 'em home.*" She stared at the clock where the arsenic was hidden, the thought of it sending a thrill through her. It was almost too perfect, too easy.

Her heart beat faster as she thought about the meal she would prepare. She manifested the looks on their faces as they ate, the oblivious smiles, the empty conversations. The image of Lafayette's smug face flashed in her mind, the way he had smiled after every lash of the whip. And Lady Baynard, watching with that satisfied grin, like she was entitled to every ounce of suffering Josephine endured. The anger surged in her cleaning. But this time, she didn't push it down. She let it fuel her, let it sharpen her focus. *Tonight*, she thought. *Tonight, everything changes.* Tonight's supper would be her finest act of service.

Josephine stood in the kitchen, her sleeves rolled up as she worked through the hours-long process of each step of the meal, just like Ruby taught her in the Raglands' kitchen. She hummed as she moved, starting with the cornbread. Her hands mixed the batter quickly, pouring it into the cast-iron skillet and sliding it into the hearth's embers. The scent of it baking filled the house. The greens came next, the leaves snapping beneath her knife as she chopped them into ribbons. She tossed them into a pot with pork fat and spices, stirring slowly, letting the steam rise around her.

The roast pork was already prepared—seasoned just the way Lady Baynard liked it, with hints of rosemary and garlic. Josephine basted it one last time, brushing the juices over the golden-brown skin. She placed it on the platter, arranging it neatly.

Then there was the tea.

Josephine paused, her hands resting on the edge of the counter as she stared at the teapot. She inhaled deeply, in the nose and out the mouth, as she turned toward the clock. Its ticking seemed louder now, anticipating what was to come. She reached up, her fingers trembling slightly as they brushed against the worn wood. The face was dull. The glass fogged with time, but it held her attention like nothing else ever had. With a quick twist, she dislodged the front panel, the sound of wood scraping. The space behind it was dark, the air was drier, desiccated, sealed off from the humidity. Nestled in the shadows was the tin can Mama Bess had spoken of. Josephine reached inside, grabbing the tin. It felt cool, almost insignificant in her hand. But as she pulled it out, she turned it over slowly, her breath catching as she felt its heft. It was bigger than she expected, but it might as well have been a cannonball. Inside, the arsenic waited, pale and fine.

The bad medicine, Mama Bess had called it. The powder inside had the gift to rewrite the narrative of the Baynard household, to make Josephine something other than the girl they had tried to break. It was justice in its purest form, contained in something so small it was laughable.

The clock ticked on behind her, louder now, each second pounding. It had always been there to mark the incessant days of servitude. But now, the ticking was hers—it belonged to her, counting down and driving her toward a future she could almost taste. She exhaled slowly, composing herself. The room held its breath with her, the faint chant of the hearth and the distant purr of the plantation falling silent. This was the moment.

She opened the tin and dipped a tip of a spoon into it, her movements careful. The powder clung to the metal, barely a pinch, and she held it over the teapot for a moment. She thought of Lafayette, his pointed teeth as he wielded the whip. She thought of Lady Baynard, her banshee laughter. She thought of the children, their flaxen hair and blue eyes, innocently cruel in their mother's image. She tipped the spoon, letting the powder fall into the steeping tea.

It dissolved instantly, disappearing into the amber liquid as though it had never been there. Josephine added a touch of cinnamon and stirred slowly, her fingers light on the handle of the spoon. She gracefully poured the tea into the porcelain cups, wiped her hands on her apron as she surveyed the meal. Everything was perfect, but still she wanted more.

Josephine sprinkled extra arsenic on the meat like seasoning, letting the fine dust settle invisibly into the rich brown gravy. She moved to the cornbread, crumbling the soft golden squares just enough to conceal the poison within. She reached for the small pot of honey on the counter and drizzled it over the cornbread, the richness pooling and soaking into the cracks. The sweetness masked everything, just as she intended. Josephine stared at the honey, light and golden. She thought of the bee from earlier today, the one that had landed on the whipping post. Honey and venom, sweetness and pain—all from the same source. The honey-glazed cornbread would be the first thing the children would reach for. Josephine allowed herself a bitter smile. *Let them choke*, she thought. *Let it rot them from the inside out.*

The greens came next, their savory aroma wafting up as she stirred the pot one final time, her fingers sprinkling the deadly powder like a cook adding salt. *They must be finished off.* They wouldn't taste it. Arsenic had no taste. They wouldn't feel it either—at least, not at first. But they would fall, one by one. This wasn't vengeance, not entirely. It was survival. She lifted the tray, her face composed, the vision of the perfect servant.

Josephine carried each dish to the dining table, arranging them with detail. The steaming cornbread sat at the center, flanked by the tender spiced greens and the roast pork, garnished with sprigs of parsley. It was a feast, a supper worthy of the Baynards' self-importance and their independence. It wasn't flames, but it would be a fire inside the Baynards.

Josephine hummed again, her voice rising slightly as she set the cups of tea on the table. There was joy in her song. The hymn's melody swirled around her, soft and lilting. Mama Bess's words, *I call it an act of God.*

She wiped her hands once more on her apron. The meal was ready, and so was she. The Baynards would sit at this table tonight, eating the food she had prepared and drinking the tea she had brewed. As they smiled and laughed, basking in their false sense of superiority, Josephine would watch. She would hum her song and wait for the bad medicine to take them.

The dining room was a shrine to the Baynards' imagined grandeur. A dark mahogany table and oil lamps cast a honeyed light. Drapes hung at the windows, the room itself conspired to isolate its horrors. Silverware sparkled beside porcelain plates. "Supper is ready," she announced, cheer in those three words. The Baynards began to take their seats. As they settled, Josephine moved with grace, serving each dish with care.

At the head of the table lounged Lafayette, his fingers tapping the arm of his chair. Lady Baynard sat next to him, her expression as stiff as the pearls tightened around her neck. Beside them were their children—a boy of fourteen with a face too sharp for his years, and a girl of eight, her cherubic features hiding a streak of malice. Their hair gleamed in the lamplight, halos of gold shrouding the gore beneath.

The boy sat with a self-satisfied smirk. She remembered every time he'd mocked her, every unkind game he'd devised to remind her of her place. He delighted in her pain, his taunts sharp as knives. "Not a proper slave child," he'd sneered once, tugging her hair until she bit her lip to keep from crying. He'd thrown rocks at her when Lafayette wasn't looking, laughed as she flinched, and gloated when she was punished.

His sister wasn't much better, her high-pitched giggles annoyingly ringing in Josephine's ears. She'd once spilled milk on her dress and blamed Josephine for the mess, watching with delighted eyes as Josephine was whipped for her "carelessness." Her small hands clutched the edge of the table now, looking with gluttony.

Josephine imagined their flaxen hair matted with sweat, their unpigmented skin wet with desperation as their faces turned a shade of gray. She saw their eyes bulging, their mouths gasping as their bodies betrayed them. She pictured the boy clawing at his throat, his childhood innocence replaced by terror. She saw the girl's hands, those dainty hands that had once pointed at her in accusation, scrabbling at the edge of the table and knocking over the teacups. The vision swirled in her mind, and for a moment, she almost smiled. But she didn't. Instead, she stepped back, her face calm and hands clasped in front of her.

Lady Baynard nodded approvingly at the display, too absorbed in the spread to notice Josephine's eyes. She stood in the corner of the dining room, far enough to seem invisible, yet close enough to watch every motion. Without even saying grace, the children dived for the cornbread. As Lafayette and Lady Baynard lifted their forks, their mouths parted to take the first bites.

An already half-drunk Lafayette stabbed at the roast pork with his fork, tearing into the tender meat like a starved animal. He shoveled the food into his mouth, barely pausing to chew, the juices dripping down his chin and mixing with the sweat on his flushed face. Grease slicked his lips as he reached for another piece, his knife clumsily hacking at the pork, sending bits of meat scattering onto the tablecloth. He gnawed at the chunk of meat, his chewing loud and wet, his throat bobbing as he swallowed greedily. Josephine was pleased. The bad medicine was there, mixed into every bite he crammed into his mouth. It would hit him soon, strong and swift.

Lady Baynard sipped her tea with exaggerated delicacy. She took small, measured sips, her thin neck elongating. She always performed gracefulness at the table, always overly rehearsed, trying to convince herself and others that she belonged among the genteel. She reached for a piece of cornbread, pinching off a bite-size morsel and placing it into her mouth. Letting each chew settle, her mouth moved in controlled motions, her lips pursed tightly to prevent even the tiniest crumb from escaping. She dabbed at the corner of her mouth with a linen napkin, her every gesture an attempt at sophistication. Josephine knew the truth behind the performance. No matter how carefully Lila Anne drank her tea or how primly she nibbled at her cornbread, she saw the cracks in the façade. She knew how Lady Baynard tore into her meals when no one was looking, finishing off the remains like a scavenger. That knowledge had been useful. Josephine had slipped a little extra bad medicine into her tea, knowing full well that Lady Baynard, so proud of her refined dining habits, would savor every drop. *Let her drink*, she thought, *and keep pretending*. It wouldn't matter soon enough.

The children ate greedily, their forks clinking against the plates as they shoveled cornbread and anything else they could fit in their mouths with their cheeks expanding. The boy chewed with his mouth open. His fork scraped noisily as he piled more onto his plate. Food fell onto the girl's lap as she stuffed herself, her lips smacking loudly with each bite. Watching them, she felt the familiar pang of disgust.

Josephine had put her soul into this meal. Every spice, every garnish, every careful stroke of the brush across the roast was deliberate. It was art, created with care that made her hands hurt. She thought of all the times she had been hungry as she watched the Baynards wolf down meals like ravenous beasts. She thought of the scraps she had been given, the leftover crumbs they wouldn't miss. She thought of the nights she and the other souls had to force themselves to sleep with a growling stomach. So, it was beautiful, the way their faces lit up, the way the muscles in their necks moved as they gulped. Each morsel was a tribute to her skill, her labor, her revenge, and her reparations.

From the corner of her eye, Josephine saw movement outside the window. Mama Bess was there, her face pressed against the glass, eyes round like a child. The lines of her weathered face mellowed. Mama Bess's joy was infectious and an affirmation. The promise Josephine had made that morning festered in her thoughts. *I'm gonna make a change there before long.*

The sun was dragging. Along the edges of the Baynard plantation, the light melted away into twilight. Inside the dining room, the kerosene lamps were the stage lights, showcasing the Baynards in domestic serenity. Parents seated at the head of the table with their dear children.

Josephine stood, her back stiff but her heart alive. The Baynards, seated at their once-pristine table now cluttered with plates, crumbs, and overturned cups, were oblivious to the growing shadows creeping around them. Their words filled the space. They talked and talked, their voices tying together in an out-of-tune melody.

Lady Baynard's shrill tones carried over the others, her sentences clipped. "You must speak to the servants tomorrow," she snapped at Lafayette. He gestured dismissively with his hand. "The tobacco isn't curing properly, and I will not have our profits squandered."

Lafayette grunted, his response muffled by another mouthful of cornbread. He wiped his hands on the linen napkin, smearing grease across its embroidery. "I'll handle it. Don't fret yourself."

The boy interrupted, "Papa, can I take the horse out tomorrow? I've been practicing my riding."

"Finish your chores first," Lady Baynard snapped. "You'll have time for such nonsense later." Lady Baynard fanned herself with her fingers. "Oh my, I do believe I have come down with a slight touch of a headache." *God is coming*, Josephine thought.

The little girl giggled, swinging her legs beneath the table. "Mama, I want another piece of cornbread," her voice slopped with the spoiled entitlement of someone who had never known hunger.

Lady Baynard smiled indulgently, reaching to tear off a piece. "Here you go, my angel." The child took it without so much as a polite thank you, forcing it in her piglet mouth.

To Josephine, their voices sounded strange, almost foreign. The words were so far removed from her reality. Days after Independence Day, they spoke of profits, of trivialities that mattered only in their world. It was a language of privilege. They talked as though the world belonged to them, as though their lives would stretch endlessly into the future, untouched by the hands of those who had served them. Here they were, chatting away about horses, tobacco, and cornbread. But this was her world now, her stage, and every word they spoke only made their downfall more satisfying. They had no idea what was next, but Josephine did. And she couldn't wait to see it. Ruby, Solomon, Luke, and Henri would be proud.

The first cough came suddenly. It was the girl, her tiny

hand flying to her mouth, her face scrunching in confusion. Josephine's sweeping gaze darted to her, the corners of her mouth twitching. The girl coughed again, harder this time, her small body jerking forward as though trying to expel something. Lady Baynard glanced at her daughter, her brows knitting together. "What's wrong, dear?" she asked, her voice edged with concern but still laced with the impatience of a woman annoyed at the slightest inconvenience.

The girl didn't answer. She couldn't. Her coughs turned into retches. The boy was next. He dropped his fork with a clatter, clutching his stomach with a groan. "Mama," he gasped, his face contorted in pain. Josephine began to hum through pressed lips to hide the grin threatening to spill over. Her girlhood, stolen and battered for years, began to unfurl inside her like a flower blooming in reverse. She felt a giddiness as she watched them—her tormentors, her captors—getting a taste of bad medicine.

Lafayette then began to cough uncontrollably, realizing something was wrong. He pushed back from the table, his chair scraping loudly against the floor as he stood. "What's happening?" he barked, though his voice cracked as he clutched his stomach. His face twisted, his mouth opening in a dry heave.

Lady Baynard's composure shattered as her little angel slumped forward; her small body fell onto the table, still coughing. "My baby!" she screamed, grabbing the child's shoulders and shaking her. The girl's tiny mouth frothed as Lady Baynard laid her on the floor. She turned to Lafayette, a dramatic panic across her face. "Do something!"

The nausea hit Lafayette, his legs buckling as he fell to his knees. His breaths came in short, rasping gasps, his hand grabbing at the edge of the table for support. "What . . . what is this?" he wheezed.

Josephine giggled, unable to contain it any longer. It bubbled out of her like a song, light and carefree, as if she were back in the fields of Magnolia Row, learning her letters and numbers in the dirt. It was the first time in years she had felt her age, the first time she allowed herself to feel joy without fear. Her laughter filled the room, cutting through the Baynards' moans.

Lady Baynard's eyes cut to her. "What have you done—" The words dissolved into a choking gurgle. She fell forward, her hands gripping her stomach.

Lafayette tried to stand, but his legs had no strength. His eyes bulging, he locked on Josephine. He pointed a finger at her, his lips moving to form words. His strength was draining fast.

The door to the big house creaked open. Josephine turned to see Old Mama Bess stepping in, her shoulders straight despite her years. Behind her, one by one, the souls of the Baynard plantation followed, their eyes burning. The sound of their feet came first. Old shoes against the wood floors, a cadence that was louder than any shout or scream. They brought with them the voices of the dead. It was the sound of history, of lives bent but never fully broken.

Lady Baynard froze at the table. Her face drained of color as the noise grew louder. One step, then another, closer and closer. She clutched her pearls, her lips twitching. "What's that?"

Lafayette's ruthless frame was reduced to a quivering heap as he uncontrollably fell to the floor. He ate so quickly and so savagely; his body was failing him. Lafayette glanced toward the sounds of the steps. "Who's there?" he rasped.

The sound grew clearer. It wasn't just one pair of feet—it was many, moving as one in a unified march. Old Mama Bess was the first to step into the dining room. She had spent more than forty years on the Baynard plantation. She had been there when Lafayette's father ran the farm. Decades of humiliation followed her into that room.

Behind her came Ezekiel. He had been sold to the Baynards at age seventeen and was now forty-two, his entire adult life spent in their fields.

Then came Ruth, a small but sturdy woman with hands cracked from years of washing, scrubbing, and plowing. She had been brought here as a child. Thirty-three years of servitude trailed her steps.

Mary followed, her face as soft as her voice, though her eyes held an animus. She was twenty-nine but had been here since she was twelve, forced into the house as a maid and later as a nursemaid for Lady Baynard's children.

James came next. He was only twenty-three but had already spent half his life under the Baynards' rule, his youth stolen by their greed.

Finally, there was Larkin, the youngest of them at just thirteen years old. Born on the plantation, he had never known freedom. His parents were sold off on a New Year's Day long ago to settle the Baynards' end-of-year debts, leaving his entire life confined to its fields and shacks.

Together, their time on the Baynard plantation added up to nearly 150 years—over a century of lives, of pain passed down from one generation to the next. They weren't bound by blood, but by something stronger: the kinship of fortitude. The generational strength in their DNA. The Baynards believed they had crushed individuality and scattered families, but they were ignorant of the community that had formed beneath their noses. They weren't just laborers. They were a people. And now, they stood together in the heart of the big house, the space where they had never been allowed to linger, let alone belong. This was the master's domain, but tonight, it was theirs. The Baynards had taken so much, but they could never take this: their unity, their unbreakable sense of one another. Here, in the belly of Lucifer, their presence was godlike.

Lady Baynard's breaths panicked as she kneeled next to her little girl. She squeezed at her throat, her pearls snapping, running away from her on the dining room floor. She looked to the souls, then to her husband. Lafayette tried to push himself upright on the floor. "Get outta *my* house!"

Mama Bess stepped forward, her old eyes locking on Lafayette. "*My* house?" she questioned. "All these years, and you still think this yours?"

"We built this house," Ruth corrected. "Every brick, every board, every inch of it."

The Baynards' fear turned to hysteria. Lady Baynard kicked her feet, her voice breaking into a soprano wail, her demure presentation falling to pieces. "You gonna burn in hell for this!"

"I already burned," Josephine responded. "Rose from the fire."

The circle of slaves and souls closed in. Lady Baynard and Lafayette gasped and writhed. The children slowly twitched, their small forms becoming limp.

For the first time, the Baynards were about to have nothing. They were at the mercy of the people they had spent a lifetime dehumanizing. And those people stood over them, watching, waiting, reclaiming the space that had always been theirs.

Old Mama Bess turned to the others. "Bring them to the center."

Ezekiel's and James's strong hands reached for Lafayette. He grunted, his body jerking as he tried to bat them away. "Get your black hands off me." His voice was barely audible over his own sickness. His protests were cut short as a retch overtook him, vomit spilling from his mouth and onto the front of his fine shirt. His boots scraped against the floor, leaving streaks of filth. Ezekiel and James hauled him to the middle of the dining room. Then Josephine saw something, *tears*. Lafayette Baynard was crying. Not the subtle tears of a man mourning his pride, but jolting sobs. He cried harder than Josephine had ever seen his own children cry, harder than she'd imagined a man like him capable of. The poisonous flames inside of him made him sob. Seeing a master so frightened that he was reduced to tears was a sight Josephine had never thought she'd witness.

"Josephine . . . please . . . begging you," Lafayette whimpered.

"Josephine? *Now* I'm Josephine?" She flicked her finger back and forth like a cat's tail. "No, no, no, *Lafayette*. Never been nothing but 'girl' or 'gal' to you. 'Less we were in the dark and you thought nobody could hear." Josephine turned to Lady Baynard. "Ain't that right, Lila Anne? How many times you sat there in that big ol' bed, knowing what he was doing? Pretending not to hear?"

Lady Baynard's breathing was rapid as Josephine remembered Magnolia Row. Mistress Kitty in Ruby's cabin after she lost her baby. Josephine on the floor watching Kitty's evil. Now Lila Anne was on the floor. Kitty and Lila Anne, just as guilty, just as compliant, just as diabolical as their husbands. "You coulda stopped it, or tried. But you didn't. You let it happen, *over and over*. You were never scared of him. You were scared of losing that pretty little life you got here. You let him take it out on me, while you laid there like a queen, pretending it wasn't happening."

Ruth and Mary grabbed Lady Baynard's arms. She fought harder than her husband, her hands trying to scratch at their faces and her legs kicking wildly. Her elegant dress tore as she thrashed, the sleeving ripping away, exposing the flesh of her arm. Then the bodice broke, baring her collarbone and part of her chest. Her slippers flew off as she let out a choked gasp.

"Drag her," Mama Bess said firmly. "She don't deserve nothing soft." Lady Baynard's bare feet kicked against the floor, splintering into the heels of her feet as Ruth and Mary hauled her forward to the center of the room, near her dying husband.

The children were next. Larkin moved without hesitation, his face hard as he reached for the boy. He may have been only thirteen, but his hands had already been shaped for battle. Larkin grabbed the boy's arms, Ezekiel his legs, and together they lifted him, his limp body swinging slightly as they carried him to the center. His eyes were half-open but unseeing. The boy was laid beside his father, his small frame a stark contrast to Lafayette's hulking, vomit-soaked figure.

Ruth and Mary turned to the girl. She was light, no heavier than a sack of grain. Mary briefly paused, her fingers grazing the soft blond curls that framed the child's face. Then Ruth's voice came. "Don't waste a thought. She just another piece of their rot." Together, they lifted the girl, her arms dangling uselessly at her sides as they placed her next to her brother, both clearly near death, their bodies settling into the space between Lady Baynard and Lafayette. Lady Baynard let out a cry. Josephine stepped to her. "You gonna watch your children die, Lila Anne."

Her cries grew more unhinged. "They're innocent!" she wailed. "They're just children! They didn't do anything wrong!"

Josephine stood over her, unmoved. "Innocent? Like the children sold from their mama's arms on your orders? Like the ones starved in your name? No, Mistress. Your children ain't innocent."

Lady Baynard's cries turned into a keening wail. She slapped the floor with her fists, incoherent words tumbling out. The circle closed tighter, the souls standing shoulder to shoulder, their eyes fixed on the center of the room. "This is God," Mama Bess said.

Lady Baynard, weak and shuddering, croaked out, "We . . . we was always so good to you . . . monsters."

Larkin was triggered. He looked to Mama Bess, who gave a nod of approval. He crouched down, bringing his face level with Lady Baynard's, her breath rank with upcoming death. "Monsters? No. Monsters got teeth. Monsters got claws. We worse, we everything you thought you owned. We all of it."

Josephine reached out, her fingers brushing Lady Baynard's cheek. "You know what the dead whisper to the living, Lila Anne? They say, 'We coming for you.'" Josephine straightened, her voice final. "Now, scream for me again, Lady. *I wanna hear what mercy sounds like.*"

Lady Baynard, now just Lila Anne, released a guttural howl devoid of respectability, going back to her trash roots. She scanned the room to escape the judgment. The mirror of her indecency reflected back at her. As Josephine looked into Lila Anne's eyes, she thought of Solomon back on Magnolia Row. His unforgettable gray eyes ruined. The eye beneath the rough patch that barely concealed the wound stared back at her in Josephine's mind. She could still hear his cries as Mr. Ragland drove the pin deeper and deeper. Solomon's torment would never be undone, and she didn't know where he was today, but here, in this moment, the scales felt closer to balance.

This wasn't just justice, it was theater, a reclamation of the space they had been denied for so long. The dining room, once a place of malevolence just earlier that morning, was now their stage. The four bodies—Lafayette, Lady Baynard, the boy, and the girl—were laid out, their faces knotted in agony. Lafayette let out a weak moan, his body finishing as more vomit spilled from his mouth. Lila Anne whimpered, her bare skin shivering. The children were still, their small forms quiet. Josephine thought of Ruby when she watched the Raglands' bodies burn. The words slipped from her lips again: "They gonna remember us." Mama Bess, Larkin, and the others stood in agreement.

The circle of souls stood unmoving. They stood as witnesses and judges, staring down at the family that had ruled over them. The children went first. The boy, his features now slack and gray, let out a final gasp. His body twitched once, twice, then went still. Beside him, the little girl followed nearly identical movements. These children, though young, had grown on the poisoned roots of their mother and father with their violence budding early. *Two less devils to reckon with*, Josephine thought, wincing at the spawn they might have birthed and the kind of adults they would have become.

Lafayette's death was uglier. His body tried to fight off the inevitable. Bile surged from his lips, spilling down his chin. His bloodshot eyes rolled wildly as if searching for a savior in the faces around him. There was none to be found.

Larkin crossed his arms. "Ain't so mighty now, are you?"

Lafayette let out a growl. With his mouth wide, his body gave one last shake, then went still.

Lady Baynard moaned and wept as she watched her darling family die. Eating so delicately gave her the pleasure of the finale. Her breaths came in pitiful gasps, her chest heaving as tears streamed down her face. "Please, Mama Bess . . ."

"No mercy here for you," Bess said, stone-faced.

Lady Baynard's body spasmed violently, skull cracking against the wood floor and her limbs whipping in unnatural angles as if pulled by invisible strings. Her mouth was pink with blood from where she'd bitten her tongue. Her hands clawed at her neck, fingers tearing at her skin. A crack echoed through the room as her head whipped back again, her veins pulsing as if they might burst. Easily, she went still. The skin around her lips darkened as her mouth opened in a wide, dry scream as her last breath. Her glassy eyes stared at the ceiling of their big house.

Their deaths marked the end of everything the Baynard family had built. There would be no heirs to carry on their lineage. What they had spent decades constructing, gone in an instant. The Baynard plantation would become a ghost. This was not just an ending, it was erasure. Their bloodlines all ended there. The Baynard name was dead.

From somewhere in the circle, a voice began to hum. Another joined, then another, until the souls were alive with song. The freed people broke into a hymn, their voices together in a harmony so mighty it shook the walls of the house. The melody was both mournful and triumphant, a song to serenade the Baynards to the hellfire they so richly deserved. Josephine's voice was high and clear, cutting through the deep timbre of the others. She looked down at the shells, the children, the mother, the father—and felt no remorse, no guilt.

The song faded into the air, leaving the room quiet. In that silence, the circle of souls stood tall, their eyes fastened on the bodies at their feet. They had borne witness to the end of a family, to the death of their oppressors. Josephine spoke the final words over the bodies. "This house was built on our blood. Tonight, it burns with yours." Josephine created her own fire.

The horse plodded slowly up the road to the Baynard plantation. Sheriff Warren Graves pulled at the brim of his hat, squinting against the light of the afternoon. It had been weeks since the Baynards had been seen in town. There wasn't so much as a plume of smoke rising from the kitchen chimney. Something about the silence prickled at him, and as he neared the house, the sound of cicadas was the only company he had.

The fields were empty and the Baynard house had its shutters sealed tight. The front door caught his eye; it was boarded up, planks nailed haphazardly across it as though to keep something inside. Sheriff Graves's hand instinctively went to the revolver at his hip. He swung off his horse. The air smelled wrong. "This ain't right," he said to himself. He approached the door cautiously, gripping the handle and tugging, only to find it firmly sealed. The boards groaned under the strain as he wedged the butt of his revolver into the gap and pried them free one by one. The last board splintered loudly, and as it fell, a stench hit him with force. He staggered back, his hand flying to his face. Warren steeled himself, pulling a handkerchief over his nose and mouth, and stepped inside. His boots clicked on the floor, the sound too loud. The windows were covered, but the sunlight seeped through in long, sharp beams. The sheriff inspected the familiar hallways; he had been in this house many times before for elaborate gatherings.

The house was sterile and still, nothing was out of place, but the stench grew stronger as he neared the dining room. He could feel his heart pounding, the revolver in his grip. The sheriff stopped. His breath held as his attention landed on the scene before him. The corpses of the Baynard family had been laid out on the dining room floor in a macabre display. Mr. Lafayette Baynard was at the head, his broad shoulders still imposing. Lady Baynard was beside him, her hands clasped neatly over her stomach, as though in prayer. The two children, pale as wax figures, were arranged side by side at their feet.

All four of them, their mouths hung agape, frozen in mid-scream. Their eyes were open wide, glazed over with a milky film. The skin on their faces pulled tight, dry and cracking, their lips shriveled into thin lines. Flies swarmed the room in a maddening buzz. Some landed on Mr. Baynard's broad chest and others crawled across Lady Baynard's clasped hands. The children were marred by the same dark whirring of insects. Around them, the dining room was in shambles. Broken plates and shattered glass were scattered across the floor, the remnants of a meal now long decayed. A chair lay tipped over near the corner of the room, its legs splintered. The tablecloth was torn and stained. The dining table was scarred with scratches and covered in dust.

The contrast was jarring: the meticulous arrangement of the Baynards' corpses against the mess that surrounded them. It was as if whoever had done this had wanted to send a message, to leave no part of the scene untouched. The symmetry of the bodies and the unnatural precision in how their limbs were positioned. This was clearly a ritual.

Warren removed his hat, his eyes on Lafayette's and Lady Baynard's faces. He had known them for many years, had shared whiskey and conversations about crops and politics. His view shifted to the children, who reminded him of his own. He backed away, his boots clicking unevenly as he stumbled into the doorframe. "Sweet Lord above," he whispered hoarsely. "It was the slaves. My God in heaven, the slaves." He took another step back, his voice rising with the horror of realization. "We're too close to the enemy. Too close by far."

The journey was grueling, but their spirits could not be stopped from soaring. Their escape was not born of luck but necessity. The weeks that passed before anyone ventured onto the plantation to discover the carnage gave Josephine and the others the head start they needed to ensure their survival. They left no trail, no whisper of their passage, taking everything they needed and leaving behind only the memory of their resistance. Days turned into weeks, weeks into months, each step a move toward freedom. The souls were clever, sharper than the men who hunted them, more skilled than those who were paid pretty pennies to doubt them. They moved as one; guided by the stars and Josephine's will, the souls journeyed through forests and across rivers that ran cold. No one was left behind. Old Mama Bess was right, Josephine was the one.

When they reached the edge of the new world, the sky opened wide above them. The air was different here, clean and full of possibility. They stood together, Josephine at the front, and embraced the expanse before them, but they would not stay together. Freedom meant different things to each of them, and so they scattered, their paths diverging like branches from the same tree. Some would find quiet lives in small towns; others would press on to the cities, where anonymity could be a shield. They carried the fire of that night with them, a memory that burned and healed in equal measure. Josephine watched them leave, one by one, until only she, Larkin—the youngest among them—and Old Mama Bess remained.

They settled in a humble cottage, perched at the edge of a field where wildflowers grew untamed, a sanctuary provided by an abolitionist group whose network stretched across Pennsylvania. These were people who worked in quiet, using secret routes to dismantle the chains of slavery. The group had heard bits of Josephine's daring escape, but were unaware of the bad medicine that provided ultimate freedom. In a cottage, Old Mama Bess found her peace, living out her days alongside Josephine and Larkin, now older but still carrying the spark of the boy. The three of them formed an unconventional family.

Josephine took it upon herself to teach Larkin his numbers, like Luke had taught her. She would tell him, just like Luke said, *Don't let them take what they can't touch.* Her determination didn't stop there, she enrolled him in a small school supported by abolitionists. She was steadfast in her belief that Larkin deserved more than survival. He deserved to thrive as a free man, just like Ruby wanted for her.

Old Mama Bess would sometimes sit on a wooden chair on the quaint porch, fingers idly tracing her cowrie shells, her eyes following Josephine and Larkin. She could sit for hours, just watching. Watching Larkin walk up the dirt path from school, his satchel swinging at his side, his head high, his young voice carrying through the air as he repeated his lessons. He always ran the last few steps, bursting into the yard, eager to tell her and Josephine what he had learned. Although they were only five years apart in age, Josephine would stop whatever she was doing, listening with all the patience and love of a mother who knew just how much this meant. It filled Mama Bess's heart to bursting. Sometimes, she would catch sight of Josephine standing in the yard, her face lifted toward the sun, arms stretched slightly, letting the warmth soak in. There was a peace about her now. Not even the sudden buzz of a bee could make her flinch; she stood her ground, calm and unafraid. The way a free woman should be.

Mama Bess would let out a long, slow breath, rocking gently, lost in quiet joy. She had lived long enough to see what once seemed impossible. She had survived masters who never believed she'd see a day beyond their grip. She had seen them die, had watched their houses crumble, had outlived their cruelty and their disbelief in her. She had seen the ones who thought she was their friend, the ones who thought she was too old, too simple, too small to resist. But she had resisted. Every quiet revolt was hers. And now, she saw it in Josephine—the same strength, the same will. Mama Bess had passed it on. She had never known her own children, never had the chance to rock them, to teach them, to watch them grow. That loss had hollowed her out for years. But here, now, watching Josephine in the sun, watching Larkin run toward her with the whole world stretched out before him, she felt—*full.* Her eyes misted, but there were no tears. Instead, she smiled. A long, deep, satisfied smile. For the first time in her long life, there was nothing left to fight for. Nothing left to hold together. She had done it. She had won.

As time ticked on, Mama Bess's days began to wane. Her frail body grew weaker with each passing season. Josephine and Larkin clung to her presence, knowing the inevitable was drawing near but unwilling to let the thought of it eclipse the life they were building.

On Old Mama Bess's final day, she lay propped up on pillows in her bed with a quilt Josephine had sewn draped over her. Mama Bess knew she was about to transition, and she was at peace. The room was filled with the late-afternoon sun through lace curtains. A gentle breeze carried the scent of blooming jasmine from outside, mixing with the aroma of lavender oil Josephine had dabbed onto Mama Bess's wrists. The window was open just enough for her to feel the world beyond, the world she was preparing to leave—a world she had fought for, bled for, and now, a world she could finally rest in. Her skin was weathered by time but still had a sheen. Her silvery hair loosely braided caught rays of light. She turned her gaze toward the open window, the bluest sky stretching before her.

Larkin and Josephine sat on either side of her bed, their hands holding hers. They trembled slightly, knowing they would soon have to let go. Josephine, her face streaked with tears, held on to the warmth of her hand, the familiar softness, memorizing the feel of it. She never wanted to forget the feeling of her hands. Mama Bess turned her eyes to Josephine and smiled. "Thanked you before, Josephine, but let me say it plain, one last time, so you never forget . . . you gave me something thought I'd never see. Gave me freedom. Not just the kind where my hands ain't bound, but the kind where my soul can rest."

Josephine choked back a sob. "You gave me just as much, Mama Bess."

Larkin swallowed hard. "Gave us all something to hold on to, Mama."

Mama Bess's gaze drifted again, her breath slowing, the light in her eyes growing distant. She looked out the window one last time, watching as a single bee danced along. A stillness settled. Not grief, but love and gratitude.

"Yes, child," she murmured. "You gotta give something. But look at what we made. Ain't it something? Ain't it just something?"

Chapter 3

Charity

"The judgment is therefore affirmed."[17]

The stagecoach rattled along the uneven road. Inside, Miss Clara Petterson sat stiffly, one hand holding the edge of the seat while the other formed shapes in the air as she spoke. She babbled a stream of words, punctuating them with animated gestures. Across from her, baby Gertrude balanced on Charity's lap, as Clara's monologue continued.

"I should have known better," she spat. "When Father told me, 'Clara, that man is nothing but a Southern charmer with more ambition than decency,' I thought he was just being dramatic. But no, Charles Petterson proved him right in every conceivable way." Charity adjusted the baby's bonnet as the wheels jolted over a rock.

17. *Butler v. Delaplaine*, 7 Serg. & Rawle 378 (Pa. 1821), Free State Slavery & Bound Labor, https://freestateslaveryproject.com/legal-materials/butler-v-delaplaine-7-serg-rawle-378-pa-1821/.

"I lost everything for him. Everything," Clara continued. "My family, my standing, my very *reputation*—all of it lost. Do you have any notion, Charity, what it means to be a Vermonter? To be reared in a household where every book, every sermon, every word spoken over supper is steeped in the cause of abolition? And then, to—to wed a *Southern* man—a *slaveholder*, no less?"

She let out a humorless laugh. "Father cast me off that very instant, disowning me without a second thought. A single journey below the Mason-Dixon Line in pursuit of my studies, and I found myself captivated by the very first Southern gentleman I encountered. Spoke sweet as molasses, promising me a life of comfort, a deceptive palace where I'd be mistress, waited on like a true Southern lady. Fool that I was, I believed him. As for his fortune, all lies. He is only a few steps away from"—Miss Clara paused and shook her head like she was talking about a disease—"common folk, barely better than middle class. I had thought—quite naïvely—that any man who held slaves must surely be of great wealth. But his station is far humbler than I had been led to believe. And I found myself little more than his handmaiden, running to his every need. A wife in name, but I was a servant, nearly a slave!"

Charity buried her disgust by fixing Gertrude's bouncy locks of hair.

"And now? After ten years, Charles has left me for some doe-eyed, feather-brained trollop barely out of girlhood." Baby Gertrude nearly fell out of Charity's arms as the stagecoach hit another aggressive bump, but Clara didn't notice.

"Ruined," Clara declared, tears welling in her eyes. "Ruined—that is what I am. He left me with that down-at-heel plantation house, scarcely fit to stand, not a penny to my name, and an infant in my arms! Oh, a gentleman indeed—so gracious as to leave me the house, a pile of debts, and a sneering little note assuring me I could 'manage on my own.' As though I have ever managed on my own! The sole consolation is the modest home he maintains here in Gettysburg. At the very least, I shall have a roof over my head while I work like a peasant."

Clara erupted into dramatic sobs, her face flushing as if painted with strokes of theatrical makeup. "And work I must, for heaven forbid a man like Charles Petterson take responsibility for the wreckage he has left in his wake. Now, I am obliged to take in sewing and alterations merely to scrape by." Miss Clara tried to breathe, patting her chest and wiping her tears. "Thankfully, there is work in Gettysburg, but it is exhausting. And do you know what Norman Bruce charged me to rent you?" She threw a glance at Charity, as though expecting her to answer. "An exorbitant sum, that's what. He was fully aware of my need for assistance with the baby, and he seized upon it without hesitation. Typical."

Charity shifted uncomfortably, trying to calm Gertrude, squirming in her lap. Miss Clara, oblivious, plowed on.

"You're a blessing, though, Charity. Truly. I can't look after baby Gertrude and work at the same time. I wouldn't trust her with anyone else. You're good with her, and I can tell you care. That's something, isn't it? Caring?" She sighed. "If only Charles had cared. About me, about our child, about anything but himself."

The stagecoach began to slow as they approached the outskirts of Gettysburg. The town was alive with activity, its streets lined with modest shops and tidy homes. Charity watched in awe. She had never been to Pennsylvania and was mesmerized by the commotion. Clara straightened her hat and smoothed her dress, then pulled a small powder box from her reticule. With a practiced hand, she dabbed her face, the powder settling over her skin, shielding her from the heat and dust of the stagecoach. "We'll go straight to the tailor shop. There's no time to waste, I have so much fabric to buy."

When the stagecoach halted, Clara opened the door, stepping out onto the cobblestone street. Gertrude's face immediately pinched against the bright sun. Charity followed, carefully cradling the baby, but enjoying the breeze. Clara turned, snapping open her parasol with a quick flick of her wrist, positioning it as a shield against the sunrays. The driver, a man with red skin and a permanent scowl, hopped down from his perch and began unstrapping their two trunks from the stagecoach. He grunted them to the ground and dusted off his hands.

"Well, I be off now," he said curtly.

Clara's mouth fell open. "Off? What do you mean, 'off,' Pedro? Aren't you going to wait and see us safely back to the house?"

The driver paused midstep. "No, ma'am. Mr. Charles's orders were to drop you here, unload your things, and head straight back. Ain't got no time to waste hanging 'round town."

Clara's parasol wobbled in her hand. "You mean to tell me I'm expected to *walk* in this heat? With an infant?"

The driver had heard enough of Clara's complaints to last a lifetime. "That's exactly what I mean, ma'am. House is just down the road and it ain't that hot. Be back here in two weeks on the dot, like Mr. Charles said." Charity studied the driver. His skin was sunburnt red, his hair, straight and black as river silt, hung neatly beneath the brim of his hat. He didn't look Southern, but his voice carried a thick drawl. Was he colored? White? Something else entirely?

Clara let out a disbelieving laugh. "You're telling me I have to trudge through Gettysburg carrying a baby and two trunks? Like some sort of . . . of *common laborer*?"

The driver smirked, adjusting his fallen-down hat with sarcasm. "Looks like it, ma'am. That's why you got Charity.

Maybe you can find one of them fine gentlemen in the tailor shop to carry your things. They ain't that heavy."

Clara's parasol snapped closed with a dramatic flourish. She pointed it at the driver like a sword. "You listen here, you insolent—"

Charity stepped closer, baby Gertrude on her hip letting out a whine. "Miss Clara," she said gently. "Maybe we should let him go. He said the house ain't far and it's not so hot with this breeze."

The driver gave Charity a grateful glance before turning back to Clara. "She's right, ma'am. House ain't but a couple miles up the road. Plenty of shade on the way." He climbed back onto the stagecoach, shaking his head. "Can't be waiting 'round here all day. Gotta get back to Maryland, like Mr. Charles told me."

Clara huffed. "Of course you do. Forever it is 'Mr. Charles this' and 'Mr. Charles that.' Heaven forbid anyone should summon the courage to think for themselves."

The driver snapped the reins, his horse trotting forward as he tipped his hat one last time. "See you in two weeks, ma'am," he called over his shoulder, his voice dripping with mock cheerfulness. "Enjoy your walk!"

Clara gripped the parasol tightly in her hand as if she might hurl it after him. She let out a long sigh, turning to Charity with a look of despair. "Miss Clara," Charity said. "Is Mr. Pedro negro?"

Clara sighed. "I don't know if he is negro or White, but he certainly isn't a gentleman! A couple of miles, he says. In *this* heat. With a child! Stay out here, I don't want Gertrude to fuss in the shop."

Clara strutted into the tailor shop as Charity stood under the shade of the awning with baby Gertrude in her arms. Charity's eyes darted nervously between the infant and the shop's door. Gettysburg's streets bustled with townsfolk. In her twenty years, she had never seen life beyond farmland. Merchants called out from their stalls, offering fresh produce and fine wares, while carriages rattled over the roads, their drivers shouting orders to the horses. Children ran between the passersby, their laughter in tune with a blacksmith's hammer and the vibrance of conversation. And there were Black men and women in crisp suits and fancy dresses, strolling with spines straight, not a single glance spared for the White faces beside them. Inside the shop, Miss Clara's voice rose and fell like the flap of a bird's wings, chattering to the tailor about hem lengths and fabrics finer than her purse could afford. Charity kept one ear on the doorway, her grip on the child.

Then he appeared.

Out of the sun stepped a tall man with broad shoulders, his silhouette sharp against the light. He wore a top hat tipped at a jaunty angle and carried himself with unhurried confidence. Charity caught him in her periphery. Her heart stumbled in her chest. She had never seen a Black man so self-assured. It wasn't just his stature or his fine, polished boots; it was the way he filled the space around him. He owned it.

He saw her and his steps slowed. His curious eyes drank her in. He saw the curve of her shoulders as she stood holding the White baby, a bundle of pink and lace that was out of place against her modest calico dress. The midday light caught the sheen of her glowing skin. Stray strands of her tightly coiled hair escaped from beneath her headscarf, framing her face. She stood with one hip slightly cocked, adjusting the baby with practiced ease. He wondered, briefly, about the arrangement—a Black woman holding a White child in this way. Was she a nursemaid? A servant?

He smiled, wide and easy. Charity felt a warmth crawl up

her neck as he stepped closer. He was taller than most men she'd seen. There was no hesitation in his approach, just a directness that settled her.

"Afternoon," he said in a deep voice.

Charity's eyes looked back to the shop door. "Afternoon," she mumbled.

"And what's your name, if you don't mind me asking?" he asked, tipping his hat slightly. Charity was struck by his pronunciation. It lacked Miss Clara's uppity affectations; his speech held a distinction unlike any Black or White man's she'd ever heard.

"Charity," she replied, her fingers tightening on the small of the baby's back.

He grinned, leaning forward just enough to make her move back. "Well, Miss Charity, it's a pleasure to meet you. I'm Larkin Butler."

"I . . . I'm waiting for Miss Clara," she said quickly, glancing toward the shop again. "I work for her. I . . . well, been rented out to her."

"Rented out?" His brow lifted. "They don't usually rent out folks in Pennsylvania. You know this here's a nearly free state?"

Charity frowned. "Nearly free?"

Larkin laughed. "Well, sort of free. Gettysburg ain't always good to free Black folks, but if a slave's been in Pennsylvania for more than six months, they are free by law. The Gradual Abolition Act of 1780." She stared, but no words came. He moved in slightly, his voice falling to a conspiratorial whisper. "Don't worry, I can teach you all about it."

Charity shook her head. "Don't know what that law's supposed to mean. Live in Maryland. My first time here."

"It means you don't need no boss lady," he said, earning a giggle from Charity. "Where you staying?"

"With Miss Clara," she said, her tone cautious again. "Only two weeks. She . . . she nice enough."

Larkin's eyes brightened but before he could reply, Miss Clara burst out of the shop, her bonnet slightly askew, struggling with bags of fabric and her expression tight with irritation. "Charity!" she snapped, glaring at Larkin. "And who might you be?"

"Larkin Butler, ma'am." He tipped his hat. "I was just admiring your fine little one there." He nodded toward the baby. "Looks just like her mama."

Miss Clara softened, but only slightly, handing her bags to Charity as she sized him up. "Well, Mr. Butler, we've no time to linger in conversation. A long walk awaits us, I'm afraid."

Larkin's smile widened. "Walk? In this heat? No, ma'am. My carriage is just down the road. Allow me the honor of giving you and Miss Charity a ride."

Clara hesitated, but she glanced at the sky, sweat already forming at her temple. "Well . . . aren't you quite something," she said, half-impressed. "This heat is quite insufferable. We're staying over on Main Street."

"Let me grab your trunks." Larkin scooped up the trunks and nodded. "Follow me, ladies."

The carriage was finer than anything Charity had seen. Its burnished wood wore a rich mahogany finish, each panel intricately etched with swirling patterns. The wheels encircled by trim, and a brawny horse with a midnight coat at the reins. The harnesses were black leather with gold accents as if they had emerged from the pages of a fairy tale. Miss Clara was now fully impressed. "Well, isn't this lovely," she said as Larkin helped them inside. His hand brushed Charity's and she felt her heart flutter again.

During the ride, Larkin kept up a steady stream of conversation. "Now, I don't mean to brag, but my blacksmith shop is the busiest in Gettysburg. Folks from miles around bring their horses, wagons, even tools to me. Always something needs fixing. So, if you need anything, you let me know."

Miss Clara blinked in astonishment. "A blacksmith shop, you say?" she repeated. "You *own* it?"

Larkin nodded, "That's right. Built it from the ground up. Keeps me busy, but it's honest work and I reckon I'm pretty good at it."

Clara, for once, was at a loss for words. She glanced at Charity, who had been silently cradling the baby. "Well," she said with a loud exhale, making Charity brace herself for what she might say next. "It is such a pleasure to meet a respectful man," Clara said, calming Charity's nerves. "Respectful and industrious. My husband—well, my *former* husband, Charles, left me not long ago, and that's the only reason I'm working now. Imagine that, after all I sacrificed for him." She gave another sarcastic laugh. "A woman like me, raised in Vermont, *abolitionists* for generations, falling for a Southern man who—"

"Left you with all the hard work," Larkin finished smoothly. "Sounds to me like Charles didn't know what he had."

Clara's head snapped up, her cheeks flushing, though it wasn't clear if it was from the compliment or the truth in Larkin's words. "Well," she said, flustered but pleased, "you're not wrong about that."

Larkin flashed that smile again, with Charity stealing glances when she thought he wasn't looking. "Takes strength to start over. Not everyone's got that kind of grit."

Clara beamed. "I suppose you're right." Struck by curiosity, she asked, "Tell me, Mr. Butler, where are you from? A man like you must have a story."

Larkin chuckled. "Well, ma'am, I'm from all over, I'll say,

moved up here about five years ago from a place called Goochland, Virginia. I was in New York City for some blacksmith work but I came back here. Been about five years now."

Clara's face lit up. "New York!" she exclaimed. "Oh, I *love* New York. The energy! Father would take me there as a young girl, and I was simply enchanted. The theaters, the parks—oh, what a marvelous place!"

"It was something. A chance to breathe, to live free without looking over our shoulders all the time." Charity's ears perked up at the word *free*.

Clara, oblivious to Charity's quiet shift, quizzed, "And why on earth did you come back here? It's hardly the bright lights of New York."

"Well, someone who was like my mama got sick. Came back here to tend to her. But blacksmithing always been in demand, and Gettysburg's been good to folks like me. I stayed after she went to glory. Decent place for free Black people to live and work." The word *free* struck Charity again.

Clara nodded approvingly. "A good place for free people," she repeated, her tone almost wistful. Then she smiled again. "Mr. Butler, I have to say, I'm quite impressed. You're a man of sophistication, and I dare say you've brought some much-needed refinement to our day."

Larkin grinned. "Well, thank you, Miss Clara. I do believe in making the best of what you've got."

Clara waved a hand, dismissing his modesty. "Nonsense. You're a credit to your upbringing, and I can't help but admire a man with such finesse. Isn't that right, Charity?"

Charity looked up briefly. "Yes, ma'am," she said quietly as her thoughts whirled.

As the carriage pulled up to their humble home for the next two weeks, Larkin stepped down first and carefully set their two trunks on the ground. He turned, offering his hand to

Clara, and then to Charity, who hesitated before accepting. The baby in her arms squealed as Larkin steadied them both with an easy grip.

"I'll see you soon, Miss Charity," he said, his eyes staying just long enough to make her cheeks flush.

Clara, adjusting her parasol against the afternoon sun, glanced between the two of them with an expression that moved from wonder to approval. A pleased smile spread across her face. "Mr. Butler, you have been so very kind to us today. Might I extend an invitation for you to join Charity and me for dinner tomorrow evening? A touch of class would do us some good, and it would be a true honor to have you at our table." Charity's head snapped toward Clara. She was shocked but overjoyed.

Larkin was unfazed. "Miss Clara, I'd be delighted. But I wouldn't come empty-handed. How about I bring a sweet potato pie? Best in the county—if I say so myself."

Clara cackled. "A sweet potato pie, you say? Well, now, that is precisely the sort of gallantry we could use more of in these parts. You shall be the first gentleman to grace my table since—well, let us not speak of *him*. We shall expect you promptly at six o'clock, Mr. Butler."

Larkin tipped his hat. "Wouldn't dream of disappointing you, Miss Clara. Or you, Miss Charity." He turned to Charity with a wink.

As Larkin climbed back into the carriage, he gave the reins a gentle tug. Clara leaned closer to Charity, nudging her shoulder lightly. "What a charming man," she whispered, her voice brimming with approval. "Wouldn't you agree, Charity? And he speaks *so* well."

Charity didn't answer. She couldn't, not with the way her pulse quickened. She adjusted the baby in her arms, her eyes following the carriage until it disappeared down the road. *De-*

light yourself in the Lord, and He will give you the desires of your heart,[18] she thought to herself.

Larkin Butler had entered Charity's world, and already it felt as if he intended to stay.

The next day dawned bright for Charity. She moved quietly, her heart thundering in her chest. She had barely slept, excitement and nervousness rushed inside of her. As she prepared breakfast for Miss Clara and the baby she tried to keep her composure. Her thoughts were consumed by the promise of Larkin Butler's return. The morning passed in a blur of tasks—tending to the baby, fetching materials for Clara's sewing, cleaning the small sitting room. Charity's hands were busy, but her mind lingered on the evening ahead. When Clara finally retired to her workbench, Charity slipped into the kitchen to begin preparing the evening meal. She chose roasted chicken, mashed potatoes, and collard greens, a hearty meal that could fill a man's stomach after a long day. She couldn't help the small smile that crept across her lips. She had never prepared a meal with this much care before, and Clara noticed.

"You're in fine spirits today, Charity," Clara remarked, glancing up from her sewing. "I daresay you're more cheerful than I've ever seen you."

Charity forced herself not to pause at the foolishness of Clara's comment. When had Miss Clara ever seen her "cheerful"—or paid enough attention to know she was mournful? Was she seriously expecting some grinning, sunshine-spitting slave? Charity focused on the mixing bowl. "Just keeping busy, ma'am."

"Well, whatever the reason, keep it up. This shabby house could use joy."

18. *Psalm* 37:4, English Standard Version.

As the sun slipped away, Charity lit the lamps and set the table with the finest dishes in the house. She adjusted flowers in the center, straightening her apron as she glanced toward the clock. The knock came at precisely six, and Charity's heart leapt with joy. She played with her hair and opened the door to find Larkin standing, dressed in a tailored but casual suit, the fabric dark and clean, his cravat tied neatly at his neck. He held a pie in his large hands, his smile as easy as ever.

"Good evening, Miss Charity," he said.

Charity stepped aside as Clara appeared in the doorway with baby Gertrude in her arms. "Mr. Butler, right on time! And what's this? Sweet potato pie?" She laughed, clearly pleased. "You're a man of your word, I'll give you that."

They sat at the table, the three of them, the conversation flowing easily. Miss Clara chattered about her work, the sewing business, and the eccentricities of her customers. Larkin listened with polite interest, occasionally interjecting with a story of his own. Charity remained quiet, her eyes shooting between them, but she couldn't help smiling at Larkin's charm and Miss Clara's unusual lightness. Charity's thoughts spun as she watched them—Larkin, a Black man, sitting at the same table with a White woman, sharing stories and laughter as if the world outside this room did not exist. She never thought she'd see such a moment, not here in Gettysburg. What would Master Bruce think of this? She could almost hear his voice, denouncing such audacity. And what of the other souls like her, back in Maryland? What would they make of this image—this mini and quiet revolt against the rules that had governed all their lives? The thought unsettled her, not because it felt wrong but because it felt too right. Larkin and Miss Clara sitting together, speaking as equals, cracked her open.

The conversation shifted as Larkin turned to Clara with a question that thickened the air in the room. "Miss Clara," he began casually, "how do you feel about your role in all this? About . . . slavery?"

Charity froze, her hand tightening on the edge of her chair. She stared at Larkin, stunned. She had never seen a Black man question anyone—let alone a White woman—about slavery. It was an act so unthinkable that it left her breathless. Could this be the end of Mr. Butler setting foot in this home? The rapport they had built over a shared meal and polite conversations was on the edge of collapse. Charity's heart drummed as she glanced at Miss Clara.

What would she do? How would she respond? Charity wasn't sure what to expect. Yes, Miss Clara had been cordial, but she still benefited from this sick institution. She was, after all, the wife—albeit estranged—of a slave owner. She had rented Charity, paid into the very system that oppressed her, and accepted the ease it afforded her life. Miss Clara might not have been as calculating as some, but she was complicit. That was undeniable. Could she endure mild questioning? The room shrank as Miss Clara adjusted in her seat, her fingers playing with the lace edge of her handkerchief. Miss Clara blinked, clearly caught off guard. She set down her fork, her lips pressing together.

"I'm not proud of it," she admitted, her voice quieter now. "When I married Charles, I thought . . . well, I thought love could excuse certain things. I was wrong. I've lived with that mistake every day, and I hope one day I can make things right."

Larkin nodded. "That's all anyone can hope for, ma'am. To make things right."

Charity exhaled quietly. Relief washed over her, though her mind was still spinning. Clara had answered thoughtfully without the defensiveness or dismissiveness Charity had feared. But it wasn't just Clara's response in Charity's thoughts—it was Larkin. My God, who *was* this man? He was unlike anyone she had ever encountered. Bold enough to pose a question most wouldn't dare utter, yet composed enough to disarm the conversation without shattering it. He wasn't just brave; he breathed clarity, a man who used his words like tools rather than weapons. Larkin Butler was something entirely new to her. Charity felt a thrill, an admiration and curiosity that she couldn't put into words.

The rest of the meal passed in lighter conversation. As Charity was clearing the dishes, Larkin asked, "Would you like to take a walk, Miss Charity?"

Charity glanced at Miss Clara, unsure, but she waved her hand. "No need to ask me. The work is done for the day. Go on."

The summer air was cool, a gentle wind rustling the leaves as Charity and Larkin walked along the dirt road outside the house. The stars were just beginning to emerge. They spoke of small things at first. Larkin's work at the blacksmith shop, the peculiarities of Gettysburg's residents, but eventually, he asked a more earnest question.

"What do you want out of life, Charity?" he asked as he slowly walked beside her.

Charity hesitated. No one had ever asked her that before—what *she* wanted. It wasn't that she didn't have dreams or longings, but she'd never been given the space to shape them into something she could say aloud. The question had to sink into her. She looked to the sky. What did she want? The answers had always belonged to others. What others needed from her, what others demanded of her. But this . . . this was different. "I want . . . a family. A home. I want to be free."

Larkin stopped walking, turning to face her. "And what does that mean to you?"

Charity looked into Larkin. "Don't remember my family . . . only plantations. One after another. I wanna be a wife. A mama. I wanna belong to no one but myself."

Larkin stepped closer. "You can have that, Charity. You deserve it."

Before she could reply, he leaned in, his lips brushing against hers in a gentle kiss. It was her first real kiss, and it stole the breath from her core. Larkin pulled back, staring into her. "A family, a home, freedom—all of it. You deserve it."

Uncertainty clouded Charity's expression. "Larkin . . . you just met me yesterday. You don't know me. Not really."

He exhaled slowly, his hand brushing against hers. "Maybe I don't know everything 'bout you yet," he admitted. "But something shifted when I saw you. It was like . . . like the world tilted, just a little. I know what I want. I've made it far, but there's one thing I don't have. A family. A place to call mine. That's what's missing. Don't wanna scare you, but I ain't gonna lie neither. I want that with you. Maybe not all at once, but someday."

Charity's eyes searched his face. "But . . . I'm not even free. How do I take what I never had? Only know what others tell me I can have."

"Start believing it's yours to take. You're stronger than the world wants you to think. And remember this—six months, Charity. Six months in Pennsylvania means you're a free woman. That's the law."

Her eyes widened. "Six months . . ." she whispered, testing the idea on her tongue.

"Yes," he said with conviction. "Add up the time. Be here for two weeks, then you come back. Keep adding up the time. Do you know your numbers?"

She blinked at the question. "No," she admitted. "Never learned."

"Then I'll teach you," he said. "It's important, knowing how to count, how to keep track of what's yours. No one can take that from you."

Charity paused. "How you learn?"

"From someone who saved my life," he said. "I escaped a plantation in Virginia, town called Goochland. Vicious place. Been ten years now. But the people there . . . they weren't just workers. They were survivors. Like family." Charity could see the past etched in Larkin's eyes. "There was Mama Bess, strongest woman I ever knew. She taught me how to hope, even when it felt like there wasn't none left. And then there was Josephine . . ." He trailed off. "She wasn't much older than me, just five years, but she looked after me like I was her own. Like I was her little brother, or her son, even. Taught me numbers, taught me how to think about the world in ways I never had before."

"What happened to them?" Charity asked.

"Mama Bess was up in years and passed. Josephine took sick before her time," Larkin said. "But she died free. Free and proud of what she had done, of what we all did together. She used to say, 'Don't let them take what they can't touch.' She believed that right up until the end."

"Sounds like folks worth remembering."

Larkin nodded, "That's how you keep people alive. You remember them. And because of her, I'm still here. That's why I'm gonna teach you, Charity. So you'll know what you need to know, so you'll have what you need to have, no matter what happens." Larkin leaned in once more, capturing her lips in another kiss, this one deeper, more certain. When they pulled apart, his forehead rested lightly against hers. "You can have it all, Charity. A family. Freedom. Me, if you'll have me."

When they walked back to the door, her heart was on overdrive. She stood in the house for a long moment, her hand pressed to her lips.

Over the next two weeks, Larkin and Charity saw each other every day. Their time together never conflicted with

Charity's work, and Miss Clara was surprisingly unbothered by the arrangement. Their courtship was filled with laughter, tender conversations, and teaching Charity her numbers and how to read. When they walked through the fields, he pointed to clusters of flowers. "Count 'em, Charity," he'd say. "How many you see right there?" He'd nudge her gently. "Ain't no rush. Take your time. One, two . . . see? You got it." He'd then make her spell *flowers*.

In the evenings, as they sat on the porch with the last light of the day, he'd trace numbers in the dirt with a stick, showing her how to write them. "This here's a five," he'd say. "Looks like an ear hanging off the side. See it?" At the market, he turned everyday errands into lessons. Holding up a handful of apples, he'd grin and ask, "How many you reckon this is? Think we got enough for a pie?" Even in the quiet moments, like when they sat by the fire at night, he'd find a way to slip in the numbers and letters. He'd place small pebbles in her hand, one by one, and whisper, "Feel that? That's one. Now two. Spell it out. You're holding five, Charity. You're holding something that's yours." Larkin never rushed her, never made her feel small for not knowing. Instead, he turned each lesson into a moment of connection. While reading was more difficult and harder to practice, slowly, she began to count the world around her, and with each number, she felt a little more like she was claiming something for herself.

Charity found herself smiling more, but the last day came all too soon. As Charity climbed onto the stagecoach, her heart ached like she hadn't expected. Larkin stood by, his hand resting briefly on hers. "See you soon," he promised.

Clara, from her seat in the stagecoach, added, "We'll be back. There's plenty of work to do."

As the stagecoach rumbled away, Charity turned to look at Larkin, he lifted his hat with a smile. She cried quietly at first but as they moved farther down the road, away from the comfort of Gettysburg, her sobs grew louder. It wasn't just the thought of leaving Larkin—it was the fear of returning to Norman Bruce. For once, Clara said nothing. She sat across from Charity, watching in silence, her face unreadable. Maybe, with only the sound of the road and baby Gertrude, Clara understood something deeper than herself. Charity's chest heaved, but she could not stop herself from wondering: Would she ever have a life that was fully hers? The open road ahead seemed endless, but it wasn't the road that frightened her. It was what waited at the end of it.

The travel between Maryland and Gettysburg became a strange rhythm in Charity's life, a cycle of hope and despair. Each time she returned to the Bruce plantation, its horrors pressed on her soul. The days filled with the barks of orders, the indignity of servitude, and the pain of longing for something she could barely imagine: a life of her own. Larkin Butler's voice was a lifeline she anchored to in her mind during those isolating days. Over the next several months, every time she took a trip back to Gettysburg, Clara praised Charity's work with baby Gertrude in the household, and this pleased Mr. Norman Bruce enough to grant her leave again and again. "She's indispensable," Clara would say, her tone light but persuasive. Norman, proud of what he saw as his "property's" value, allowed the trips, unaware of the rebellion unfolding beneath his nose.

Each time Charity traveled the familiar route, her eyes always found the same marker—the white chimney with the black top rising against the sky. She had learned early that when she saw it, she was about to cross into Pennsylvania, stepping into where freedom lived. During her weeks in Pennsylvania, Charity and Larkin stole every moment they could together. They walked the fields near his blacksmith shop, talking about their lives, their dreams, and the possibilities of a future together. But Larkin avoided revealing too much of his yesterdays. He did not speak of the liberating details about fleeing the Baynard plantation in Goochland, Virginia. Charity sensed there was more that he was not ready to say. She knew he was trying to protect her from something—perhaps to protect himself too. Still, with each talk, her curiosity only grew stronger, leaving her certain that she had only just begun to see the man Larkin truly was.

Charity was struggling to learn her letters and was outraged by the frustration of being unable to write to Larkin during their separations. Charity soaked up everything Larkin showed her, but it wasn't enough. She needed more help, quicker. She was hungry to learn. During one of the long rides back to Gettysburg, Charity inquired about the book Clara was always reading. Clara lit up. "Oh, Charity, it's called *Sense and Sensibility* by Jane Austen!" Clara exclaimed, pulling the book to her chest. "Miss Austen is *exquisite*. Her wit, her insight into human folly—it's simply divine."

Charity was unsure how much Clara was willing to do, but she decided to take a chance. "I'd like to learn to read, ma'am," she said softly, her stare dropping to her hands. "If you'd be willing to teach me."

Clara gasped, her excitement almost childlike. "You want to read *Sense and Sensibility*? Charity, this is marvelous! Of course, I'll teach you. It would be a crime against art not to."

Her enthusiasm was genuine, but there was something else beneath it, a bit of understanding that Charity couldn't place. This offer felt like a small act of sedition. Clara was no stupid woman; she knew what teaching Charity meant, but she didn't vacillate. Instead, she savored the opportunity. The lessons began immediately. Clara was dramatic, theatrical even, as she read passages aloud, insisting Charity mimic her pronunciation. "No, no, dear, *ennui* is pronounced *on-wee*. Now try again!" Clara sighed dramatically, whining about how Charity's "stubborn tongue" refused to pronounce certain words.

Charity couldn't help but laugh at Clara's over-the-top instructions, but she was grateful for the effort. With patience, the letters and words began to make sense. Larkin's earlier lessons merged with Clara's more structured ones, and soon Charity was deciphering sentences on her own. Whether Clara fully understood the implications of her teaching, Charity didn't know, but the lessons became a strange bond between them—a rebellion shared on their rides and evenings by the fire. For Clara, teaching Charity was not just about education. It was a way to challenge the forces that had instructed her life. Charity sensed that each page turned, each word learned, was as much a defiance of Clara's past as it was a gift for the future. For Charity, it was freedom, one word and one day at a time.

As the months passed, Charity and Larkin's bond deepened. Their love grew, first in glances, then in kisses, and finally in the tender intimacy of their nights together. They discovered a closeness neither had known before, and for Charity, those moments with Larkin were a revelation. For the first time, she felt not just wanted, but cherished. Then came a new revelation. Back in Maryland, Charity missed her cycle. The morning sickness and faint swelling of her belly confirmed what her heart already knew. She carried Larkin's child. The news filled her with both fear and joy. She counted the weeks desperately, her growing belly pressing against the time she had left before returning to Pennsylvania.

Finally, after two agonizing months—the longest she had been forced to wait—Charity boarded the carriage for Gettysburg, her heart racing with anticipation. She had news to share with Larkin. The familiar fields and winding roads of Pennsylvania beckoned her, each mile drawing her closer to the life she deserved. When the stagecoach pulled to a stop at Miss

Clara's, Charity wasted no time. She set down her trunk, saw to baby Gertrude, and hurried through her tasks for the day. Clara, preoccupied with her latest seamstress orders, barely noticed Charity's distracted demeanor. Every stitch and errand Charity performed was with the quickness of her mission: to see Larkin. The moment Clara excused her for the evening, Charity slipped out of the house and rushed down the path to Larkin's blacksmith shop.

The clang of metal against metal rang out as she approached. The brightness of the forge spilled into the darkening evening, framing Larkin's broad body as he worked. He looked up, wiping sweat from his defined jaw. His face lit up when he saw her.

"Charity," he called. He set down his tools and strode toward her. Charity paused as she placed a hand over her belly.

"Larkin," she began softly, taking his hand and placing it against the slight swell of her abdomen. "I'm with child." For a moment, he stared, his hand resting gently against her. Then, a broad smile broke across his face, his joy radiating like sunlight. Without a word, he dropped to his knees, resting his head against her belly as if to feel the life growing within.

"Charity," he said, "then let me do this right." He took her hands in his own. His gaze met hers, full of love. "I don't have a ring, but I promise I'll spend my life proving how much I love you. Charity, I want you as my wife."

Tears streamed as she laughed, overwhelmed by the moment. "Yes, Larkin," she whispered. "Yes." The two stood, wrapped in each other's arms.

The next morning, Charity woke with a renewed sense of purpose. These two weeks would mark not only her sixth trip to Pennsylvania, but—when added to her previous visits—would total over six months spent in the "nearly free" state—183 days exactly. She had crossed into freedom. For months, she had meticulously tallied each day with Larkin's help.

Now, at last, she was free by the law of the land. Charity was overflowing with elation and anxiety. She would have to tell Miss Clara, who had been many things to her, sometimes kind, always complex. Would she understand? Would she be angry?

Over the next two weeks, Charity's thoughts churned with these questions. Clara, as always, demanded her share of attention, keeping Charity busy with the baby and seamstress errands.

Each evening, Charity saw Larkin. His confidence steadied her, his belief in her strength giving her courage she didn't know she possessed. The night before she was scheduled to return to the Bruce plantation, they stood under the stars, the cool air brushing against their skin. Larkin took her hands in his. "You'll tell her, Charity. Tell Miss Clara. You're free now—no one can take that from you. Do you want me with you when you tell her?"

"No. I should tell her on my own."

He nodded, his eyes searching hers. "I understand. But just know it's not just your freedom at stake now, it's our child's."

Charity's every nerve sang with the tension as she nodded.

Larkin gave her hands a reassuring squeeze. "You'll be alright. And I'll be waiting for you."

His words stayed with her as she made her way back to Clara's. The night was quieter than usual, as though the world was holding its breath. The baby had long since fallen asleep. Charity paused at the threshold of the small sitting room where Clara sat by the firelight. She held a cup of tea in one hand. *What a long two weeks in Gettysburg*, Clara thought to herself. Her fingers ached from the seamstress work.

Charity gathered her thoughts, her hand resting briefly on her swelling belly to remind herself why she had come. Inhaling deeply, she stepped into the sitting room.

"Miss Clara," she said softly.

Clara turned, startled for a moment. "Charity," she said, setting her teacup down on the table beside her. "What are you doing up at this hour? We have a long day ahead of us tomorrow."

Charity stepped closer, her hands in front of her. "Need to talk to you."

Clara raised an eyebrow. "About what?"

Charity didn't sit. She stood near the lamp with her head down. "About tomorrow. About going back to Maryland and Mr. Bruce." This was her first decision as a free woman, she lifted her head, chin high, speaking with the diction she learned from *Sense and Sensibility*. "I will not be returning to Maryland."

Clara blinked, her face stiffened in surprise before a strained laugh escaped. "Not going? What do you mean you're not going? Of course, you're going. We leave in the morning."

Charity shook her head. "No, ma'am. I've been counting. Since the first time we came to Pennsylvania. It's been six months, Miss Clara. That means I'm free."

Clara sat up straight. "What are you talking about?"

"The Gradual Abolition Act of 1780," Charity said calmly, a term she first heard Larkin say over a year ago, not even knowing what the words meant. Now she was living those words. "Larkin told me. He has been teaching me, said if I stayed here for six months, I'd be free. And I keep track every single day. We've been here on and off for over a year. But it's been six months, all the numbers added up. I don't have to go back, Miss Clara."

Clara's mouth opened, but she was speechless for a few seconds. She hunched over, trying to process the revelation. "Larkin," she said finally. "So, this is his doing . . ."

"My doing," Charity replied. "Larkin told me about the law, but I made the choice. Kept count."

Clara stood, pacing toward the window. "Charity, do you

fully comprehend what this means? What Norman Bruce will do should he discover you've remained—should he learn that I permitted it—" She pressed a hand to her forehead. "He shall lay the blame squarely upon me, you realize that, don't you?"

Charity didn't waver. "I know. And I'm sorry for what this means for you, Miss Clara. But I can't go back. I won't. This is about me. About my life, and . . . my child's life." She placed a hand on her belly.

Clara's eyes dropped to Charity's hand. "Your . . . your child?" she sighed.

"I'm with child. And Larkin asked me to marry him."

The room sank into quiet again as the two women stood facing each other. Clara's shoulders slumped slightly as she side-eyed Charity. Carefully, she moved to sit back down, her hands clasping in her lap. Clara's mind was a snarl of thoughts she couldn't untangle. Charity's pregnancy struck a strange chord within her, an alien ache that Clara could not name. It wasn't as if Clara had ever felt true solidarity with the likes of Charity; that was impossible. She participated in a system that had always been hers to navigate, manipulate, and benefit from. This wasn't about Charity, not entirely. This was about Clara herself. Something had been festering inside her, a revolt against the life she had led, the world she had helped maintain. Her mind reverted to moments she rarely allowed herself to remember, the screams she had once ignored and the way Charles had spoken of "discipline" as if it were justice.

Clara wasn't ready to call it guilt. It felt more like exhaustion, a spreading loathing she couldn't shake. Clara didn't profit like she thought she would. Slavery had never been a cage for her. She had been its enforcer. Now that it was inconvenient for her—and only her—could she push back. Her own narcissism might have spared Charity. Whatever Clara thought of herself, surely she wasn't one of *them*—was she? "I ought to stop you," Clara stated firmly. "I ought to summon the authorities, to alert the slave catchers. That is precisely what Charles or Norman would do, what they would expect me to do." Clara then remembered telling Larkin, *I hope one day I can make things right.*

Charity didn't flinch. "But you won't."

"No," she said. "I won't. Because they've taken everything from me—Charles, Norman, men like them. I won't take anything from you. Not your freedom, nor your child."

"Thank you, Miss Clara."

Clara shook her head. "Do not thank me yet, Charity. I cannot prevent what they may do if they discover the truth. But I will not be the one to hinder you. You have found love. I will not destroy that, not after all I have lost myself. Live the life I could never have, but for heaven's sake, tread carefully. Men like Norman Bruce are not inclined to forget."

"I know," Charity responded. She knew more than Clara could imagine. "But I have to try."

Clara reached for the small, wooden box resting on the nearby table. She lifted the lid, withdrawing a well-worn book, *Sense and Sensibility*, the book that Miss Clara had used to teach her how to read. "Take this," she said. "It has served its purpose for me. I have no further use for it." Charity hesitated, but Clara let out a sigh, as though shaking off any dramatics. "My address in Vermont is written there. I do not know how much longer I shall remain in the South, but should you ever have need of me, you will know where to find me."

Charity turned the book over in her hands. "You taught me to read with this," Charity murmured. "I . . . I don't know what to say."

"Then say nothing," Clara said crisply. "Merely take care. Love is a fragile thing, and men like Norman Bruce are adept at crushing that which they do not understand."

With that, the two women sat in calmness for a while longer. They were so different—one nurtured to privilege, the other bred as chattel—yet, in this moment, they had accomplished something extraordinary, almost impossible given their circumstances. They had crafted an alliance. Charity's strategic break from slavery did not impede Clara's life. Charity was inspired by Larkin's freedom and the power of reclaiming what should never have been stolen. Clara, stripped of the illusions of her former life, chose not to wield the power given to her as a weapon but as a shield, refusing to be an instrument of further harm. One couldn't help but wonder: If more stood together as they did, how swiftly might oppressive institutions crumble?

In the dark, they proved what could be possible when those marginalized, no matter how small or vast, refused to turn on one another. By working together—or simply by refusing to stand in each other's way—they could subvert the forces that sought to pit them against one another. Clara shifted in her chair, distant but reflective. Charity, one hand resting protectively over her new life, stood with peace.

The next morning, the red-skinned driver arrived promptly. Clara stood on the porch, her expression pinched but composed, her parasol resting at her side and baby Gertrude on her hip. As he finished loading the stagecoach, the driver glanced up. "Where's the gal?" he asked in a blunt tone. "Ain't she coming back with us?"

Clara's hand gripped the parasol so firmly that her knuckles whitened. "Hush," she said. "Mind your business and see to the ride."

The driver blinked, perplexed, but her words left no room for argument. "But, ma'am—"

"I said hush," she snapped, cutting him off before he could say more. "We must leave at once. I need to get back to Maryland without delay." Still confused but unwilling to press further, the driver climbed onto his seat. Clara followed, her movements brisk, though her face betrayed the turmoil roiling beneath her. As the horses began to trot, she sank back into her seat, her eyes on the passing landscape.

The wheels on the road were louder without Charity, each bump a reminder of the decision she had made. Clara's thoughts reeled with second-guessing as she stared into baby Gertrude's eyes. Had she made a mistake? Should she have insisted that Charity come back with her? The thought clawed at her, but then, another voice surfaced. When Charity spoke of freedom, of her child, of Larkin, she had made her choice, and Clara had chosen not to be a blockade. As the ride jolted along for hours, Clara leaned her head back against the seat and rested her eyes. She allowed herself to admit the truth: She had done the right thing. Charity's freedom was not hers to deny, nor was it hers to safeguard.

Her thoughts shifted, circling back to Charles, the man she had once sacrificed everything for. What had her devotion to him gained her? Ruin, heartbreak, and endless regrets. She had given her loyalty to a man who had never deserved it. She would return to Maryland, to the home Charles had left her, and she would find a way to rebuild. Maybe write Father and ask to return to Vermont. Charity had shown her something—freedom didn't have to look the same for everyone. For Clara, it meant starting anew and refusing to let men like Charles dictate her worth.

Mr. Norman Bruce rode up to the fading plantation home of Clara Petterson. The once-proud house was a sad defeat with peeling paint and sagging shutters. There were no souls working the fields. Charles had taken his property, human and otherwise, leaving Clara with nothing but the shell of a farm she had no means to manage. Dismounting his horse, Norman adjusted his coat with an agitated tug—one of many small compensations for his small stature—before climbing the porch steps, his short legs working harder than he'd ever admit. According to the driver, who worked for both Norman Bruce and Charles Petterson, Charity had not returned with Clara. The very thought was absurd. Surely, the girl was back, tucked away somewhere on this dilapidated estate. Clara, for all her dramatics, wouldn't have dared defy him, he told himself. Yet, the driver's report curdled in him. *Damn fool women, always taking it into their silly heads to run off and make trouble.*

Drawing a breath, Norman rapped on the door. Clara firmly pulled it open. There she stood, a touch taller than him, her face the picture of serene indifference. She held baby Gertrude on one hip, her other hand rested lightly on the doorframe.

"Mr. Bruce," she drawled, her voice caked with charm. "To what do I owe this unexpected pleasure?"

"Come for Charity," he said, looking in her home, hoping to see her there. "Assume you brought her back as agreed."

Clara quickly nodded her head. "Charity? Oh, yes. Lovely girl. Helpful too. But, you see, she's not here."

Norman felt anger rise. "What you mean, not here?"

"She stayed in Pennsylvania," Clara said casually, stepping to invite him in. "Simply refused to leave. What could I do? You know how these young girls can be." The words came light, almost playful.

"What you mean, she refused? That gal is *my property*. You were supposed to bring her back, like you always do." He walked in the house, inching closer to Clara. "That was the arrangement."

Clara shrugged. She moved toward a quaint table where a pitcher of sweet tea waited, pouring herself a glass. "Arrangements change, Mr. Bruce. She's a stubborn one, that Charity. Must've got it in her head to stay. Maybe she met someone."

Norman's hands balled into fists. "Met someone? What in God's name are you talking about?"

Clara's tone shifted, the sweetness giving way to steel. "A man named Larkin Butler," she said, sipping her tea. "Seems he took a shine to her. Handsome, *tall*," she said, scanning Norman from head to toe. "And I can't blame her for wanting to stay. Pennsylvania's a fine place, don't you think?"

Norman's face turned crimson. "You playing a dangerous game, Clara. That girl was rented to you on and off for over a year. *Rented*, at a fine price, might I add. And you let her go."

Clara huffed. "A fine price? Overcharged me is more like it. Do you know how much you *men* bleed us dry? You and your kind—my good-for-nothing husband included."

Norman's mouth twisted. "Watch your tongue, woman!"

Clara set her glass down with a loud clunk. "Why? Are you going to tell your dear friend, my husband Charles, how I failed to bring back your precious girl? Oh, I'm sure he'd love that. Assuming you can find him. Perhaps he's off ruining another young woman's life as we speak."

"You gone and made a mess of things," Norman said with a pointed finger. "And you'll answer for it!"

"Oh, Norman, you do have a knack for theatrics. I didn't 'make a mess.' Charity decided to stay in Pennsylvania. Who am I to deny her that? After all, Pennsylvania is a lovely place"—she took a pregnant pause—"to raise a child."

Norman's head jerked toward her like a dog catching a scent. "What you say?"

Clara took another sip of her sweet tea. "This tea is just lovely, so refreshing."

"*Clara*," Norman Bruce said through clenched teeth.

"A child, Norman. Charity is with child." She let the statement land, basking in the way it hit him. "And again, Pennsylvania is wonderful for children. I always admired Governor

William Johnston. Such a sensible man. I'd surely have voted for him, had I the right to vote—being a woman and all."

"That child belongs to me! That's my property, Clara!"

Clara barked a laugh. "Property? That's all you can think about, isn't it? A life growing inside a woman, and you reduce it to property. Perhaps you're just angry you didn't get the chance to impregnate her yourself. It wouldn't surprise me, considering the wretched ways of men like you."

Norman's hand slammed against the side table, the pitcher rattling violently, but Clara didn't budge. She leaned forward. "You're nothing but a sad *little* man."

"You're trash, Clara," he spat. "Always acting like you're the queen of something, but you ain't nothing but bitter. That's why Charles left. Sick of your high-siddy nonsense. You're old, you're plain and think you're better than us."

Clara turned icy. "I do think I am better than you. I *know* I am better than all of you. What a pity I wasted my life falling for Southern scum like Charles. Maybe if I crawl on my hands and knees, my family will take me back. A proper Northern lady, redeemed from the filth of you and your kind." Norman took a menacing step closer. "And where is your wife, Mr. Bruce? Where is your lady of the house? Oh, that's right. You don't have one, do you? Too busy sniffing around other men's messes. Or, perhaps, you and dear Charles might find comfort in one another's company. What interesting bedfellows you two would make."

Norman came a trifle nearer, hand raised, but Clara was faster. She swept baby Gertrude into the bassinet with one arm and moved to the dresser with the other, drawing a revolver in one fluid motion.

When she turned, the barrel was aimed squarely at his bony chest.

"Touch me," she warned, her voice like a whip, "and you'll regret it."

Norman was motionless, his breath coming in bursts. Overpronouncing each word, he said, "Put that down. You're just mad because Charles left you."

"Could be. Or maybe I've simply grown weary of men such as yourself presuming to instruct the course of my life." She cocked the gun, the *click* echoing. "I've endured quite enough of your kind."

"You'll regret this," he growled, moving toward the door. "I'll get Charity back, and make sure you pay every cent it costs to collect her."

Clara lowered the revolver slightly, her death stare never wavering. "You can try, Mr. Bruce. But I'd think long and hard before you do. My aim is unerring."

Norman stumbled out the door, slamming it behind him. Clara stood there for a short moment, the gun still in her hand, before she turned back to the bassinet. Baby Gertrude's tiny fingers were grasping at the air.

Clara placed the revolver back in the dresser. She knelt beside baby Gertrude, patting her soft curls. "Men like that think they hold all the cards," she said. "They don't know a thing about strength or survival. But I believe now is the time to return home to Vermont. There's simply no possibility Father will turn away his own grandchild. You, my dearest, shall be the one to secure our freedom."

Norman Bruce gripped his seat for hours, the road jostling him as the wheels bounced over rocks and potholes to Gettysburg. His mood grew darker with each lurch. The driver said nothing.

"Pedro, why didn't you insist Clara bring Charity back with her?"

"Well, sir," he began cautiously, "Miss Clara, she's . . . a determined sort. Wasn't in a position to argue."

Norman Bruce glared at him. "You should have done more

than argue. You should've demanded it. That girl is my property, and you let her slip away."

The driver kept his eyes on the road ahead. "Begging your pardon, sir, but Miss Clara didn't seem the sort to take orders."

Bruce let out a humorless laugh. "You Indians as dumb as negroes. A White man would never let a *woman* tell him what to do. Dumb as a negro."

Pedro stared at the road ahead, refusing to let the insult settle in his bones. *Dumb as a negro*. One day, men like Norman Bruce would travel down roads that wouldn't carry them so easily, Pedro thought. He swallowed his fury, forcing his voice into something even. "Reckon a man don't always get to decide who listens to him, sir." Norman snorted in irritation.

Word had already spread that Clara had returned to Vermont, taking nothing with her but baby Gertrude, her revolver, and clothes. Charles, her ex-husband, said she left a note behind. In classic Miss Clara style, it read: *May she find satisfaction where I could not, though I suspect your true desires lie elsewhere entirely.*

The remainder of the ride passed in tense silence, the stagecoach rattling its way into Gettysburg. Norman Bruce stepped out as soon as he arrived, dusting off his coat and scanning the town. He approached the first White man he saw.

"I'm looking for someone," Norman said. "A colored blacksmith by the name of Larkin Butler."

The man raised an eyebrow but nodded. "Larkin Butler? Best blacksmith in Gettysburg. You'll find his shop down the main road, just past the inn."

Norman didn't thank him. He turned on his heel, his boots striking the ground. The shop was easy to find, the clang of metal-on-metal echoing down the street. Smoke rose from the forge, and the heat was palpable even from a distance. He pushed the door open without hesitation. Inside, Larkin Butler stood at the anvil, his powerful arms swinging a hammer in strokes. He looked up as Norman Bruce entered, his face calm but watchful.

"You Larkin Butler?" Norman barked.

Larkin set the hammer down slowly, wiping his hands on a rag. "That's right," he said. "What can I do for you?"

"You can hand over what's mine," Norman said. "Charity. She belongs to me."

"Charity doesn't belong to anyone," he shot back. "She's a free woman."

"You hiding her? I know she here. Don't think you can fool me, *boy*."

"She ain't hiding. She's here because she chose to be. And she's free by law. You've no claim on her, *sir*."

Norman Bruce's temper flared as he jabbed a finger at Larkin's solid chest. "If we was a few hours away in Maryland, I'd have had you strung up on a tree."

Larkin stood as tall as an oak, looking down on Norman Bruce, who barely reached his biceps. He didn't raise his voice. "If we were a few hours away in Maryland," Larkin said, "you'd find yourself on the wrong side of a fight you ain't prepared for. I'm not a man who's ever feared pale foolishness dressed up as power." Larkin didn't give him the chance to react. He stepped back, his movements unbothered, and picked up his hammer again as though Norman's threats were nothing more than a buzzing fly. "Now," Larkin said, striking the red-hot iron on his anvil with a clang, "you're in Pennsylvania, not Maryland. And here, the law doesn't bend to men who think they can own what they don't deserve."

"This ain't over," Norman Bruce spat, pointing a finger at Larkin. "You'll regret this."

Larkin watched him storm out, the door slamming shut behind him. Larkin turned to the corner of the shop, where Charity stepped out from her hiding place, her face in distress.

"Don't know why you're hiding. You're free," Larkin assured.

"He'll come back," she said softly.

Larkin nodded. "Then we'll make sure he can't do a damn thing when he does."

The law office of Thaddeus Stevens was modest but meticulously ordered, shelves lined with leather-bound books and a sturdy desk at its center. The space showcased intellectual rigor, yet the scent of pipe tobacco and the worn furniture hinted at a man who valued utility over pretension. Behind the desk sat a sharp-tongued secretary, Mrs. Wilhelmina Clarke, whose cutting tone was often enough to deter unannounced visitors. Norman Bruce, however, was not easily deterred.

He pushed through the front door, his small boots tapping loudly against the wooden floor. Mrs. Clarke didn't bother to stand for the tiny man, instead peering over her spectacles. "And just who do you think you are, barging in here like a bull in a china shop?"

"Here to see Mr. Stevens," Norman snapped. "It's urgent."

Mrs. Clarke arched an eyebrow, unimpressed. "And does Mr. Stevens know you're coming? Because he's a very busy man, and he doesn't entertain just anyone who waltzes in off the street."

Norman's Southern drawl dripped with impatience. "I assure you this is a matter of utmost importance. Fetch him at once."

Mrs. Clarke leaned back in her chair, folding her arms. "Mr. Stevens doesn't 'fetch,' nor do I. If you've come without an appointment, you can turn yourself right back around, he has no availability until next month."

"Listen, gal—" Norman snapped, making Mrs. Clarke's eyes grow like saucers.

"Mrs. Clarke," came an authoritative voice from behind the door to an inner office. Thaddeus Stevens emerged, leaning on his cane. "What's all this commotion?" Norman turned, momentarily taken aback by the man before him. Thaddeus Stevens's clubfoot was immediately noticeable and his ill-fitting wig perched awkwardly atop his head. He looked weak and passive, nothing like the lawyer of formidable reputation he had heard described. "I heard the shouting from my office. It seems there is a guest who believes himself too important for protocol. But let him in, Mrs. Clarke."

With a gritted exhale, Mrs. Clarke waved Norman toward the door. "Don't say I didn't warn you, Mr. Stevens. This one's trouble." She gave Norman one more look and mumbled under her breath, "Tiny little man."

Norman stepped inside, glancing around the room before finally settling on Thaddeus Stevens. "I hear you're the leading lawyer in the state." His tone was grudgingly respectful.

Thaddeus leaned on his cane, studying Norman with amusement. "You flatter me, Mr.—?"

"Norman Bruce," he said, puffing his chest slightly. "I've got a case here in Pennsylvania that needs handling. And it's a damned mess, thanks to your state's damn Abolition Act."

Thaddeus Stevens gestured for Bruce to sit as he sat in his leather chair. "Ah, the Gradual Abolition Act. An elegant piece of legislation, if I do say so myself. And what about it has brought you all the way to my door?"

Norman sat. "It's about a wench—Charity. She's one of my slaves. She thinks she's free because of this Act, claiming she's been in Pennsylvania long enough. She tallied it up. Can you believe that? A slave, doing math!" He bit out the words, his face red with anger. "Now she got with some free negro named Larkin Butler, and she's with child. I own that child in her belly, Mr. Stevens! And I want Charity back."

As Norman Bruce spewed his claims, Thaddeus Stevens

could not ignore the familiar name—Larkin Butler. He straightened slightly as Bruce ranted about a "free negro." He had hired Larkin on more than one occasion, a man who had earned his respect through diligence and skill. Thaddeus recalled the first time he'd met Larkin, a charming man who had rebuilt a fence on his property with such precision that it outlasted every other in the neighborhood. Larkin had worked in Gettysburg for years, and his reputation as a capable craftsman preceded him. They had shared polite conversations over the years, Thaddeus Stevens always appreciating Larkin's unassuming intelligence and forthright nature. And now, as Norman rambled on, Thaddeus Stevens remembered seeing Charity on a few occasions; she was a woman whose poise was memorable.

"I know Mr. Larkin Butler," Thaddeus began. "He is a fine man. A man who has earned the respect of many in this town—including mine. And Charity . . . I've seen her. Mr. Butler is a steadfast man who has done nothing but contribute to this community." Thaddeus Stevens rested his hands on the top of his cane. "But let me get this straight, you've come to me to argue that a negro who, by your own admission, has done nothing but follow the letter of the law should have her freedom stripped away. Is that about the size of it?"

Norman Bruce bristled. "Don't patronize me, Mr. Stevens. The law is on my side if it's applied correctly. The time should be consecutive. This piecemeal counting—it's hogwash! What's next? Letting slaves argue for freedom because they breathed in a free state? Charity has broken the law!"

"The law is clear. Six months, Mr. Bruce. It doesn't stipulate consecutively, as far as I recall."

Norman Bruce's fists pressed into the desk. "But it should. And you, Mr. Stevens, are the man to argue that it must. Everyone says you're brilliant. If you're as good as they claim, you'll find a way."

Thaddeus Stevens leaned back, unimpressed. "And why,

exactly, should I care about your grievances? Slavery is dying, Mr. Bruce, whether men like you wish it or not. Why should I invest my efforts in your . . . nostalgia?"

Norman Bruce let out a bitter laugh. "You care because I'm offering you opportunity. I hear you're a man with ambitions beyond this law office. A man who might one day find himself in the halls of power. Winning this case would prove that Thaddeus Stevens knows how to wield the law to serve his clients. It would make you look very important to men of influence."

Thaddeus remained impassive, but Norman Bruce was pressing where it mattered. Ambition. Power. The chance to cement his name in the legal annals of Pennsylvania. The opportunity was tempting.

Norman Bruce sensed he'd struck a chord. "And let's not forget the precedent this would set. It would clarify the law, an act of intellectual brilliance, surely. Isn't that what you lawyers live for?"

Thaddeus's expression showed no inner conflict; he was indifferent. Much like Clara, he had been born in Vermont, the first state to abolish slavery in the Union. Thaddeus had grown up insulated from the institution's brutal realities. Even Pennsylvania, his adopted home, had passed the Gradual Abolition Act of 1780, signaling the institution's eventual decline. Slavery had always seemed like an outdated practice to Thaddeus, a stain whose eventual erasure was inevitable. That said, it was not a major problem in his mind; it was a distant, moral inconvenience he assumed history would correct in due time.

In the comfortable bubble of his upbringing, Thaddeus had thought little of "the negro problem." He saw slavery as morally abstract, a mild evil that did not intrude upon his daily life. Yet, as he considered the case before him, he realized it wasn't just about legality. For him, the law—even with its flaws—stood above moral concerns. Slavery was immoral, but legality must prevail. The case had the power to bring him into the spotlight as the premier defender of law and order.

Then there was Larkin Butler. A good man in the community. And Charity. She had a bearing about her that was hard to forget. As Norman Bruce continued to rant about "his" property, Thaddeus felt something he rarely allowed himself to indulge in: doubt. Was it possible to argue for the law while ignoring humanity?

As Norman Bruce waited for a reply, Thaddeus Stevens was forced to confront the question of whether the law, as it stood, could truly serve justice—or if justice itself demanded something more.

After a long pause, Thaddeus Stevens finally spoke. "It'll cost you dearly, Mr. Bruce. My services, should I agree, will not come cheap."

Norman Bruce stood. "I don't care what it costs. I'd rather see every penny gone than let that wench think she won. She's mine, Mr. Stevens."

"So, you'd impoverish yourself just to strip a woman of her freedom? Fascinating. And yet, that tells me all I need to know about you." He paused, tapping his cane against the floor. "Very well." Thaddeus rose slowly. "I'll draft my terms, and Mrs. Clarke will see you out. But let me leave you with this, Mr. Bruce, be careful what you wish for. Sometimes, even victory has a way of feeling hollow."

Norman Bruce nodded stiffly. "I'll be back tomorrow to sign the agreement."

As the door slammed shut, Thaddeus sank back into his chair. The case offered a chance to prove his skill. Still, a nagging lassitude settled in his chest. For all his ambition, the thought of aiding a man like Norman Bruce left a bad stench. He leaned back, his cane resting against the arm of his chair. Larkin and Charity were good people, but goodness alone didn't win court cases. The law did. And the law, as it was written, might be on Norman Bruce's side. Whatever personal feelings he had for Larkin and Charity had to be set aside. Thaddeus Stevens worshipped the law, its order, its logic, its capacity to provide structure in a chaotic world. To allow emotion to sway his actions would be to betray everything he believed in.

For Larkin Butler, the news that Thaddeus Stevens, a man he had worked for and respected, would be representing Norman Bruce stunned him. He stood in the middle of their small kitchen while Charity sat nearby, her hand resting on her belly, her face stressed with concern.

Larkin's voice quivered with anger. "I've lived here in Gettysburg for years. I've worked for that man—*that man*—on his own property. Repaired his fences. Fixed his tools. And now, he's going to stand in a courtroom and argue to send my future wife into slavery?" A harsh laugh escaped him. "God Almighty, the man wears that rug on his head like a possum crawled up there and died of shame—and he dares preach about what's lawful?"

"Larkin," Charity said, "we knew this fight wouldn't be fair. It's not about who we are. It's about what they see when they look at us."

"What they see?" he questioned. "No matter what I've done, no matter how many times I've proven myself, men like Thaddeus Stevens will *always* side with men like Norman Bruce. How many White men have stood by us when it mattered? Even Thaddeus Stevens. I thought . . . I thought maybe he was different. But no. The first chance he gets, he turns around and stabs me in the back."

Charity didn't let her fear show. She had been a slave, a soul bound by chains both visible and invisible. Nothing about Thaddeus Stevens's betrayal surprised her. There was no shock, no disappointment, only the understanding of a truth she had carried her whole life: The promises of fairness and justice were not meant for people like her. Larkin's anger, his disbelief, even his sense of betrayal, these were luxuries Charity had never been afforded. Although he was once enslaved, he had lived a life where hard work earned respect, where decency could buy trust. Larkin's world had cracks, but hers had been nothing but a chasm, a world where freedom was so fragile it could shatter at the whim of a man like Norman Bruce. This wasn't new or a faded memory to her; it was the world she'd always known, the fight she'd been born into.

Larkin's shoulders slumped. "To know a man you respected could look you in the eye one day and argue to destroy your family the next. Makes you wonder, doesn't it? If there's a White man alive who won't sell his soul for a few coins?"

Charity stood, wrapped her arms around him, holding him tightly. "Then we fight, Larkin. We fight like we always fought. And if they won't do right by us, then we show them we can do right by ourselves."

Larkin nodded, his anger simmering, but his determination hardening. "We'll fight. And no matter what happens, they gonna remember us." As the words left his mouth, they sounded familiar, like an echo. And then it hit him—it was Josephine. She had said those very words when they watched the Baynards die over a decade ago. The memory gripped him. He turned to Charity. "Never told nobody this," he began. "Some things, you keep to yourself. But you need to know why I fight, why I know how to fight."

Charity knew there was more. There was more to all of us. "Remember I told you about Goochland? Josephine and Mama Bess?" Charity nodded. "I was born and raised in Goochland, didn't know my mama or my daddy—just me, my hands, and the work. I was on the Baynard plantation." He paused. "Josephine poisoned them all. The master, the mistress, two nasty children, all of them, gone. Poison in their supper. We saw them, all of us, laid out in that house, stiff as a board. Never forget it. Josephine . . . she said it then, just like I said it now: 'They gonna remember us.' "

Larkin took a breath, his Southern inflections thickening. "Before freedom came, before the papers said 'free,' I saw my freedom. When I saw the Baynards die, that's when I knew. Didn't need no paper to tell me I was free. That's when I saw it—clear as day—freedom was mine to take. And Josephine said, 'They gonna remember us.' They did. The Baynards all dead, but we lived on. All of us made it up North with Josephine."

"Josephine," she said softly, as if tasting the name. "Wish I could've met her. She must've been something."

"She was. She didn't bow, didn't break. She saw what needed doing, and she did it. So, I know what it means to win." He grabbed her hands. "To take back what they tried to steal. She got sickly and passed too young, but she taught me they can beat you, starve you, strip you bare, but they can't touch what's inside you unless you let 'em." He lightly tapped Charity's chest, just over her heart. "Don't let them take what they can't touch."

Life in Gettysburg settled into a new rhythm for Larkin and Charity. Their days were filled with the euphoria of building a life together, one brick, one meal, one moment at a time. After their marriage in a small church just outside of town—a ceremony attended by a few trusted friends who knew the risks Charity had taken to claim her freedom—they moved into a modest but sturdy house that Larkin had built with his own hands and the help of others. Each plank of wood and nail an example of his dedication, not just to his craft, but to their future. The house stood proudly near his blacksmith shop, a comforting backdrop to their lives.

Their life together blossomed with the births of their

daughters, first Harriet, and later Sophia. Harriet's birth was a moment of revelation for Charity—a glorious, overwhelming experience. Holding her newborn daughter for the first time, Charity felt only hope, her tears mingling with Harriet's first cries. She marveled at the tiny fingers that wrapped around her own, promising herself that her child would never know the chains that had once bound her. Larkin's proud smile and the gentleness with which he cradled Harriet were forever in her memory. Sophia's arrival two years later was no less profound. By then, Charity had grown into her role as a mother, her confidence blossoming alongside watching Harriet take her first steps and speak her first words. In their home, with Larkin's hand on hers, Charity felt their family grow stronger, their love deepening with each new life they brought into the world.

These experiences bound them in ways words could never capture. The sight of Larkin holding his daughters reminded Charity of all they had fought for and all they would continue to protect. Their love was a partnership, one built on respect and an understanding of the scars they both carried. Charity, who had spent so much of her life being silenced, found her voice in Larkin. Larkin, who had long been accustomed to working in isolation, found purpose in the home they created together.

Harriet and Sophia had spent many days in the blacksmith's shop with their daddy, despite Charity's constant protests. Their mother worried, always fretting that they would burn themselves on the hot iron or cut their fingers on the edges of his tools. But the girls loved to watch Larkin work, loved the way his strong hands moved over the metal, shaping it, taming it, making it into something new. He could take a useless lump of iron and turn it into a horseshoe.

Larkin never shooed them away, never told them they didn't belong. Instead, he let them stand close, their small faces lit by the forge, their wide eyes reflecting the dancing embers. Sometimes, when he wasn't too busy, he would hand them a hammer to tap gently against a softened piece of iron, guiding their hands as they shaped the metal. More often than not, they spent their time cleaning up after him, wiping down his workbench, stacking the tongs, sweeping the dust and ash into small piles at the edges of the shop.

Charity would shake her head whenever she found them there, hands on her hips, exasperation pulling at her features. "They ain't boys, Larkin," she'd mutter under her breath, but he would just smile, shrugging in that smooth way of his.

"Don't matter none," he'd say. "Fire don't care if you're a boy or a girl. It just cares if you are strong enough to stand in it." And so they learned. The rhythm of their father's hammer, the way the fire pulsed. They learned the smell of metal burning, the sound of iron screaming as it was bent and shaped under heat.

In Gettysburg, Charity made the community her own. She volunteered at the local church, taught other freed women to read, often reflecting on Clara's lessons in the carriage rides. These acts of service brought new meaning and connected her to a growing network of people who believed in the promise of freedom. At night, when the girls were asleep, Larkin and Charity would sit on the porch as they talked about more dreams for the future. "Speak the dream out loud, so the Good Lord can hear you," Larkin would say.

But throughout the years, Charity and Larkin found themselves in a painful cycle of court appearances with abolitionist lawyers by their side. The question of leaving Gettysburg arose more than once, but their counsel cautioned against it, arguing that such a move could further complicate matters. Charity's legal status remained precarious at best under the prevailing laws. Her freedom was uncertain and subject to challenge anywhere she might go. A change in jurisdiction could render her a fugitive in the eyes of the courts, placing her at even greater risk of returning to bondage. After yet another failed hearing, with no ruling in her favor, the possibility emerged that the case could ascend to Pennsylvania's Supreme Court. Charity began to wonder if the law offered any hope at all. Would it be safer to trust the courts, or to flee—leaving behind the legal wrangling that was designed to trap her, not free her?

"Larkin," she said as they sat on the porch watching the girls chase fireflies in the yard, "what if we moved farther up North? New York? You lived there before. And we wouldn't have to live under . . . under *his* shadow anymore."

Larkin turned to her, his expression serious but calm. "I've thought about it," he admitted. "But, Charity, we're free. We've built this life here, and it's ours. I don't want to run from it."

"It wouldn't be running," she said. "It would be protecting our girls. What happens if Norman Bruce doesn't stop, Larkin?"

Larkin reached for her hand. "Norman Bruce doesn't get to decide what we do, Charity. I ain't running. Not when we've done nothing wrong. This here's our home. We built it with our own hands, piece by piece. We earned it, fair and square, and I'll be damned if I let him take that from us. The law's supposed to be on our side, and I ain't about to live like a fugitive in a place that's rightfully ours."

Charity nodded, though her heart remained heavy. She admired Larkin's refusal to let fear dictate their lives, but the dread clung to her. A verse stirred in her mind, *For freedom Christ has set us free; stand firm, therefore, and do not submit again to a yoke of slavery.*[19] It was an anthem that stuck with her.

19. *Galatians* 5:1, New Revised Standard Version.

For well over a decade, they were working closely with abolitionist lawyer Parker Harris. Charity, desperate to defend her freedom and the life she had built, begged to testify in court. Her ability to do so, however, was fiercely contested. Thaddeus Stevens argued that the testimony of a Black woman against a White man held no legal weight. After heated deliberations, the court allowed Charity to submit a written statement rather than testify in person, a concession Thaddeus agreed to, confident the judge would dismiss it as inadmissible.

With the help of their lawyer, Charity poured her heart into the statement. She recounted her nearly fifteen years of freedom, the life she had built with Larkin, and the daughters she had brought into the world. "I am free," she wrote. "Free in my mind, in my body, and in my spirit. My daughters have never known the chains I once wore. My husband and I have worked tirelessly to build a life of love and dignity. To take that from us now is to shackle not just me, but everything I have ever hoped for my children. This is not justice. It is cruelty."

The letter continued. "I invoke Pennsylvania's Gradual Abolition Act of 1780, a law meant to ensure that no person would live in bondage on this soil without conditions for freedom. By the terms of this law, I have properly added my time, years of residence and work far beyond the six months the law requires for my freedom. It has been over a decade. Over a decade of liberty, proving that I belong to no one but myself. I have exceeded every measure of time required by the law. Now you tell me that these years mean nothing? That the very law that gave me the courage to escape is powerless in this courtroom?"

Charity struck like a hammer. "This court must answer a question not just of law, but of humanity: Do you value a life built on love, work, and freedom? Or do you return me and my children to chains, as if these years never existed?"

Her words were powerful, but as Thaddeus predicted, the judge dismissed the statement entirely. "The law is clear," the judge declared. "Sentimentality has no place in this courtroom."

Larkin stormed out of the courthouse with Charity close behind him. "Larkin, please," she begged. "Stay calm. We need to think of the girls."

Behind them, Parker Harris followed, quickening his pace to catch up. "Larkin, let it go for now. You can't argue with the ruling. Not like this."

Larkin stopped abruptly on the courthouse steps. He turned to Parker, "*Let it go?* You think I can just walk away after what they've done?"

Then he saw him—Thaddeus Stevens, standing near the bottom of the steps, leaning on his cane as he spoke quietly with Norman Bruce. He had seen him countless times over the years in and out of courtrooms, but now the sight of him made Larkin's blood boil. He squared his shoulders, keeping his anger in check. Charity placed a hand on his arm.

"Mr. Stevens!" Larkin called out. Thaddeus Stevens looked up, his expression detached, though his grip on the head of his cane tightened. Norman Bruce began to speak, his smug grin barely hidden.

"Mr. Stevens, don't waste your time on him," Norman sneered. "The man—"

Thaddeus interjected, "Mr. Bruce, I suggest you refrain from commenting further. Anything you say here could be detrimental to your case." Norman Bruce mumbled under his breath but hushed.

Larkin descended the steps. He stopped a few feet away, his hands at his sides, his voice pained. "Mr. Stevens, how could you do this to my family? I've known you for years here in Gettysburg. You hired me for jobs at your own home. You watched me work for this town, for my wife, for my daughters. And yet, you stood in that courtroom today and argued to ruin us."

Thaddeus Stevens met Larkin's gaze, his clubfoot bore more of his weight than usual. "Mr. Butler," Stevens began, his tone measured, "this is not personal. I upheld the law as it stands. My responsibility is to argue the case before me, not to rewrite the statutes of this country."

Larkin took a step closer. "Not personal when you're trying to condemn my wife and children to slavery? We live free. We work, pay our dues, raise our daughters, all while believing in this town, in this state. *Free*. You argued against that—that's not what a man of justice would do."

Charity spoke softly. "You saw us, Mr. Stevens. You knew what this meant for us. How could you look at my girls and argue they were anything but free?"

Thaddeus Stevens's fingers squeezed the top of his cane. "Again, the law," he said, his voice quieter now, "does not bend to sentiment. If it did, it would no longer be the law."

Larkin shook his head slowly. "Then the law is broken. And so are the men who stand behind it."

Parker Harris stepped forward, gently placing a hand on Larkin's forearm. "Come on, Larkin. There's nothing more to be done here. Not today."

Larkin glared at Thaddeus Stevens, his eyes laden with profound disappointment.

As they walked away, Norman Bruce smirked at the departing family, but Thaddeus Stevens didn't share his satisfaction.

The case inched up the legal ladder, all the way to Pennsylvania's Supreme Court, Thaddeus Stevens's first case to reach the state's high court.[20] Driven by ambition and Norman Bruce's demands, he mounted a ferocious legal battle. His arguments were precise, exploiting every possible loophole. The fight culminated in a devastating blow when Thaddeus presented a pivotal argument, supported by cold legal logic: "*As to continued residence for six months, it is clear that a slave who happens to come with his master on different visits, which may on adding up the time of their duration exceed six months, cannot be contemplated by law.*"[21]

Thaddeus argued that Charity's belief in her freedom, based on the years she had lived as a free woman in Pennsylvania, was irrelevant under the law. He argued that her initial claim to freedom had been made unlawfully. By declaring herself free and leaving Norman Bruce's custody, she had violated the very legal frameworks she now sought to invoke. "This court cannot condone lawlessness," Mr. Stevens insisted before the panel of justices. "Charity's years of residence in Pennsylvania, while seemingly in accordance with the Gradual Abolition Act, are overshadowed by her unlawful act of self-liberation. No one, regardless of sentiment, may claim the benefits of a law they themselves have broken."

20. W. U. Hensel (1906, September). Thaddeus Stevens. BEGINS PRACTICE IN ADAMS COUNTY. INCURSIONS INTO POLITICS. IN THE CONVENTION OF 1837. REMOVED TO LANCASTER. SOMETIMES HIS OWN LAWYER. HIS DEFENSE OF FUGITIVE SLAVES. THE "CHRISTIANA" RIOT. A GREAT "COUNTRY LAWYER." HIS QUALITIES AS A LAWYER. WHEN HE LEFT THE BAR. *The American Lawyer (1893-1908), 14*(9), 394, https://www.proquest.com/magazines/thaddeus-stevens/docview/125701896/se-2.

21. *Butler v. Delaplaine*, 7 Serg. & Rawle 378 (Pa. 1821), Free State Slavery & Bound Labor, https://freestateslaveryproject.com/legal-materials/butler-v-delaplaine-7-serg-rawle-378-pa-1821/.

The Supreme Court's ruling reflected Stevens's unyielding logic. The judges, swayed by the technicalities, deemed that Charity's freedom did not grant her permanent liberation. They upheld Norman Bruce's claim, citing the strict interpretation of the law. The court's statement was final and chilling: "*The judgment is therefore affirmed.*"[22]

The words exploded in the small courtroom, sealing their fate: Charity, Harriet, and Sophia were declared the legal property of Norman Bruce. All four of them—Larkin, Charity, and their two daughters—had been ordered to appear in person for the ruling, a spectacle meant to finalize their humiliation. The ruling would go into effect immediately. Larkin sat like a statue, his mind spinning as the judgment settled in. Charity wept silently beside him, clutching a handkerchief to her mouth to muffle her tears. Their daughters, Harriet and Sophia, sat between their parents, grasping the nightmare. The already small room closed in, every creak of the benches like a nail in their coffin.

Thaddeus Stevens gathered his papers with an air of triumph, but even he hesitated as Charity's eyes blazed into him.

Larkin stood suddenly, his chair scraping loudly against the floor. He drilled into his attorney, his voice rightfully bitter. "You told me we could win!"

Parker Harris's voice cracked as he replied, "I thought we could, Larkin. I believed it."

Larkin turned to Charity and their daughters, his face marked with despair. "We'll find another way," he said, though he wasn't sure what that way could be. Charity nodded, her face soaked with tears.

Larkin tried to contain the storm inside him. "No!" Lar-

22. *Butler v. Delaplaine*, 7 Serg. & Rawle 378 (Pa. 1821), Free State Slavery & Bound Labor, https://freestateslaveryproject.com/legal-materials/butler-v-delaplaine-7-serg-rawle-378-pa-1821/.

kin's voice roared through the courtroom. "This ain't justice! This is theft! Stealing my wife! My children! My life!"

As a guard rushed to Larkin, the judge slammed his gavel.

Larkin pointed a finger at Norman Bruce. "You're no man. You're a coward. Hiding behind lies and laws written by men who don't even see us as human."

Norman Bruce didn't respond, his eyes sinister and victorious.

Larkin turned his wrath toward Thaddeus Stevens, who stood visibly tense. "And you," Larkin hissed, "you made this happen. You took a pen, some words on paper, and turned them into shackles. How can you stand there on your cane, knowing what you've done? How can you call yourself a man of law when that law is poison?"

Thaddeus Stevens averted his face.

Charity stepped forward with her daughters pulling at her. "Look at me, Mr. Stevens." Before she could say more, guards moved in, grabbing hold of both Larkin and Charity. Their hands on her arms made Charity gasp as Larkin struggled against their grip, his voice lifting in rage.

Thaddeus Stevens raised a hand, his voice commanding. "Enough!" he barked. The room froze, the guards immediately released Larkin and Charity. Thaddeus's authority was absolute, his reputation as a powerful man evident in the way his single gesture ceased the chaos. The courtroom fell still, all eyes on Charity.

"Look at what you done," Charity continued, tears carving her cheeks. "I was free. My children were free. And now . . ." Her voice broke. "Now we'll be torn apart, all 'cause you thought the law mattered more than our lives."

Thaddeus shifted on his cane. He said nothing, his silence louder than any defense he might have offered. What could he say? That logic had prevailed? The guards moved in, grabbing Charity by the arms, then snatching up her children. Her voice rose. "Your law's wicked, Mr. Stevens! You hear me? It's wicked. And you better repent! Repent, or you will burn in the hell you made!"

Larkin surged forward for his family, his panic overflowing. A guard slammed a hand against his chest, shoving him back with brutal force. He stumbled but didn't fall, his hands outstretched. "Charity!" he cried. "I'll come for you. I swear it."

Charity turned her head. "Larkin!" Harriet and Sophia screamed as they were pulled toward their mother. Harriet, her hands reaching for Larkin, sobbed uncontrollably. "Papa! No! Don't let them take me! Please, Papa, please!" Sophia, only two years younger than her sister, clung to Charity's leg, her fingers digging into her dress.

Larkin fought with everything he had, but the guards overpowered him, their hands pulling, tearing, dragging Charity and her girls away inch by inch. "You can't take them!" Larkin roared. "My *babies*! They're free!"

Norman Bruce stood at the edge of the chaos. His demented joy in the suffering of this family on his face.

The guards forced the girls into Charity's arms. She held them tightly, her own sobs wracking her body as she was dragged toward the door. "Larkin, my love," she screeched as she looked at him one last time.

"Don't let them take what they can't touch!" Larkin screamed. "Don't let them take what they can't touch!" he roared again. Larkin collapsed as the door slammed shut, his daughters' cries ringing in his ears. His body convulsed with sobs, his fists pounding the wood as though he could crack the earth itself and pull them back. *I'll make 'em pay*, he said to himself. *I'll get my justice. Tried doing it the right way, played by their rules, and look where it got me, empty-handed and full of regret. Never again.*

The courtroom fell into an eerie quiet, shook up only by

Larkin's ragged breathing. Norman Bruce stepped to Thaddeus. "You said to me, 'Sometimes, even victory has a way of feeling hollow.' Don't feel hollow to me. I feel mighty full. Mighty full. Thank you, Mr. Stevens." Thaddeus could only watch as Norman Bruce strode out of the courtroom. Thaddeus's cane dug into his palm. It was *he* who felt hollow, a victory in name alone. The image of Larkin, Charity's raw agony, and the terrified cries of Harriet and Sophia seared themselves into him. For the first time in his career, Thaddeus Stevens doubted everything—the law, the system, and his place within it. The gavel had fallen, but what had it wrought? Not justice. Only devastation.

Thaddeus Stevens returned to his law office that afternoon, his steps slow, his cane dragging against the floor. He did not head straight for his back office but instead collapsed into the first chair in the lobby. Mrs. Clarke observed him with an arched brow.

"How was the ruling?" she asked idly.

Thaddeus did not immediately respond. His finger trembled as he unbuttoned his coat. His lips parted, but no words came. The law had been upheld, but he felt no triumph. He lowered himself into the chair, his body heavier than it had ever felt.

Mrs. Clarke clicked her tongue, folding her hands over the desk. "Well?" she prompted, her voice edged with impatience. "Surely it went as expected."

Thaddeus exhaled, rubbing his temple. "As expected," he murmured.

Mrs. Clarke nodded as if that settled the matter. "Justice served, then." She reached for a stack of correspondence, flipping through the envelopes.

"Was it?" His voice was distant.

Mrs. Clarke set the papers down, studying him over the

rim of her spectacles. "You upheld the law, Mr. Stevens," she said carefully. "And they are just negroes."

Thaddeus's eyes snapped up to her. "Mrs. Clarke," he said. "Would you say the same if it were you on the receiving end of that law?"

She blinked, caught off guard. "That's hardly— "

"But it is," Thaddeus interrupted. "It is precisely the matter at hand." He leaned forward. "I saw no justice today."

Mrs. Clarke hesitated before scoffing lightly. "And what would you have done differently, Mr. Stevens? The law is the law."

Thaddeus stared at her. "Then what is the point of me?" he asked.

For the first time since she had met him, Mrs. Clarke had no reply. Thaddeus rose slowly. Without another word, he turned and walked to his office, closing the door behind him. Inside, he leaned against the door, his head falling back as he let out a long breath. He moved toward his desk but did not sit. Instead, his gaze swept the room until it settled on the chair across from his desk. He remembered Norman Bruce sitting there—smug and entitled. Thaddeus turned away, squeezed his eyes shut, but Mr. Bruce's face lingered. He had watched the verdict with gross satisfaction. He had left the courtroom like a conqueror. Thaddeus collapsed into his chair, rubbing his temples again. He could still hear the echo of Charity Butler's fierce words. "*Your law's wicked, Mr. Stevens! You hear me? It's wicked!*"

The office walls felt too close. He gathered his coat and left, retreating to the solitude of his home.

Days later, a telegram arrived, but he did not open it. It sat on his desk untouched for hours, then days. He waited until he was home and away from the world, before finally picking it up. The house was dark, except for the fireplace. His hands felt cold as he broke the seal and unfolded the telegram.

Mr. Stevens,
My gratitude for your services in ensuring justice prevailed. The outcome has served my interests well. May history remember the law and those who uphold it.
Mr. Norman Bruce

His grip tightened until the paper crinkled under his fingers. He strode toward the fireplace and threw the telegram into the flames. The edges curled inward and crumbled into ash. The fire did not cleanse, nor did it absolve. The words, the trial, and the faces would never burn away.

Larkin sat in the dark. Not as a man sits, but as a soul flattened by grief. The house was too big now. The walls listened, the floors sighed, and the air carried memories that stung. Weeks passed, but time had no shape. There was only before and after. Before—his daughters, their laughter, their feet pattering against the wood. Charity's voice, sweet in the mornings, reading passages to herself from that old book, the one she never let go of. After—silence that crawled along the baseboards and into his bones. His body had become something separate from him, a thing that lay when it should rise, that shook when it should hold steady. He had not eaten. Had not washed. Had not spoken to another soul. He lay curled on the floor, chanting their names in prayer. "*Charity. Harriet. Sophia.*" Over and over. But there was no answer.

The rage came in waves. One moment, he was drowning in sorrow. The next, he was standing outside, watching himself slip into Thaddeus Stevens's home with a blade. Larkin saw it so clearly: the thin slice of steel against the flesh, the hot spill of blood onto white linens, the gurgle of a man whose power would mean nothing if the night took him.

"*What would Old Mama Bess do?*" She would have whispered in his ear. Told him how to make the cut. How to keep it quiet. Or maybe she would have done it herself. He thought of Josephine, how she had slipped poison into the Baynards' cups, how she had watched them drink. He longed for her wisdom. He had tried to do things right. Trusted the system. Look where it got him.

Then he thought of that old book. It sat untouched on the bedside table since his wife was returned into bondage. The pages were worn and the edges curled. *Sense and Sensibility*. Charity had read it a thousand times and encouraged him to do the same. He reached for it, pressing his palm against the cover. He wanted to feel her, just for a moment, to trick his body into believing she was near. He opened the book. There was a name on the inside cover, faint but legible. "Clara Petterson." And beneath it, an address in Vermont.

Larkin stared at the ink, his pulse heavy in his ears. He had not spoken Clara's name in years, though she was mentioned in the courtroom more times than he could count. She had been there at the beginning, when he first met Charity. His fingers traced the letters, memorizing them. A shift. Small, but there. For the first time in weeks, he sat up. And for the first time in weeks, Larkin knew what he had to do.

The road back to hell was unmerciful. Charity had lost count of the miles, hours, and places they passed. It didn't matter. There was only the destination, looming like a specter in the distance. Her stomach clenched as her eyes caught the familiar white chimney with the black top rising against the horizon. The sight had once meant something else—it had once been her quiet marker that she was leaving Maryland for something better, even if only for a short while. But now it meant the opposite. Now, she was going back. When the carriage turned the final bend, the house came into view, rising from the land like a thing that should have crumbled long ago. It was smaller than she remembered. Age had bent it; the weather had beaten it. The once-proud columns now leaned inward, the wood split and splintered, a house breaking beneath its weight. The porch railings were crooked, some sections missing entirely, and the paint had long since peeled away, exposing the raw gray bones beneath. The windows were thick with grime, the glass cracked in places, and the roof sagged in the center as if it, too, was tired of standing.

Charity shook her head as she saw the ruin, the place she had fled but never truly escaped. The front door was the same one she had walked through a thousand times before, the same one she had been dragged through when she was too weak to walk. The steps still bore the grooves of boot heels, the marks of men who had come and gone, of women who had been forced to stay. Beyond the house, the land stretched wide, modest rows of fields that had once been full of cotton and corn but now stood half-tended, patches of weeds in the soil. Once upon a time, the Norman Bruce plantation had been known for its yield, for bringing in enough profit to make its master believe himself a great man. Norman Bruce never accumulated a large number of souls, preferring to rent them when he needed labor and rent out those he owned when he didn't. A man who believed in ownership, but not responsibility. That had always been his way, taking, using, and discarding.

The blacksmith's shed stood off to the side, hunched in the shadow of the main house, the roof patched in places where the rain had eaten through. She remembered it well. She had hated that place and feared it. The only five cabins behind the shed were worse now, but they had always been wretched. Over 15 years ago, they had been little more than shanties, their walls warped and splintered, the wood gnawed at by rats and termites. She had slept in one of those cabins for years, her body tight against the chill, her skin crawling with lice and fleas that bit her in the night. She would wake to the scuttle of roaches across her face, their shells brushing against her lips, and the scratch of rodents in the corners, their teeth eating at the rotting wood.

It was in that cabin that she had caught a sickness, one that had left her weak, her body wracked with fever. She had coughed until her throat was raw, her lungs burning as though they were filled with fire. There had been no medicine, no comfort, only the cold floor beneath her and the sound of the wind howling through the gaps in the walls. She had thought she might die there. She wondered how many souls had died in these cabins over the years. Charity clenched her fists, her nails pressing into her palms as she stared. She had left this place, but it had never left her. It had followed her in nightmares.

The carriage doors smacked open. Hands grabbed Charity before she could move, yanking her from the seat. Her legs buckled. The ground rose to meet her as she crumpled into the dirt. "Mama!" Harriet screamed. Sophia's small hands clutched at her dress. The girls wailed, but Charity couldn't move; a slap cracked against her cheek, jerking her head to the side. Norman Bruce stood over her.

"Get up," he spat. Charity felt nothing. Her body had absorbed too much pain to register more. "Take 'em to the cabin," he ordered to the other souls, none of whom recognized Charity; she had been gone too long. "All three of 'em can stay in the one with all the critters. Need her to teach them girls how to work. Free negroes always lazy."

The cries of her daughters were distant. Hands dragged Charity forward as her mind drifted and then fractured. She once wanted to live, but now she was ready to die without Larkin.

Time blurred into an arduous march. Charity rarely spoke. Barely moved. She sat in the cabin, watching but not seeing.

Breathing but not living. Harriet and Sophia brought her food and pressed tin cups of water to her lips, but she could hardly swallow. *Nothing matters, nothing left*, Charity thought.

Harriet and Sophia refused to break. At fifteen and thirteen, they had become parents, stepping into roles too heavy for children and carrying burdens meant for those far older than them. Their mother was weak, barely able to rise in the mornings, unable to work the modest fields, incapable of cooking even the simplest meal. Some nights, she lay so still that Harriet placed a hand over her chest to make sure she was still breathing. And oddly enough, Norman Bruce never laid a hand on her. He enjoyed watching her decline. His work had already been done.

Sophia stood outside the cabin, arms crossed, the last slivers of daylight spreading across the dirt yard. "Mama ain't eat again," she said. "Won't even sit up when I put the plate down."

Harriet leaned against the wood of the cabin. "Mama *hasn't* eaten again," she corrected softly.

"Sorry," Sophia said with her eyes down. Harriet and Sophia were literate, educated. Larkin and Charity had them reading as soon as they could walk and later enrolled them in a school run by abolitionists. As the older sister, Harriet knew her father would not want them to forget their lessons.

"It's okay, sister. We can't let them take anything away from us. We are still free, I don't care what that judge said."

Sophia kicked a stone, sending it rolling toward the trees. "I'm scared for Mama."

Harriet watched the sky, the way the color bled from blue to violet. "Mama used to be the strongest person we knew," she said.

"Is she dying?" Sophia asked.

Harriet turned to look at her, at the worry written over

her face. “I think she’s already gone in her mind,” Harriet admitted.

Sophia sniffed, wiping at her nose with the back of her hand. “I hate him,” she said. “Hate that he took us. Hate that he watches us, like he waiting for us to slip. Hate that he took Papa from us.”

Harriet quickly nodded. “I hate him too.”

Sophia exhaled through her nose. “We gotta take care of Mama.”

Harriet nodded. “Yeah, Sophia. We do.” They were not born to this, not raised under the lash, not bred for obedience. They had their father’s fire in them, and it burned.

Charity sat in the dirt outside the cabin, staring at nothing. The day was slipping into dusk, but she hadn’t moved in hours—maybe longer. She didn’t know how long she had been on the Bruce plantation. Weeks. Months. In the distance, metal against metal rang out from the blacksmith’s shed. That’s where the girls were. In fear of being rented out like the other souls, Harriet and Sophia had offered to work in the blacksmith’s shed, hoping to stick together. Norman Bruce said no at first, but then he remembered their father. He had been one of the most respected blacksmiths in Gettysburg.

Two girls who knew how to shape metal? Not that he cared that they were girls. To him, they were only property. So, he put them to work, always with an older soul nearby to lift the heavy loads. The forge dominated the blacksmith’s shed, its brick-and-stone hearth darkened with years of soot. The chimney stretched high, built to funnel thick, choking smoke, though stray wisps clung to the rafters. A heavy iron bellows hung near the hearth, suspended from thick wooden beams. It was Harriet and Sophia that fed the fire, their hands that pulled the iron from the flames and shaped the tools. The older men were impressed. The girls were good at what they did. They didn't need to be told twice. They were obedient, bending to the work without complaint. And because of them, the work got done three times quicker. Although the work was harsh, being in the blacksmith's shed made them feel closer to their father.

The sound of metal would also calm Charity's mind. If she let herself believe, Larkin was there. As Charity hummed to the clanks, she felt someone standing over her. Then, a nudge, a boot-tapping against the side of her foot, not rough but enough to pull her back to herself. She blinked, tilting her head up.

The sun cast his face in shadow, but she knew that skin, much older now, but the deep red tone, the slant of his cheekbones, the black hair slicked back beneath his fallen-down hat. When the voice came, she remembered it well.

"Got something for you." She blinked again. Pedro. The driver. The one who had taken her and Miss Clara back and forth to Gettysburg all those years ago.

He crouched low, his voice quieter. "A letter."

She didn't reach for it at first. He didn't force it. Just held it out, thin and folded, waiting for her to take it.

"Read it in private," he firmly said. "Tell no one. If they catch us, we both gonna be skinned alive." She wrapped her fingers around the paper. As quickly as he had come, he was gone.

That night, by candlelight, she unfolded the paper. Her hands shook as her eyes traced the words.

My Dearest Charity,

It has been far too many years since last we spoke. My heart is burdened beyond measure to learn that you have been cast once more into the clutches of that reprobate, a man devoid of all decency and virtue. I tremble to think of the suffering you have endured. Do not despair, for you have not been forgotten. Mr. Larkin Butler sought me out, his words steeped in anguish, pleading for aid. He has not relinquished hope. Nor shall I. I can only pray this letter finds its way to your hands, for within it lies the means of your deliverance. There is a way, if you have the courage and strength yet to take it. I have written to trusted friends, those who labor in secret for the cause of liberty. If you can make your way to a safe house at the Maryland border, 145 River Road, you will find righteous souls who will shelter you and see you and your daughters safely northward. The driver is known to us; you can place your trust in him, but you must undertake the journey without him. You know the way—it is long, but the same path we often traveled to Gettysburg. You will know you have arrived when you see a chimney of white bricks crowned with a black top. If you can reach them, I swear before Heaven and Earth that we shall see you to Vermont. Tell them Miss Clara sent you. You and your dear girls will have a home here, where no man shall lay claim to your freedom again. I implore you, hold fast, my dear. Your story is yet unfinished, and Providence does not forsake those who seek the light.

With steadfast hope and the deepest affection,
Clara Petterson

Charity pressed the letter to her chest. If only it had come sooner. How could she run, weak as she was? She wanted to feel hope, she wanted to believe, but all she felt was despair. A tear slipped down her cheek, falling onto the paper.

Harriet's voice cut through the silence. "Mama?" She reached forward and pulled the letter from Charity's grasp. Sophia crawled onto Charity's lap, her small hands pressing into her mother's arms for reassurance that she was still there. Harriet smoothed out the creased paper.

Harriet's eyes moved quickly, absorbing the meaning, parsing the message before she spoke it aloud. Harriet looked at Sophia, then back at their mother. "Mama, who is Miss Clara Petterson again? I remember hearing the name." Charity just stared. Harriet's fingers tightened around the letter. Sophia's lower lip trembled as she looked from her sister to their mother. They both knew what this letter meant, but they also knew their mother's condition.

"Mama," Harriet pleaded. "Mama, we can get back home to Daddy." Charity did not blink.

Harriet pressed the letter into her hands. "Please, Mama. Please, we can leave this place. We can see Daddy again." Her voice cracked, but she pushed forward. "I know you're tired, I know you're hurt, but we need you." Nothing. Harriet's frustration flared. "Mama, do you hear me?" She grabbed Charity's shoulders and shook her gently, then harder. "Mama, please! Say something!" Still, Charity only stared. Harriet let out a shaky breath. She turned to Sophia. "Stay with Mama."

"Where are you going?" Sophia cried.

"To the well for some water to wash up." She walked fast. Her fear and desperation all crashing together. *How could Mama just sit there? How could she not want to go?* The thought made her sick as her vision blurred with unshed tears. She ran, letting the moonlight guide her to the well. Harriet nearly ran straight into him; she yelped—Norman Bruce.

The kerosene lamp in his hand, a glow over his face, deepening the shadows in his sunken cheeks. His grin stretched too wide. He was small with a wiry frame, almost childlike in its frailty. His bony arms hanging too loose at his sides, the lamp making his knobby fingers twitch like spider legs. His clothes hung off him, too big for his body, and his pants were cinched tight at the waist to keep them from slipping down his twiglike hips. Harriet was taller than him and she could see it now, how weak he truly was beneath all his posturing. An inadequate man built on cruelty instead of brawn. His power had always been stolen. Without it, he was nothing but a heap of bones waiting to be broken. He was standing near the well, where the land sloped down into the trees. "Now, what's a thing like you doing out here all by herself?" His voice was unusually friendly. He stepped closer. "Was you trying to *run*, girl?"

Harriet gulped. "No, sir," she said quickly. "I just—"

"You just what?" He took another step. "Seems awfully late for a stroll."

"Mama isn't feeling well. I was just getting some air," she lied. Harriet didn't want to admit she was going to the well, which would force her to walk closer.

Norman Bruce's eyes trailed over her face, then dropped, dragging down the length of her body. She felt his unclean look. Harriet was big for fifteen, not as malnourished as the other souls. They'd been on his plantation for only a few months, but she still looked healthy, full in the hips, and her body was taking on a shape. She filled out in ways that made his pulse throb in his temples. His sick desires bloated in his belly like spoiled milk.

"You getting grown every day, ain't you? Ain't a little girl no more. You 'bout a woman now."

"I . . . I gotta get back to Mama," she said, stepping back. "She's real sick."

Norman Bruce stared at her, a hunger in his eyes. "You tell your mama she best not go dying on me just yet." Harriet turned and walked back toward the cabin, fast but not too fast, not wanting to give him a reason to follow. She could feel his eyes on her.

It was the way Harriet could feel him before seeing him. She learned it like a second sense. She'd turn her head, and there he'd be. In the doorway of the blacksmith's shed, leaning against the frame with his arms crossed. She kept her head down, her hands busy with the iron, but the forge's heat couldn't chase away the chill. When she went to the outhouse, she hurried, but he was there, standing at a distance. At the well, she'd see him only a few feet away, watching with wolf-like eyes.

Harriet tried to talk to Charity, her voice soft, as Sophia slept soundly beside them.

"Mama . . ." Harriet whispered. "He's watching me." Charity's eyes didn't blink. "He's following me," Harriet tried again. "By the outhouse, by the shed. He . . . he looks at me like I'm something to take."

Charity looked past her, eyes fixed on something only she could see. "Mama, please. Say something," Harriet begged. Charity sat still, her face a mask of nothingness. Harriet reached out and cupped her mother's face, desperate to break through the silence. She thought she saw a spark for a moment, but then it was gone.

Harriet sat there a long time, pushing the critters of the night off her, hands curled around her mama, waiting for something to come back. She felt more alone than she'd ever felt before. Norman Bruce's eyes were everywhere and Charity's were nowhere. Harriet pulled her knees to her chest and stared at the wall.

The days bled into one another as a cruel summer dragged on. The blacksmith's shed had been the worst of it, air so dense with smoke and soot that every breath felt like swallowing embers. Harriet and Sophia worked because they had to, because it was easier to move than to stop and think about what waited beyond the shed walls. But at least they had each other. They didn't know how long that would last. The souls whispered that the end of the heat meant something was coming. A sale. A swap. A decision made in the dead of night that none of them had a say in.

Charity had her good days and her bad ones. Some days, she was almost there, her eyes clearer, her hands steady as she lifted a spoon to her lips, eating without needing to be coaxed. Then, just as quickly, the fog would return. There were nights she seemed catatonic, her eyes empty as if part of her had left this place long before her body could follow. Harriet would sit with her, whispering words she wasn't sure her mother could hear, pressing small bites of food against her lips, hoping and praying.

The season shifted. The heat finally began to lift with the wind whispering of something colder yet to come. The scent of the fields changed, the sun sinking earlier, the sky bruising to deep purples before slipping into night. It was one of those early-autumn evenings when you could feel the rain coming. Harriet and Sophia had been ordered by the older souls to clean up for the day, their hands moving quickly to tidy the tools. Hand hammers, sledgehammers, tongs, and pokers, all returned to their places. The fire in the forge still burned, flashing against the walls, creating a yellow and red glow. The older men had left, their voices fading into the distance, running to their cabins before the downpour began, leaving the sisters alone with the quiet and the heat.

Sophia sniffled, rubbing at her eyes with the back of her hand. "Hate it here," she mumbled. Harriet set down the last of the tongs. She turned to her sister, the firelight catching the wetness on Sophia's cheeks. "If Papa was here, we wouldn't be stuck in this place. We wouldn't be— " Her voice caught and she dropped her head.

Harriet reached for her, pulling her close, wrapping her arms tight around her little sister. "Shhh," she said, rocking her gently. "Daddy's still with us. You hear me? He's in us. We have his blood, and as long as we have that, he isn't gone. Don't let them take what they can't touch, right?"

Sophia clutched at Harriet's arms. "I don't want to be here no more."

Harriet closed her eyes. "Me neither."

"You think he's gonna sell us?" Sophia asked with concern. A striking of thunder exploded through the sky followed by the sound of rain.

Harriet's stomach knotted. "Don't know . . . but we better hurry, a storm's coming."

Sophia pulled back; she could see her father in her sister's beautiful face. Now Harriet was the strongest person she knew. "Are you scared?"

"Yeah," she admitted. "But I'm not gonna let us get sold."

Sophia sniffed. "What if he starts renting us out? How are you gonna stop it?"

"Don't know yet," she said. "But we're never gonna be apart. You hear me?"

A slow creak split through the shed. The door eased open, the hinges squealing, and both girls jumped. Norman Bruce appeared in the doorway, his diminutive frame lit up by the forge. He stepped inside, his wet boots heavy on the dirt floor. Sophia froze, her eyes darting to Harriet.

"Sophia," Norman said, "go check on your mama. She been looking poorly."

Sophia didn't move, her eyes stayed on Harriet, wide and fearful. "But . . . it's raining."

"Go on now," Norman snapped. Sophia took a step, then another, like she was walking through water, passing by Norman Bruce as he turned to look at her. Sophia glanced at Harriet one last time before slipping out the door, leaving it slightly ajar. Norman Bruce closed the door behind her with a weak latch that clicked like a trap.

Norman turned to Harriet, his tongue hung like a mutt tasting the air. "Your mama," he said, stepping closer, "cost me too much. Too much to get what's rightfully mine. You know that? She made me pay. But you . . . you ain't gonna cost me nothing."

Harriet backed away until she touched the wall of the shed. She had known this was coming. From the moment they were dragged to this cursed place, from the first time Norman Bruce laid eyes on her, a warning was always in the back of her mind. She had spent nights lying awake, terrified of the day he would make his move. And now, here it had come, and she was alone in the blacksmith's shed. The rain came down harder as he reached for her, his wet fingers brushing her arm as she flinched.

"Don't," she whispered, her voice breaking.

He laughed an ugly sound as thunder boomed again. "Don't what? Don't touch what's mine?" His slimy hand moved to her dress, tearing the cloth as she screamed. Although he was a tiny man, he still had strength. He smacked her, his palm against her face echoing like a gunshot. White light burst behind her eyes as she stumbled, but he caught her, his fingers digging into her arms. She fought, kicking and scratching. "You a strong, big gal, ain't you?" he growled. He let go just long enough to grab a poker from the forge right beside them. The tip glowed red hot like a burning eye. He held it up between them, grinning as he watched her panicked chest rise and fall.

"Get on the ground," he ordered. "Spread them legs."

Harriet's body locked. She wanted to fight. She had always fought, but something inside her, something she hated, began to fold. Her knees trembled. Her arms felt like lead. She felt herself giving in. Inside, she screamed for her daddy. Begged for him to come charging through the door, for his strong hands to pull her up. She cried for her mother, for Charity to rise, to come alive again, to pull her into her arms and whisper that everything would be all right. But there was no hero. Harriet began to cry and beg.

Sophia could hear the screams and sobs of her sister. She never left the shed. She had been right outside the door, now soaked and shivering from the rain, with her body pressed against the rough wood. She knew her sister was in danger. She pulled at the door, her fingers scrabbling against the wood, pounding her fists against it, but the latch held. She hollered for help, but the other souls couldn't hear her over the storm. Sophia yelled for her mama with a breaking wail. She threw her body against the door, her frame colliding with the wood and her palms bruising. One more time. Another. The door let out a creak under the force, the latch straining against the hinge. Sophia braced herself, sucked in a breath and with her thirteen-year-old strength, she hurled herself forward. The weak wood snapped simultaneously with the whip of more thunder, the latch giving way, as Sophia stumbled into the shed.

Sophia saw Harriet was on the floor, one hand clawing at the dirt, the other pinned beneath the weight of Norman Bruce with a hot poker in his hand. His body hovered over her with his knee, forcing her legs apart. Sophia didn't think—she moved, her eyes locked on a small, rusted sledgehammer leaning against the wall. She seized the handle with both hands and dashed to Norman Bruce, her feet barely touching the ground. The steel slammed into Norman Bruce's back. He jolted, his body arching in agony, the poker slipping from his fingers, falling onto the dirt floor, just inches from Harriet's face.

Harriet scrambled and snatched a large, warm hammer from the forge. The first swing crushed Norman Bruce's knee. Bone splintered and cartilage ruptured with a crunch. Norman folded, collapsing onto his back. Harriet jumped on top of him as the tiny man screamed and cried. She raised the hammer high, the blow landed where a man fears most. The fabric of his trousers did nothing to stop the splintering impact. A wet, pulpy sound followed, a mix of tearing cloth and a smashed organ. He howled, sounding far from human, but Norman Bruce was never human. Harriet stepped back and let the hammer slip from her fingers. Straightening, she looked down at Norman Bruce, a whimpering mess at her feet.

"Gonna kill you gals," Norman Bruce wheezed. Harriet and Sophia didn't hear him. Or maybe they did, but it didn't matter. He reached out, grasping at the hem of Harriet's dress. She reached for the poker lying on the ground—the same one he had tried to use against her—its glow dimming with the fading heat. She thrust the poker back into the forge. The embers roared as the metal met the fire, spitting as it drank in the heat. She pumped the bellows with one hand, feeding the flames, watching as the poker's tip went from dull to furious.

Harriet thought of her father, his hands as he worked the forge, his voice calm as he taught her the craft. She could almost hear Larkin now, a divine condescension instructing each move. The tip glowed a molten orange. Sophia stood motionless and looked to Harriet, watching with an intensity as the poker hovered in the air, a seraphic weapon of retribution.

Harriet drove the poker down, piercing his chest with a scorch. Norman screamed again, his eyes rolling back to their whites. Harriet yanked the poker free, the tip dripping a gooey red. She plunged the poker into his stomach. His body jerked violently, his hands clawing as if searching for something to hold on to, but there was nothing. Sophia wanted more.

Sophia grabbed a branding iron from the forge, its end glowing like a star. She turned, her body shaking but her grip firm. Harriet took it, fingers locked around the metal shaft. Norman Bruce writhed beneath them, like a smashed bug. He was still here, still living, just barely. "Brand him, sister," Sophia demanded.

Harriet pressed the iron against his chest, right over his pale heart. At first, there was resistance, the fabric of his shirt stiffening under the heat before it gave way, shrinking, blackening as the fire chewed through it. The smell of charred cloth filled the shed. His skin then took the burn, flesh blistering beneath the iron, the heat burning further, through skin, muscle, tissue, marking him in a way that could never be undone.

Norman Bruce came alive for another dance, his lower back arching off the floor. His skin bubbled like fat in a pan, the branding iron sinking into him, carving justice. Harriet thought, *How many before me? How many had been held down, bound, stripped of their names, their homes, their dignity, burned like this, their flesh marked as someone's property?* To know, in his last moments, what it was to be branded. To be owned. To be nothing. Harriet exhaled, her grip loosening on the iron.

A sound came from the doorway. Harriet looked up, the iron still clutched in her hand, and there, in the entrance of the blacksmith's shed, stood Charity. Through the storm, she had heard the cries of her girls and forced herself to the shed. Charity, face and body drenched from rainwater, stared at Harriet and Sophia.

Blood was smeared across the dirt floor, pooling around

Norman Bruce's body. Steam still rose from the brand seared into his chest.

Sophia stood with her fists clenched at her sides. Harriet was at the center as if she were forcing the violence back inside her. Her forehead wrinkled, cheeks blotted with dirt and blood.

Charity took it all in. Something that had been buried beneath grief and silence began to stir. She stepped forward, the wetness of her dress making a sound with each movement, her eyes on Norman Bruce. Her toes sunk into the bloody dirt. She came to stand over Norman Bruce, staring down at the wreck of a man who held power over them. Now, he was nothing more than a pile of broken, bloodied limbs, his body barely clinging to life.

His swollen eyes opened. He saw her. He saw *Charity*.

His lips trembled. "C-Charity . . ."

Charity tilted her head, a life force returning to her. For the first time in a long while, her eyes were clear. She was here. *Fully here*. Norman Bruce's mouth gaped, sucking in air that would do him no good. You could see the demon leave his body, earning a place in hell.

"Mama." Harriet's voice was frantic as she set the iron down, her hands shaking. "He came after me. It was the only way, Mama." Charity marveled at her daughters. They had their father's spirit and strength. She had raised them to survive, had taught them what it meant to hold on to themselves. And now, she remembered who she had taught them to be. *You cannot make a slave.* That was the flaw of this institution, the big lie that had held it together for generations. It was built on the breaking of spirits, on the belief that a person could be stripped down to nothing and reshaped into obedience. But no whip, no chain, no branding iron could turn a soul into property. No master could own what was never meant to be owned. They had tried to break her. They had tried to break Larkin. And now they had tried to break her daughters.

Charity, galvanized by the deeds of her daughters, stared at the girls she had carried, and said, "Put him in the fire." Harriet and Sophia looked at their mother. The woman who was drained of all life was no longer there. In her place stood the mother they had known in their earliest memories. Killing Norman Bruce had brought her back.

The forge still smoldered, but it wasn't roaring. The iron bellows hung beside it. Harriet grabbed hold of the wooden handles and pulled, once, twice, forcing the forge to breathe. The forge was hungry.

As the storm continued to unleash, Harriet, Sophia, and Charity grabbed Norman Bruce's shoulders, dragging his dead weight toward the forge. His small body was heavier than it should have been, its resistance unnatural. But it didn't matter. They would finish this. Charity looked to her girls. "We take him apart, piece by piece . . . same way he tried to take us." They stripped Norman Bruce down to his underpants, revealing his thin, pale frame. His body was riddled with wounds, his insides exposed like a gutted pig.

Harriet and Charity worked in tandem, the tools of the forge becoming the tools of justice. Limbs broke, bent and splattered. Sophia grabbed a long blade from the workbench, one used for cutting thick straps of leather. The beast's head needed to be removed.

Charity aggressively lifted his chin as Harriet took the saw from Sophia's hands. With a firm grip, she pressed the jagged teeth against Norman Bruce's throat. The first pull tore through skin, a red line blooming before the blade bit deeper. Sinew and muscle resisted, stretching and fraying with each motion. Bone, skin, and the crack of Norman Bruce's skull echoed as it caved beneath the force. Blood slicked Harriet's fingers as she worked, the saw catching, jerking, until with a shuddering snap, the vertebrae gave way.

Harriet lifted the head, the severed stump dripping. Sophia took a step back but did not look away. Charity reached, holding Harriet's grip as they placed the head on the fire bed. For a moment, nothing. Then the heat took hold.

The flames licked at the broken skin, burning the edges of his gray hair into black wisps. The skin around his face tightened, shrinking against the bone before it cracked and peeled away. The whites of his eyes clouded, then burst with a *pop*, releasing a foul steam that touched the rafters. His lips, twisted into a half smirk in death, burned away next, exposing teeth that had blackened. The fire crackled louder as they fed it more. Harriet stoked the flames, forcing them higher, pushing them deeper into the ruins of him.

Piece by piece, they fed him to the flames, watching as the fire ate through muscle, organs, and reduced him to brittle. By the time the fire had done its part, what remained had to be broken down. The larger bones, including the skull, were too thick to burn through completely. Harriet took the blacksmith's hammer, once used to mold iron, shattering his stubborn skull. There was nothing left but ashes and chunks of bone. Charity wiped her hands on her dress and exhaled through the front, then out the back of her heart. She turned to her daughters. "Judgment affirmed."

The forge still crackled, but there was no time to watch it burn. They had to move.

Charity, Harriet, and Sophia rushed into the storm that was pummeling through the Bruce plantation. They scrubbed their faces, heads up to the thunderous sky and rain, washing away the evidence of what had just been done. There was no one in sight; the other souls were hunkered down in their cabins praying the rain wouldn't cause the shacks to fall on their heads.

Moving steadily, they reached the cabin, already leaking from the wood ceiling, hoping no one heard the screams. But perhaps they heard the reckoning through the storm, perhaps it was a symphony to them as well. Stillness from the souls, Charity thought, is also rebellion. After all, even the Psalms spoke of silence: *Be still, and know that I am God.*[23] Stillness was not surrender; it was a trust that the scales would balance in their own time.

They peeled off their clothes, the fabric on their skin stiff with dried blood and sweat. They reached for the only rags they had left, dressing quickly. Harriet dug beneath the floorboards and pulled out a small bundle of food. It wasn't much, some stale cornbread, a few dried strips of meat, a jug of water, and a sliver of soap worn down from use. It was enough to last them a few days, maybe longer, if they stretched it. "I've been getting ready," she said to her sister and mother. "Didn't know when we'd need it, but I knew it was coming."

Charity's arms reached out and pulled Harriet into her embrace. It wasn't weak, wasn't distant like it had been in those long months. It was strong. Harriet clung to her, eyes squeezed shut. She had dreamed of this moment. Had begged and prayed. Now, Charity was here, flesh and blood, mind clear. "You're back, Mama," Harriet said.

Sophia pressed her body between them. They held one another, the three of them locked.

Charity pulled back. There was little time for lingering. She moved swiftly to the wooden box near the bed, lifting the lid with careful hands. Inside, folded and creased, was Miss Clara's letter.

"145 River Road . . . You will know you have arrived when

[23]. *Psalm* 46:10, New Revised Standard Version.

you see a chimney of white bricks crowned with a black top." Charity had seen the white chimney many times over the years, its pale column rising through the trees.

Charity ran her fingers over the words. "I know the way," Charity said. "Gonna be hard in this storm, but that means nobody's looking for us anytime soon. God—or whoever's listening up there—He'll cover us. Might take days, but we'll make it."

"Storm's just noise," Harriet said. "We've been through worse."

They stayed off the big roads but close enough to the path. The storm was howling. Rain lashed their faces, cold and sharp as broken glass, while the wind screamed through the trees, bending them double. The chaos of the forest was barely visible through the sheets of rain. Branches snapped and flew like arrows, and the trees groaned as if they might uproot themselves and run with them.

Charity led the way, her clothes soaked through and clinging to her skin, ripped in places where the underbrush had clawed at her. Every step was a fight, against the mud that sucked at their thin shoes, against the roots that tripped them, against the cold that made their hands stiff and clumsy. But they kept pushing. The storm's violence was a mirror of the world they were trying to escape. Harriet could see the determination in her mother's steps, the way her fingers squeezed the sack she carried. "We coming home, Larkin," she would say to herself whenever a wave of fatigue hit her.

By the next morning, the rain had calmed, but they were still far from safety. They could hear activity on the road nearby, forcing them to hide in the trunks of trees, shaking off bugs and holding their breath when they heard someone or something pass. They moved by night, sleeping in brief, uneasy stretches beneath the cover of thick brush. When they found streams not far from the path, they washed their faces, pressing cool water against their swollen feet. They ate sparingly, stretching each bite as far as it would go.

Days continued, who knew how many, and doubt crept in their hearts. Their bodies fought back pains from the endless push forward, from sleeping on a frigid earth, from the fear that every snapping twig, every distant voice in the wind, was the sound of their doom. Charity had led them this far, but she feared she had taken them the wrong way. Had she led them deeper into danger? And, most of all, could Miss Clara truly be trusted? She was once an owner of souls, including hers.

Every morning was bitter. Their rags did little to keep them warm, the threadbare fabric barely shielding them from the wind that bit at their exposed skin. Their breath came out in thin white wisps, vanishing into the air as quickly as it appeared. The last of their food had been rationed down to near nothing, scraps of stale bread and a few kernels of corn they had picked from the roadside. Their water was nearly gone, a few drops that remained were sloshing at the bottom of the jug. Still, they walked. All three of them limped now, their bodies worn down to raw, blistered feet. Every step was painful. The road had taken its toll, and yet Charity worried the worst of it wasn't behind them. She was sure someone had found what was left of Norman Bruce by now. They were being hunted. She could feel it by the prickle at the back of her neck, in the way the trees seemed to close in around them. It was coming.

Charity's mind began to slip, thoughts unraveling into half-formed fears. She squeezed her eyes shut, shaking her head to ward off the thing that clawed at her mind and dragged her toward blankness. *Dear God, please don't let it come back. Dear God, keep me strong. Keep me here*. She forced the words between her chapped lips.

And just when it felt impossible, on the verge of collapse, finally—there. Just beyond the bend in the road. *You will know you have arrived when you see a chimney of white bricks crowned with a black top.*

The stark white bricks, rising against the horizon. The chimney, capped in black, stood tall, a dark crown atop a house that meant everything. The wood of its beams was dark, strong in the way that things built to last must be. The windows were shuttered and the curtains drawn. Freedom. Safety. Defiance. Harriet reached for her mother's hand. Charity wrapped her fingers around Sophia's wrist, whose body was spent.

As they made their way through the morning lull, Charity prayed that inside the house righteous souls were waiting. People who had risked everything to stand against the wickedness of the law. People who, no matter what happened in that courtroom with Thaddeus Stevens, had chosen justice over silence. The house was a hope that after everything, after blood, fire, fear, and flight, they had persevered.

They made their way to the door, their bodies shaking with despair and cautious optimism. Charity feared someone would see them. Did anyone know about this house? Were bounty hunters in the area waiting for souls to approach the house with the white chimney? Charity hesitated, staring at the wooden door, her fist hovering before knocking. Harriet squeezed her mother's hand and glanced behind them, terrified a band of White men would appear. Sophia wrapped herself around Charity's leg. They had defied the law again, but had they won? Charity thought.

Charity knocked. They heard footsteps. Someone looked out of the window behind a curtain. The door slowly opened.

The man who stood before them was tall, his beard streaked with white, his face lined with years, his clothes plain. Charity tensed. All she saw was his whiteness. The world had taught her to fear men who looked like him. Then she remembered Miss Clara's letter. *Trusted friends, those who labor in secret for the cause of liberty.*

She squeezed her daughters' hands. "Miss . . . Miss Clara sent me."

An understanding passed through his eyes. He stepped aside, opening the door wider.

"Welcome. You're among friends."

CHAPTER 4

NATHANIEL

"His conduct became so notorious that he lost the confidence of slave owners and respect of negroes, who several times tried to murder him."[24]

Charleston, South Carolina, was no stranger to contradictions. The city's stately streets teemed with the moral perversion of commerce and its stone-laid paths betrayed the layers of brutality in pseudo-elegance. Beneath polished mansions and well-tended gardens, the labor of enslaved Black bodies formed the city's very foundation. Here, in the cradle of aristocratic mercilessness, Nathaniel William had built a small empire.

Nathaniel stood in front of the heavy oak door of his big house, its surface polished to a white sheen. The door was solid, strong, and a symbol of his reign, the threshold he

24. Calvin D. Wilson (1912, November), "Negroes who owned slaves," *Popular Science Monthly 81*, 487.

crossed daily as a master. Its iron hinges were thick and sturdy. The carved panels carried the marks of age but showed no weakness. The wood itself defied time, as did his neatly ordered aisles of crops. The chill in the autumn air nipping at his cheeks brought memories of falls long past. It was nearly the end of harvest season. As a young man, he had once worked the fields, but his life had changed when he was rented out to a White man who was a cotton gin maker. Those machines would devastate Black lives, making the demands even higher, but for Nathaniel they provided a narrow path to freedom. Quickly, the cotton gin maker noticed his keen intelligence and took him under his wing, teaching him skilled trades, reading, writing, and bookkeeping.

Despite these privileges, Nathaniel remained enslaved and was often sent back to work the fields. He knew hunger, weariness, the aches and pains, and the ire of the enslaver. Years passed—more than ten—without any sign that his master intended to grant his freedom. Whispers circulated that this same master might be his father, though no one dared confirm it. Determined to liberate himself, Nathaniel stole and saved every penny he could. By the time his master lay dying and debt-ridden, Nathaniel was ready. He bought his freedom and, in doing so, took the first step toward creating an enterprise. His Charleston plantation.

Freedom had not brought peace; it had sparked an insatiable yearning for power. Nathaniel used what little savings he had to purchase the farm, a modest plot on the outskirts of town. Yet each seed he planted, each acre he claimed, only deepened his drive to control whatever lay before him. He was a master of the field, skilled at picking cotton, curing tobacco, and wielding a blacksmith's hammer. But he couldn't do it all alone. He began to acquire souls to work the farm and tend to the livestock, taking on the roles he knew better than anyone. Investing in free labor was a divine blessing. An ordained path to prosperity. Yet, the real profit lay in the resale—a trade he entered with no conscience. Profit became his life's sole ambition.

When White men acknowledged his tenacity, extending him a sliver of respect, Nathaniel clung to it like scripture. *Maybe I am one of them*, he reasoned, *after all, what negro gets this type of respect?* He prayed with every fiber of his being that his father had been his former owner after all. That close to whiteness, that possibility of White blood coursing through his veins. He believed he was destined for superiority. He wanted to be superior. *From cotton to master*, Nathaniel thought.

At the edge of the veranda, Nathaniel surveyed the land and grinned with his gummy smile. As for all this Civil War, it was nothing but a nuisance to him. South Carolina, his home state. The first state to secede from the Union. A state that would never fall, no matter how many Northern soldiers marched its way. The backbone of the South. *If those negroes had any sense, they'd stop stirring trouble, stop dreaming of freedom they couldn't handle. They'd settle in their place and make the best of it. Freedom for negroes was absurd*, he thought. *If negroes wanted to be free, they would, they too comfortable. There was no such thing as oppression. Just fools too sorry to lift their own heads out of the dirt.*

Nathaniel believed himself to be a special negro. His truth? *Most negroes weren't built for freedom. They were shiftless, always begging for scraps, always asking for what they hadn't earned.* Nathaniel shook his head. *Abolitionists clamoring to end slavery didn't care about the negro*, he thought bitterly. *All they cared about was poor Whites rising up without slave labor undercutting them. If these negroes were let loose, it would be chaos.* "White supremacy," he muttered as he smacked on tobacco. "Free them damn slaves, and we'll have negro supremacy. God help us then." He'd built his castle with his own hands, risen above the lot of them, Black and White, and he wouldn't let it be taken from him. Not by the war, not by the Union, and certainly not by the idle hands of men who'd rather beg than fight.

The wind tugged at his worn but sturdy coat as he spit out the tobacco in a cup. His wide-brimmed hat sat precariously on his bald, round head, barely concealing his shining scalp. Nathaniel's chunky, tall frame strained against his clothes, hips too wide and belly too big. His small, yellowed teeth flashed whenever he spoke, and his fat cheeks gave him the deceptive look of an affable man. But those who worked under him knew better. Nathaniel's power didn't lie in his hands or his body—it nested in his craving to be the *only* one. No one else but him.

From the doorway of the house, Solomon paused to glare at Nathaniel. It had been thirty years since that night on Magnolia Row, and time had not been kind to Solomon. He wasn't as old as he appeared. His body, battle-scarred by years of punishment on plantation after plantation, each one worse than the last. His limp had worsened, dragging with every step like a ball and chain. He went through countless eye patches to cover the wound so repulsive that it drove away anyone who dared to glance at it. Many had escaped Magnolia Row that fateful night, but Solomon hadn't been one of those lucky souls. He had been caught, sold, and sold again from one hell to another. But the William plantation was a unique hell. The man wasn't just a grifter or a sellout; he was worse than any White master Solomon had known and he had seen plenty.

Nathaniel was one of the few Black slave owners in South Carolina, though most who shared that distinction owned their kin to protect them. Not Nathaniel. He had no kin. No compassion. Nathaniel knew what it meant to suffer, and yet he inflicted pain with the vehemence of a man terrified to lose his place. In Solomon's eyes, Nathaniel was far more detestable than most White men. A former slave always trying to top White men's evil to prove he was just like *them*. Just the sight of Nathaniel standing as if he were some benevolent patriarch was enough to make Solomon's belly ache.

Nathaniel's thoughts were interrupted. He turned to see Solomon emerging from the house, balancing a basket of apples and peaches in his hands. Solomon's face was carefully neutral. He placed the fruit on a small table and stepped away to a respectful distance, avoiding direct eye contact.

"The fruit you asked for, sir."

Nathaniel plucked an apple from the basket and turned it over in his hand. He examined it carefully, his fingers pressing into the skin. He sniffed it, then glanced at Solomon.

"You ain't tried slipping anything into these, have you, Solomon?" Nathaniel's tone was mocking.

"No, sir," Solomon said. "Nothing wrong with the fruit."

Nathaniel took a bite, chewing slowly. The sound of his teeth crunching through the apple was unnervingly loud. He stared into Solomon's one good eye. "Where you get them gray eyes from? You got that White blood in you?"

"Don't know," Solomon said, looking away.

"Damn shame, you black as tar but got them gray eyes. The one good thing on you and you don't even have both of 'em!" he said with a repulsive laugh. "How you lose that eye?"

"Don't remember," Solomon lied.

"Tell me something," Nathaniel said. "You been a slave all your life?"

"Yes, sir."

Nathaniel cocked his head. "How many years you got on you?"

"Think I'm almost at fifty years, sir."

"Thought you had sixty or seventy years on you," Nathaniel chuckled. "Funny thing is, I'm no slave and I'm younger than you. I be forty in September. Bought my way out. Yet here you are, still wearing that same old yoke. Makes a man wonder why. You ever think 'bout buying yourself free?"

Solomon frowned slightly. "Never had the chance, sir."

Nathaniel snorted. "Never had the chance? Or maybe you just ain't got the spine for it. Comfortable, ain't it? Somebody telling you what to do, feeding you, keeping you in your place." Nathaniel relished seeing Solomon's discomfort. "We both colored, Solomon, but look at us. I'm a free man, a master, and you? You *still* a slave, same as always. Makes me wonder . . . maybe you ain't meant to be free. Maybe you exactly where you belong. Maybe this whole thing called slavery is a *choice*." The other souls nearby could hear. "Negroes like you, Solomon—naturally dumb. White man's got it right about most of y'all."

Solomon nodded once, a small, almost imperceptible gesture, then turned and walked away.

Nathaniel watched him go. "That's right, keep your head down," he said, taking another bite of the apple. "No room at my table for fools like you." He tossed the half-eaten apple into the yard.

Nathaniel knew that Solomon, like all of the souls on his plantation, despised him. He was one of them—but he wasn't. He shared their complexion, but he had abandoned the spirit that bound them as a people. His blackness made him an aberration. He was an enemy dressed in familiarity. What made Nathaniel even more dangerous was that he knew them in ways White folks never could. He had lived their lives, suffered their chains, and sung their songs. He recognized the understated rebellion behind a sideways look, the restraint in a fist and the meaning of a pitch-perfect song. To Nathaniel, these were not signs of resilience or hope; they were weaknesses to exploit. Unlike the clueless White owners who dismissed these subtleties, Nathaniel saw through the smallest gestures, the faintest shifts in body language. He knew when a soul was planning to run, when their spirit was breaking, and when they were too timid to fight back.

Nathaniel snuffed out hopes with a sterile precision that left even seasoned overseers in awe. He saw himself as smarter, stronger, better than any of them. As he stalked the fields, his presence was a reminder that he was more than a master. He was a predator who was once the prey. The enslaved loathed him not just for what he did but for what he represented: the ultimate desecration.

Nathaniel squinted into the distance, his eyes catching movement near the tree line. He tipped forward on the porch. He spotted a female figure stumbling through the underbrush, clutching a toddler tightly to her chest. *Smell like gold to me*, Nathaniel said to himself. "Abram!" Nathaniel yelled to the young, wiry man who was too juvenile to refuse orders and could still be trusted.

"Sir?"

Nathaniel pointed toward the woman trying to not be seen. "Go fetch her! Be quick 'bout it!"

Abram nodded and sprinted toward the tree line. The woman was startled. She held her child tighter, her body tense with fright.

"Don't hurt me," she begged. "Please, don't hurt my baby."

Abram softened his voice. "Nobody gonna hurt you. You on the William property now. You safe." Abram could feel the heat of Nathaniel's staring. One wrong move and his day could end terribly. She trusted the young boy's eyes and she was beaten down from fatigue. She also couldn't see a White man in sight. Abram urged her to follow him. When she reached the porch, Nathaniel William flashed his smile, showing more gums than teeth.

"Welcome, miss." His deep Southern drawl lent familiarity. "You safe here. Nobody gonna hurt you or your child on my land."

"Who . . . who you?" she asked, her voice shaky.

Nathaniel spread his arms in a gesture of hospitality. "Name's Nathaniel William. This here's my land." Nathaniel saw her confusion. A Black man owning land? "Ain't what you think. These folks here, they my kin. My family. Every last one of 'em."

"You . . . you a master? Never heard of a colored master."

Nathaniel guffawed. "Not like the ones you running from. I protect my people, give 'em a place to stay. A roof, food, safety. You and your little one, you can stay here too, if you like."

The woman's grip on her child loosened slightly. "I . . . don't know how to thank you," she whispered. "Been running for days. Name's Evalina, and this here's my boy, Thomas."

"Well, Evalina, you safe now. That's all that matters. How many years is your boy?"

"Four years."

"Looks like a strong boy. You hungry? Got plenty to eat." He nodded to Abram. "Give her some fruit . . . And don't you worry 'bout nothing. You can rest here tonight, and in the morning, we see where you can fit in." The other souls watched, but Evalina didn't notice, she was too focused on the kindness in Nathaniel's voice and chewing on an apple. She shared a piece with Thomas. "Abram will take you to one of the cabins, it ain't much but it'll do." Evalina took another look. Nathaniel's words had been so welcoming, but they didn't match what she saw around her. He had called them his family, the people working silently. Yet, if they were family, why did they live in cabins while he stayed in a big house?

She took in the structure behind him; its tall windows and fresh white paint stood in contrast to the rough-hewn cabins she could see scattered along the edge of the property. But as quickly as the thought came, she shoved it to the back of her mind. She was cold, tired, and desperate. This place felt like safety, at least for now. She pulled Thomas closer, feeling his tiny body against hers. Questions could wait, rest couldn't.

"Thank you, sir."

Nathaniel nodded. "No trouble at all."

Evalina followed Abram, never letting go of Thomas as they approached one of the cabins. She couldn't shake the feeling of eyes on her. But when she stepped inside the clean, small room, with its modest bed of hay, blankets, and a lantern, she allowed herself a moment to breathe. Evalina sank into the makeshift bed, her body queasy with weariness. It didn't matter why things were strange or why the man's "family" lived in drab shacks. For now, all that mattered was that she and Thomas had a roof over their heads. Nathaniel watched the cabin door close behind her.

The next morning, Nathaniel sat in his favorite rocking chair on the porch. A steaming cup of mint tea rested on the table beside him. His fastidious eyes were on every inch of his property, taking in the stirrings of the day. He didn't need an overseer. He always watched. Nothing escaped him. Abram approached, his body drowning in an oversized shirt hanging off his shoulders. Nathaniel noticed him but didn't speak.

"Sir?" he said.

"You find out where she from?"

"She didn't wanna talk at first. She was scared. But . . . I got it outta her." He was ashamed, but his choices were limited. "She from Mr. Zeb Turner's plantation." He'd betrayed Evalina, like he had so many before. It was always his job to break runaways, to dig out their secrets and deliver them back to chains. He hated himself for it, hated Nathaniel even more. Yet there was no way out. Nathaniel William turned them into traitors, made sure their hands were as dirty as his.

Nathaniel took a sip of his mint tea. His fingers tapped a rhythm on the armrest. "Well, now, ain't that something?"

A knock startled Evalina. The door opened with a squeak to reveal Nathaniel. "Good morning," he said, calm and pleasant. "Figure we talk a bit before the day starts proper. Mind if I come in?" Evalina nodded, shifting Thomas to her lap. "You rest all right?" he asked, folding his hands behind his back.

"Yes, sir," Evalina said softly.

Nathaniel waved off the formal address. "No need for that, now. I told you, we family here. So, how long you thinking of staying? You got plans, or you looking to settle?"

"Don't know yet," she admitted. "Just needed to get away . . . somewhere safe."

"Safe, huh? There's a story there." He took a pause. "You trust me enough to tell me what happened? I can help, but I need to know what you running from. I don't want no White folks coming here looking for you." What Evalina didn't know was that no White folks ever came onto his land searching for runaways. No bounty hunters were necessary, since Nathaniel would return those who came to him seeking shelter—for a fee, of course. The selling of souls kept his land safe.

Her eyes filled with tears. "Couldn't stay there no more."

"Go on," he urged.

Her words poured out in a rush, yet she carefully avoided mentioning Zeb Turner's name. "He . . . he been doing ungodly things to me. And Thomas"—she glanced at the boy in her arms—"he his child." Nathaniel's eyes fell on the yellow-skinned child cradled in her arms. He admired his mop of curly hair, the curve of his nose, the olive undertone of his skin that hinted at the blood running through his veins. *That White blood*, Nathaniel thought.

"That's why you left?"

Evalina nodded. "When Thomas finished breastfeeding, he said he was gonna sell him off. But he's mine. Couldn't let him do it."

Nathaniel rested a hand on her shoulder. "You did what any mama would've done," he said. "You saved your boy. And you don't have to worry 'bout him here. You both safe."

"Thank you so much."

Nathaniel offered her a smile. "No need to thank me. Like I said—family. And we all help out around here, like family does. There's work to be done, but it ain't slavery. You won't be treated like that here. Just pull your weight, and you'll always have a place."

Evalina nodded, relief washing over her face. "Yes, sir. Do whatever I can." Nathaniel left the cabin with a wink. Still, there was something unsettling about the way he spoke—about "pulling your weight." *But it ain't slavery.*

Evalina sat for a moment, her fingers absently brushing Thomas's curls. A knock at the door made her jump. Abram stood in the doorway. In his hands, he held a neatly folded set of clothes. "These for you," he said, eyes skimming just past her face. "And something for the boy too." Evalina accepted the bundle with quiet thanks. The fabric was rough, simple, but clean—better than what she'd been wearing. Abram gave a small nod, then gestured outside. "Gotta show you where you work."

Out in the fields, Abram explained her tasks. "Weeding mostly, keeping the rows clear. The tools are over there, and you can let the boy stay close. If he don't bother no one, it be fine. Just . . . keep to yourself, work hard. Harvest season almost done. Ain't much else to it." His voice was pleasant enough, but his eyes never met hers. He wasn't the only one evading her. Evalina noticed the other workers moving nearby, shoulders hunched like the living dead.

Evalina and Thomas washed up in a small basin of water and dressed quickly. Thomas giggled at first, tugging at the oversized sleeves, but the sound faded as they made their way into the fields. Abram handed her a hoe and walked away without speaking another word. The other workers moved with swift hands. There was a silence broken only by the occasional sound of tools striking the earth.

As Evalina worked, a thin woman with ebony Black hair in intricate braids managed the row beside her. Her movements were efficient, but her eyes shot toward Evalina. When she got close enough, she spoke quickly: "Don't trust him." Evalina's hands stopped in midmotion.

"What you mean?" she asked, glancing at the woman.

"He negro," she said, "but he really a White man inside. Run now, while you can."

Evalina blinked. "What you talking about?" she asked, but the woman had already turned back to work. Evalina watched, waiting for more, but the woman said nothing else. Evalina glanced toward the big house in the distance. She dismissed the woman's cryptic warning. *He saved us*, she told herself. *Where would we go? Maybe they ain't his family, but this place is quiet enough. Better than Zeb Turner.*

Emma Jane shook her head. *They never listen.*

Nathaniel rode his horse along the wide dirt path leading to Zeb Turner's plantation. The estate was twice the size of Nathaniel's and he was envious. *If I work a little harder, I can have even more*, he thought. He stepped down from his horse, dressed in his absolute best, a wine-colored velvet suit that was far too loud for the plantation grounds. Gold buttons gleamed, running the length of his jacket, which was cut just a bit too tight for his fluffy frame, and a thick gold watch chain swung from his waistcoat. His outfit screamed excess, a pitiful flaunting of wealth and importance. It was the same kind of garishness that had left Zeb Turner unimpressed whenever he saw Nathaniel in town.

Mr. Turner's White overseer emerged from the house, his face grew grimmer as he recognized the visitor. Disdain was in his eyes, but he said nothing, stepping aside as Mr. Turner himself appeared on the porch. His beady blue eyes swept over Nathaniel, perturbed by the velvet and gold.

"What brings you here, Nathaniel?" Mr. Turner called out, purposely calling him by his first name.

Nathaniel tipped his hat as he approached the steps. "Zeb—"

"It's *Mr. Turner*," he corrected.

Nathaniel paused with his gummy grin. "Yes, Mr. Turner, I do apologize. Always a pleasure to see you. I assure you, this is a matter of business."

Mr. Turner crossed his arms. "What sorta business would bring you to *my* doorstep?"

Nathaniel delivered his words carefully. "Well, sir, it's come to my attention that a certain piece of your . . . property has found its way onto mine."

He paused. Zeb knew of the mousetrap on Nathaniel's land. All the White folks did, but none of his property had fallen into Nathaniel's hands to date. "Who?"

"Goes by Evalina," Nathaniel said with false cordiality. "Got a young boy with her. Seems she ran off some time back and thought my land was safe."

Mr. Turner stepped down from the porch. "How many hidden negroes you got over there on that meager land, boy?"

Nathaniel raised his hands in mock innocence. "Now, hold on, Mr. Turner. I don't hide nothing. Found out she was yours, and I came straight to you."

Mr. Turner huffed. Evalina, and especially the boy, were prime property. "You trying to sell me back my own damn property?"

"Well, Mr. Turner, you know how it is," he said with an

exhale. "I could send her down South, fetch a pretty penny for her and that boy. But figured I give you the courtesy of first refusal."

Mr. Turner bristled. "You think you got leverage over me? I could call the sheriff right now and have you locked up."

Nathaniel didn't budge. "You could," he said. "But I'd remind you, Mr. Turner, the sheriff is a mighty good friend of Minister Woodward, who is a business associate of mine. He the one who helps me sell property like Evalina when the situation arises. Now, do you wanna risk losing her to the auction block, or do you want her back where she belongs?" Minister Woodward wasn't just a preacher, he was a businessman camouflaged in scripture. From the pulpit, he preached of submission, quoting the Good Book to condone their sins wrapped in statute books.

Mr. Turner's face flushed red, but Nathaniel wasn't done. "And let's not forget, I been feeding her. Feeding that boy of hers too. Keeping her calm, talking her down so she don't bolt again. You know as well as I do, runaways don't stop running easy. Done the work to make sure she stays put, to make sure you ain't chasing her halfway across the state again. That's time, effort, and money, Mr. Turner. A debt that needs paying."

The veins in Mr. Turner's neck popped. "You got some kinda nerve, bringing up debts to me. You keeping my property."

"Oh, I didn't keep her, Mr. Turner. I preserved her—for you. She still yours, but let's be honest here. If I hadn't stepped in, who knows where she'd be? Up North living free? I saved you the trouble and brought her back to you in one piece. That's worth something, ain't it?"

Mr. Turner inhaled deeply, wrestling with the insult of having to negotiate with Nathaniel. "What's the price?"

"For Evalina and that boy of hers," Nathaniel said. "Five

hundred will cover the cost. Fair, given the trouble I've saved you."

"Five hundred dollars for my own property?" he hissed. "You lucky I don't put you in the ground for this insult!"

Nathaniel's smile didn't budge. "Mr. Turner, let's not get hasty. This ain't just about property. It's about the time. Pay me what she's worth, or you take your chances with the auction block."

Mr. Turner glared at Nathaniel. "Fine," he bit out. "Five hundred. I'll be at your land by sundown to collect."

Nathaniel tipped his hat. "Pleasure doing business with you, Mr. Turner. I'll have her ready and waiting." Mr. Turner turned sharply on his heel, walking back toward his house. Nathaniel climbed back on his horse. *Five hundred*, he mused. *And a reminder of who really got the upper hand.*

The quiet of the late afternoon was disrupted by hooves on the dirt road. Nathaniel stepped onto the porch, the wooden planks creaking under his boots. Unlike his usual flashy ensembles, Nathaniel had dressed down, choosing attire he believed befitted a planter ready to conduct a transaction, not a negotiation. A plain linen shirt, slightly rumpled. His trousers were a dark cotton, tucked into scuffed boots that looked like they had seen more dirt than polish—a choice to project the image of a man familiar with hard labor, though Nathaniel rarely dirtied his hands with anything beyond a pen. To complete the look, he wore his wide-brimmed hat, its brim slightly frayed.

Dust rose until it revealed itself as Mr. Zeb Turner in his grand carriage. It was a sight designed to impress: a glossy black body polished to a mirror sheen with brass fittings. The wheels, rimmed with iron, turned as a chestnut-colored horse pulled the carriage, its bridle adorned with silver buckles. Beside Mr. Turner, his White overseer with a scowl. There was no mistaking the envy that crept within Nathaniel. *That carriage. That wealth.* Nathaniel hated it. And yet, there was no denying how he wanted it. He coveted the shine of brass, the respect that followed a man who stepped out of such a carriage. He was more and more like Zeb Turner than the slave he used to be, but it wasn't enough. *From cotton to master.*

Out of the carriage stepped Zeb Turner. He had never been on Nathaniel's land. He took in everything before him—land, labor, people. "Nathaniel," Mr. Turner said, omitting any hint of respect. "Where is she?"

Nathaniel tipped his hat. "Mr. Turner, welcome. Always a pleasure to—"

"Where's the gal and the boy?" Mr. Turner cut him off.

Before Nathaniel could respond, a scream erupted from the fields. All heads turned to see Evalina. She had spotted Zeb Turner and scooped Thomas into her arms, holding the boy to her chest.

"Grab her!" Nathaniel demanded. The other souls moved toward Evalina. Their faces were obvious with apologies, but their bodies were driven not by choice. Two strong men reached her first as they pried Thomas from her arms; the child's wails pierced the air. "Mama! Mama!" His small fists flailed. Evalina fought as they pulled her toward the waiting carriage, her bare feet scraping the ground.

In her anguish, she didn't hear the whispers, faint and mournful. *"Be calm, sister,"* the men who carried her whispered. *"Nothing you can do now. Don't let him see you break. Breathe, child. He can't take your spirit, no matter what he takes from your hands."*

Evalina wailed, her voice rising to the gods. "Don't give my baby to him! Don't take my baby!" Thomas's cries matched hers. Yet still, the whispers flowed. *"Hold on, child. Hold on. He doesn't own your soul."*

Zeb Turner watched the scene with satisfaction, his overseer stepping forward with chains in hand. Evalina's struggle intensified as the cold metal was fastened around her neck. The overseer tugged the chain roughly, forcing her to her knees before yanking her back to her feet.

"Now," Nathaniel said to Zeb Turner. "We had an agreement. Five hundred dollars for the woman and the boy."

"You'll get your money," he snapped, reaching into his coat for a pouch of coins. He handed it over without another word. Evalina's tear-streaked face turned toward Nathaniel. "How could you?" she choked out. "You lied. You said we was safe. You said we was family!"

Nathaniel sneered. "These people out here my workers, not my kin. You were just a deal waiting to happen."

Evalina cursed him to hell as she was dragged into the grand carriage, her chains clinking. Thomas was pushed into his mother's arms, eyes red and raw, his tiny sobs muffled against her shoulder. Solomon, Abram, Emma Jane, and the other souls watched. They had seen this before, too many times to count, but never with a child. Nathaniel William had perfected the art of treachery, using his skin to lure in those needy enough to trust him. Runaways came to him seeking refuge, clinging to the hope that someone who shared their suffering would help. He would offer food, shelter, and false promises. While they rested and their guards were down, he would order the other souls to dig. Quietly, persistently, they would ask questions—where they had come from, who owned them, and what price their lives might fetch. The answers determined their fate.

If the reward was high, he sent them back in chains, pocketing the money without a shred of shame. If the price was too low, he sold them elsewhere. Every transaction lined his pockets. The souls watched Evalina's cries fade as the carriage disappeared down the road. They knew better than to speak out, better than to let their hatred show. But inside, they boiled over. Nathaniel was a man who used the one thing that should have united them—their shared skin.

Nathaniel turned to the souls. "What you looking at? Get back to work! Now!" Reluctantly, they turned away. Nathaniel stood tall on the porch, his face proud without remorse. He glanced at the coins in his hand. *A good day's work*, he thought, turning back into the house.

Light struggled to stretch long across Nathaniel William's dining room. He sat at the head of a table, the only one who ever did. No wife, no children, no other family. He preferred it that way, or so he claimed. On rare occasions, another man—a White one, of course—might share a meal. But tonight, Nathaniel dined alone, save for Abram. Nathaniel allowed only one servant in a room with him while he ate. He didn't trust any of them. He could see it in their eyes. He could read their thoughts as easily as if they were spoken aloud. *They think I'm a traitor. They think I'm worse than the White man. Maybe I am.*

Abram stood just outside the dining room. He couldn't get Thomas, the child, out of his mind. The image of Thomas sobbing, his hands reaching for his mother as they were taken away. He was ashamed of his participation in Nathaniel's evil. He couldn't take it anymore. He had listened as Solomon spoke about fires and poison, the ways souls had turned the tables on God's order. Solomon hadn't given instructions outright, but his words came with urgency. As the primary house servant, Abram knew he was the only one who could do it. Poison couldn't be too hard, Abram thought. A sickly stew would do the trick. His fingers had plucked deadly mushrooms from the garden earlier that day. The lye, stolen in small amounts over weeks, had been stored in the corner of the pantry. *Not too much, just get him sicker day by day, a slow, natural dying.*

But as Abram stood, his youth betrayed him. The confident talk in his head didn't translate to his body. The tray he held rattled as he set it down in front of Nathaniel. His fingers fumbled slightly as he adjusted the placement of the bowl full of his favorite stew, a motion that should have taken a second but stretched into an awkward eternity. Sweat beaded on Abram's forehead, despite the coolness of the evening. A single drop trailed down his temple. Abram wiped it away hastily with the sleeve of his shirt.

Nathaniel missed nothing. He watched the boy. He knew he was angry about Evalina and was waiting for when he would turn on him. Abram's every twitch, shift, and glance, all of it spoke volumes. "Sit down, boy," Nathaniel commanded.

Abram stammered out, "G-Got work to do, sir."

"No harm in sitting for a moment, is there?" Nathaniel's finger tapped. Abram's nerves were something deeper, he was frozen still.

"Too much work to be sitting, sir." Nathaniel had learned long ago that fear like that had only one source: *guilt*.

"Why those hands shaking like a leaf? You cold? You nervous 'bout something?"

"J-Just the cold, sir. It's right bitter tonight."

"The cold, you say? Feels just fine to me. Real warm, in fact." He dipped the spoon into the stew, lifting it and letting the thick liquid slide back into the bowl. He dropped the spoon in the bowl. "You made this yourself?"

"Yes, sir," Abram said, his voice strained. "Wanted to fix your favorite, sir."

"My favorite, huh?" Nathaniel said, resting his elbows on the table. "Ain't that thoughtful of you." He stared at the stew for a long moment before lifting his eyes back to Abram. "Go on, then."

Abram blinked. "S-Sir?"

"Go on and have some. You oughta be the first to taste it, seeing as how you worked so hard on it."

Abram's breath stopped. "Already ate, sir. Had my supper earlier."

"Ain't that convenient? But I ain't asking if you hungry. I'm telling you to eat."

Abram shook his head. "I . . . I can't, sir."

Nathaniel stood up. "Can't? What is it you can't do, boy? Swallow your own cooking? Or maybe . . ." He stepped closer. "Maybe there's something in that stew you don't want in you. Is that it? Think I'm too stupid to see it? You gonna eat this, every damn bite, and you gonna swallow it down."

Abram shook his head frantically. "Please, sir, I—"

Nathaniel's hand shot out, grabbing Abram by the collar. "Eat it!" he roared. He shoved Abram's face down to the bowl, the steaming stew splattering on his cheeks. "Open your mouth!"

Abram whimpered, his knees buckling as he tried to pull away. Nathaniel's grip was iron. He forced a spoonful of the stew into Abram's mouth, the young man choking as the liquid slid down his throat.

"Taste good, don't it? Next time you think twice 'fore you try something stupid."

Abram collapsed to the floor, coughing and gasping for air. Nathaniel dropped the bowl beside him. The stew spilled across the wooden planks, pooling in uneven patches of thick, greasy liquid. Nathaniel stood over him. He pointed to the mess on the floor. "You gonna eat every last bit of that stew right off the floor. Go on, lick it up like the dog you are. And if you even think about refusing, I'll take that hand of yours and chop off one of them fingers. Reckon you won't need all ten for what little work you do anyway."

Nathaniel's foot slammed down hard beside the mess.

"Now!" Nathaniel barked. "Get to it, or it's your damn finger. Hell, maybe I'll start with two."

With shaking hands, Abram bent his head, his lips grazing the splattered stew, and began to eat.

"That's it," Nathaniel said. "Lick it clean, boy. Every drop. Don't leave none behind." Abram crawled, dragging his tongue through the muck. Nathaniel crouched, his face on Abram's. "If you get sick, if I so much as hear you cough, I'll know what you was trying. And if that happens . . ." He paused, his heated breath against Abram's ear. "I'll take that head of yours clean off your shoulders and post it right out front of the big house. Let everyone see what happens when you cross Nathaniel William."

Nathaniel gestured to the mess with his finger. "Finish it up. Don't let me see a drop left when I come back." With a final, mocking chuckle, Nathaniel turned and strode out of the dining room.

Nathaniel stood on the front porch of his house, his hands resting on the railing. It was time to make a change. The group he had wasn't working anymore. They were sloppy, tired, or maybe just too comfortable in their misery. It was dangerous to let people think they were irreplaceable. Maybe he'd keep Solomon, he had been with him for years—old and broken as he was, the man at least knew his place. Solomon didn't talk back or challenge him. He was predictable, a quality Nathaniel valued more than strength or skill. But the rest? Useless. He'd clear them out, one way or another, and bring in fresh blood. Harvest season was almost over, a perfect time for some adjustments.

There, among the rows, he spotted Solomon moving, his limp making his progress uneven but determined. "Solomon!"

"Yes, sir," Solomon said as he reached the steps.

"Go inside and check on Abram. Wanna see if he's near dead yet. Wouldn't surprise me none, the weak little bastard.

If he is, clean up whatever mess he left. Can't have the stink hanging around the house." Solomon paused and said nothing for a moment. "You got something to say, Solomon?" Nathaniel growled.

Solomon turned. "No, sir. Just making sure I understand you right."

"Then get on with it."

Abram lay slumped atop a hay pallet on the floor, his body slick with sweat. His stomach fought nausea. Every few minutes, his thin frame jerked with dry heaves that left him weaker than before.

Emma Jane knelt beside him. She was older but still a young woman with a thin frame, hair always in braids; she arrived on Nathaniel's land only a few months ago. She lifted a jug of water to his lips. "Drink, Abram," she urged. He turned his head away, but Emma Jane pressed the cup closer. "You gotta." Abram groaned but finally took sips. Emma Jane shook her head, she didn't have much sympathy. "You a fool, Abram. No other word for it. You don't go messing with poison unless you know what you doing."

Abram wheezed. "I . . . I didn't put enough in to kill him outright. It was . . . it was s'posed to be slow. Make him suffer, like he done to us."

"Slow?" she repeated. "Boy, you barely know how to piss on your own and you out here trying to play God?"

Solomon entered the cabin and took in a sigh when he laid eyes on Abram. He admired his effort but was disappointed in his secrecy. "Why didn't you tell nobody, Abram? Why you go and do this alone?"

"After . . . after Evalina and her crying baby," he said, swallowing hard, the effort costing him. "Was angry. Wasn't thinking clear. Just . . . just needed to do something. Couldn't stand looking at him no more. Couldn't stand it."

"Anger will do that to a man," Solomon said. "Make you blind. But, Abram, you gotta think before you move."

Emma Jane huffed. "Anger or not, this was dumb. You ain't just risked yourself—you risked all of us."

Abram turned his head away as he coughed weakly. "I know it was stupid. I just . . . I couldn't take it no more. Evalina, and that boy of hers . . . they ain't deserve what he done to them."

Emma Jane softened slightly but didn't relent. "None of us deserve what he do, but you gotta be smart. You don't fight a man like Nathaniel with half a plan."

"You alive, and that's what matters right now," Solomon said. "Next time, you come to us first. You hear me?"

Abram nodded, "You think he gonna kill me?"

"No way he's killing you," Emma Jane said in a firm voice. "You too young, too much value to him. You *property.*" Emma Jane looked to Solomon. "But we find another way. Nathaniel William must meet his Maker. Ain't no question 'bout that."

"Burn it all down," Solomon said. "We could burn it all down. Saw it happen once . . . in Virginia. Set fire to the house, to the fields."

"You ain't thinking either," Abram said to Solomon. "What happens after, huh? We burn it down, then what? They hunt us down. We burned alive or worse."

"But some of 'em got away, Abram," Emma Jane said. "Maybe we all won't make it, but if just a few of us did, wouldn't that be enough? And what's better? Staying here, living in chains, watching him do worse?"

"I didn't get away, I couldn't." Solomon looked down at his foot, the shape of it a frustrating reminder. Solomon had run with the others. For a while, he kept pace, adrenaline numbing the familiar pain in his twisted foot. But the rocky ground betrayed him, and his limp dragged him down. As he struggled, he knew the others were moving ahead without him. He had shouted after them, "Go on! Don't wait for me!" The group hesitated, but Solomon waved them off again. "Don't waste your freedom on me!" And so they left, while Solomon found refuge beneath an old tree, its roots curling protectively around him. He'd hoped it would be enough, that the hollow would hide him until the patrols moved on. But by morning, they found him, and he was soon on an auction block. Solomon knew he'd never run again. Too many months and years later, time hadn't just aged him—it had worn him down into something smaller. Maybe Abram was right. Solomon's chance was gone, buried under years of suffering, but the boy still had something—like Henri, Ruby, and Luke, many years ago on Goochland's Magnolia Row.

Abram broke up Solomon's thoughts. "But . . . what about this war? Ain't the Union fighting to end all this? Frederick Douglass got Lincoln to let colored men fight. I heard Nathaniel babbling about it to himself. He sure hates Frederick Douglass."

"That war ain't for us," Emma Jane said dismissively. "You think Lincoln care about us? He just like all the rest. My mama got snatched up on account of that runaway slave act. You know who backed that? Lincoln, that's who."

Abram frowned. "How you know all that?"

Emma Jane shook her head. "'Cause I listen. Always watching and listening. You gotta know what's going on. It's the only way to stay ahead."

"But . . . from what I'm hearing," Solomon said, "the war ain't going well for the South."

"Maybe, maybe not." Emma Jane shrugged. "But freedom ain't coming quick enough for us, not with Nathaniel. That man's destroying us now, and if we wait for the Union or Douglass or Lincoln to save us, we all be dead before they do." Abram nodded weakly, his hands trembling as he drank more water. Emma Jane watched him with a mix of frustration and tenderness, before she turned and motioned for Solomon to follow her outside.

It was a moonless night. Emma Jane walked a few paces ahead, lantern in hand, leading the way. Swathed in a thick blanket, the hem of her dress peeked out beneath. Solomon trailed her, shoulders hunched in his coat. Emma Jane did not meet his eyes right away, only nodded toward the path leading beyond the row of shacks.

"Come," she whispered.

"Where?" Solomon asked.

"Something I must do." They walked in silence, Emma Jane adjusting her pace to match Solomon's. They moved toward a half-forgotten corner of the William plantation. A graveyard.

Emma Jane squinted at him. "Our own buried out here?"

Burial grounds weren't something you talked about. Not in front of certain folks. His mouth opened, closed, then he spoke, nodding toward the tree line. "They out there, where the brush grows thick. I build the boxes and lay them west, so they face east in the next world. That's the one thing Nathaniel let me do, give a proper burial."

"Take me there," Emma Jane ordered.

They reached an untamed edge, where thin clumps of fern crowded around weathered wooden markers stretching beyond the trees. No stone, no marble, just rough planks and a bit of carving to mark who rested beneath. As Emma Jane shined the light, Solomon reflected on the small mounds and shallow dips in the earth, trying to remember how many he'd placed here. How many tiny coffins for newborns barely given a chance. *More babies and children than grown folks*, Solomon thought.

Emma Jane shivered. "I can feel them," her voice barely above a breath. The way the blanket clung to Emma Jane's bony, pointy shoulders gave her an otherworldly presence like she had been sculpted from the black night itself. Her ageless face was silvered by the lantern's light. Solomon shifted uneasily.

Without another word, Emma Jane crouched and set down a large mason jar she had carried snug against her hip. "Hold this," she said, giving the lantern to Solomon. From within her dress, she carefully withdrew four long nails, dark and irregular. Then she produced a straight razor, its handle dull with age. She held it up, letting the light catch its blade. Solomon's stomach tightened when he saw the dried smears on it. "That's Nathaniel's razor," Solomon said, worry knotting his voice. "Why . . . why you have that?"

Emma Jane's eyes pinned him. "Every morning, he uses this against his own flesh. Nicks himself, leaves a bit of himself behind. His life clings to it."

Solomon's heart thrummed like a rabbit's heart in the dark. "Emma Jane, this ain't . . . this ain't what we s'posed to be doing. Christ, you scaring me."

She began to scrape at the earth with her fingernails, pushing aside leaves and brittle twigs. "Maybe all that Christ-like talk is what's keeping us weak and waiting," Emma Jane said as she dug deeper, her fingertips darkening with soil. "We need something else. Something that reminds him he ain't above judgment."

Emma Jane pressed her hand into the dirt, cupping it carefully and lifting a good measure into the mason jar. The soil came loose in clumps, as the scent of earth rose between them. "The dirt from the grave of a warrior. Every slave is a warrior." She took the four nails and pushed them in, their heads gleaming before they disappeared into the dirt in the mason jar. She slid Nathaniel's bloodstained razor into the jar, the blade angled downward as if anchoring everything else in place. She shut her eyes and lowered her head, whispering words too quiet for Solomon to catch. The wind hissed softly, and he felt certain that if he leaned in, he might hear the pulse of the dead. Emma Jane's face grew fierce. Not belligerent but focused, as though summoning something mightier than anyone living could remember. Something that lived in the marrow of bones, in the songs of the dead before their time.

When Emma Jane looked up, there was a gleam in her eyes that made Solomon's heart skip. "Can't fight him alone," she said with conviction. "We need them. They will help us now."

Solomon bowed his head. The fields were quiet, yet it felt as though a hundred whispers had begun moving through the branches overhead. He did not know if this was right or wrong, but he knew that Nathaniel's cruelty had to end. If this was a way to call forth justice—if this could help them endure, resist, survive—then it needed to be done.

Emma Jane sealed the mason jar, pressing it tight, and stood. She held it close to her chest as the lantern's light caught her face again, stern and beautiful. She turned to Solomon. "Come," she said. "We must leave them in peace." Without another word, they stepped through the underbrush, disappearing into the dark.

The plotting began. Each person had a role. Emma Jane would gather supplies from the main house under the guise of fetching linens. Abram, weak but determined, would scout out Nathaniel's routines. Solomon played docile but was analyzing when Nathaniel was the most vulnerable. But every step brought more complications. Nathaniel's routine shifted unexpectedly. He was perpetually alert, always calculating. Nightly, they gathered to reassess, but there was invariably a different turn from Nathaniel. He sensed the undercurrent of tension on his plantation. He could feel it in the chatter that stopped the moment he appeared and in the unnecessary kindness from the souls. A curtsy or a too-wide smile did not fool Nathaniel.

Nathaniel penned a letter to Minister Woodward, the preacher man who handled his sales. He had plans to expand his holdings, to procure a larger property nearby, and the timing couldn't have been more perfect for a shake-up. He had seen too much camaraderie. That kind of closeness was dangerous. It bred disobedience. It was time to scatter their bonds. Abram, for one, had become a thorn in his side. The boy had never been properly punished for that foolhardy poisoning stunt. Abram should have been made an example of then, but now the opportunity was ripe. Selling him would be an unmistakable message to the rest. It was a twofold plan: extinguish any sparks of rebellion and profit from the purge. When the minister arrived, the plantation would not just be shaken, it would be reforged. Examples would be made, and Abram might very well be the first. Nathaniel signed the letter to Minister Woodward, sealing it with wax.

Nathaniel William paced the front porch of his house, his hands nervous with anticipation. Minister Woodward wanted to come to see the property up close and even agreed to a meal. Though he had entertained White men before, hosting a man of the minister's stature made his chest swell with pride and greed. *A White man in this house! Sharing a meal!* It was more than an honor; it was validation.

Nathaniel ran down the orders. "You there! Get those floors scrubbed till they shine! And you, fetch the best wine. Best, you hear? None of that cheap swill!" His eyes scrutinized the kitchen, where pots clanged and steam billowed from the windows. "Move faster! Ain't got all day!" The minister was no ordinary guest. He was a man of God, a neighboring plantation owner with a reputation for efficient operations. Even more tantalizing, Minister Woodward was in the market to buy slaves to ship further south.

Everything was ready for the minister's arrival. The house was cleaned to perfection, the finest linens adorned the dining table, and the dining room carried the rich aroma of roasted chicken, fresh bread, and spiced apples. When the minister's carriage finally rattled up the long dirt drive, Nathaniel sprang into action. Minister Woodward was a man of contradictions. Tall and imposing, with a mane of silver hair that glinted in the sunlight as a false halo. He carried himself with divine authority. His tailored suits were immaculate, accented by the white collar. But it was his voice that truly set him apart—a booming baritone that reached into the malformed hearts of his diaphanous congregation. His sermons were theatrical, his hands gesturing toward heaven as if God himself had placed the whip in his hand. The congregants, wealthy planters and merchants, nodded fervently, assured that their sins were virtues in Woodward's gospel. For them, he was not just a preacher but a prophet, justifying their demand for gain with the infallibility of divine will. He hosted gatherings where the wealthiest men of Charleston would dine and discuss which families to tear apart next, all under fellowship and faith. To them, slave markets were a holy place, a site where they enacted God's will on earth. These were the gatherings Nathaniel prayed on his knees to be invited to.

The minister descended from the carriage, his eyes casing the surroundings before seeing Nathaniel. "Minister Woodward!" Nathaniel greeted him with an exaggerated bow. "An honor, sir, an absolute honor to have you here!"

The minister nodded curtly, allowing Nathaniel to lead him inside. The souls lined the path, heads low, their presence a display of Nathaniel's "success." Inside, the dining room shined with the effort of hours of scrubbing. Nathaniel gestured to the table, where a fine meal was laid out.

"Only the best for you, sir," Nathaniel said, pulling out a chair for Minister Woodward at the head of the table.

The minister sat, his posture straight. He took in the room, dissecting every detail, red wine already poured in glasses, the candelabra, and most notably, the enslaved who served along the edges of the room. Nathaniel, ever the eager host, gave a wide smile that didn't reach his eyes. "How was the ride? Not too rough, I hope?"

Minister Woodward, always the drinker, took a sip of his wine before answering. He caught a look at Emma Jane standing against the door, sizing her up from the braids in her hair to her feet. "Smooth enough, though these roads don't get any better, do they?" He turned to Nathaniel. "Your place here, though—it's fine. Real fine. House is sturdy, clean. You keep it well."

Nathaniel's chest swelled at the compliment. "Only the best, sir. Make sure of it. Ain't no sloppiness tolerated 'round here."

Minister Woodward nodded, his eyes shifting to the men standing by the wall. "Strong stock. How many you got working these fields?"

"Only eleven to be exact," Nathaniel said as the food was placed on the table. "Each one knows their place, knows what's expected. I like a small group. How I keep things running smooth. Don't even have an overseer here. I'm the overseer."

The minister raised an eyebrow, his fingers tapping on the stem of his wineglass. "If they don't respect you, they'll walk all over you."

"Oh, they respect me, all right. No question 'bout that!"

Minister Woodward cut into his roast as his eyes went to Emma Jane, mentally cataloging her again. Emma Jane stared back. "You breed any?"

Nathaniel bit into his roast, only after Minister Woodward, wiping his mouth with a cloth napkin. "I do. Ain't nothing wasted here. You tell me what you need, and I make it happen."

Minister Woodward settled in his chair. "You're a businessman, Nathaniel. I like that." The minister gestured with his glass toward the field visible through the window. "This land of yours," his tone probing, "it's good land. Fertile. But it takes the right kind of hand to make it work. You ever think 'bout what'll happen if those Yankees get their way in this Civil War? This talk of abolition?"

Nathaniel scoffed, shaking his head. "Abolish slavery? Madness. Colored folks ain't got the sense to work on their own. Ruin the economy. You let 'em loose, they'll be wandering like sheep without a shepherd."

The minister chewed slowly. "Well, slavery isn't just the backbone of our economy—it's the will of God Almighty. The Good Book says it plain: '*Servants, be obedient to them that are your masters.*'[25] Without our guidance, these poor souls would indeed wander, lost and aimless, like the Israelites in the wilderness."

"Oh, yes, sir. Amen!"

"Ain't often you meet a negro who . . . understands the value of God's work."

"I see it clear. We tear it down, and everything falls."

"I've always said there's value in letting a handful of coloreds own slaves. Just a few crumbs. Gives them a stake in the institution, see? Makes them less likely to side with abolitionists. But—" He studied Nathaniel. "It's a rare breed that can pull it off. Most don't have the stomach for it."

Nathaniel chuckled. "Well, sir, I'm cut from different cloth."

Minister Woodward lifted his wine. "But the Confederacy's taking a beating. We lost New Orleans awhile back. An embarrassment. Our grand General Lee isn't the man we prayed for. He's stumbling 'round like a drunk in Sunday

25. *Ephesians* 6:5, King James Version.

clothes. Keep this up, he'll be crying surrender before the next harvest."

Nathaniel stiffened, trying to keep his face smooth. "I . . . I wouldn't count us out yet. I'm sure slavery will remain."

"You think so?" He leaned forward, his demeanor shifting, elbows on the table, ignoring the fine manners Nathaniel worked so hard to uphold. "You think just because you bought your freedom and got a few slaves chained under your roof, you'll be safe?" Nathaniel stopped chewing. "You might know how to count your coins, but you don't know how White men do their business behind closed doors. That's why I came here today . . . To remind you."

Nathaniel glanced nervously at the minister's hands resting near the polished silver. He could feel the tension knotting in his stomach. Maybe Zeb Turner had gotten to the minister and complained about the terms of their trade. "What y'all doing behind closed doors?"

Minister Woodward laughed spitefully. "Slavery ending, all right. 'Great Emancipator,' Abraham Africanus himself already thinking how to coddle us after this war, handing out pardons like candy, making sure the Confederate boys can come home. You think we'll just vanish?" He spread his hands wide, smirking at the fine tablecloth. "That is not God's will. We'll ditch the word *slavery*—call it something else—and keep these folks shackled by debt and circumstance, tied to this land like a mule to a plow. Looks pretty on paper, but nothing will change."

Nathaniel's throat tightened. "And . . . what about me? I'm free, got property. What's that mean for me in this new . . . arrangement?" Nathaniel had not felt the sting of the whip in decades, had not stood shaking in a field while a White overseer rattled orders, had not tasted blood and sweat just to draw another breath. He had grown used to the idea that his papers, his property, his ability to own, would shield him and only him. But according to the minister, once the old system fell, it would be reassembled with new chains. And when that time came, if those who held true power decided they no longer needed a man like him—this unusual figure who served their purposes only as a showpiece—his flimsy documents and carefully cultivated airs would mean nothing. He could easily find himself back at the margins. Nathaniel's hand hovered over his fork, but he no longer had any appetite.

"You have an unimpeachable reputation," Minister Woodward said. "Unimpeachable. But when all this is done, when this war is lost and we dress up the old ways in new clothes . . . well, we'll see how unimpeachable you really are."

A clatter broke into their conversation. Abram stumbled, dropping a bowl of gravy. The dish shattered, splashing onto Minister Woodward's lap. The souls froze. Emma Jane squeezed her eyes shut. Solomon shook his head. Abram dropped to his knees, stammering apologies as he tried to clean up the mess. The minister's face darkened and his eyes shot toward Nathaniel. Minister Woodward's expectation was obvious.

Nathaniel stood slowly. He grabbed Abram by the collar and yanked him to his feet. Nathaniel turned to Minister Woodward.

"You see," Nathaniel began, his voice measured as though this were a rehearsed performance. "Discipline is the foundation of order. I don't tolerate laziness or disobedience. These people"—he motioned dismissively to Abram—"they require a firm hand. No softness." Solomon and Emma Jane locked eyes.

Minister Woodward dabbed at his soiled pants with a cloth. Nathaniel continued. "Minister Woodward, I think it's only proper we step outside. Lessons are learned best in the open air." He grabbed Abram by the arm and pulled him to his feet.

The trio stepped out as the other souls watched from the

window. Emma Jane chanted in her mind while Solomon prayed. Nathaniel yanked Abram toward the whipping post, tying the young man's wrists to the wood. The minister stood a few paces back. His eyes followed Nathaniel's every move, noting the finesse, the ceremonial way he handled the whip. Minister Woodward had witnessed many whippings in his time—too many to count—but this felt different. There was . . . joy.

Nathaniel ripped off Abram's shirt and cracked the whip against the ground. He glanced back to the minister, flashing his gummy, crooked-tooth grin before delivering the first strike. The whip sliced through the air with a whistle, landing with a thwack against Abram's back. He cried out, his body jerking against the restraints. Nathaniel's eyes burned. He wasn't merely punishing; he was performing. Each strike was exaggerated. He was drunk on absolute power.

The minister's minor smile faded. The display unsettled him in a way he didn't expect. He had seen plenty of White men use the whip, but there was something pestilential about seeing a negro deliver such punishment. It wasn't just the viciousness, but the way Nathaniel feasted on it. Nathaniel was too invested in his authority, too consumed by it. *What if this power turned inward?* the minister thought. *What if this negro decides one day he's above not just his own kind, but the rest of us?*

Nathaniel delivered one more resounding blow, stepping away and admiring his work as if he'd completed a masterful painting. Abram slumped against the post. Nathaniel turned to the minister. "Discipline," he said, his voice self-assured. "Discipline is what keeps order. That boy won't forget this lesson anytime soon."

Minister Woodward's thoughts were elsewhere. "Discipline's one thing. But don't forget who you are."

Nathaniel's smile faltered. "Simply saying," he stated cautiously, "that we share the same philosophy. Hard work, discipline—these are the marks of a good master, wouldn't you agree?"

Minister Woodward knew Nathaniel needed a reminder. He didn't listen to Zeb Turner, but he would listen to him. "No matter how many slaves you own, no matter how brutal you get, you'll never be one of us. You might wear fine clothes," the minister continued. "But don't forget, you're still a negro. You were born a negro, and you'll die a negro. And when you do, your body will rot in a negro's grave."

Nathaniel's nostrils flared, but he took a breath. He wanted to scream. There had to be a way to make the minister see—make all the White men see—that he was not just another negro. He was a man of wealth, of power, of means. He had fought for everything he had, clawed his way up from nothing, and had done so with the success that rivaled any White planter. *From cotton to master.* But Nathaniel couldn't let himself dwell on it. He wouldn't let his mind turn against a White man, a man whose approval still mattered to him. Instead, his thoughts traveled elsewhere. Maybe it was his slaves. Yes, that had to be it. They hadn't performed well enough. They'd embarrassed him, made him look weak. That was the problem. Not Minister Woodward. Never Minister Woodward.

"Well," the minister said. "It's time for me to depart."

Nathaniel begged, "Surely you don't have to leave so soon. There's still a fine meal waiting on the table—even a peach cobbler. Made sure everything was prepared just right for your visit."

"I appreciate your hospitality, but as you can see"—he gestured to the stain on his pants—"this isn't the kind of evening I care to extend."

Panicked to regain some footing, Nathaniel begged. "Allow

me to walk you to your carriage, sir," he offered. "It's the least I can do."

"No need for that," he said. "Tend to your mess here. You got plenty to clean up. Good day."

Nathaniel nodded. "Good day. Safe travels."

Minister Woodward didn't look back as he climbed into his carriage. "Keep your place," he called over his shoulder. "You'll live longer, by the grace of God."

The Whites in Charleston, South Carolina, had turned on Nathaniel William. He'd thought he was one of them—or at least, closer to their favor than any Black man could expect to be—but Minister Woodward had made it plain otherwise. He refused to sell any of Nathaniel's slaves. Zeb Turner, ever eager to stir trouble, had gone further, ensuring the slave patrols stayed close to Nathaniel's plantation. "Don't want none of them ending up in William's hands. He ain't getting a dime from us."

Even worse, Minister Woodward demanded Nathaniel repay Zeb Turner for selling Evalina and her child back to him. Notices began arriving with regularity, each one more insistent than the last. The first was almost polite:

Mr. William,
You are hereby reminded of the outstanding debt owed to this parish for the transaction regarding Evalina and her child. The sum of $1,000 is now due to the parish. Please remit payment promptly.

They had doubled the price. Due to the ongoing war, whatever wealth he'd once claimed was tied up in slaves he couldn't buy or trade. Minister Woodward's tone shifted with the second notice:

Mr. William,
Your failure to pay the sum owed has not gone unnoticed. This parish does not tolerate dereliction of duty, particularly when it concerns matters as delicate as the purchase of labor. You will remit payment or face an announced visit to settle the debt by other means.

Minister Woodward's note was clear. If Nathaniel could not pay the debt, they would take what he had—livestock, tools, anything of value to settle the balance. Zeb Turner had ensured Nathaniel's name was poison in Charleston.

With every passing month it became clearer that the Confederacy was faltering. Word filtered back of battles lost, of cities falling, of the Union's advance. Then came the stories of Black troops, their numbers swelling, their bravery turning the tide. The sight of Black men—some fresh from plantations—marching under the Union banner was a blow the South hadn't anticipated, many of them ordered to go to abandoned or barely functioning plantations. It wasn't just the manpower they brought; it was the symbolic destruction of everything the Confederacy stood for. But the likes of Zeb Turner and Minister Woodward were preparing.

Nathaniel wouldn't believe it. Not South Carolina. "The first to secede shall be the last to fall," he said to himself often, gripping his shotgun tighter as he paced the front porch. He refused to acknowledge the signs, even when the distant boom of battle reverberated through his land. Then the Union blockade choked Charleston's ports. The news of plantations burned, their masters driven out. Even as the Confederate currency lost its value and deserters swelled the countryside, Nathaniel clung to his delusion.

Moreover, he was forced to live with the few slaves he still had—Solomon, Emma Jane, Abram, and the others—and every day he trusted them less. Paranoia consumed him. Nathaniel began cooking all his meals himself, barring anyone from the kitchen. He kept a shotgun by his side at all times, even while he slept. The house grew silent and still. The fields went untended, the estate slipping into disrepair as Nathaniel spiraled further into his own mind.

Emma Jane loved to watch him. "Man done lost his mind," she said one day, twisting the lid off the mason jar with the graveyard dirt. She turned it slowly, her fingers methodical as she pulled out the nails. "Twist it slow, make sure it stays in place."

Abram, restless and simmering with anger, would tell Emma Jane, "We gotta strike now. He weak. What we waiting for?"

"Patience, young man," she said. "Ain't no sense in rushing when we can do it right. You want him gone, don't you? Gone for good?"

Solomon nodded. "Emma Jane's right. You rush, you risk everything. We been waiting this long. We can wait a little longer." They weren't waiting for outside liberation or salvation of any kind. Emma Jane's plan hinged on Nathaniel's complete vulnerability. She wanted him cornered at his weakest point, when he'd be less likely to fight back or summon help, when no one would dare come to his rescue. Maybe he'd be too far gone in his own arrogance to sense the threat gathering around him. Whenever that moment arrived, they'd be ready. Emma Jane's calm certainty kept the others prepared.

So they waited, watching as Nathaniel's worry deepened. His footsteps would fill the house as he paced. The once-immaculate corridors now held the stale stink of rotting food. Gone were the days of his careful grooming and pressed linens. He moved through the rooms in a daze, shirtless, his belly straining outward in an ungainly curve. Always with a bottle of whiskey in his hand, grease and crumbs clung to his chin, and where a starched collar had once encircled his neck, only a ring of old skin oil remained. He was unraveling, body and mind both slipping. "Can't trust none of 'em," he grumbled. "All gonna turn on me, every last one." He paused, glancing out the window at the fields, now overgrown and wild. "First South Carolina, now my own damn house. Ain't nothing sacred no more."

The mayor of Charleston, South Carolina, surrendered the city to Union Brigadier General Alexander Schimmelfennig on a frigid morning in February 1865. The heart of the Confederacy was crashing, its grand cities falling one by one. The war was nearing its bitter conclusion, but the isolated souls on Nathaniel William's plantation had no idea how near the forces of freedom were. The signs of collapse had been there for months. Union victories were everywhere. But the plantation, secluded and consumed by Nathaniel's paranoia, remained cut off from the world.

It was Solomon who saw them first. Three Union soldiers approached the house on horseback. All three were Black men in Union blue. The uniforms fit like they were made for kings, the indigo wool pristine. Gold buttons ran in a line down their chests. Each man wore a hat tilted low over their faces. Across their backs, rifles rested, and leather straps cut diagonally across their broad shoulders. On horseback, their boots, black and shining, hit the stirrups. Solomon had never seen Black men like this before. These weren't men under someone's thumb. These men weren't just soldiers. They were freedom personified.

These Black men had come to this land, their presence alone a rebuke to everything enslavers stood for. They were the reckoning. Solomon saw what freedom looked like, and it was Black, shining, and unstoppable. Solomon's legs felt weak beneath him, his good eye brimming with tears that threatened to spill. The others gathered quickly, Abram smiling for what felt like the first time in his bound life.

Only Nathaniel balked at the sight, wrapped in a moth-eaten wool coat, its seams frayed and collar stained with sweat and old tobacco. Gone were the velvet suits and gold watches; now his shirt hung untucked, its yellowed linen streaked with grease, and his suspenders sagged over his fat shoulders. He stood on the porch, shotgun in hand, squinting in fury. The sight of Black soldiers approaching set his blood to boiling. These uniformed men with their heads high and their spines straight were an insult, a direct challenge to the world he had shaped. Their coats were clean, their boots steady against the dirt of *his* land. It was all wrong. Black men were meant to serve, to toil, to lower their eyes when men like him passed. Not this, not marching onto *his* property as if they had any right, claim, or authority.

"This my property!" he roared, his voice cracking. "I own this land, this house, everything here!"

The shorter soldier dismounted, his boots against the gravel as he leveled his rifle at Nathaniel. "Put that shotgun down." The two other soldiers, still on their horses, grabbed their rifled muskets. "South Carolina has surrendered. There will be no more slavery in this state."

Nathaniel tightened his grip on the shotgun. "Got nerve stepping foot on my land! Don't care what uniform you wear, this is my property! I own this house, this land! I'll die 'fore I let you take it!"

The shorter soldier had confusion on his face with the rifle still pointed at Nathaniel. "You own this land?" he asked. "A colored man, owning land?" He looked Nathaniel up and down, then glanced back at his two comrades on their horses. "Never seen no colored man like you. Most we seen own their kin, trying to protect 'em. And when we show up, they're glad to see us. But you? You got the stink of something else."

"That's right. I'm the master, same as any White man! This

land! These people! They mine! Built this with my own hands!"

Abram stepped forward. "Yes, yes, he a slave owner—just like the White man, but worse! Made Black folks think this land was safe, but it was a trap! He sell 'em back, for a fee, back to the White folks!"

Emma Jane, her slender frame towering, stepped beside Abram. "He ain't no better than the devil himself," she said with the dirt-filled mason jar in her hand. "Talking 'bout owning us, like we ain't flesh and blood, like we ain't his own people. He worse than a master, he's a monster."

"You best think real hard about what you do next," the soldier said to Nathaniel. "Drop that shotgun, or I'll make sure you ain't standing to pick it up again."

Nathaniel hesitated, sweat beading on his shiny forehead as his grip on the shotgun loosened. He held it for a second longer before letting it clatter to the ground. "There," he spat.

"Now, we gonna have a little talk about what you been doing on this land."

Solomon was in a trance as he stared at the other two soldiers on horseback. The world blurred around him—the voices, the fields, even Nathaniel—all of it faded. His good eye remained fixed on the taller soldier, scanning every detail as if his mind couldn't quite trust what it was seeing. He slowly limped forward, making the soldier turn to him.

Solomon blinked hard, willing himself to focus, to separate reality from the tricks his beat-down mind might be playing. He'd imagined plenty over the years. But this? This felt different. The way the soldier sat in the saddle, the set of his shoulders, the shape of his face—it tugged at a memory buried so deep, Solomon wasn't sure it was even real. His eyes felt like family. Then the soldier turned his head to look at his fellow soldier.

With the turn of the head, Solomon saw it. The jagged scar

of a half missing ear, a mark decades had not erased. The sight jolted Solomon like a lightning strike. His vision tunneled on that scar as if it were the only thing in the world.

"Luke . . ." Solomon whispered. His legs moved before his mind could catch up. "Name Luke?"

He stared at Solomon for a long moment. There was something familiar in the way the man stood. Disjointed memories began to surface, the limp, the eye patch that left only one stormy gray eye visible. That gray eye was in his mind like a phantom. There was only one man he'd ever known with eyes like that. A name was on the tip of his tongue. Was this man someone he once knew? *Maybe you come back for me, one day*, he remembered hearing eons ago. Before he could form the thought, Solomon reached up, pulling off his dirty eye patch to reveal a scarred socket. "It's me," he said. "It's Solomon . . . Magnolia Row, in Goochland."

Luke's breath caught. He dismounted, his boots hitting the ground. The other soldier lowered his rifle and followed suit. "Solomon?" Luke repeated, his voice breaking.

The two men closed the distance between them to embrace, their souls intertwining across three decades of survival.

Luke pulled back, his hands resting on Solomon's shoulders, his eyes taking in every detail of his face. They were nearly the same age, but Solomon was worn down. He could have passed for Luke's father. Luke had seen men march through bullet wounds, through fever, through hell itself, but human slavery was worse than war. Decades in this machine of misery had bowed Solomon's spine. But it was his eye that haunted Luke the most. One remained steely, still a beautiful stormy grey. The other was lost, a reminder of Montgomery Ragland's cruelty, the price Solomon paid for trying to escape Magnolia Row. "It's been thirty years . . . what happened to you after Magnolia Row?" Luke asked.

Solomon's face cracked into tears. They weren't the tears of an old man, they were the cries of his boyhood. "Tried to run," he choked out. "But couldn't keep up. My foot . . . it wouldn't let me. Told 'em to go on, don't wait for me. They left, and the patrols found me. Been all over since then. Sold off to anyone who'd take me. I'm useless, Luke. This limp, this eye . . . what good am I? Just ended up here. No place else for me."

"Not useless," Luke said fiercely. "You survived, Solomon. That's more than most of us can say." Solomon shook his head. "I made it, all the way up to Massachusetts," Luke revealed. "Built a life there. It wasn't easy, but it was better. I worked, saved up, and when the war broke, I joined the Union Army—when Lincoln let us fight. Thought if I could fight, maybe I could make something right."

Solomon blinked through his tears, staring at Luke like he was a ghost. "You . . . you made it all the way up there? How? How'd you do it?"

"Ruby, it was all her," he said. "Ruby was with me. She knew which way to go. Took a woman to lead us. We made it out together. She's good, Solomon. Married now, got herself a husband who loves her, and she fights against slavery every day. Every single day."

"I . . . I remember Henri dying. All that blood," Solomon said.

Luke gave a knowing nod. "Don't let them take what they can't touch . . . you remember Josephine?"

"Course I do. How could I forget?"

"We lost Josephine that night . . . all the chaos. We searched for her, but we couldn't find her. Broke Ruby for years. Thought we'd never know what happened." He gestured to the soldier standing nearby, a presence of charm and swagger. "This here is Larkin Butler. Turns out . . . he met Josephine on another plantation in Goochland. She got him to freedom."

Larkin tipped his hat slightly, his voice rich. "It's true. Josephine told me about Magnolia Row and about the fire. She said y'all had lit the way for us. She got me out of the devil's hands and into freedom, but . . ." He paused. "She fell ill not long after. Stayed with her as long as I could. She didn't make it, but I made her a promise: I'd keep fighting. For her. For all of us."

Solomon's eyes brimmed with tears. "Josephine . . . that's why you fighting in this war?"

Larkin nodded but paused. "Didn't stop losing people. After Josephine, I found a wife, Charity. Got her free up in Pennsylvania. We had two little girls—my whole world. But that devil of a man, her old master, come claiming she was his, and so were my babies." He shook his head. "Had some fancy lawyer, too—fellow who's up in Congress now, talking high about ending slavery like he doesn't have blood on his hands. Like he didn't tear my family clean apart."

His voice shifted to pure strength. "But I got them back. I worked with some abolitionists to get them free. We live in Vermont now," Larkin continued. "But when they said colored men could fight . . . I knew I had to join. Couldn't just stand by, it's for them. For Charity. For my girls. For Josephine."

"Me and Larkin—God brought us together in the Colored Men's Fourteenth Infantry," Luke said to Solomon. "I didn't even know he knew about Magnolia Row, but when we started talking . . . it was like we were always meant to meet. Like everything from that fire got us together."

One flame, one uprising, had set an entire generation ablaze with audacity. The story traveled farther than the ashes of the plantation itself, from one plantation to the next, passed through the Underground Railroad, and told in campfires among soldiers who'd once been enslaved. The Black Union troops that raided plantations knew the stories. Many of the men had come from places just like Magnolia Row, where violence reigned but hope had never died. Now, they sought justice, not just for themselves, but for those who had never lived to see freedom. Many former slaves with muskets in hand were ordered to raid these plantations, knowing they could talk to the enslaved in the ways White soldiers couldn't. And they did so with purpose, striking back at the so-called master class.

"What do you reckon we do here?" the other soldier asked, with Nathaniel still held at gunpoint on the porch.

"Hold on, Private Irvin . . . who's the master here?" Luke asked Solomon. "Are they telling the truth?"

Solomon turned his head, his good eye locking onto Nathaniel. "It's him . . . Nathaniel William. Black man owning Black people. Everything Abram and Emma Jane said true. He worse than the Whites."

Luke marched toward the porch with Larkin following. They stood over Nathaniel as he sat against the door of his house. "You want to be a White man, don't you?"

Nathaniel backed farther against the door. "I-I own this land!" he cried. "You got no right!"

Luke drew up his rifle. "I'm going to give you a bullet right between the eyes."

Nathaniel's body pressed against the oak door. His face twisted as he looked to the souls staring at him: Abram, Emma Jane, Solomon, and the others. "Clothed you! Fed you!" he spat, his voice rising, his entire body shaking with fury. "You ungrateful *bucks!* You be *dead* without me! Who kept you all together? *Who?*" His voice cracked, his spittle flying, his eyes wild as he swung his gaze between Luke, Larkin, and the others who had gathered. "Ain't none of y'all nothing but a pack of low, thieving *darkies!*"

Luke's rifle didn't move.

Nathaniel's fingers twitched. "You think 'cause you got on

that blue coat you something? Think you better than me? You ain't nothin' but a *coon* prancing 'round in Massa Lincoln's rags! A pig in silk, it's still a pig! And you"—his eyes flashed to Larkin—"you no better than a damn field *buck*, swinging that rifle, acting like you worth more than the dirt you sleep in! You a bunch of wild African moon crickets!"

He let out a strangled, bitter laugh, his teeth bared like a cornered animal. "Look at you, thinking you free! Ain't *none* of you free! All of you on the Yankee plantation!" Luke pulled back the hammer of his rifle with a click.

Solomon stepped up to the porch, his right leg dragging slightly with the familiar limp that had plagued him for years. He moved closer, eyes locked on Nathaniel. He stopped just inches from Nathaniel's face, so close their noses nearly touched.

"Always thought you could be one of *them*," Solomon said. "Walking 'round here, putting on airs, but you ain't *them.* You ain't never been *them.* And look at you now." Solomon laughed. It was the first laugh he'd had in years. "Ain't never seen no White man backed up against his own damn door, whining like a stray." Solomon paused, his lips in a smile, and then he spat. The glob of saliva struck Nathaniel's cheek, sliding slowly down his skin. Nathaniel's entire body jerked.

"You bastard!" he shrieked. "You damn, filthy coon! After all I done for you negroes!"

Luke had had enough. He took the barrel of his rifle and pressed it hard against Nathaniel's forehead, forcing his head back. Emma Jane watched. This—*this*—was the moment she had been waiting for. Watching the great Nathaniel William, the so-called master, going to hell on his grand oak door. It was better than anything the ancestors ever whispered, but she wanted more.

Luke was ready to pull the trigger as Emma Jane stepped closer. "Stop!" Emma Jane snapped as she stood below the porch steps, the mason jar in her hands. She looked to Luke, Larkin, and Irvin. "Bullet's too easy. Too quick. He made us all suffer. Not gonna let him go with a single shot. That ain't justice. That's mercy. And this man? No mercy." She climbed one step, then another, holding the mason jar as she stood next to Solomon. "You see this?" she said to Nathaniel. "Not just nails and dirt—this every life you took, every chain you kept locked." Solomon, Abram, and the other souls stood behind Emma Jane, murmuring in agreement.

Emma Jane looked to the souls. "Let this devilish house bear his mark forever. Fix him to the door."

The soldiers stepped back as the souls forced Nathaniel's body up and slammed him against the oak door of his wretched house. It was more than a door. He had worshipped that oak door, the threshold he crossed as a master, standing tall and self-assured while others cracked under his rule. That porch, with its warped boards and sagging steps, had been his throne, the place where he issued orders and punished dissent. It was where he had stood, shotgun in hand, declaring his damnation over the souls he had claimed as property. Now, the door would become his grave.

A soul grabbed one of Nathaniel's flailing arms and wrenched it outward, pinning it flat against the door. The other souls helped. They held Nathaniel firm as they forced his body into position. His other arm was stretched out wide, his feet spread apart. Nathaniel screamed, thrashing in vain. Luke, Larkin, and Private Irvin stood, rifles raised but unmoving.

Emma Jane's eyes sparkled as she unscrewed the lid of the mason jar. The four nails were comfortable in the glass, and the grave dirt inside shimmered with Nathaniel's used razor deep at the bottom.

"Put this dirt in his mouth," Emma Jane said to Abram. "Make him feel it."

Abram scooped a handful of the grave dirt from the jar and

slammed it into Nathaniel's mouth. He could still see himself on the floor of the kitchen. The poisoned stew that Nathaniel forced him to eat like an animal. He remembered all of the filthy things that came from his lips, deceiving Evalina, her child, and selling so many others.

Nathaniel gagged and choked, his body convulsing as he tried to spit out the dirt. Solomon, his face ossified with years of pent-up rage, stepped away briefly and returned with a hammer he retrieved from the dying garden. Leaning on his good leg, Solomon stood beside Nathaniel, pulling a dirty nail out of the jar. "Hold him," he ordered as the others tightened their hold.

The first strike of the hammer shattered the air, the sound of metal driving into his palm, blending with Nathaniel's unholy screams. Blood spurted, pooling on the peeling paint of the bright white door. Solomon didn't pause, his strikes meaningful, the hammer driving the nail deeper into his hand, until it embedded fully in the wood. Solomon passed the hammer to Emma Jane.

Emma Jane looked to the soldiers and nodded. She wanted their help. *Every slave was a soldier.* Larkin let out a breath before stepping forward, remembering his years in Gettysburg. "I never figured I'd use my blacksmith's swing on flesh."

Larkin took the other palm. He placed the nail against Nathaniel's skin. The nail bit into him, already slick with sweat, the veins bulging like ropes. With one swift motion, he raised the hammer and brought it down. The sharp clang of the nail punctured skin and tendon. Blood cascaded as Nathaniel let out a bombastic roar. Droplets splattered across Larkin's blue uniform, staining the gold buttons. The blood streamed down Nathaniel's arm, filling the crevices of his elbow before dripping onto the porch. The door splintered faintly but held firm. Luke nodded with approval.

Emma Jane grabbed the hammer's worn handle. She bent over Nathaniel's right leg, pulled from his body, gripping his ankle with one hand to keep it still. His foot jerked, toes curling in an attempt to escape, but the souls held him. She pressed the nail against the center of his foot, feeling the pulse beneath the skin. She lifted the hammer high. Nathaniel screamed before the strike came. The hammer came down in one smooth, brutal arc, ringing out like a church bell. Blood welled instantly, pouring in ribbons. His body shook against the door as he wailed. Emma Jane still had a craving. She raised the hammer again. Another blow. The nail sank deeper, officially fastening him to the wood. Only then did she step back, her fingers tightening around the hammer as she passed it to Luke.

Luke knelt at Nathaniel's feet, seized his left leg, and yanked it outward as the souls kept him still. Nathaniel fought, continued to yell about coons and bucks, but Luke didn't hear him. His mind flashed with images of the past—Henri, his mother, the father he never met, Josephine, and so many others in his nearly fifty years. Luke placed the nail at the center of Nathaniel's foot and raised the hammer, his heart pounding like a war drum. The strike echoed across the veranda. Blood wrapped around Nathaniel's ankle and soaked into the wood. He hadn't seen blood like this since the night he sent Junior to hell in his own bed on Magnolia Row.

With another blow, he saw Henri, broken and bleeding on the porch of Magnolia Row. Luke's teeth ground together. This wasn't just about Nathaniel. This was about everyone—Black or White—who had upheld this vile institution. The hammer connected again and again, the sound of breaking bones mingling with Nathaniel's tortured screams. Luke's face was mottled with blood. With one final, bone-jarring strike, the nail drove into the oak, pinning Nathaniel's body in place.

The door's strong frame refused to break, as though it, too, demanded retribution.

The porch fell silent, save for the sound of Nathaniel's ragged breaths. Blood seeped from his wounds, dripping slowly into the cracks of the wood. Luke stood back, the hammer slipping from his bloodied fingers to the ground with a thud. His eyes didn't leave Nathaniel's broken form, arms and legs splayed and nailed to the door in the shape of an X, like a gnarled ornament. He looked up, past Nathaniel's bloodied face, and felt the presence of something greater. God? Justice? Vengeance? It didn't matter what name it carried.

Solomon stood beside him, his eye locked on Nathaniel's limp body. He thought of the years, the pain, the hopeless nights he'd spent praying for something—anything—to change. Now, here it was, finally delivered. He didn't know if this was God's work or the devil's, but for the first time since he attempted to escape Magnolia Row with his dear friend David, he felt a lightness in his soul.

Abram, standing behind them, crossed his arms over his chest. He'd grown up hearing whispers of a God who saw all, who counted every tear and remembered every injustice. Now, as his eyes burned into Nathaniel, he felt that God was watching. This was divine, holy vengeance.

Emma Jane was satisfied. The mason jar, empty now except for the razor blade, dangled from her fingers. Not one moment of revolt could compensate for a lifetime of betrayals, but satisfaction had arrived.

Larkin stood off to the side. His thoughts drifted to Norman Bruce, the man who had destroyed his family, and to Thaddeus Stevens, the White congressman who now preached abolition. Charity flashed before him—the fire in her eyes as she fought back, the emptiness that came when she was taken, and the joy when she returned with their girls. Nathaniel was still alive, moaning through the dirt in his mouth. The portrait of him nailed to the door of his great house was a vision. "God has showed up," Larkin said aloud.

No one heard the hooves until it was too late. A shriek broke through the chaos, causing everyone to spin around. A man sat atop a horse, his figure draped in the robes of a clergyman. The souls recognized him instantly. It was Minister Woodward. He had come to collect his debt, undeterred by South Carolina's fall or the Union soldiers' presence. Perhaps he thought he aimed to strip the plantation bare before the Yankees got to it. But one look at the scene before him—Nathaniel nailed to the door—stopped him cold.

"What in God's name . . ." Minister Woodward's voice quivered, his fingers on the reins as he saw three Union soldiers and the souls surrounding Nathaniel.

Emma Jane yelled and pointed, "That's the evil preacher man! He sells us off in the name of God!"

The soldiers turned their rifles on him in unison, the metallic clink of muskets being readied. Luke stepped forward, his voice commanding. "Off the horse, now!"

Minister Woodward's eyes spun wildly. "What's this madness?"

"Down!" Luke ordered.

Minister Woodward yanked the reins. He spurred the horse, attempting to flee, but before he could make it far, Larkin's rifle cracked through. The bullet struck the horse's flank, and with a cry, the animal collapsed to the ground, throwing Woodward violently from the saddle.

As he scrambled on the ground, his back in excruciating pain, Emma Jane ordered, "Get him!"

The soldiers seized Minister Woodward. "Release me!" he demanded. "You don't know what kind of trouble you're stirring up. I've got the sheriff's office, the judge, and half the county on my side. Let me go, or I'll bring hell down on every last one of you!"

Emma Jane stepped closer. "He gotta be buried. Get the shovels and follow me."

Luke and Larkin exchanged a glance. What happened here at the William plantation could never leave this place. The generals would never condone such acts, no matter the justice they felt they were delivering. "Private Irvin," Luke ordered, "stay here at the house with the others. Keep watch."

Irvin nodded, not fully aware of what was happening. "Going to the graveyard. Not far," Emma Jane said.

Luke, Larkin, Abram, and Solomon—limping but pushing—dragged the screaming preacher across the brisk plantation. Emma Jane took the lead, she and Abram snatching up shovels along the way. Minister Woodward's head struck against the rocks scattered across the ground, each impact sending pain through his skull. The sharp edges sliced his scalp, smearing streaks of blood. His fingers clawed, gravel embedding themselves under his nails as he tried to slow their march. His nails tore through a patch of brittle cotton stalks with dried plants scratching at his legs through the fabric of his trousers. He quoted scripture in a bid for mercy. "For God shall bring every work into judgment! With every secret thing—whether it be good or evil!"[26] Minister Woodward's feet kicked up dirt, his cries growing hoarse as the graveyard came into view. It was there that Emma Jane had gathered her sacred dirt. Now it would serve another purpose.

They worked quickly as a shallow grave was dug for the man of God. Movement caught Solomon's eye. From one of the shallow dips, something emerged, pale and shining, curling itself from the ground. A pink snake. The serpent pulled

26. *Ecclesiastes* 12:14, King James Version.

him back across decades, to Magnolia Row. Henri's face in the light of the cabin, seeing the snake on its belly, grabbing it and wringing its life out with one grip. The serpent was something more, how Henri saw the world. How he squeezed the existence out of anything that was dangerous, venomous, and deceptive. Solomon gritted his teeth and brought the flat edge of the shovel down on the serpent, splitting it in two. Solomon scooped its pieces into the minister's grave as he continued to scream with madness, "The Lord sees! The Lord sees!"

Emma Jane stood over him as he lay sprawled in the dirt, the grave being dug beside him. "The Lord saw what you did to us," she said. "And now He gonna watch you meet your reckoning."

Minister Woodward was tossed in the grave, landing on his aching back as the first shovelful of dirt hit him. The soil clung to his clergy robe, staining the white collar and smearing his sanctimonious image. He screamed, clawing at the loose soil, moving the dirt away from his face. "Deliver me!" he rasped. "Oh, Lord, deliver me!" He broke into a sob. "Please, I'll pay—whatever you want!" The dirt began to fill his mouth as they chuckled at the irony of his greed saving his soul. Stinking soil slid into his nostrils, forcing him to cough and sputter.

Each of them took turns with the shovels. The grave dirt wasn't just earth—it was packed with the carcasses of those who had been buried without ceremony. Now, it coated Woodward's throat. His lungs fought and hands raked at the sides of the grave. Minister Woodward's fingers curled as the dirt rose higher, creeping over his lips and pressing into his cheeks. His movements grew weaker. He was collapsing against the pressure of God's great earth.

Emma Jane's voice rang out. "The wages of sin is death. And you've earned every last grain of this dirt." The final shovelfuls came quickly, closing over Minister Woodward.

No prayers were said. No stones marked the site. By the time they returned to the house, his ungodly screams were nothing more than a memory in an unmarked grave.

Luke and Larkin took in the William plantation. It looked like so many others they had seen on their journey south. Yet this one had a black face at its helm. *I'm the master! I'm the master!* Nathaniel said. A dire parody of a man so consumed by the mechanism that enslaved him that he became its most faithful servant. Their eyes moved to the house, standing tall, its faded white paint peeling like a shedding skin. A carbon copy of every other plantation house. They were all the same, some more extravagant than others. Columns that strained to look dignified, porches that pretended to welcome, and doors that opened to horrors.

He thought of Henri. His love's blood on the porch of another house like this. His voice, *Burn down master's house. Burn it down, Luke.*

Luke turned to the others. "This house," he said, loud enough for all to hear. "No different than the rest. These houses can't stand." He looked to Solomon, who knew. "Fire is the only cleanser." Although Luke was a soldier, and his actions went against the orders he'd been given, he was far more than a uniform and a rifle. He was a former slave, and his true allegiance lay with his own people rather than the Confederacy or the Union. No one would care, not even the Confederate soldiers, about the estate of a Black slave owner. As for Minister Woodward, buried deep in the graveyard's cursed soil, White folks would never be smart enough to find his body.

The freed people moved as one, gathering what they had: kerosene, rags, and matches. Emma Jane handed out strips of cloth as she wrapped them around wooden torches they fashioned. Luke was first to spark a flame. He struck a match and lit his torch, holding it high as if it were a beacon. Then Larkin lit his, then Abram, then Emma Jane, Private Irvin, and the others. One by one, they formed a ring around the great house and set the beams and dry planks alight. Flames took hold in seconds, crackling and snapping as the fire spread. The house groaned, the fire swallowed in a ravenous embrace. The heat warped the glass windows until they shattered, sending shards raining down in a symphony of destruction. Smoke, thick and choking, coiled into the sky, a signal to the heavens that another comeuppance had arrived. The roof, once proud and whole, began to buckle. Sparks burst into the air, caught in the dance of the inferno, swarming like fireflies in the wind. The fire was beautiful in its destruction—merciless, cleansing, final.

And then, the fire found Nathaniel nailed to his oak door. The flames kissed the soles of his bare feet. The skin blistered in an instant, blackening as the fire curled up his ankles like creeping ivy. His tendons snapped, muscles lurching against the heat's grip. His chest jerked, the last instincts of survival. His eyes—rimmed in white terror—searching the faces in the fire. There was no mercy from any of the souls. The fire climbed his legs, wrapping his calves in orange and blue. The fire reached his waist, curling around his stomach, the heat warping the fabric of his shirt until it melted into his skin. His body seized, the pain beyond comprehension, his head snapping back against the door. His mouth stretched open, but his voice had abandoned him. The fire spread across his torso, ribs, and arms. The flames crept higher, pecking at his jaw, prancing along his cheeks and filling his mouth. His lips curled away from his teeth, gums sizzling, his bald head wearing a crown of flames. The wooden door behind him rumbled, the heat weakening its structure, the flames turning it into a funeral pyre. The house collapsed, its cracks locking Nathaniel in his tomb.

Emma Jane wrapped herself around Abram, cupped his face in her hands. "You free now."

Larkin watched the flames and thought of that horrific day in the courtroom when he lost Charity and his daughters. There was a promise he made. "Got my justice," he said to himself, the words rough on his tongue.

Solomon remembered Magnolia Row and knew this time his ending would be different. No running. No hiding. With Luke beside him, he'd found his family again. The loneliness that once ate at him now lay dead.

The flames reflected in Luke's eyes. There hadn't been a single day in the thirty years since the fires on Magnolia Row that Luke hadn't thought of Henri. Without him, Luke wouldn't have known freedom on their nineteenth birthday in Goochland, Virginia. One flame sparked a resistance. One act of love lit the road to liberation. Henri had been more than a comrade, he had been Luke's heart. Their love blazed in rebellion, fueling the courage it took when the souls rose up and burned their master's house to the ground.

But the fight wasn't finished—there'd be more wars to come.

"This is not the end," Luke said, almost to himself. "They'll keep trying. But every time they build, we must burn it down. Not just the house, but the whole foundation. We can't just rearrange the furniture and slap on fresh paint." The others nodded as the flames spread to Minister Woodward's fallen horse and the fields. "We must take it down," Luke declared. "Start over. Purification."

The Nathaniel William land was ash, and within two more months the Confederacy would surrender. Secrets spread about that day. A Black enslaver burned alive on his own plantation. Some say it was a myth. Others claimed they killed the right man in the end: For all his efforts to become like the White men he worshiped, not a single one of his "brethren" rose to defend him. Even in death, his so-called heroes turned their backs, sealing his fate with a final dismissal.

The South, its soil soaked with Black, Brown, and White

blood, would attempt to rise under different names, different regions, different politics, and different faces. These false prophets—modern strongmen who wrap themselves in old flags and old lies—will stand again, demanding a return to what was. The presidents, prime ministers, oligarchs, demagogues, and an alliance of dictators will thrive by turning neighbor against neighbor to deflect their own sins. But the spark has been lit and there will be dissenters who refuse to bow.

No more apologies while wishing for retribution.

No more waiting for allies or accomplices.

No more mercy; the demise of those who oppress won't be accidental, it will be intentional.

We will answer with fire.

AUTHOR'S NOTE

Burn Down Master's House began over twenty years ago with a short story I penned titled "Magnolia Row" about two enslaved men who fall in love. I was inspired to write this story after reading two sentences in slave narratives, Henry Bibb's *Narrative of the Life and Adventures of Henry Bibb, an American Slave* (1849) and Harriet Jacobs's *Incidents in the Life of a Slave Girl* (1861). I first read these accounts in Charles Clifton's essay "Rereading Voices From the Past: Images of Homo-eroticism in the Slave Narrative," which appeared in the 2001 collection *The Greatest Taboo: Homosexuality in Black Communities*; men named Luke and Henry were both mentioned on page 356.[27] The stories of Henry (whose name I render as "Henri") and Luke never left me.

In Bibb's narrative, he wrote, "I have been dragged down to the lowest depths of human degradation and wretchedness by slaveholders . . . which I consider too vulgar to be written."[28] In the Harriet Jacobs story, she described an enslaved person named Luke who was chained to the bedside of his owner. She wrote, "Some of these freaks were of a nature too filthy to be repeated. When I fled . . . I left poor Luke still

27. Delroy Constantine-Simms and Henry Louis Gates Jr., *The Greatest Taboo: Homosexuality in Black Communities*, First Edition (Alyson Books, 2001), 356.
28. Henry Bibb, *Narrative of the Life and Adventures of Henry Bibb, an American Slave*, Lucius C. Matlack, editor (New York: H. Bibb, 1850), 14.

chained to the bedside of this cruel and disgusting wretch."[29] Although Henry Bibb only hinted at events "too vulgar to be written," he offered no further context, and Luke vanished from the historical record. However, I saw a connection and began writing a story titled "Magnolia Row."

Sexuality among enslaved people has rarely been explored beyond the context of assault by White enslavers; I wanted to give these two men love and justice. In this novel, I have reimagined their lives, placing them in Goochland, Virginia, where my own family was once enslaved (many of the supporting characters in the book are named after my ancestors in Goochland), and using them as the anchor for future revolts. By showing how one flame inspired a thousand fires, I hope to immortalize both Henri and Luke.

A similar process brought me to Josephine. Her story is drawn from two people, both named Josephine—how ironic—who were accused of poisoning their owners in separate incidents, one in Maryland and the other in Mississippi. The Maryland case, documented in the *Baltimore Sun*, was from July 7, 1855, and involved a fourteen-year-old girl named Josephine Webb (I have her as eighteen for continuity purposes). According to the article published that same year in the *Baltimore Sun*, Josephine, who was quoted as wanting to "make a change there before long,"[30] decided to kill her master after being physically assaulted by the mistress. Another enslaved individual reportedly encouraged her to commit the act. Josephine volunteered to prepare the family's meal, secretly adding arsenic extracted from a clock. The poison failed to kill the mistress but instead took the life of another person who was eating with the family and died the following day.

29. Harriet Jacobs, *Incidents in the Life of a Slave Girl* (Boston: Thayer & Eldridge, 1861), 289.
30. "Distressing Homicide," *Baltimore Sun*, July 18, 1855.

Josephine was convicted of second-degree murder and sentenced to eighteen years at the Maryland Penitentiary. Little is known after that, but she died on January 10, 1867.[31]

The other was Josephine of Mississippi, similarly implicated in a poisoning. Scholars like Alexis Wells-Oghoghomeh, a Clayman Institute faculty research fellow and assistant professor of religious studies, recovered her life and testimony. In a lecture titled "The Ethics of Revenge: Enslaved Women and Poison in the American South," Wells-Oghoghomeh researched Josephine's 1857 trial for poisoning her owner Lafayette Jones and his family, who, according to the records, "became violently ill immediately after drinking a tea that was allegedly served and prepared by her, the family's new cook."[32]

At the time of Josephine's trial, enslaved people could not testify in court. When convicted of a capital crime, death was the usual sentence, and even if exonerated, enslaved defendants often faced "social death," being sold away from their family and community. Therefore, it is rare that any record of Josephine's testimony exists. Purchased by Jones in New Orleans in February 1857, two weeks before the alleged poisoning, Josephine had previously been in Kentucky, where she may have worked as a nurse caring for children.[33] She owned a surprising amount of jewelry, and Wells-Oghoghomeh ar-

31. Maryland State Archives, *Josephine Webb (b. 1841 – d. 1867)*. Archives of Maryland (Biographical Series). Accessed January 8, 2025. https://msa.maryland.gov/megafile/msa/speccol/sc5400/sc5496/002900/002965/html/02965bio.html.

32. Fatima Suarez, "Poisoning as revenge for intimate violence against enslaved women," *Stanford University Gender News*, June 1, 2022, https://gender.stanford.edu/news/poisoning-revenge-intimate-violence-against-enslaved-women.

33. Michael P. Mills, "The trials and tribulations of Josephine," *Racism.org*, March 24, 2012, https://racism.org/articles/citizenship-rights/slavery-to-neoslavery/slavery-2/119-articles-related-to-slavery/456-slavelaw03.

gued this suggests Josephine was "a very highly favored enslaved servant," possibly coerced into serving as a sexual consort.[34]

Josephine and another enslaved person, George, stood accused of poisoning Lafayette Jones, his second wife, Eliza, and their infant daughter Lelia Virginia. Though the Jones family's eldest son and dinner guests, who allegedly did not drink the tea, remained well, Lelia Virginia died, and Josephine was tried for homicide by poisoning. Lafayette Jones sexually assaulted Josephine two days after purchasing her, and again the day before the alleged poisoning. On the morning of that meal, Josephine prepared a badly cooked breakfast; when Eliza confronted her about the poor meal, Josephine responded "impudently and saucily." Eliza reported this to Lafayette, who whipped Josephine. Shortly thereafter, Josephine openly defied Eliza by making a face and overturning a chair, prompting Eliza to summon the overseer for another whipping. Not even two hours later, Eliza called Josephine to prepare dinner. It was at this point, according to the trial records, that Josephine poisoned the family's tea.[35]

After four years of trials and mistrials, Josephine and George were shockingly exonerated. However, according to Alexis Wells-Oghoghomeh, it is unclear why.[36] Nonetheless, Josephine fought back and won.

34. Fatima Suarez, "Poisoning as revenge for intimate violence against enslaved women," *Stanford University Gender News*, June 1, 2022, https://gender.stanford.edu/news/poisoning-revenge-intimate-violence-against-enslaved-women.
35. Michael P. Mills, "The trials and tribulations of Josephine," *Racism.org*, March 24, 2012, https://racism.org/articles/citizenship-rights/slavery-to-neoslavery/slavery-2/119-articles-related-to-slavery/456-slavelaw03.
36. Alexis Wells-Oghoghomeh, email message to Clay Cane, January 9, 2025.

By blending these two Josephines into one figure—connected to the reimagined Lafayette Baynard, a composite master from archival fragments—I aimed to amplify her. What we know of these women comes primarily from legal records and slaveholders' documents, which so often muted their true voices and experiences. My Josephine, inspired by the fire of Luke and Henri, refuses silence. She exists as an expression of resistance to that which sought to erase her autonomy and humanity.

Charity Butler is inspired by the true story of a Black woman who challenged her enslavement under Pennsylvania's gradual abolition statutes of 1780 and 1788. Charity was born enslaved in Maryland and belonged to Norman Bruce. Bruce leased Charity to a man named Gilleland (also recorded as Clelland). Soon after this agreement was reached, however, Gilleland separated from his wife. His estranged wife—on whom the fictional character Miss Clara is based—moved near the Pennsylvania line and took Charity with her to care for her infant child. Nearly destitute, the wife traveled frequently to find seamstress work, bringing Charity along for weeks at a time. Charity tallied the days spent in Pennsylvania. Since state law decreed that enslaved people who resided in Pennsylvania for six months or more would be freed, Charity didn't return to Norman Bruce.

This led to the case of *Butler v. Delaplaine*, originating in the Court of Common Pleas in Adams County, Pennsylvania. Thaddeus Stevens, a lawyer who would become a famed abolitionist and congressman, represented Charity's enslaver. Stevens argued before the Pennsylvania Supreme Court that the law required six months of continuous residence for emancipation. The court agreed with Stevens, concluding that fragmented visits, no matter how they added up, did not meet the law's criteria for freedom. Charity, after a decade of freedom, was returned to slavery. Her two daughters, who had known only freedom, were also enslaved and became the property of Norman Bruce.[37] For this story, Charity's journey is reimagined in the late 1840s. To expand her daughters' narratives and age them appropriately, Charity now has 15 years of freedom rather than ten.

Historically, Charity's fate was sealed by legal technicalities and her resistance overshadowed by Thaddeus Stevens. Charity, her husband, Henry Butler (to avoid having two Henrys in the book, his name has been changed to Larkin—an homage to my ancestor from Goochland, Virginia, whose recorded name was Patrick Henry Larkin), and their two children, Harriet and Sophia, have disappeared from recorded history. In this fictional reimagining, however, Charity and her daughters reclaim their freedom. By intertwining these historical fragments and personal connections, the story restores Charity's voice and highlights the complexities of the very legal structures that shaped her family's life. Also, to remind people that regardless of Thaddeus Stevens being an abolitionist, his betrayal of Charity should be remembered.

The final chapter draws on one of the most unsettling aspects of American slavery: the small number of Black slave owners who, rather than using legal ownership as a means to protect family members, exploited the system just as viciously as White enslavers. Two individuals, Nat Butler of Maryland, and William Ellison of South Carolina, inspire the events depicted here, and the chapter references their known histories.

According to an article titled "Negroes Who Owned Slaves," by Calvin D. Wilson, published in *Popular Science Monthly* in 1912:

37. *Butler v. Delaplaine*, 7 Serg. & Rawle 378 (Pa. 1821), Free State Slavery & Bound Labor, from https://freestateslaveryproject.com/legal-materials/butler-v-delaplaine-7-serg-rawle-378-pa-1821/.

"There was a negro named Nat Butler who lived near Aberdeen, Harford County, Md., who owned a small farm and bought and sold negroes for the southern trade. This sharp and noted fellow would persuade a slave to run off and hide for a few days at a place prepared by Butler, who would in the meantime see the master of the runaway and learn the price he would take for him. If the owner had little hope of recovering his slave and so placed the price low, Nat would buy him and resell him to slave dealers who knew Butler's rendezvous for hidden negroes. His conduct became so notorious that he lost the confidence of slave owners and respect of negroes, who several times tried to murder him."[38]

This reveals how Butler was notorious enough to inspire multiple attempts on his life. While I could find no record of Butler's fate, these violent reprisals underscore that those he terrorized recognized his complicity and that he had to die. This guided the portrayal of Nathaniel William in the story's final chapter, highlighting that some Black people, like Butler, actively profited from the trade in human beings. I did not use the last name Butler because of Charity Butler.

The second figure is William Ellison, originally born April Ellison around 1790. With the help of a White "master craftsman,"[39] Ellison worked in a gin shop. It was there he learned reading, writing, bookkeeping, and cotton gin craftsmanship. By 1816, Ellison had saved enough money to purchase his freedom. Circumstances suggest that the man who owned him, likely his father, refused to free him so he had to buy his

38. Calvin D. Wilson (1912, November), "Negroes who owned slaves," *Popular Science Monthly 81*, 487.

39. Johnson, Michael P., and James L. Roark. *Black Masters: A Free Family of Color in the Old South.* New York: W. W. Norton, 1984, 11.

freedom.[40] Ellison chose to perpetuate the barbarity of slavery rather than challenge it. Historical sources reference his presence as a major enslaver as "even amongst his White peers, was seen as a particularly cruel master. Due to his constant effort and drive towards wealth and prestige."[41]

By the beginning of the Civil War, Ellison owned approximately fifty enslaved people,[42] demonstrating that his quest for wealth and status led him to embrace the very institution that once bound him. I chose Charleston, South Carolina as the setting because it had a significant population of free Black people, which led to a small number of Black enslavers. I could find no record of black slave owners in Goochland, Virginia, and in Maryland, only Nat Butler. Again, for most Black slave owners, holding their own relatives in bondage was a means of protection rather than profit. In South Carolina, however, formally emancipating an enslaved Black person was nearly impossible. In 1800, the state passed a law requiring any owner seeking to free an enslaved individual to petition a court and attest to that person's "good character."[43] Given the entrenched racial prejudices of the time, a Black slave owner's testimony on behalf of another Black individual would likely have been dismissed, making formal emancipation highly improbable. By 1861, there were 171 Black people

40. Johnson, Michael P., and James L. Roark. *Black Masters: A Free Family of Color in the Old South*. New York: W. W. Norton, 1984, 15.
41. Zachary M. Saddow, *Black Joining the Ranks of White: Black Slaveowning in 1800s South Carolina* (master's thesis, Winthrop University, 2023), 32, https://digitalcommons.winthrop.edu/cgi/viewcontent.cgi?article=1154&context=graduatetheses.
42. Zachary M. Saddow, *Black Joining the Ranks of White: Black Slaveowning in 1800s South Carolina* (master's thesis, Winthrop University, 2023), 3, https://digitalcommons.winthrop.edu/cgi/viewcontent.cgi?article=1154&context=graduatetheses.
43. Johnson, Michael P., and James L. Roark. *Black Masters: A Free Family of Color in the Old South*. New York: W. W. Norton, 1984, 15.

who owned slaves in South Carolina, many of them based in Charleston.[44] However, these numbers declined rapidly toward the end of the Civil War, likely reflecting the imminent end of slavery.

As for language, I avoided leaning into a hyper-Southern, stereotypical accent often associated with literature about enslaved people. Contrary to popular portrayals, the speech of enslaved individuals varied widely depending on numerous factors: their place of origin, the region where they lived, and even the specific plantation or community they were part of. Not all enslaved people spoke in the exaggerated "yessuh massa" dialect commonly depicted. Some spoke with accents similar to their enslavers. Additionally, free Black people living in slave-holding areas added another layer of linguistic diversity. Many slave narratives written by Black people display beautiful, nuanced language that defies the stereotypes often associated with the era. These complexities in language reflect the depth of the people who lived through slavery, which I wanted to honor in this book.

Another conscious choice I made was to exclude the N-word *entirely* from the book. I didn't want to write a novel about slavery that drowned in its usage. Historically, there's some debate among scholars about how frequently the N-word was used during slavery compared to the Jim Crow era and modern pop culture portrayals. For example, in *Narrative of the Life and Adventures of Henry Bibb, an American Slave*, the N-word does not appear once. In 1849's *The Life of Josiah Henson, Formerly a Slave, Now an Inhabitant of Canada, as Narrated by Himself*, the N-word is not used. In *Narrative of the Life of Frederick Douglass, an American Slave*, one of the definitive slave narratives, the N-word is written on only five

44. Larry Koger, *Black Slaveowners: Free Black Slave Masters in South Carolina, 1790-1860* (Jefferson, NC: McFarland, 2010), 18.

pages. This is not to deny the existence of the word in history, but rather to emphasize that the experience of slavery cannot be reduced to the N-word. Slavery was a framework of dehumanization and brutality, and centering the N-word risks diminishing the broader scope of that experience. Instead, I chose to focus on the individuality of the enslaved, ensuring their stories remain the focal point.

In the end, each of these historical fragments—Luke and Henry, the two Josephines, Charity Butler, Nat Butler, William Ellison—represents people whose stories have been partially buried by time and erasure. Historical fiction allows me to bond their lived experiences into a coherent story. I don't believe uprisings are isolated incidents. They are all connected via the souls who were long denied a free life.

Acknowledgments

Writing *Burn Down Master's House* has been one of the most fulfilling journeys in my professional career. It is the book I always wanted to write but was always told no. Having the freedom to choose what I wanted to write is a blessing I've worked to earn. This book would not have been possible without the support, inspiration, and guidance of many incredible people.

My mom, my dad, my second mom Ann, Nicole Ray, Karen Hunter, Reecie Colbert, Monroe France, Antar Bush, Lurie Daniel Favors, Michael Griffin, Dr. Omekongo Dibinga, Dr. Barbara Foley, Dr. Zain Abdullah, Dr. Koritha Mitchell, Brandon Proia, Jameson Bennett, Stephanie Buscetta, Amina Talat, Steve Robinson, Ted Winn, Keith Boykin, Jeremiah Jones, Erica Savage, Dennis Williams, Derick Monroe, and all of my ancestors from Goochland, Virginia, to Philadelphia, I am eternally grateful for all you have given me. Lastly, to my love, my dear friend Alexa Muñoz: this book would not have been completed without you. My life has been reshaped and reordered with you by my side. Your loyalty taught me so much. I'll never waste time on those who don't give love in return. Rest well.

A special thank you to my incredible literary agent, Mark Gottlieb, and the entire crew at Trident Media Group, as well as Dafina Books and Leticia Gomez. From the first read, your belief in this book has meant the world to me. All it takes is for one person to say yes.

To the historical fiction novelists whose work inspired me many years ago at Rutgers University: Arna Bontemps (1902–

1973), Richard Wright (1908–1960), and Margaret Walker (1915–1998)—their legacies remind me of the power of storytelling to challenge, teach, and inspire.

Lastly, to the SiriusXM Urban View family and every listener of *The Clay Cane Show*, your unwavering support stays with me. You've lifted me with your energy, prayers, and belief in me. I never take it for granted.

And you know the deal—*I ain't ever really gone.*

Discussion Questions

1. The book opens by detailing how misinformation reshapes our understanding of history. After reading *Burn Down Master's House*, what are your thoughts on the importance of confronting the challenging aspects of historical events, even the painful ones like chattel slavery?

2. The main characters were inspired by real people whose names history has forgotten. How does the novel remember and honor these forgotten spirits? In what ways does fictionalization serve to bring these stories to light?

3. The title of the book, *Burn Down Master's House*, suggests an act of destruction. What do you think this phrase might symbolize in the story? How does the "house" represent more than just a building?

4. In the Author's Note, Clay Cane explains his deliberate decision to exclude the N-word from the novel. How did this choice impact your reading experience?

5. What significance does Luke and Henri's relationship hold within the oppressive context of chattel slavery? How might their relationship be interpreted as an act of resistance or a reclaiming of humanity in a system designed to dehumanize them?

6. The scene between Luke and Henri at the riverbank is charged with intimacy and vulnerability. What did this moment reveal to you about love, desire, and agency under slavery?

7. Examine the significant relationships Josephine shares with Ruby and Old Mama Bess. How do these women provide Josephine with support, knowledge, and the tools for resistance? What does this reveal about the importance of women's networks and intergenerational wisdom within enslaved communities?

8. How does *Burn Down Master's House* tackle the struggles and strengths of enslaved women? Through the characters of Ruby, Josephine, Old Mama Bess, Charity, and others, how does the novel contrast their resistance with the complicity of the White women characters?

9. Considering Thaddeus Stevens's historical role as a prominent abolitionist, how should we understand his actions in *Burn Down Master's House*, where he advocates for the return of Charity Butler and her freeborn children to slavery based on legal technicalities? Does this historically documented act tarnish his legacy, or do his broader contributions to abolition outweigh the trauma inflicted on Charity's family?

10. Facing the imminent threat of assault under Norman Bruce, Harriet and Sophia commit a brutal act of retaliatory violence. How does their revolt reflect the legacy of resistance inherited from their parents, Charity and Larkin?

11. Is Miss Clara a villain, a guilt-ridden narcissist, or something in between? Do her actions reflect true remorse, self-interest, or both? Do you see her as redeemed, or is her complicity too great to overcome?

12. How does the character of Nathaniel William serve as a representation of people who inflict harm upon their own community in pursuit of power and acceptance from the dominant group? Are there similarities be-

tween his perspective and those of controversial figures today?

13. What social, economic, and psychological forces might have driven individuals like Nathaniel, modeled after historical figures Nat Butler and William Ellison, to participate in the very system that once enslaved them? Is Nathaniel purely insidious, or is he, in some ways, also a victim of the institution of slavery?

14. Reflecting on Solomon's journey—his early escape with David, his alliance with Luke and Henri, the impact of his assault, and his eventual arrival on Nathaniel's plantation—how do these different phases of his life show ways enslaved people survived, even after experiencing profound trauma?

15. How does *Burn Down Master's House* challenge caricatures of enslaved people, such as the "noble savage," the "obedient servant," or the "loyal caretaker"?

16. The phrase "don't let them take what they can't touch" appears multiple times, spoken by different characters across varying circumstances. How do you interpret this phrase within the narrative, and what role does its repetition play in highlighting the book's themes of freedom and identity?

17. How does *Burn Down Master's House* depict violence—not just as suffering, but as defiance, and consequence? How do the acts of enslavers and the actions of the enslaved reshape our understanding of survival and what it means to be free?

18. The book shows that people resisted in different ways, from small acts to large rebellions. What were some of the different ways characters in the story showed resis-

tance? Which of these actions stood out to you the most, and why?

19. How does *Burn Down Master's House* portray traditional African faith and spirituality, and in what ways can its preservation be seen as an act of resistance—perhaps even a form of "burning down master's house"?

20. The novel ends with: "*We will answer with fire.*" How do these words resonate with the political and cultural climate? What do they suggest about resistance—both in the past and in the present?